THE LIST MAKER

FRANCES COWIE

D2S MEDIA

THE LIST MAKER
Published by D2S Media

Copyright © 2017 Frances Cowie
www.francescowie.com

The moral right of Frances Cowie to be identified as the author of this work is hereby asserted.

ISBN: 978-0-473-36268-3 Paperback
ISBN: 978-0-473-36269-0 E-book

A catalog record of this book is available from the National Library of New Zealand.

The List Maker is a work of fiction. Apart from certain aspects of geography, the characters, locations, products, incidents, and events in this book are either used fictitiously and/or are a product of the author's imagination. Any resemblance to persons, living or dead is purely accidental.

Cover Design: Steven Novak / www.novakillustration.com

110720

To Kevin

CONTENTS

THE LIST MAKER

OBSERVATIONS

IT WAS THE PERFECT VIEW. A beautiful woman—tight skirt, silk tunic, slingback kitten heels—strolling into the bar with the crowd. Her relaxed and confident smile set alight an otherwise uneventful night.

She removed her scarf, draped it over a leather chair and raked her fingers through the mass of dark curls framing her face. Her tunic reminded AJ of a pigeon's nape and hackle. Predominantly molten gray with undertones of emerald green and warm violet, the silky fabric shimmered under the low-hung ceiling lights of the moody bar.

An undeniable sense of familiarity made AJ wonder where their paths had crossed. Had they spent a night together? Surely he'd remember. He'd noticed her here before—more than once. The expressive dark eyes and hands that danced when she spoke were hard to forget.

AJ grabbed his Corona off the bar and took a swig. The lager soothed his throat, and while he welcomed the bitter taste, the thick fog outside suggested a smooth whiskey may have been a better choice. Something to warm his insides.

He tried not to stare, but the shape and form of the human

body, both male and female, had always fascinated him. Not only the bone structure and physique, but also, the way emotions were conveyed by a continuous array of expressions. For the first time in weeks, the need to paint overwhelmed him. But AJ hadn't touched a brush since his friend Cathy passed away, her generous bequest having the opposite effect of her intention. The studio, once vibrant with anticipation, sat empty. Fumes and blank canvases locked away with his inspiration.

Leaning against the bar, he watched the woman stand, her gaze directed his way. When he offered a slight smile, her perfectly shaped brows knitted together, and she walked straight past him. Not an expected reaction.

He stepped forward. "Excuse me. Have we met before?" His inquiry was genuine, but his purpose questionable. "You look vaguely familiar."

She flashed an amused smile. "Really? Is that the best you can do?"

"You think I'm trying to pick you up?"

"Aren't you?"

"Wouldn't dream of it."

"Good, because my mother warned me about speaking to strangers."

"And you never rebel against your mother's advice?"

"On the odd occasion."

She handed over her credit card and thanked the bartender with an unmistakable Australian or possibly Kiwi twang and a bright smile. As she turned to walk away, she stopped short with a second thought and looked downward. "Nice boots," she said. "And no, we've never met."

When AJ joined his friend Chris at a nearby table a few minutes later, easy conversation meant a shift in focus. Even so, every time he glanced her way, her head would lift to attention as if they shared a connection, and she would glance back, her smile laced with amusement. She had gorgeous lips, distinct and full, and painted in a muted dark rose lipstick that begged to be kissed off. Lips that told tales of possibilities.

"So, all set for the big trip?" Chris asked.

AJ pushed the slice of lemon further into the neck of his beer. "Not yet. Plenty of time."

"When are you leaving again?"

"Eight days."

Chris followed AJ's line of sight. "Who are you eyeing up?"

"That woman. The one in the gray tunic. I feel like I know her."

The woman cocked her head to the left, looked him in the eye, then flicked her lashes downward before turning back to the conversation at the table. To anyone else, the gesture would appear dismissive. AJ didn't see it that way. She liked his boots. At least he had one skinny straw to clutch on to.

"Yeah. She looks familiar."

AJ glanced back at Chris. "Any update on the house?"

"Not really. We can't move forward until they finish the dig. They're now talking eighteen months to two years."

"Shit. Two years? What are we supposed to do in the meantime?"

"Sit tight while the lift in the London property market doubles our investment."

AJ took a long drink of his beer. "Let's hope."

"Look, if you want out, I'll talk to Ryan. We may be able to buy your share."

"No. I'm in."

"I know it hasn't been easy for you lately, with what happened to Cathy. This trip will do you good." Chris hailed the server for another two beers. "Reevaluate, and you'll return with a renewed purpose."

"When did you get so philosophical?"

"It's an occupational hazard. Anyway, how have you been?"

"Up and down. I had no idea Cathy had cancer when we first

3

met." AJ paused, massaging his fingers through the week-old growth on his chin. "Shit. I should've known."

"Would it have made a difference? You weren't in love with her. Cathy knew that."

"I know, but I could have supported her as a friend."

"You were there for her in the end."

AJ nodded. "Yeah, and she left me her studio. And for what? Being her fuck buddy?"

"Don't be so hard on yourself, mate. Cathy wouldn't want that."

"Yeah, but guilt's a bitch."

Chris smiled. "Yep. And regret's a bastard."

On the short walk home, AJ imagined what his friend Nate would say about the beautiful woman in the silk tunic. Nate, a mixture of British Isles descent, with an English rose mother and a father born and bred in Dublin, would have three words for him. 'Feck off, mate.' He'd go on to explain that the woman in question was way out of his league 'mate' and remind him that casual often led to complicated.

Nate would be right.

In the back of his rational mind, AJ reminded himself casual sex was off the menu. He'd set himself a task, and the reason behind that task was why the woman with the delicate hands and high cheekbones had to stay the object of his fantasies, nothing more. That didn't stop his imagination running wild, but the dream of taking her to bed, where there would be no conversations of the past or future—no plans made—had to stay just that. A dream. The days of sowing his wild oats in whatever field that suited him were over.

Six weeks ago, the thought of unlocking the door to Cathy's studio filled AJ with dread. But as he stood outside the paint-blistered door the following day, a flash of inspiration hit him head on.

The studio occupied the entire top floor of a small commercial terrace. On the way in, he'd stopped to say hello to the ground floor tenant, a horizontally challenged woman in her mid-sixties who ran a bookshop filled with female-friendly erotic literature and other items of that nature. She'd agreed to keep an eye on the studio while he was away, and AJ knew he could rely on her.

As he stepped into the stairwell and switched on the dim ceiling light, a dank smell clung to his nostrils with a sting. Making a mental note to hire someone to repair the roofing tiles, he bounded up the stairs two at a time. When he reached the landing, he stopped. The door, half-ajar—the lock also in need of repair—served as a barrier to his unease.

Inside the studio, stale remnants of musk oil, cigarettes, and weed—Cathy's drug of choice and the main reason AJ ended their liaison—added to the feeling of closeness. She'd insisted smoking weed eased the pain of an old back injury from her ballet days. He'd always wondered, and by the time they parted ways, he'd feared her lack of motivation had little to do with her pain, and much to do with her drug habit. Now he knew better.

After she died, her family had spent several days cleaning out the space—storing brushes into old paint cans and hanging tubes of paint by bulldog clips on a sheet of pegboard. But now, the neatness of the room seemed out of place. Like the essence of Cathy had been stripped bare.

They'd left only one completed canvas, a reclining nude AJ had posed for. Now, every time he looked at the nude, he recalled Cathy painting it—when they were lovers, seemingly without a care in the world.

Dumping his backpack on the trestle table desk, AJ took a deep breath. Everywhere he looked, small splatters of paint littered the whitewashed floorboards. The flecks of color comforted him. Cathy's spirit dominated this space as much now as it did before.

When AJ checked his reflection in the large mirror above the desk, he imagined her behind him, her voice—husky courtesy of a passion for cigarettes—whispering in his ears. "Close your eyes, Anthony. Feel the work in your soul before you make any attempt to marry the paint to the canvas."

AJ opened the door to the storage area. He grabbed a large mounted canvas and placed it on the side wall, then stood before it, deep in thought. When he was younger, he thought people who talked to the dead were batshit crazy, but since Cathy's death, he'd spoken to her many times. He muttered under his breath, "Show me," and closed his eyes. After several minutes of concentration, he grabbed a palette and brush, and attacked the stiff white textile as if his life depended on it.

The next time he checked his watch, six hours had passed.

2

A STRANGER'S GLANCE

BEFORE ARRIVING IN LONDON, Liz Dobson imagined she'd walk straight into a job and be inundated with affiliate marketing opportunities, along with a potential list of new clients hungry for her services. The reality had been very different.

She strolled west along the Embankment toward home. Up ahead, an ice cream truck displayed the usual signs—*Freshly Made Ice Cream* and *Mind That Child*. It reminded her of her childhood, hot summer days, and *Greensleeves*. She stopped. Glanced at the menu. Stood in line.

Cone in hand, Liz sat on a wooden bench and watched small watercraft carve rippled vees on the surface of the River Thames. Behind her, workers replaced cobblestones in one section of the pavement, and a yellow concrete-mixing truck came and went. She checked her phone, smiling at a text from her friend, Penny, suggesting they meet for a drink.

Her cone finished, Liz headed home past rows of uniform houses until she reached her tree-lined street. The narrow terrace house owned by her cousin, Nate, was typical of the area. It stood with an understated air, coupled with a black ironwork gate and small box hedge that created an insignificant barrier between house and pavement. A sticky front door proved a challenge every time Liz opened it, and as she inserted her key in the lock, today was no exception.

The door gave way the same time as her phone rang.

"Where are you?" Penny shouted over raucous background noise. "Aren't we meeting for a drink?"

"I'm just home. Be there shortly. I need a quick shower."

"Okay, we're at Munro's. Bring that spunky cousin of yours. I could do with a bit of eye candy in the form of Nate O'Loughlin tonight."

Liz laughed as she rushed into the bathroom, stretching her neck from side to side to relieve tension. "Okay. I'll text him."

Standing in a dream as the hot water cascaded over her back and shoulders, Liz washed away the fumes and grime of the city with a soap-filled sponge. She loved London, but some days, it's closeness engulfed her.

The choice of clothes in her closet left a lot to be desired, and lack of cash meant the usual jeans, floaty top, and jacket combo would have to do. After all, she was only meeting Penny, not some gorgeous man who would sweep her off her stilettos. Liz had first met Penny on the cramped flight from LA to London. Their differing personalities clicked the moment Penny grabbed Liz's hand during takeoff, and they'd been friends ever since.

Liz just about knocked Nate off his feet as she hurried down the stairs.

"Where are you off to in such a rush?" he asked.

"Meeting Penny at Munro's. Keen?"

"Sounds good. As long as she keeps her hands to herself."

Liz chuckled. "You love the attention. Go on, admit it."

"My self-inflated ego does. My rational self, not so much. I'll just get changed."

"Make it quick. Penny's already stalking me."

When they arrived at Munro's Bar and Grill twenty minutes later, the place was packed, and the smell of steaks on the grill reminded Liz she should eat. Nate made a beeline for the bar while Liz weaved her way toward Penny's table.

"How are you, angel?" Penny planted two air kisses on Liz's cheeks.

"Good." Liz smiled as Penny scanned the room before turning her attention back to Liz.

"How's the job hunting?"

"It's not. My one and only hope, where they insisted I was their ideal candidate, chose a 'more suitable' applicant. I'm over it. I've applied for at least forty jobs. It's depressing."

She grinned at Penny's expression.

"I know," Liz said. "Laugh and the world laughs with you, cry and you're a lonely loser."

"Totally. Usually while watching sad movies and balancing half a tub of ice cream in your lap. Still, at least you have your waitressing job. Something will turn up. Where's Nate?"

"He's here somewhere."

Penny scanned the bar again. "There's the sexy devil. And check out the hottie at six o'clock." She looked the men up and down. "Wow. Cute times two divided by sex on the first date."

Liz cocked her head, eager to see whose good looks held Penny's attention as she caught an uneventful back view of Nate's companion. "Who, Nate or the other guy?"

"Both. Get me details on Mr. Man Bun, stat. Three words: Good, fling, prospect." Penny counted the words on her fingertips.

"Who for, you or me?"

"Me. Don't you have that Peter guy sniffing around?"

"Kind of. I'm not sure if he's interested, or more to the point if I'm interested in him. But he does check all the boxes on my 'Hell Yeah' list."

"You have a 'Hell Yeah' list?"

"And a 'Hell No' list. Don't you?"

"I love all sexy men. You know that. Wait. Don't tell me you keep your lists on a vision board?"

"No. My vision board and I parted company when I left New Zealand. It was time for us to break up. But I kept my lists."

"Just as well." Penny grinned. "Those vision boards are a stark reminder of your failings. Anyway, back to check-all-the-boxes Peter. I thought he seemed keen."

"Me too, but he's pretty full of himself. Just when I think otherwise, he makes a smart remark and I'm reminded to stay away. And he's a no touch kind of guy."

"What? No hanky-panky-spanky?"

"I've only had lunch with him twice. It's a bit early for fornication." The thought amused Liz. The fact she couldn't imagine hanky, panky, *or* spanky with Peter should have raised a red flag. "What I mean is, he doesn't touch at all. Not even a hand on the back or kiss on the cheek."

"You can't be serious."

"Yeah, I'm not sure what his deal is. A little dose of tactile flattery never goes amiss. I don't necessarily want a full-on relationship, but still, it's always nice to feel desired."

"I agree." Penny sucked on the straw of her cocktail. "Get rid of him. He sounds like hard work."

"Maybe, but all I want is a bit of fun."

"Same. A little fling with a solid piece of morning wood would brighten up my day no end."

Liz burst out laughing. "Your poor mother must lie in bed worrying about you all night long."

"She thinks butter wouldn't melt in my hot little mouth." Penny raised her eyebrows and giggled. She cocked her head around Liz, her attention on Nate and her ideal fling prospect. "They've spied us. Call them over."

Liz turned and froze as her eyes locked with Nate's friend. She quickly looked away. "I know him," she whispered. "The hunk with the stylish boots. He's always staring at me with those crazy-colored eyes. Maybe he's seen me on Nate's Facebook page. I'm not sure about guys who look like the back end of a horse."

"What?"

"He's got the whole ponytail thing going on."

"Well, he doesn't look like the back end of a horse to me. He's hot as liquid toffee with a skin color to match. Gorgeous!"

Liz tried to keep a straight face. "You think?"

"Not in a traditional way, I grant you. But still—dark and broody, a mixture of saint and sinner. And it's not a ponytail, it's a man bun."

"Anyway, looks don't make the man."

"No, but they certainly help when you're doing it with the lights on. I can just imagine his hair fanned out over the pillow while I straddle his pony and whip his tight ass."

"Stop it. They're coming over." Liz took a gulp of wine, eager to hide her amusement as she watched Penny's interest flit between Nate and his friend with her 'take me now but not forever' eyes.

"And who do we have here?" Penny offered her hand as she looked Mr. Man Bun up and down. "I'm Penny."

They exchanged a warm smile. He'd probably met hundreds of girls like Penny in his lifetime. Fun girls with knowing smiles that would take him straight to the bedroom. "Anthony. Friends call me AJ." He reached for Penny's hand, pulled her in close and kissed her on both cheeks.

AJ turned to Liz. He shot her a knowing smile, the kind of smile that tips a girl sideways with a jolt. "We meet again." He looked her up and down through lazy eyes fringed with thick black lashes. Penny had hit the nail right on the head. Saint by day, sinner by night.

"Meet my cousin Liz," Nate said.

AJ nodded slowly. "I thought you looked familiar. Now I know why. You and Nate have similar facial features. It's the cheekbones."

Nate offered a wry smile. "I'll take that as a compliment."

AJ didn't shift his gaze off Liz as he offered his hand. "Fully intended." He had a firm grip—too firm. "AJ Tanner. Nice to put a face to the name finally."

He didn't lean in for a cheek kiss and Liz wondered why. AJ had flawless olive skin and a height that would make a tall girl feel petite. He reminded her of friends from home with a touch of Māori or Pacific Island blood running through their veins. However, the shape of his nose didn't fit with South Pacific heritage.

"Likewise, Anthony." She committed his nickname to memory, thinking of an association to go with the initials. The first one to pop into her head was 'another jerk.' However, AJ didn't look like a jerk. Not one bit. Liz quickly dismissed it for apple juice.

"Please, call me AJ. Only my mother calls me Anthony."

"And what does the J stand for?" Penny asked.

"Guess."

He had a gorgeous smile and straight white teeth. Liz liked men with beautiful teeth. Yet the rest of his persona wasn't her type. A tattoo down his right arm was the first distraction. It was almost obscured under his sleeve, but as he grabbed his drink, his T-shirt strained to reveal black ink on light olive skin.

His hair, long and slightly unruly, sat in the infamous man bun at the back of his crown, and a few weeks of unclipped growth prickled his jawline. Still, he was neatly dressed and well-groomed, with artistic hands and finely tapered fingers. His mouth intrigued her the most. Full of color, distinctively outlined, and almost too pretty—a contrast to his somewhat rugged exterior. The AJ paradox. Liz quickly reminded herself that long hair and tattoos were on her 'Hell No' list.

But all lists need reevaluating at times, right?

AJ slipped into the booth, his legs wide. A physical display of male dominance wrapped up in a pair of designer jeans and leather boots. Liz tensed at the thought and gave herself an imaginary slap to prevent further hijinks from playing in her mind.

"So, what do you do in London?" AJ asked. His knee touched her leg more than once. He didn't seem to notice. The fact that she did bothered her.

"I'm a waitress."

"Anywhere I know?"

"*El Beso*." Liz noticed his amusement at her clipped pronunciation of Spanish and felt herself blush with embarrassment.

"Ah, *The Kiss*. One of my favorites. They have the best tapas in town."

"Yeah. It's a good place to work." Liz smiled politely, but the effect of his stare unnerved her.

"And you? Where do you spend hours nine to five?" Penny asked, doing her best to sound interested as she checked out his physical attributes.

He fiddled with the coaster in front of him, turning it end for end. "I'm an accountant. Nate and I went to university together."

He didn't look like an accountant to Liz. Still, what did an accountant look like? Apparently not the stereotypical image she'd conjured up from the accountancy firm her parents used. If their accountant had looked like this, Liz would've gladly taken over the accounts for the orchard.

"Isn't it a tad boring, crunching numbers all day long?" Penny asked. "Two of my accountant friends were over it after only a few years."

"Yep." AJ sipped his beer, then sucked the residue froth from his mustache. "I'm one step ahead. Leaving for Japan in a week for an extended trip around Asia."

"Really?" Penny asked. "Why Japan?"

Liz watched in amusement as her friend worked her magic. Penny never stayed at home on the weekends with rom-coms and ice cream for company. She always had somewhere to go. And more to the point, someone to go with.

"I'm taking a pilgrimage."

"Which one?" Liz asked. "Not Shikoku?"

"You know it?" He sounded surprised.

"A friend did it last year. I know it's a cliché to say he found himself, but he really did."

"So, there's hope for me yet." AJ flashed a smile in her direction. "To find myself, I mean."

A woman understands when a man is sensing her. Liz felt it—that curiosity, that interest. And while she wouldn't admit it to Penny, she welcomed the attention of this interesting man. The more AJ talked to the group, the more attractive he became. Even so, Liz suspected when it came to her, Anthony Tanner had only one thought on his mind. The last thing she needed was a fling with her cousin's friend who was leaving London on the road to self-discovery and worldly enlightenment. She had conveniently forgotten he wasn't her type for the moment.

As AJ moved away from the table, Liz studied him with a critical eye. He looked like an arty type rather than a businessperson. A complex soul. A man who wouldn't tell his story to just anyone. Liz had a habit of judging people at first glance and while she was usually right, she found London men harder to read than the average Kiwi guy. Peter's image flashed into her mind accompanied by a touch of unease. Sometimes, when it came to smooth operators with easy smiles like Peter, Liz ignored her own advice to trust her instincts.

On first impression, AJ's good looks could never be described as traditional, with eyes that narrowed under prominent hooded brows and his nose slightly off-center. However, when those imperfect features gelled together, they formed a striking package. When he smiled, the moody look of arrogance completely disappeared in favor of glinted amusement.

Of course, tonight wasn't the first time AJ and Liz had played glance at a stranger. The pair began shooting glances at each other weeks ago when he and his stylish leather boots intrigued her as she walked past him in a moody bar.

Yet as the evening progressed, Liz became acutely aware of

AJ's aloofness. He seemed totally relaxed flirting with Penny and the other girls in the group as he drank beer and chatted with friends. However, apart from a few words of polite small talk, it seemed that Liz had slipped off his radar.

She stood to leave just as Nate wandered back to their table.

"Stay for another round," he said.

"I should get going." Liz hesitated as she weighed up her options. She needed a solid eight hours sleep to cope with her workload. Socializing would have to wait. "I'm on a morning shift."

"You don't usually do Saturdays."

"I've been roped into extra shifts this weekend." Liz picked up her bag and jacket, and maneuvered out of the booth. "See you next week, Penny. Bye, guys."

As she crossed the floor toward the exit, Liz peeked at AJ at the bar, his flirtatious eyes locked with a redhead while he leaned in a little too close to her ample boobs encased in a low-cut top. She wouldn't have the chance to say goodbye or wish him safe travels.

A rush of disappointment surfaced as Liz pushed through the door and out onto the street. It was still early, just after ten, and the night was alive with life. Red double-decker buses, sometimes two deep, crawled into the curb of Putney High Street, but she couldn't face a bus ride home.

"Liz." She turned to see AJ, his hands in his pockets as he strolled toward her. "Let me walk you home."

His face held no hint of a smile and for a second, Liz tensed with a touch of unease. "Thanks, but I'll grab a cab."

"At least let me see you to your door. I'll get the cab back later."

She hesitated as a cab pulled into the curb. "That's so sweet of you, but there's no need. I hope you find what you're looking for, with the pilgrimage."

She slid into the back seat and closed the door, a small smile on her lips.

———

AJ watched the cab slip out of view, wondering what had just happened. He'd been interested in the Liz Dobson package since the first time their eyes met across a sea of unacquainted faces several weeks before. He could have sworn she felt the same way. It wasn't like him to misread suggestive glances from a beautiful woman.

As he returned to the bar, AJ couldn't get the image of Liz out of his mind, and her rejection away from his bruised ego. And while he'd promised himself he wouldn't pursue casual sex before his trip, especially now he knew Liz and Nate were cousins, the imagined scenario chipped away at his resolve.

"You having another?" AJ asked Nate as he joined him at the bar.

"Yeah, why not."

He hailed the bartender, ordered two beers, then turned back to Nate. "What's with your cousin? Is she stuck up or just playing hard to get?"

Nate couldn't hide his amusement. "You prick."

"What?"

"Don't tell me you hit on her?"

"Okay, I won't. Anyway, she blew me off."

"New experience for you, mate. Welcome to the real world." Nate chuckled. "She's not stuck up, she's just shy. And to be fair, she watched you flirt with half the girls in here. Also, you're leaving next week. Hardly makes you a candidate for the date of the month award."

"Purely a technicality. And who mentioned dating? We could have fallen in lust, made out in that tiny terrace of yours, and waved goodbye on Monday."

"There's no way you're making out with anyone in my home, especially Liz. Anyway, I've never known her to do the casual thing, and there's some guy after her. Peter Nichols. I'm not sure about him though." Nate scanned the bar, checking to see who was within earshot. "I've never seen him out of a perfectly tailored suit, tie, and expensive cufflinks. And he drives a late model Porsche. Something about him doesn't add up. Still, it's not my business."

"Competition with a Porsche. Damn. I don't stand a chance. What's her story?"

"Arrived in London a few months back. Moonlighting as a waitress while trying to launch her business."

"What sort of business?"

"She's a dot-com whiz with an internet list and a few affiliates. Has an honors degree in marketing."

"Not another blogger. Shit, the world's full of them. She's got amazing eyes though. Like burnt amber." AJ wanted to say more but stopped himself. Nate didn't need the details of how he'd taken an instant liking to her pert body and amused smile weeks ago.

"Feck off, mate. Don't even think about it."

AJ laughed as he recalled his thoughts on Nate's opinion, and that was before he knew Liz and Nate were cousins. "How old is she?"

"Twenty-three. So keep your hands off."

"Really? She seems older—got that whole sophisticated air thing going on."

"Anyway, Penny has you in her sights."

"Not my type." AJ raised his bottle to his mouth. "Too forward." He took a sip.

"What? Since when?"

"I told you, I'm turning over a new leaf."

"Yeah? Whatever."

CHEMICAL REACTIONS

AROUND MID-MORNING, a party of eight—including a tall, dark-haired Adonis with a man bun—arrived at *El Beso* for brunch. Liz made her way over to explain the specials, her focus on the group, not on AJ Tanner.

"Welcome to *El Beso*." Everyone looked her way and a familiar clench of uncertainty held her gut as she wrestled with shyness. Liz went over the menu, not stopping to catch AJ's eye. He didn't seem to notice as he joked intimately with the same redhead from the night before. His nonverbal communication came through loud and clear. The idiom 'treat them mean, keep them keen' jumped into her thoughts. "Are you ready to order or shall I come back in five minutes?"

AJ looked up. "We're ready."

"Okay, what can I get you?" Liz asked the first woman to her right, then continued around the table until she reached an attractive male with sandy-colored hair and a neutral expression.

"I'll have you served on French toast with dripping hot butter and sprinkled with blueberries, sugar, and cinnamon." The guy didn't smile, just leaned forward with his elbows on the table and expression serious as if he'd ordered scrambled eggs and bacon with a side of toast.

AJ leaned back and shook his head, a suppressed grin firmly in place. "Ryan, cut it out, mate," he said. "Pull your head in."

Liz and Ryan locked eyes for several seconds. "Please excuse me for a moment."

She made her way to the window of the kitchen, spoke to the chef, then returned to the table. "I'm sorry. The chef said we're all out of dripping hot butter. Is there something else you'd prefer?"

Ryan offered a smile, albeit a slight one, as the rest of the table laughed loudly.

"Don't be a jerk, Ryan," said a woman in a broad Scottish accent. "Ignore him, love. He's hungover and feeling sorry for himself."

"You're so beautiful," he said. The compliment traveled on a whisper. Even so, everyone at the table, including AJ, heard it.

Liz turned to face him, the heat rushing up her neck. "Ryan, isn't it? Do I make you uncomfortable? Would you rather one of the male wait staff serve you?" she teased.

"Not at all." He grinned at her response. "I promise to behave if you bring me the big breakfast."

"Good, because I pride myself on being courteous to my customers. Sometimes it's a challenge, as you may well imagine." Liz looked at an amused AJ. "What would you like?"

"The Spanish omelet thanks, Liz. And a tomato juice."

So, he did remember her.

Finally finishing around two, Liz dumped her apron in the laundry chute on her way through the back alley, greeting the crisp but sunny afternoon with a smile. She checked her phone for a text from Peter. Liz enjoyed Peter's attention, even with the uncertainty accompanying it. The fact he didn't want a purely sexual encounter was a conflicting plus—or minus, depending on the day.

So far, he'd been the perfect gentleman on the two occasions they'd met for lunch. Yet Liz wondered if a perfect gentleman fitted her requirements. Science wasn't her thing, but when it came to her limited knowledge of the opposite sex, she understood the importance of chemistry, just like the next girl. Passion always had its place.

As Liz walked past the restaurant entrance, she turned to see AJ leaning against the wall of the building, one heel—again clad in a fashionable boot—kicked up against the brickwork. She stopped, slipped her bag over her shoulder, and rubbed her hands together, expecting the friction to ease the chill of the early afternoon air.

"Hi. How was your brunch?" she asked, determined to keep a chaste distance between them.

"Great, as always." His smile, warm and infectious, lit up his face. A different version of the face she experienced the evening before. "I want to apologize for Ryan. He can be inappropriate when hungover, or drunk for that matter. He's going through some stuff, but that doesn't excuse what he said."

"It's not up to you to apologize. I thought I handled it okay."

"You did. Still, you must get guys hitting on you all the time."

Liz slipped her hands into her coat pockets, searching for warmth from the satin lining. "Not really."

"No?" He raised a brow.

His style intrigued her. Dark-washed jeans rolled at the bottom, those infamous boots, a white T-shirt, and a thick plaid jacket left undone. With a sloppy beanie covering his hair, he looked like a farm boy with a fashion edge. Organically sexy as hell.

"Shall we walk? I live a few blocks past Nate's." He motioned her forward, and they fell into step. "Any plans for this afternoon? We could hang out."

"Actually, I have an appointment with the bathtub and a hot guy on my e-reader."

"Sounds good. We could watch a movie after I've helped you wash your hair. I've heard those e-reader guys have little substance when it comes down to the nitty gritty."

Liz stopped and turned his way, amused at his attempt to make a joke. "Are you always so forward with women you hardly know?"

"Not always, but I'm off in a few days. I thought it's about time to break free of my usual restraints. Besides, our eyes met across a crowded room of drunken bastards weeks ago, so we're hardly strangers."

His smile could melt chocolate quicker than a microwave, she thought, then chuckled at how food was always her analogy of choice.

"Are you laughing at me, Lizzy?"

AJ's use of her childhood nickname amused her. Her brother Mitch always called her Lizzy-boo. "A bit. I'll pass on the invitation."

"Let me walk you home, anyway. Give you time to reconsider."

They chatted all the way. Small talk about the London weather, what sights she'd seen, and her job, and reached Nate's place in no time. Liz turned to speak. "This is me, obviously."

She offered her hand. His intense stare held hers. He was the kind of guy who, when he looked at you intently, reminded you something was missing from your soul.

Something immense and important.

He leaned closer, so close she could feel the heat of his breath on her ear. "I'd like to spend time with you."

His power surrounded her, and she struggled to break the charge. "Um…I really should go in."

"Okay. Later? Dinner?"

"I'm pretty sure I have plans."

"Pretty sure? Has your boyfriend not contacted you today?"

"Not yet. And he's not my boyfriend." Liz scolded herself for offering too much information.

AJ took several steps forward. Liz stepped back. The smell of fresh paint tickled her nostrils as his frame loomed over hers and her butt bumped against the newly painted, high gloss front door of number thirty-five. He rested his hands on either side of her. Confinement never felt so good. She held her breath as any awareness of activity on the street vanished. He considered her, his pupils dark and full and a half smile tugging at his lips.

"Therefore—" AJ brushed a lock of hair from her face in the gentlest of gestures. "He doesn't deserve you." He leaned in closer, flicked his line of sight unashamedly between her lips and eyes and asked, "May I?"

The kiss took her by surprise. Not because he dared to kiss her, but the intensity of the feelings it aroused. This type of kiss soared straight from her imagination—soft and fluid, alternating with demand and determination. She stood, struggling to calm her breath as his dark stare requested a response and her lips dripped with fire.

"I have to go." Liz fumbled in her purse for her keys, not trusting herself to speak further.

"No, you don't. You have a free afternoon. You just said so."

"Did I?" She made eye contact, gently chewing her bottom lip for the body language effect. "I'm not thinking straight at the moment."

"Pity." AJ stepped back onto the narrow path and slid both hands into his jacket pockets as a token of retreat. "Enjoy the rest of your day."

Liz inserted the key in the lock with a shaky hand, and, not looking back once, opened the door with a pull and a push. Her keys and bag found contact with the hall table. She made a beeline for the guest bathroom where she splashed her face with cool water, struggling to get a grip.

One kiss!

No other man in her entire dating life had made her feel like AJ Tanner had at that moment. The intensity stunned her. If she imagined her life as a movie, which she occasionally did, AJ would certainly be cast in the lead. Liz hadn't enjoyed orgasmic sex in a long while—suppression remained her default setting of the moment. Now one kiss threatened to disrupt everything.

However, instead of the afternoon she craved, Liz flopped down on the living room sofa with her phone and a mug of hot chocolate, and waited for Peter to have the decency to pick up the damn phone and call as promised.

Around eight-thirty, Peter texted, full of apologies about being caught up. He offered no other explanation. Liz stared at the TV, flicking through channels for something decent to watch. Within half an hour, she padded into the kitchen for a glass of water, then went to bed.

She didn't bother with dinner or ice cream.

4

SPLINTERED HEARTS

SLEEP WAS a restless affair for Liz that Saturday night. She tossed and turned, worrying about Peter, her To-Do list, and the kiss at the door of the tiny terrace from the man with the stylish boots and clever tongue. After finally drifting off just after two, she slept through her alarm when she hit *off* rather than *snooze*. Sunday would be a long day.

Around midday, AJ arrived back at *El Beso* with two young women. They sat at a table for four by the window. From this vantage point, he had a clear view of the restaurant and everyone in it, including Liz. She wondered if the girls were his sisters by the way they interacted in a relaxed and affectionate manner.

Liz asked one of the other servers to work the table and avoided eye contact with AJ. The few times she dared look his way, he looked right back. When the chef dinged the bell indicating service for table eight, she steadied two of the large plates along her left arm and picked up the other in her right hand, then moved toward them.

"Good afternoon. Who's having the baked eggs?"

"That's mine." AJ smiled. "How are you today, Liz?"

"Great, thank you." Liz placed the two seafood salads in front of the girls.

"Say hi to my sisters Anna and Charlotte. Liz is Nate's cousin," AJ offered as part of the introduction.

"Pleased to meet you both." Liz greeted the girls grinning up at her. Good looks ran in the family.

"You're from New Zealand, right?" Charlotte asked.

"I am. I guess you both know Nate. Everyone seems to know him around here."

"I was in love with him years six through sixteen. He said I was too young to be in a relationship," Anna said. "Broke my little heart into splinters. I've never forgiven him, and he's never so much as even kissed me."

Liz laughed. "I think lots of girls have loved my cousin from afar. Please enjoy your meals."

"Thanks," AJ said. "We will."

"O.M.G. That's the girl you have the hots for," Anna said as Liz walked away from their table.

"Really?" AJ chuckled at the look on his sister's face. "I only met her three days ago, so keep your voice down."

"Nate's cousin, you sly fox," Charlotte teased. "She's pretty, stunning in fact." Charlotte's gaze followed Liz around the restaurant before she leaned over the table and whispered, "Have you slept with her yet?"

"What? You can't ask me that. And even if I had, I wouldn't discuss it with anyone, let alone you two."

"You've kissed her, though. I can tell," Anna joined in. "It's written all over your face."

AJ couldn't hide his amusement. "Would you two stop trying to run my love life. I told you, I'm having a break from women for now."

"So, what's she like, as a kisser?" Anna asked.

AJ let out a throaty laugh and shook his head, not shifting his sight off Liz for a moment. Why not, he thought. "Incredible."

"It's a pity you're leaving town," Anna said. "You guys could have dated. It's about time you had a proper girlfriend."

"Not my style, you know that. Anyway, she has a boyfriend of sorts, and she doesn't seem like the cheating type."

"You can't tell that about a person by just looking," Charlotte said. "How serious are they?"

"No idea." AJ tore a slice of bread in half and topped it with beans. "Can we change the subject?"

Liz didn't return to their table, leaving the job to one of the male staff. Yet, every time she glanced his way, he'd stare and occasionally, she'd stare back. By the time he and the girls had finished lunch, thoughts of *why the hell not* and *no way* conflicted in his conscience. He sipped his juice while weighing up the pros and cons, the sharp taste of grapefruit cleansing the chorizo from his palate. He decided to wing it. If the opportunity arose, surely one small indiscretion wouldn't hurt.

As Liz turned into her street later that afternoon, she noticed AJ leaning on the gate, his hair covered with the same loose beanie. His stance matched that of the day before. A foot kicked back on the pillar, one hand in his pocket and the other on his phone. Saint, ready to move over to the dark side.

He looked up. "Liz. What a nice surprise."

Really? She strolled toward him, keys ready and waiting. He flashed his signature flirty smile, hot as hell and twice as sexy. "Hi. Are you looking for Nate?"

"Yeah, we'd planned to have a beer, but he just texted to say he can't make it. Fate seems to be pushing us together, so I'm free if you are."

Liz didn't reply as she pushed the gate open and walked up the path to the house. He followed. She stopped at the doorstep. "I don't think fate has anything to do with it. I'm kind of seeing someone. I told you."

"And I told you he 'kind of' doesn't deserve you. We're ships passing in the night. And if the way you kissed me yesterday was any indication, you want to cruise on my boat just as much as I want to cruise on yours." His smile held, ensuring the banter stayed lighthearted.

Liz enjoyed the flattery, even if she knew better. "Is that right?" She smiled at the boat metaphor, then reached into her purse for her keys, forgetting they were already in her hand.

"Come on, Lizzy. Meet me halfway. You won't regret it."

"Sorry. But I'm not the kind of girl who sleeps with a guy just because he pushes me up against my front door and kisses the heck out of me."

"That's good." He leaned in closer. She positioned the key in the deadbolt and pulled the door toward her to free the sticky lock. "Because I'm not the kind of guy who's offering sleep."

The door opened right on cue. She turned to face him, his line of sight unashamedly focused on her lips. "What are you offering? No strings sex to keep the wind in your sails until you reach Japan?"

AJ leaned on the door frame and slipped his hands into his jacket pockets while eyes the color of a dried-off meadow held her attention. "I'm offering you an experience you won't forget."

He wore the sexy male look well—that look of lust. Hooded eyes that smoldered her way coupled with determined lips. The look that's usually over the minute they've finished groaning their release.

"Sailing makes me a little seasick unless I'm at the helm." Liz didn't feel insulted. She didn't understand what she felt, so her answer held no sting in the tail, just a touch of tease. "Now, please leave and take your spinnaker-sized ego with you."

He laughed. "You're breaking my heart. Let's spend a few hours together. You can be at my helm any day of the week."

"I don't think so. Thanks for the dose of flattery, though." Liz smiled warmly, still enjoying the moment. "Safe travels."

He nodded, then turned and walked away. Only when he was halfway down the street did she shut the door, leaning on it for support as arguments flew back and forth in her mind. The intensity of his smell and touch smothered her. Liz tried to convince herself her decision-making process was sound. Anthony Tanner was a shameful player. A player who'd use her before leaving for the airport with another notch in his expensive leather belt. Once in Japan, he'd forget she even walked the face of the earth. AJ was definitely a 'hell no' kind of guy.

And yet...

Liz plodded into the kitchen and took a loaf of grainy bread from the pantry. She sliced it thickly and spread it with copious amounts of butter and a touch of Marmite. Taking a bite, she slouched in front of the TV, checked her social media, and waited for Peter to call.

Her phone lit up with a text. She glanced at the unknown number on the screen.

Friday night? Bon Voyage soiree? AJ.

She placed her phone on the coffee table. *Bon Voyage soiree? Interesting.*

The week passed without a word from either AJ or Peter. The Peter situation played on her mind with a confused hand. He'd seemed keen initially, but his interest had apparently waned. Oh well.

AJ was a different story. His sexuality 'shone like a beacon on a dark and blustery night' as Penny so aptly put it. But Penny said that about lots of men. In fact, every handsome man she met.

Even though AJ was skipping town within the week, thoughts of him consumed Liz. How would it feel to be delivered from sexual obscurity—just once, or maybe twice if he could manage it —by such a man? A man who wasn't afraid to flaunt his experience. A man whose hands could tell tales.

In the days that followed, would snippets of their liaison slip in and out of her consciousness, like an inspiring book or movie you can't stop thinking about? She decided thoughts of AJ and her doing the wild thing must stay exactly that—thoughts.

However, when Friday arrived, her imagination was still running wild. The night before, the manager of *El Beso* persuaded her to work another day shift. Working a Friday, usually her day off, didn't appeal in the slightest, but the prospect of extra cash held the upper hand.

The day started with a crash and a bang when Liz, armed with a stack of dirty dishes, bumped butts with a customer. Plates and silverware flung through the air and landed in a shattered heap on the tiled floor. When he called her a clumsy idiot, it only added to her distress.

The place was busy and short staffed, with the head chef in a blue mood turning to dark gray as the morning progressed. Liz had worked on her internet business until after midnight the night before, so by the end of her shift, the thought of a bathtub of steaming hot water excited her more than anything.

Not having the energy to walk one more step in the stuffy afternoon air, she caught the bus, sandwiched between a guy who hadn't discovered the virtues of antiperspirant, and an elderly woman dressed to the nines who reeked of stale garlic.

When Liz finally rounded the corner into her street, there he was again. The handsome, expensive-boot-wearing Mr. Tanner, his sight set on the screen of his phone. He glanced up as she approached. Liz spoke first. "Hi. Are you waiting for Nate? He's away this weekend."

"I know." AJ looked her up and down, his intention plainly evident. "I've just dropped some books off for him. They're around the back. And anyway, don't we have a date?"

She nodded, her top teeth absently scraping across her bottom lip. "Didn't you get my return text?"

"No."

"That's because I didn't send one."

"I thought that meant you were keen."

He flashed his signature smile and for a moment, Liz wanted to lose herself in his warmth. To forget about her day and her reasons for keeping him at arm's length. "Anyway, it's been a long day and I have a date with the bathtub."

"What is it with you and that bathtub?"

Liz smiled back.

"Okay. I've a couple of last-minute things to do. Have a soak, and I'll be back around seven with food."

"I don't think—"

"It's just dinner, Liz," he interrupted. "No ulterior motive intended. My flight leaves in the morning. I don't want a late night."

He stepped closer, his space dominating hers. The offer of a takeout excited her almost as much as the thought of other things. Almost.

She huffed a sigh as she considered his offer. "Okay, but you have to be gone by ten."

"Eleven at the latest." The sparkle in his eyes danced into mischief. "Any preference food wise?"

"Turkish, Japanese. I eat anything."

By the time he returned, Liz was starving. She'd left her hair curly and had pulled on a comfortable combo of soft denim jeans, slashed at the knee, and a light gray sloppy sweater.

He stepped back as she opened the door, letting out a soft whistle while he looked her up and down. "I know I said this was just dinner, but with you looking all flushed and sexy, we may have to reevaluate."

"Stick to the plan and come in, or reevaluate and leave. Your choice."

"What kind of choice is that?" He walked through the door, across the living room and into the kitchen as if he owned the show. "You're the one looking hot. I'm purely an innocent bystander."

"You may be many things, but innocent?"

"My mother used the term occasionally, back in the day. Anyway," he said, unpacking the bag onto the booth table. "I have lamb kofta, pilaf, dolma, and flat bread, *and* yogurt sauce to complement the lamb. I even thought of dessert." AJ put down a small container and opened the corner for her to take a peek.

"And, to add to the ambiance of the evening, a smooth Spanish red." He pulled a bottle of red wine out of the bag and moved to the cabinet for two glasses.

"Yum. I'm in heaven."

"Not yet, babe," he murmured.

AJ's playful side amused Liz. And yet, his brooding intensity tipped her slightly off balance and made her question several items on her 'Hell No' list. Still, it was nice to know his personality contained a certain complexity. "Would you behave? Let's enjoy our meal and engage in stimulating conversation without the innuendo."

"I'll try. Can't promise though. Especially when you're tossing words like *stimulating* around." AJ held up two glasses. "Wine?"

"Half a glass, no more. You certainly know your way around the kitchen."

"I come here a bit. We have boys' nights where we watch the

rugby, eat pizza, drink beer, and talk bullshit." He cocked a brow. "I've even slept in your bed on the odd occasion."

"So, you're the one who left the large indentation in the mattress?"

AJ threw his head back and laughed. "Liz Dobson, you're a shameless flirt. Who would have thought?"

Her cheeks flushed with uncomfortable heat. "I meant the bed has a distinct sag. I've ordered a new one, but it hasn't arrived yet."

"Pity. Still, what's a little roll together between friends?"

"Let's eat. This conversation is taking all kinds of turns in the wrong direction."

He motioned her toward the booth. "Sit, I'll grab some plates."

"Looks delicious. I don't know where to start. You choose for me."

AJ dished food onto two plates, handing one to her. "Tell me about dreams that have passed you by, and ones you have for the future."

Liz thought for a moment. He seemed genuinely interested. "I never wanted to be a princess when I was a little girl. I wanted to be a digger driver. To dig to London."

"Dig to London?"

"Yeah, you know that kid's game—digging to the other side of the earth with a shovel from the tool shed."

"I remember it well. Why London?"

"The streets are paved with gold, aren't they?"

A smile lit up AJ's face as he reached for his wine. "You realize that's just a rumor from an old fairy tale."

"A happy ever after fairy tale."

He offered his glass in a toast. "To happy ever after."

5

UNSPOKEN EXPECTATIONS

BY THE TIME they'd finished the meal and polished off the wine, the best part of four hours had vanished. They'd recounted trivial tales about their lives with much amusement, tasting from each other's plates while the Spanish red relaxed their inhibitions. Occasionally, they ardently disagreed on a topic of the moment, which only added to Liz's interest in AJ.

"Thanks for the lovely evening," she said. "I can't remember when I enjoyed myself more."

"Sounds like you're ready to show me the door."

"You did say you'd be gone by eleven. It's now half past."

"Breaking rules is one habit I never plan to break." AJ cleared the table, loading the plates and glasses into the dishwasher. "Coffee?"

"Not for me. I'd be up all night."

He slipped into the booth beside her, sliding his arm along the back of the seat. "That was the idea, but maybe you're right. No coffee."

Liz inhaled an unsettling breath. "You're awfully close."

He moved forward a fraction. "Am I?"

AJ ran his hand through her hair, using his index finger to trace the spiral of a curl. "Sometimes"—he brushed his thumb over her cheek—"it's nice to sit next to a beautiful woman, to feel connected and enjoy comfortable conversation."

He certainly has the gift of the gab, she thought with an inward smile. "So what are you saying? You have no expectations?"

"Not necessarily. I find you incredibly attractive." He whispered the line as if telling a secret no man had ever told her before. "I want to sit with you wrapped in my arms and lie with our legs entangled, even if it's only for one night out of our entire lives." AJ leaned forward and let his lips lightly brush against hers. Liz smiled. He moved closer in response, and for the second time in a week, caged her against the wall, his lips moving to take what he wanted.

Aided by the effects of the wine, Liz responded in kind. In less than a heartbeat, she'd taken the first step onto the gangplank of his boat. The boat that dragged anchor in rough waters. The boat she had no business being on.

"Let me stay?" His whisper brushed her earlobe with a soft breath.

"You really should go." Liz felt obliged to at least make the suggestion. "I've had too much to drink and don't feel in total control."

"You hold the power here, Liz. I'm not some asshole who will coerce you into doing something you don't want. We can just make out." He bent down and kissed the side of her neck. "Because even before we met, we connected."

She lifted her chin. "Did we?"

"I recall one particular evening." He skimmed his lips across to her earlobe and gave a little tug. "We were at a small bar down from Putney Bridge. It was bitterly cold outside, remember? You floated in on a whoosh of cool air with a group of friends, wearing a dark gray silky tunic and a pencil skirt. And we played the game. The glancing game."

Her eyes held the smile her lips suppressed. "I don't recall."

"Is that right? I talked to you at the bar. You commented on my boots. You looked familiar, but I couldn't remember where we'd met."

"Because we hadn't."

"No. But you and Nate could pass for siblings." He stood and offered his hand. "Let's go to bed, just to cuddle. Anything else is a bonus."

She followed him up the stairs to her bedroom, took a detour to the bathroom and shut the door. The Liz in the mirror's reflection wasn't an easily recognized version of herself. She didn't do casual sex. Didn't give herself to a man when the odds of them having a relationship were zero to none. This Liz was not the Liz Dobson she knew and respected. That Liz played it safe, always did the right thing. And yet, just for tonight, she wanted to let go. To feel reckless and alive and sexy under the touch of this good-looking man, without worrying about what her friends or family would say. No one would ever find out.

When she stepped from the bathroom a few minutes later, AJ was already lying on her saggy bed, naked from the waist up. What she saw didn't disappoint. Tight muscular definition, nipples covered in a scattering of hair, and a distinctive tattoo on his left pec and shoulder, all went together nicely with the sexiest happy trail she'd ever seen.

He watched her move across the room. "You okay?"

"Yes, fine."

He smiled. Liz returned the gesture. She sat on the bed, anticipating another kiss. AJ didn't kiss like other guys in her intimate back story. He had an amazing way of darting his tongue in and out of her mouth. It drove her crazy. He scooted closer and kissed her, then slowly guided her hand toward his fly.

"Do you want to do the honors?"

Her hands moved to the top button, but her fingers struggled to release it from the buttonhole. She looked up. "I want to take it slowly."

"Of course. But if you're any slower with that zipper, the denim may rip of its own accord."

Liz didn't find his manner domineering. Sure, he acted forthright and determined, but he did so with humor and patience. He tugged his jeans down, taking his boxers along for the ride. Her hand flew to her mouth.

He threw his head back and laughed. "Cover your eyes if you don't want to see me naked. Not your mouth."

"I didn't expect you to strip completely."

"Sorry, physical modesty's not my strong point." AJ grabbed the top sheet and covered his lower torso. But it was too late. She'd seen the beast, and what a beast it was.

"Obviously."

Liz enjoyed the visual of the naked male form, but decorum demanded she pretend otherwise. She reached over to flick off the lamp, the glow of the streetlight casting a forgiving shadow across the room. Standing, she rested her hands on his shoulders to steady herself.

He clutched the bottom of her sweater and pulled it up and over her head before his fingers made quick work of her jean zipper. Strong hands slid into the space between the back waistband and her underwear, cupping her bottom enclosed in thin lace. "No G-string?"

"I'm more of a vintage kind of girl."

"Let me see." He pulled her closer and planted a soft kiss on the top of each breast, the roughness of his beard scraping over the lace of her cami. "I love vintage underwear."

AJ flicked the bedside lamp back on and watched her tug off her jeans. Liz stood before him in a see-through lace cami and panties to match in shades of soft caramel. He puffed out a deep breath. "Shit. You invited me over wearing that, and now you're pretending you don't want sex."

"The choice of my underwear had nothing to do with you. I just like the feel of it. Now shift."

He moved over, taking the covers with him. "I love a strong woman, especially when I'm in bed with them naked."

"About that. At least put your boxers back on."

He shook his head. "Why would I do that?"

"I won't get any sleep at all if you don't."

"You're right about that. We have some serious making out to do."

He leaned over, taking her face in both hands and did the tongue flick thing repeatedly, his fingers raking through her curls as the tip of his erection brushed against the sheerness of her panties. Sultry kisses trailed down her neck and over the contour of her collarbone. His talented lips moved down to her breasts. His hands followed suit. "I'd never take advantage, though. The choice is yours."

"I don't usually...do this. But..."

Expert thumbs connected with both nipples. He worked back and forth, so softly she could barely feel the touch. And as the pressure increased, so did the heat and her breasts tightened of their own accord.

"But?"

Outside, an early spring shower turned into persistent rain, joined by the occasional dull flare of lightning and the distant rumble of thunder. Liz hardly heard it. "You're an amazing kisser. Oh...holy shit..."

AJ teased down the top of her camisole and licked his way around each breast—hand on the left, mouth on the right, then vice versa. "Babe, I haven't even started yet."

"It's just... It's been...a while... And I..."

He sucked the indent at the base of her throat, then blew his soft breath over the wet smudge left by his tongue. "You what?"

"It feels so good."

His fingers raked through her hair. He massaged her scalp and tugged gently. "I love your hair. All these curls."

"Really?" The word barely left her lips.

"I really do." AJ rested his forehead on hers and inhaled. "You okay? We can stop right now."

"Um… No. Don't stop."

She felt like a horny teenager shacked up in the back seat of a car, his musky aroma enticing as she nuzzled into his neck. He kissed and caressed and sucked her breasts through the lace, leaving his barely wet imprint. His hands stayed above her waist. She wondered why he didn't touch her hips, thighs, or elsewhere, when she clearly craved it. Only when she took the lead, guiding his hand with hers, did he make his move. His determined fingers found their place of worship as his throaty voice whispered erotic commands against her neck, and his erection pressed fiery hot against her.

"You sure?" he asked again as he reached for a condom from his wallet on the nightstand.

"I…yes." Liz wasn't sure of anything apart from the aching need consuming her.

AJ took his time. Tender hands touched, a watchful gaze gathered clues and, all the while, he uttered words of want and praise into her neck and throat. When her legs tightened for the second time—his name whispered on a husky breath as she slipped from his grasp into pleasure—only then did he gently move forward, allowing her to consider.

"You feel so beautiful. Every curve, every hollow." He paused for a moment, tilted his head, and looked at her, smiling softly. "You okay?"

"Yes." She rocked downward in consent. "I want this. I do."

Long fingers trailed over the soft skin of her backside, digging in tight as he pulled her closer. "You do? And you're okay with the position?" His voice held a trace of amusement as he grabbed her hands and held them above her head.

"Yes."

"You want it bad, Lizzy?"

"Yes!"

"Say it. Tell me you want it bad."

Concerned brows knitted together. Dominant AJ was introducing himself in no uncertain terms, and his demeanor left no room for doubt or regret. "I want it bad."

Lips slammed into lips, his tongue hotter and stronger than she could ever imagine. He sucked her in, claiming her breath and her soul, then pulled back and looked at her, his eyes dark with want. "You're full of surprises." His hands caressed both sides of her face as he stared into her eyes. "Let's make beautiful sex."

Like a tango dancer guiding his partner through a dance set to a sensual melody, AJ took a dominant lead. Words of desire puffed across her skin as he entered her. The force had her arching off the bed as every inch of naked skin tightened under his touch. By the sound of the gasp emanating from deep within his throat, his experience mirrored hers as he rocked her to heaven and pushed her over the edge.

AJ collapsed on top of her, his face buried into her neck and his lips soft on her skin. They stayed tangled together for some time—he still inside of her—their bodies slick with sweat and hearts beating in an accelerated, but unsynchronized tempo.

He moved onto his back, one hand still entwined with hers, and rolled his head on the pillow to look at her.

"I'll be back in a sec." AJ's smile didn't quite reach his eyes, and Liz noticed an immediate shift. He closed the bathroom door, staying there for several minutes.

It gave her time to think, or rather to chastise herself for making a poor judgment call. She'd just experienced a mind-blowing liaison with a guy she never intended to liaise with. The possibility of seeing AJ again was slight. That bothered her. However, when he returned, smiled down at her and slid into bed, his arms wide, all thoughts of impropriety were tucked away for later.

"That was incredible. I hope I didn't come on too strong." He pulled her closer and kissed her with soft lips. "Are we good?"

Liz snuggled in close, an emotional lump forming in her throat. "Yep."

He rubbed his hands up and down her arms, his concern genuine and yet, somehow aloof. "You don't sound convinced."

"No, we're good." Liz wondered if he noticed the hesitancy in her voice. "I'm just not used to this. It feels a little foreign."

AJ held her with firm tenderness, the heat of his body helping relax her disquiet. "I like you. I'm not just saying it. If things were different, who knows…"

"I understand." The sentiment didn't quite reach her soul. "What time do you have to leave?"

He checked the clock on the nightstand and stretched over to turn off the lamp. "Way too early."

"Have you set your alarm?"

"Yep."

"Will you wake me before you go?"

"Of course." AJ rolled onto his side. The barrier created by this simple act screamed of indifference. Instead of snuggling into his back, Liz curled herself into a partial ball beside him as she wished he didn't have a plane to catch.

Would they ever see each other again?

Liz woke around four to an empty bed and knew he'd gone. Maybe it was better this way. She didn't have to face him or listen to lame excuses of how 'if things were different' blah, blah. Restless and moody, she snuggled under the covers. When sleep didn't return, she flicked on the bedside lamp and reached for her e-reader.

It was just after six when Liz dragged herself out of bed and stood naked in front of the bathroom mirror. The presence of AJ's lust tingled between her legs, his mark blatantly obvious on both breasts. Not having the energy to shower, she returned to her room and flopped on the bed. The smell of AJ lingered.

The sheets came off with a flourish, landing in a heap on the floor. She collapsed on the mattress cover, grabbed the duvet, and pulled it over her head. His scent remained.

The faint chime of a text alert woke her several hours later. She reached under her pillow, grabbed her phone, and glanced at the unknown number.

Don't forget me, Liz. AJ xx

6

DELIBERATION

As AJ snuck out the door of number thirty-five and into the predawn of the city, he did his best to discount the tightness in his chest at the thought of leaving Liz without waking her. They'd spent one night together. But he knew when he sat in the bathroom afterward, struggling to get his shit sorted, that Liz Dobson would hold a special place in his story among the many rumors and regrets.

He shouldn't have left without saying goodbye. He'd stuffed up, and as he said to Chris the week before, 'guilt's a bitch.'

AJ caught the tube to Chris's apartment, his London home for the past few months, and let himself in. Chris sat at the table eating breakfast, dressed and ready to go. "Hey, you're back. All set?"

"Yeah. I appreciate this, mate." AJ zipped his backpack and clicked a small padlock into place. "Didn't want the family at the airport. Mum was bad enough when I phoned her yesterday."

"No problem. It's on my way to Slough."

"Remind me why you're going to Slough again?"

"To run a clinic. Come on, we'd better go, or I'll be late."

The men braved the fresh morning air, jumped in Chris's SUV

and made their way through already congested traffic toward Heathrow.

"What happened to you last night?" Chris pulled onto the M4. His amused smile said it all. "Got lucky or what?"

"Got lucky isn't an accurate description of the events. Stuffed up more like it."

"Care to share?"

"Not really," AJ sighed, "but I went home with Nate's cousin and played naughty naked teenagers in her saggy bed."

Chris chuckled. "You can't be serious? At the tiny terrace?"

"Yep." AJ removed his sunglasses and rubbed his fingertips over closed eyelids. Never one to regret a night of sensual stimulation, he understood why this time he felt differently. It wasn't because Liz and Nate were cousins, or even because his trip meant he couldn't see her again. AJ had disappointed himself on a self-indulgent whim. "I can't keep my dick in my pants long enough to save myself. Not proud of it either. Seemed like a good idea at the time, though. There's something about her. Shit."

"You can't beat yourself up over Cathy forever."

"It's only been eleven weeks. You think I'd at least keep myself in check for eleven lousy weeks. But no, I had to have her, just like the old days. And she's Nate's cousin. Shit, shit, shit." AJ returned the sunglasses and stared out the window as the consequence of Nate's reaction hit him. "He's gonna kill me."

"You're too hard on yourself. It's not like you've screwed half the girls in Putney. No harm done."

"That's not the point. The night before Cathy slipped into a coma, she told me she loved me as much as any of her men, including her deceased first husband. I never knew. Thought it was a bit of fun. Her cougar moment. It never occurred to me she'd fall in love. Or get hurt."

"At least she got the chance to tell you."

"Yeah. Still, I set a goal, and as soon as a beautiful woman crossed my path, I ate the marshmallow on a sexual impulse."

Chris laughed. "You've always been a marshmallow kid. No self-control."

"Thanks for your opinionated vote of confidence."

"So, Nate's cousin, eh? What's her name again?"

"Lizette." AJ closed his eyes momentarily and leaned back on the headrest. "Beautiful Liz. I left without saying goodbye. What kind of dick does that? I'll be on the top of her bastard list by now."

"We've all been at the top of someone's bastard list at some stage."

AJ never imagined Chris being a bastard in any way. "Not you, surely."

Chris shrugged. "But just remember, your past doesn't have to control your future." He pulled into the passenger drop-off point. "Right, on that piece of sage advice, I'll have to drop you and run. Otherwise, I'll be late."

AJ opened the door and remove his bag from the back seat. "Thanks, I owe you."

"My pleasure. Say hello to Bali from me."

"Will do. I'll be surfing in Kuta in ten weeks time."

Chris chuckled. "A real test for you and your marshmallow dick."

"Thanks. For a doctor, you're no help at all. See you in eighteen months." AJ shut the door and slapped the roof of the SUV twice. He watched Chris drive away.

After a breakfast of airport bacon and eggs and a half decent coffee, AJ sat in the departure lounge flipping his phone end for end and wondered if he should text her.

Or not.

He replayed their episode several times in his mind, blaming his lack of judgment on the wine, then on his nonexistent sexual activity of late, and lastly, on Liz herself. Why was she so reticent initially? Didn't she realize men want what they can't have, feel the need to conquer? He slipped his phone into his pocket, then grabbed it again and keyed in the passcode.

Don't forget me, Liz xx

7

SUBTLE MANIPULATIONS

LIZ SUMMED up Peter Nichols from the first moment they met. He thought of himself as a distinguished man about town. The fact his ego didn't quite match his package obviously had never occurred to him. Even so, she found him pleasant company when they were alone, and handsome, in a preppy kind of way. Not that looks made the man, but maybe Penny was right about doing it with the lights on. He definitely checked several points on her 'Hell Yeah' list.

The week after AJ left for Japan, Peter finally got his act together and issued a dinner invitation for the following weekend. Initially, after her regretful—albeit entirely memorable—night with the infamous Mr. Tanner, Liz appreciated the mild interest Peter showed.

AJ leaving at the crack of dawn without saying goodbye put a distinct dent in her self-esteem. Her Granny repeatedly told Liz and her sisters that men were 'only after one thing and one thing only.' The problem was, Liz wanted that one 'thing' as much as AJ did. What would Granny have to say about that? She'd label Liz a *wanton hussy* for sure.

If AJ hadn't left the country, the option of spending time with Peter would have been even more difficult. But as AJ told no lies and gave no promises, Liz knew he'd only walked into her back-story for an instant, never to return. Penny would say he'd tiptoed into her world to leave a lesson. Liz wasn't convinced.

However, when she thought about it, maybe the lesson was: never sleep with a handsome stranger after one too many wines. It only made you question your principles and some days, questioning principles was a pointless exercise.

Peter collected Liz around eight. His smile matched hers, and an easy conversation flowed as they drove toward the city center.

At the restaurant, Liz glanced around at the starched white tablecloths offset by the high-gloss black and concrete gray interior as an enthusiastic waiter ushered them to a table for six.

Introductions were made as two other couples joined them. When one of the men asked Liz the generic question of 'what do you do in London,' Peter spoke before she'd even swallowed.

"Liz is university educated," he said, as if that was the be-all and end-all of one's existence. "But she works in a restaurant at present."

There it was—the 'but' of her life.

"You're not using your degree?" the same guy asked. "What a pity. It's a brave move in a town like this. You don't want to stay out of the workforce for too long."

Peter continued to speak for her as Liz shifted in her chair. She hadn't even had a chance to open her mouth. "It's just until your company hits the big time, isn't it, Liz?"

"A girl has to eat." Liz downed the rest of her wine, then excused herself to the restroom where a series of deep breaths accompanied a little pep talk of 'I'm good enough, and I won't let anyone tell me otherwise.'

Still, the fact remained. Peter's social set were sophisticated London businesspeople, and she was a waitress at *El Beso*. A hope-less romantic who cried in soppy movies, and a dreamer of big dreams whose sole ambition as a child was to drive a digger.

After the meal, Peter drove Liz back to the tiny terrace through tree-lined streets and late evening fog. He talked about himself all the way.

"Thanks for seeing me home. Would you like to come in for a coffee?" Liz asked as she rummaged through her bag for the front door key.

"Do you always invite first dates in for coffee? Next you'll be expecting me to spend the night, and that's not my style. Especially when we've only just met."

You could've knocked Liz over with the tail feather of a baby sparrow. Maybe he'd forgotten their lunch dates. "I haven't been on a date in a while, so I'm a bit rusty in dating etiquette. I meant coffee, nothing more."

"I see." He stepped away, his hands in his pockets as he studied her. "I appreciate the offer, but I should go. You wouldn't want me jumping to conclusions, now would you?"

Liz hesitated. He must be joking. But no. He was treating her like a naughty kid. She decided to drop it. If Peter didn't want to jump to conclusions, he could make his own damn coffee. "Thanks for dinner."

"You're welcome. I have your number. Is it okay if I call you sometime?"

"Um...I'm not sure. I have a busy few weeks coming up."

He lingered, his hands still in his pockets. "Okay, goodnight."

Later, while sitting at the island eating ice cream smothered in chocolate sauce, Liz realized loneliness sometimes made for bad judgment calls and fickle friendships. There would be no more dates with Mr. Nichols.

However, when he texted her the following week, she decided there was no harm in giving Peter another shot.

———

When Penny arrived at the tiny terrace for a wine several weeks later, it wasn't long before the conversation centered on Liz and Peter's dating life.

"Okay, tell me everything." Penny always wanted to know the details, sordid or otherwise.

"Well, the first date wasn't the best. I didn't even get a kiss goodnight."

"Foolish man."

"Dates two through six followed a similar pattern, although there was a little doorstep activity, just to keep me on my toes."

Penny pulled a face. "And?"

"He finally made it through the front door after date number seven. Once inside, he talked non-stop, mainly about his favorite subject, himself, then said goodnight with a little half-hearted second base action and a few soft kisses."

"Is he a decent kisser?"

"Not the best in the world. Nothing like the talented mouth of Mr. Tanner, but he's improving. And he smells fantastic."

Penny nodded. "I've had to give a few kissing lessons in my day. It's not the end of the world."

"At first I thought he might be asexual. He doesn't seem to have the time or energy for sins of the flesh."

Liz thought about the time it took Peter to make a move and smiled. Still, his personality was growing on her. Each time they met, she liked him a little more. She'd had her fair share of unwanted male attention in the past, so Peter and his apparent lack of sexual interest was a welcome deviation from the norm.

"Really? I've never met a guy like that. Most guys can't wait to invite you to the bedroom. Or the bathroom, the hallway, or the back seat of his car."

"Tell me about it. He intrigues me. He has a wide circle of friends and is the perfect gentleman, but he's kind of pompous around them. Still, he's very caring when we're alone."

"Always a plus. And what about the list?"

"I'm not sure. It may need a tweak here and there. Anyway, the next day he sent me a bunch of gerberas spiked with bits of green stuff and a card that simply read, *best, Peter*. I'd never put him down for a man of so few words. Usually, he won't shut up."

"Gerberas?" Penny made another face. "What on earth did you do with them?"

"They graced the windowsill of the downstairs bathroom for a few days."

"Good spot."

Liz giggled. "Yeah, I thought so."

"Have you had date number eight?"

"Yes. Last Friday. He arrived with a takeout in one hand and his phone streaming a movie in the other. We cuddled on the sofa, had a little kiss. It was nice. But it didn't go so well once we made it upstairs."

"Why not?"

She hesitated. "He didn't... He's kind of..." Liz giggled. "Um..."

"So, you didn't float to paradise wearing wet panties, then?"

"Penny! Stop it."

"What? That's what sex is all about, isn't it? Floating away to paradise for a few minutes before the world crashes down around you again."

"Not always. Sometimes it's just nice to be held."

8

FROZEN WATER PEOPLE

From: Anthony Tanner
To: Mum and Dad
CC: undisclosed-recipients
Subject: F it's hot.

Kansai International Airport hums with hustle and bustle like any other. The irony of it being stuck out in Osaka Bay, joined by a long stretch of highway that leads only to the airport, is not lost on me. I feel the same. Like I'm stuck out on a limb in the middle of nowhere.

The flight passed in a flash as thoughts of 'what on earth am I doing' barged into my rational mind.

The first thing that hit me on arrival was the oppressive heat. Maybe I should have waited until autumn, but sometimes in our haste to experience new moments, planning is left to chance. I'll stay in Osaka tonight, then catch the bullet train to Hiroshima for a night or two.

Take care,
AJ

From: Anthony Tanner
To: Mum and Dad
CC: undisclosed-recipients
Subject: One down eighty-seven to go.

I stayed in Hiroshima for two nights. What a sobering place. Man's inhumanity to man. It certainly makes you wonder about the world.

On return, I spent a couple of hours in Tokushima, then took a slow bus and train to Bando Station. From there it's a short walk to Temple 1.

It was good to get started. I like the fact there are eighty-eight main temples, eight being my lucky number. Must be a sign.

I've met a nice Canadian girl called Alice. We rarely walk together but meet up sometimes.

Thought for the day:

Life is a journey of self. Learning to enjoy the voyage with others is a gift to be mastered.

Love and peace,
   AJ

From: Anthony Tanner
To: Mum and Dad
CC: undisclosed-recipients
Subject: Thank God for little old ladies.

It's easy to underestimate how much water I need in these temps. A little old lady noticed me on the side of the road and stopped to say hi, giving me an orange and a bottle of frozen water.

The locals are warm and friendly and go out of their way to look out for you. It makes me appreciate my friends and family that have my back, no matter what. My frozen water people. I'm truly blessed.

Thought for the day: I have to keep reminding myself that I'm a lucky bastard, even when sweating like a pig.

Take care,
AJ

From: Anthony Tanner
To: Mum and Dad
CC: undisclosed-recipients
Subject: Sometimes I wonder...

...what the F I'm doing here? The walking is not always leisurely, especially when you're not used to it. I thought I was fit, but maybe the mental strain is taking its toll. A big part of the struggle at this end are the long distances combined with a lack of amenities. Still, I'm over halfway, and meeting up with Alice occasionally, keeps me going. I plan to visit her in Canada on my way home.

Thought for the day: Balance is the key to staying on the edge of the cliff, so step carefully and keep your focus forward.

Have a great day,
AJ

From: Anthony Tanner
To: Mum and Dad
CC: undisclosed-recipients
Subject: Nothing's going on.

To answer your question, Anna. Nothing's going on between Alice and me. We're friends, and she's on a much more enlightened spiritual path than I could ever hope to be. She's an inspiration.

Thought for the day: Surrounding yourself with inspirational people can be a tonic or a poison. It's all about attitude.

All my love,
AJ

From: Anthony Tanner
To: Mum and Dad
CC: undisclosed-recipients
Subject: Cooling down.

The days have cooled, which makes walking more bearable. I'm not sure I'll make it in under forty-five days, but it no longer matters. We are so captured by the hands of time in our everyday lives that learning to let go of the concept can be a struggle.

Thought for the day: Learning to let your muddled thoughts go for ones less complicated is a skill of the truly blessed.

Missing you all,
AJ

From: Anthony Tanner
To: Mum and Dad
CC: undisclosed-recipients
Subject: Expectations.

During my days on the trail, I expected to feel Cathy's spirit around me. I find myself mentally talking to her sometimes. But the fact remains. Cathy's spirit doesn't roam the temples and shrines of Eastern lands. Cathy's spirit lives in Putney. At the studio where she spent her days, the bars where she drank Pimms with slices of cucumber peel striping down the glass, and the tiny outdoor table of her favorite coffee shop, where she held court with friends over espresso and end-on-end cigarettes.

In many ways, I never belonged to Cathy's world. The world of the avant-garde, where innovators of their craft push boundaries of acceptability and surprise. My upbringing has been too mainstream for that.

I'm forever grateful for all of you and the example you, Mum and Dad, have set for us. The bar is high, but I aim to reach it, always.

Thought for the day: Sometimes we're so consumed with what we know, we forget to keep learning, to grow, and to understand.

Take care of one another,

AJ

9

SANCTIMONIOUS SUGGESTION

MONTHS LATER

LIZ GLANCED at the caller ID of her phone and inhaled deeply. She smoothed her hands over the rich leather inlay of her desk and leaned back in her new chair before picking up.

"What's this I hear about you having an actual office?" Peter's voice boomed into her ear as she pressed the speaker icon. He always shouted into his cell phone, even when out in public.

"I mentioned it weeks ago."

"I thought you were joking. Didn't think your business could afford such an expense. Text me the address. I'll pop over after work with a bottle of champagne."

Liz did as she was told, even though the thought of seeing Peter didn't thrill her.

However, when he arrived, his mood jovial and his hug comforting, she relaxed.

"Well, well, well. My little Kiwi girlfriend has finally hit it big in the city. Congratulations."

"Thanks. It's great to have somewhere to go during the day."

He leaned in for a kiss. "You look especially beautiful today."

"Really? Thank you."

"So, I know it's not necessarily my business," Peter said as he opened the champagne and poured it into two glasses, "but is your revenue stream high enough to afford this place?"

"It is."

Peter's face held a frown of superiority as he waited for her to elaborate. Liz accepted the drink and took a relaxing sip.

"I've been thinking." He reached for her hand across the table. "Why don't I come on board as a director to handle your investments? Keep you on the straight and narrow, so to speak."

Liz narrowed her eyes. She sucked in a breath while considering his sanctimonious suggestion.

"What do you say?" he continued. "I'll get my team on to the details tomorrow. Where's your company listed?"

She ignored his question and pulled her hand free. It was no business of his where she'd listed her company. "Thanks for the offer but taking on a director is a big step. I'll talk to Ivan about it."

"Ivan? Who the hell's Ivan?"

"My lawyer. At Ivan Kingston Law."

"IKL are a large firm. Why would you need their legal advice?"

"They were recommended to me." Liz knew Peter wanted to ask more, but he changed tack.

"Anyway, I'm only suggesting an advisory role," he said. "I'll let you handle the day-to-day."

"Thank you for that consideration." Her sarcasm slid right off the duck's back.

"It's a win-win. I have skills. You underestimate me sometimes."

"Not at all, but I'll need time to consider it."

"Of course. Take the weekend, but we need to move. It's not every day you receive an offer from someone like me."

Liz quickly changed the subject. "I bought a new car today. A Range Rover Evoque."

"What? Without asking my advice. Cars are my thing. I could have helped negotiate a finance deal."

"I paid cash."

"Cash? You paid cash for an Evoque? But they're nearly fifty thousand pounds."

"I got a good deal on an ex-demo. Nate has a friend in the business, and I've always wanted an SUV. I'm off to Scotland soon, so thought I should bite the bullet."

"Scotland? When?"

Liz drew a steady breath, determined not to let Peter intimidate her. Her trip to Scotland wasn't his business, not that she'd go without telling him. Still, she'd had plenty of chances to discuss it and chose not to. And now she knew why as a flash of hesitation gripped her gut. "Next month. With Penny and two of her friends."

Peter's face held a somber expression as he stared at her. "I understood we were in a relationship here. Now I find out you've bought a jolly expensive vehicle you can't possibly afford, and plan to go off on a road trip to Scotland with your friends."

"It's only for a few days," Liz disregarded his annoyance. "I was going to tell you this weekend."

"Well, now you don't have to bother."

Liz rushed to leap to her own defense, then thought better of it. She watched Peter stand and step toward the door.

He grabbed his coat from the rack, shrugged it over his shoulders and turned to speak. "I'm late for a dinner appointment. I'll call you next week if you're not flitting all over the UK in your new Range Rover."

As Peter left the office, Liz poured another mouthful of champagne and gulped it back in a single swig. When the liquid courage finally calmed her, she pressed her lips together as a lone tear slipped down her cheek.

She recalled the first time they met, how friendly and agreeable he seemed. How flattered she'd been when Peter, a successful London businessman, wanted to date her. She'd learned to read him over the last few months and half expected him to barge back in and apologize for overreacting. But the door stayed shut.

It hadn't taken long for cracks to appear in their relationship and over the next few weeks, Liz and Peter spent less time together. But when they did, Peter took small but skillful hits at her self-esteem. Not the type of hits where bruises show, but rather, a flicker of tightness in the chest, a squirm of the gut, and an insignificant push on the swing of her emotions.

After each date, she'd retreat to her small bedroom—with its walls of duck egg blue and floaty off-white curtains—and watch trees from the street cast shadows across the ceiling. She'd analyze the situation until nothing made sense and make plans for a life without him. But a few days later, he'd call, talking gently into the phone as he connected the disconnected.

Peter usually waited two weeks between dinner invitations, but this time, it had only been five days. When Liz opened the door, he looked her up and down and shot straight to a critique. "What on earth are you wearing?"

Liz stood in the hallway, dressed in a fitted jersey V-neck number with long sleeves and a sexy gather at the right hip. She loved the fabric—the feel and comfort of it and the rich navy color—not to mention it was a designer label she'd snapped up on sale, saving over two hundred pounds. Still, Peter always dressed impeccably. Should she trust his judgment, even when it hurt?

"Don't you like it?"

"It's not that, Liz. It's just unflattering. Maybe you've put on a few pounds, do you think?"

Liz ran her hands over her hips and looked side on in the entry mirror, searching for the additional pounds mentioned. "No, I don't think so."

"Why don't you let me pick something? The drop earrings are a nice touch, though."

Climbing the stairs to her bedroom, he glanced back and asked, "Are they real antiques or a knock off from the High Street?"

"They were my grandmothers."

"Thank goodness for granny."

The situation didn't improve over dinner. Peter ignored her throughout the evening as he and his friends shared jokes, talked British politics, and ribbed each other in overtly intellectual banter while the gin and tonics flowed. The only time he paid her any attention was when it came to ordering dessert.

Peter held the dessert menu and considered the options. "Let's share, shall we." His smile told her it was a forgone conclusion. Her opinion didn't matter.

Liz noticed one of the other women at the table—a slightly overweight lawyer—raise an eyebrow before ordering a tarte tartin. Peter picked a chocolate fondant and asked for two spoons. When it arrived, he condescended to give Liz a taste. The small spoonful lost all its calories on the journey from the plate to her mouth. Still, she didn't argue. How can anyone reason with a man who's had too much to drink?

There was no sex that night.

Peter's foot returned to his mouth the next day as they loaded the dishwasher after breakfast.

"Have you ever thought about a boob job?"

Liz stopped mid rinse and looked at him. She loved her breasts. They were smallish, but pert and firm. "No, never."

"You could easily go up a couple of cup sizes. You can afford it now your business is taking off."

She inhaled slowly and clenched her teeth. An ache formed along the entire length of her jawline. "I guess, but I don't want to subject my body to an anesthetic for the sole purpose of increasing my breasts with a manmade product."

Peter huffed. "It would be an improvement, that's all I'm saying."

Hell No!

Over the next few weeks, Peter's unhealthy interest in all things Liz Dobson intensified. Nothing escaped his attention, including her company as he offered pointers—like a business guru coaching a naïve newbie on how she should expand her markets. He questioned her style of dress, told her what to wear when they went out, and picked small but pointed holes in her appearance as his hands flicked through her closet looking for the perfect dinner dress.

On the day of reckoning, Peter called at her office unannounced under the pretense of missing her, although he didn't even offer a kiss hello.

"I have a business dinner Friday night," he said before he'd even sat down.

"I have something on as well."

"I need a date. It's black tie. Maybe you could shout yourself a padded bra and tame those curls for once."

Liz felt her jaw clench. "Sorry, did you hear what I just said?"

He frowned a question.

"How long have you known about the dinner?" she asked.

"A few weeks."

"And you didn't think to ask me earlier."

Peter huffed. "We are moody today, aren't we? What do you want me to do, take someone else?"

"You do that. And while you're at it, maybe we should have a break."

"What? Over one jolly dinner date. Don't be ridiculous."

"It's not only the dinner. I'm not what you need. You make that very clear." Liz stood. She smoothed her hands down her skirt, then fiddle with the chain around her neck. "I'm not enough for you."

"Surely I should be the judge of that. The trouble with you, Liz, is you believe all that romantic bullshit the media feed you."

"Maybe I do."

"Right, well. I'll get out of your hair for a while." He stepped toward the door, then turned to face her, an angry finger pointing her way. "But make no mistake. If I have to take someone else to that dinner, I won't look back. Understand?"

MOLTEN GRAY

MANY MONTHS LATER

AJ STROLLED through light London fog to MoMo, a bustling dumpling joint less than a dozen blocks from Nate's terrace house. An imposing cloud of *what now*, made more intense by the weather, weighed him down. He grabbed a table near the window, ordered for them both, and like every other lone diner, checked his phone as he waited for Nate to join him.

Nate appeared a few minutes later, all rugged up in a pea coat and scarf, and weaved his way through the busy lunch crowd.

"Do you have a job yet?" Nate asked before he'd even pulled out a chair or removed his coat.

"You mean a nine to six daily grind kind of job that sucks the life out of your soul? Or a job where I paint passionate imaginings onto impossibly large canvases?"

Nate grinned as he sat down. "No, one that pays the bills, you dick."

"Not yet. I've only been back two weeks. Definitely on my 'To Do' list."

"Good, because I want you to consider something. And please," Nate added, "do so with an open mind."

"Should I show my intrigued face?"

"You should." Nate waited as a server placed a bamboo steamer of dumplings in the center of the table and set down two side plates and two pairs of chopsticks. "Do you remember my cousin Liz?"

AJ looked up from his plate. A wry smile followed. "Ah, the elusive Liz Dobson, destined to be admired from afar."

"The very same. Anyway, she needs a business advisor, slash CFO, slash man Friday."

"Man Friday? You realize that's a politically incorrect term that reeks of sexism and British colonialism."

"Of course." Nate tucked into a dumpling with gusto and grinned. "I'd never utter it in public."

"So, she's still in London? Is she single?"

"Still in London and seeing someone. Well, off and on, so get your mind out of the bedroom for a moment."

"Too late. Sensual Liz just walked into my fantasies, chewing her bottom lip and—"

"Stop. I don't need the visuals. I thought you came back enlightened."

"Yeah, but I have needs just like the next bloke. Not that I can act on them right away. I'm still in sexile. And she's with someone, so…" AJ shrugged.

"Probably just as well. As I was saying before your sexual fantasy rudely interrupted, her business has taken off and she's in burnout mode. If she doesn't get help soon, her decision-making process may be compromised."

AJ leaned back in his chair. "And? Your point?"

"You're looking for something part-time, she'll pay well, and it will free up the rest of your week to play with your arts and crafts."

"I don't *play* with my arts and crafts, I create. I'm an artist in waiting." AJ laughed, chewed, and thought for a moment. "So, have you discussed this with Liz? She won't be keen."

"Why not?"

64

AJ hesitated. He wasn't one to screw and tell. "We kind of had a thing before I left. I haven't heard from her since."

"What the...? You slept with her? That's like me sleeping with one of your sisters."

"Anna's keen."

"So I've noticed." Nate laughed. "I might be shy, but I'm not blind."

AJ picked up another dumpling and popped it into his mouth. "Don't even think about it."

"All that aside, are you saying you and Liz slept together...in my house?"

"I'm not saying anything, mate."

"You don't have to," Nate replied. "It's written all over your smug face."

"Moving right along. What's her deal?"

"Her boyfriend, Peter 'the dick' Nichols, is doing a real number on her. They broke up for ages but are back together after he chased her for months with phone calls and flowers arriving on the doorstep every other week. If you ask me, she took him back out of loneliness more than anything else. He spends all his spare time shooting his pompous mouth off, telling anyone who'll listen he taught her all she knows."

"And did he?"

"It's pure, steaming hot bullshit. What concerns me is whether he's about to wheedle in on her assets. And I don't mean the physical kind."

AJ surprised himself by actually considering Nate's suggestion. "Sounds fun. I love a good old-fashioned asset fight."

"To tell you the truth, she's an emotional mess. There's a good chance I'll get the Moscow job, so I thought—"

"No way—"

"You could move into my place while I'm away, keep an eye on her and work a few hours a week in her business. Thoughts?"

"So, basically you want me to babysit a grown woman. A

woman I may or may not have had a history with, while I sort out her financials on the side."

"About covers it."

"While I appreciate your attempt to mind-map my messed-up life, it's not happening. We wouldn't be a good business fit."

"Why not?"

AJ shook his head. He wanted to see Liz again, but the last thing he needed was to play secretary in her business. "Do I have to spell it out? My dick would be doing all the thinking. I've been in that position with her before. Besides, I've had other offers."

"You think she's hot, so what? Doesn't mean you won't work well together. At least consider it?"

"You're asking me to live and work with her. How would I stay on my side of the landing with her sleeping naked a few feet away?"

"I told you, she's already in a relationship. You're perfect for the job and the job's perfect for you. And you're broke."

That was an understatement. "You're right, but no."

"Cheap rent, a decent hourly rate, long weekends in Cambridge. What more do you want?"

"So, if the package is so good, why don't you do it?"

"Because we're family and my career is upwardly mobile."

"And mine's not?" AJ said, mocking offense.

"We want different things. I'm the first to recognize your talents lie…elsewhere and well done for following your dream. In the meantime, you still have to eat."

AJ realized Nate had made some serious positive points. "Can she afford me?"

"Very much so."

"Any idea of her yearly revenue?"

"Not specifically, but it's up there."

AJ cocked a brow as he grabbed the last dumpling. "What, for a one-woman internet business?"

"She's hit an affiliate goldmine. Doing very well for herself.

And I mean *very well*. Look, why don't you let it simmer for a few days?"

"Shout me another plate of dumplings, and I'll think about it, but the answer will still be no."

"Where do you put all the food you eat?"

Just on dusk, AJ stood in front of the large canvas leaning on the back wall of his studio. Apart from an initial frenzy before he'd left for Asia, it remained untouched. The only hint of progress, a thread of spider's silk linking the painting to the casement window that overlooked the street below. He closed his eyes, trying to recall her essence. Her complexity.

AJ longed to see Liz again, and now, Nate was practically serving her up on a platter. However, he didn't want to work with her, he wanted to consume her. To start over where they'd left off eighteen months before. To take her in his arms, kiss her tenderly and learn her secrets. The secrets he didn't have time to explore the first time around. Then, he wanted to throw the tender bits out the window while they devoured each other between crumpled linen sheets—on what he remembered would be her new bed, their bodies slick with passion-induced sweat.

Several months after they'd first met, AJ noticed a photograph of Liz on Nate's Instagram feed. In the image, Liz stood in profile. Her slender neck—pale and creamy—was offset by the color of the same silk tunic she wore that night in the bar.

He'd studied the photo repeatedly, as he planned the evolution from screen to canvas. But now, he struggled to mix the colors of her tunic. The molten gray was simple. The green and violet, not so much. He started with viridian, an intense pure secondary color close to dark spring green and mixed with more blue than yellow, but no red. For the violet, he blended a base of French ultramarine, adding a bit of this and that in search of the perfect shade. But as hard as he tried, he couldn't bring the intensity of the color palette to life.

AJ surveyed his work, not in admiration, but in harsh critique. Portraying Liz on canvas continued to be a challenge. And after what happened between them, working for her would be a challenge as well.

Unable to secure a cab, Liz boarded the bus at the stop down from her office on Putney High Street, alighting several blocks from home to walk the rest of the way in the brisk London air. By the time she breezed through the door, thoughts of affiliate products, email lists, and Peter had all but disappeared.

Nate stood in the kitchen with a cleaver in hand and dressed in a T-shirt that said: *If you want to fall asleep, ask an accountant about their day*. Liz loved it when Nate cooked. He placed all the ingredients into small bowls lined up along the kitchen counter in order of importance, just like on a cooking show.

Liz sat at the booth and opened her Facebook page, idly glancing over pictures of new babies, a recipe for raw brownie, and the various political posts on her wall. A friend request caught her eye.

AJ Tanner.

Liz shivered as she recalled the man's talent for certain things. She'd often wondered if their paths would cross again. But why, after the way he left, would he send her a friend request eighteen months later?

Now that Peter was back on the scene and seemingly more into her, she had no other option than to hit the decline button before she even considered the possibility. AJ Tanner and Liz Dobson would never be friends, Facebook or otherwise.

"What are you frowning at?" Nate asked.

"A Facebook friend request."

"A stalker?"

"No, nothing like that."

With AJ on her mind and half a glass of juice in hand, Liz watched Nate spread redcurrant sauce in the center of two white plates with as much flamboyance as a Michelin star chef. Next, he layered a sweet potato cake on each, topped it with a rare fillet of beef, and added a side of green beans and buttered bok choy. He reached for two placemats and set the warm plates on the table of the booth.

"Would madam like a glass of wine? I have a Central Otago Pinot Noir breathing on the table, delivered all the way from the Southern Lakes district of New Zealand. Well, according to the guy at the liquor store."

"Lovely. Thank you." Liz hadn't been in a drinking mood for months. In fact, not since that night with AJ when she compromised her integrity with a third glass of Spanish red. But a beautiful meal and a glass of Pinot went perfectly together, and she was in safe company.

Memories of that night surfaced. Looking back, she wouldn't change a thing. Having her inhibitions shattered by AJ was the best sexual experience of her life. She often wondered what might have been if they'd spent more than one night together.

"Earth to Liz?"

She looked up. "Sorry, I was miles away."

"I want to talk to you about something." Nate took a sip of his wine, sat the glass on the table, then ran his thumb and forefinger up and down the stem. "I have a new job."

"Really? I didn't know you were looking. Have you been head hunted?"

"Kind of. I'm moving to the Moscow office for a two-year contract."

Liz looked at him in disbelief but recovered quickly. Nate deserved this promotion and had worked hard to get it. "That's great news. Are you happy about it?"

"Sure. The package is hard to resist, and the perks are even better. Also, an apartment is part of the deal. You'll have to come over once I'm settled."

"I'd love to. I've always wanted to visit Moscow." Liz cut into the beef and closed her eyes briefly as she took a bite. "This is so good."

"Thanks. Are you happy to stay here while I'm away?"

She glanced up from her meal and grinned. "So, you're not throwing me out then?"

"Of course not." He hesitated. "But you'll need a housemate to help with expenses."

"I can afford to live alone."

"Okay. We'll sort out the details later."

With the main course over, Nate collected the plates from the table and rinsed them in the sink. "I've made an apple tart. Keen?"

"I really shouldn't."

"Why not? Dessert is one of life's great pleasures."

"Not according to Peter." She smiled. "Any cream?"

"Of course." Nate plated the rustic tart, adding a dollop of cream to the top and ice cream on the side. "Speaking of Peter…"

Liz didn't want to discuss Peter with Nate. She knew he didn't approve, and on the subject of her relationship with Peter Nichols, they'd agreed to disagree. "Yes?"

"Remember how we discussed a CFO for your company? Have you given it further thought?"

"I have, but I'm not a team player, you know that."

"Still, you've experienced a dramatic increase in your revenue stream and your investments need attention. I'm not sure Peter has the necessary skills to advise you."

Liz frowned. Nate was right, but the situation was complicated.

"Just because he's your boyfriend doesn't mean he knows what's best for your company."

"Okay. Where's this coming from?"

"Look, I may be overreacting, but Peter seems to be offering you more and more financial advice. In my opinion, you'd be wise to maintain a dissociation in that regard. Strategic planning is imperative to your ongoing success. Mixing business with pleasure can work, but only under certain circumstances."

Liz suppressed a smile. "I love it when you go all accountant on me."

Nate chuckled. "But seriously, be careful of the guy. Especially if you're thinking of doing business together."

"I know you don't approve of Peter, but he has a sweet side behind closed doors."

"All the same, whether I approve or not doesn't matter."

"Okay," she said, sighing. "All that aside, do you have someone in mind, for the job I mean? Who do I trust besides you and Ivan?"

"Do you remember Anthony Tanner?"

A flutter in an obscure corner of her mind reminded her in no uncertain terms. "Are you kidding me? AJ the sexy egomaniac? Isn't he away finding himself while he screws his way around Asia?"

"He's back, and in my opinion, completely trustworthy."

Butterflies fluttered in her stomach. "He's back?"

"Look, I know you guys have a history."

"Who told you that?"

Nate hesitated. "He did."

Liz knew her night with AJ would come back to haunt her one day. She waited for Nate to elaborate. When he didn't, she asked, "What did he say? I hope he didn't boast about me."

Nate sliced another serving of tart and smothered it with whipped cream. "Not his style. What do you think? Could he be a candidate?"

"Definitely not. Hell would have to freeze over, and you know I can't ice skate. Definitely not," she repeated with increased emphasis.

"Why not?"

Liz didn't want to go into the details. Didn't want Nate to know she couldn't trust herself in the same room as the guy. "I thought he hated accountancy."

"Sure, traditional accounting. But he's brilliant at what he does. The CFO position may be the challenge he's after. He has other interests, so twenty hours a week is his max." Nate paused again, a soft smile moving into form. "I can't believe you guys slept together. Well, I believe it of AJ, not so much you."

"Excuse me. I don't make moral judgments about who you sleep with." She did, but it was manners to pretend otherwise.

"You do so. What about Carol?"

"She wasn't your type. It's a wonder you didn't suffocate in those fake boobs of hers."

"And AJ? He was your type, was he?"

Liz thought back to the feeling of being caged against the door as AJ kissed her with his gifted mouth—and the rest—and smiled. "Purely for a moment in time." She flushed at the memory of AJ's tongue flicking into her mouth, the taste of mint, and the scrape of his beard against her skin. "He has an unforgettable personality."

"Not you as well. When we were younger, all the girls in our group wanted to marry him and have his babies. It used to piss me off. He always got the girl while I stood back, too shy to speak." Nate laughed at the recollection.

"Come to think of it," Nate continued, "nothing much has changed. Still, underneath his good looks, he's a great guy. But one word of advice. I've never seen him in a long-term relationship. I'm not convinced commitment is part of his deal. Sure, he'll make you think you're the only one for a brief period when you're on his radar, but once he's focused on another target, you'll be off the map before you can even say blip."

Liz pretended to check her phone, more to hide her surprised disappointment than anything else—Nate's warning a timely reminder to keep her guard up. "What are you? A frustrated naval operator? Anyway, I'm in a relationship and I've already experienced the AJ effect. It didn't go so well."

"At least you're not bitter about it."

"There's no point. Now, pass me that tart. And the cream."

"I love seeing you in a relaxed mood. Haven't seen you relax much lately."

Liz ignored his concern, steering the conversation in a different direction. "I hope you haven't discussed this with him already."

"I might have mentioned how busy you were. He's tossing options around. Actually, Ivan suggested he touch base with you."

"AJ knows Ivan?"

"He's Ivan's nephew. Ivan wanted AJ to follow him into Law, but he barely finished his accounting degree. He still managed honors, but university bored him to tears."

"Him and I both." Liz thought for a moment, daring herself to consider Nate's suggestion.

"Just think about it," Nate said. "If you continue to run your company on your own, you'll burn out. You work way too many hours a week as it is. It's not healthy. Work life balance is the key to success. It's not always about the money."

"Ha, you think. You're a fine one to talk. And you know I don't do it for the money."

"I know, but shit, you need to protect your assets and put them to work."

"What are you saying? I need protection from Peter?"

Nate replied with a shrug. Liz understood if he opened his mouth and verbalized his distaste for all things Peter Nichols, he wouldn't stop.

"Maybe you're right," Liz said. "Not about Peter, but about the independent help. How will I manage when you're in Moscow?"

"You'll be fine. Just give AJ serious consideration. Do it for your cuzzie bro."

Liz laughed at Nate's attempt to talk Kiwi slang.

"But you'd better move fast because he has other offers on the table," Nate continued.

Liz's insecurities clouded her judgment for a moment. She

understood the importance of first instinct and her first instinct told her to go for it. But what if she took one look at him and recalled every touch, every whispered command, and the flick of his tongue as he traveled down her body?

Or worse—what if her imagination didn't do him justice? What if he was a total jerk? A jerk she'd spent an incredible night with before he snuck out of her life without even a polite *ciao*.

"I'll need a few days to decide." She stood and placed her plate in the dishwasher. "Right, on that note, thanks for the beautiful meal. I'm off to change into my PJ's. I need to ditch these jeans before they burst."

Climbing the stairs, thoughts of AJ flitted in and out of Liz's mind. And later, as she slipped into bed, she chastised herself for thinking of him and not Peter. A mental list of pros and cons followed, the pros taking the lead more than once. Liz wondered if maybe, just maybe, AJ could make a difference.

However, with the clarity that morning often brings, Liz pushed all thoughts of AJ aside. Having him in her life, albeit professionally, was a bad idea. The worst idea ever.

11

MONOSYLLABIC MONOTONY

LIZ SAT on the banks of the Thames and watched the sunset, her enthusiasm for her business at an all-time low. The day before, a major client had pulled out of contract negotiations, and her pitch for a new affiliate campaign failed to take. Now Peter had summoned her for an after-work drink.

Patrons overflowed onto the street as Liz pushed her way into Munro's, and the waft from the grill reminded her of her hunger. She grabbed her phone out of her bag to text Peter just as a firm hand pulled her aside.

"You've finally decided to grace us with your presence, have you?" Peter rarely kissed her in public, so his lack of affection didn't surprise her. "What are you drinking?"

"I was about to text you. I might call it a night. I have a splitting headache."

"It won't hurt you to stay for one drink." He didn't bother to hide his annoyance. "Come on, Liz."

"Okay. I'll have a lime and soda, thank you."

"Why didn't you return my call?"

"Sorry, I've had a busy day. You said this morning you'd meet me here."

"It's still manners to confirm."

Peter paused, like he was waiting for another apology. Liz wasn't about to offer it again.

"Anyway, no matter," he continued. "I'm a bit short of cash and cards take forever. Loan me twenty quid, and I'll shout you that drink."

Liz fished in her purse and pulled out a twenty-pound note. She joined Peter's friends at a table against the whitewashed brick wall. When he returned with her drink and another gin and tonic paid for with her money, all answers to questions about his week were met with monosyllabic monotony.

His indifference annoyed her more than usual. She finished her soda, excused herself and pushed through the crowd to the restroom. The line ran down the corridor and as she waited, Liz checked her phone like everyone else. When she finally entered a stall, she sat for a moment, her hands massaging tender temples while a knot of emotion tightened in her throat.

Usually, Liz wasn't a crowd scanner—a people watcher like Penny. Yet, as she made her way back into the bar, she felt an insistent need to glance up, straight into the gaze of AJ Tanner. Wearing black jeans, boots, and a white T-shirt underneath a distressed leather jacket, he'd dressed down for the occasion of Friday night drinks in a city bar. He looked different; thinner, almost gaunt. His beard—now in full flight and thick and bushy—rested below his Adam's apple in a straggle, and his long hair sat in a topknot like the first night they'd met. The word 'shit' nearly escaped her lips. No doubt about it, the man had a presence. Memories of the evening she struggled to forget screamed at her to recollect.

AJ's lips held no smile as he stepped forward to greet her. Liz stiffened as he reached for her hand and kissed her lightly on both cheeks. His cologne reminded her of happier times, and as the noise of the bar faded into the background, all she heard was, "Liz, hi."

She pulled back. "AJ. It's been a long time."

"It's great to see you again. What are you drinking?"

AJ had a smile that could melt a girl's heart, but it was still nowhere in sight. He didn't let go of her hand, and as she glanced over at Peter's questioning stare, she felt the slight pressure of his thumb as he rubbed it across her knuckles.

She pulled her hand free, but not before her fingertips traced lightly over his. "Thank you, but I'm here with someone."

AJ followed her line of sight and Liz knew instantly he understood. He stepped back. "Pity. Maybe another time."

She walked away.

"Who was that guy?" Peter leaned in close as she sat back down in her chair. He slid his arm around her waist, staking his claim.

"A friend of Nate's." Liz pulled away slightly, her gaze drifting back to the bar. AJ's stare stalked hers. He frowned. She felt herself blush like a shy schoolgirl, a response at odds with her resolve.

"I don't like the look of him. Doesn't he own a jolly razor?" The thump of Peter's beer bottle on the table startled her. "Right. We're off to a party. Keen?"

"I might call it a night. It's been a busy day."

Peter looked at her for a moment. Her stomach tensed as he moved closer.

"I'm sorry I was short with you before," he murmured. "Got a lot on my mind. It's been one hell of a day."

She relaxed. "No problem."

"You should head home. I'm not keen on you staying here alone."

"Do you want to walk with me?"

"You're a big girl. I'm sure you can find your own way."

Liz stayed seated as the group stood to leave, and as she watched Peter move through the door, she wondered why he didn't kiss her goodbye.

Nate slid into the chair beside her. "Hey. You okay?"

Liz covered her disappointment with a smile. "Yes. But it's been a long day."

"Come and have a drink with us. AJ's here."

Her gaze flitted back to the bar. AJ was now otherwise engaged, talking to a woman with raven hair and a loud throaty laugh. He turned, gave Liz his attention for a moment, then with a dismissive nod, returned to his friend.

"I'm not good company right now. I need food and an early night."

Nate gave her shoulders a quick squeeze. "Come on, I'll walk with you. I could do with an early night too."

Liz relaxed, grateful Nate understood her need for support.

On the way home, they stopped at the supermarket for chicken and vegetables, and as soon as they walked in the door and dropped their coats, Nate had the wok heating on the gas. Liz poured two glasses of Pinot Gris and handed one to Nate. She kicked off her shoes and lay back on the sofa, glad to be home.

Nate talked about his day as they ate. He always had funny stories to tell about his co-workers. Liz wondered how long it would take him to steer the conversation around to AJ. She didn't have to wait long.

"What are your thoughts on AJ and the job offer?"

"Bad idea. I wouldn't feel comfortable dealing with him in a business capacity. He won't be interested anyway."

"He's interested. He asked me about it again tonight."

"What? Are you serious?"

"Look, you slept together, so what? It's not like you had a torrid affair where your passion destroyed any future contact. Maybe it's time to move on."

Liz disagreed. Her night with AJ certainly felt torrid to her, and she still had the emotional scorch marks to prove it. Seeing him tonight threatened to ignite the fire all over again. And where there was sexual fire, intense heat followed. "Maybe, but I don't need that complication right now."

"I understand." Nate didn't push the point. "I'll tell him you have it covered."

"Thanks."

And yet, as soon as the words left her lips, an imposing disappointment surfaced. Liz knew instinctively AJ may be the solution to her problems, but before she let the possibility linger, she turned on the TV, snuggled down on the sofa with a bar of chocolate and lost herself in a chick flick playing on the BBC while Nate, who insisted Liz have a night off, cleaned up the kitchen.

AJ had promised Nate he'd give Liz Dobson's employment opportunity consideration. That's all he'd agreed to. Even so, he couldn't wait to hear her reaction to Nate's suggestion. The days were cooler now, the daylight hours shorter as winter approached through autumn's back door. A certain moodiness washed over him as he met Nate at Wandsworth Park for a jog along the river walk.

Nate frowned as he looked AJ up and down. "Maybe we should skip the run. Go to the pub for a steak instead."

"Yeah, I've lost a few pounds. My personal trainer has got me onto a pea-based protein powder between meals." AJ grimaced. He shook the restlessness out of one leg and then the other. "I have a long way to go, though."

"Sorry, I didn't mean to judge. It's more noticeable in your training gear."

"No problem. Did you talk to Liz?"

"I did. She's not keen. Doesn't want it to be weird between you."

AJ nodded. "Yeah, I left without saying goodbye. Not my finest hour. But I never let my professional life interfere with my private parts." AJ chuckled. "You know that."

"Maybe, but that particular romp in the hay is coming back to bite you on the ass and leaving a severe bruise."

"Everything else around is so freaking boring. These corporates, they expect you to work six days a week, and instead of church on Sunday, want you back at the office to worship at the altar of commercial complacency. Some days, I wish I was still in Bali, surfing my life away."

Nate slapped AJ on the back and laughed. "Shit, you have it bad. So Liz is a last resort?"

"Not necessarily. But the money would come in handy. Why I ever invested in that damn property deal, I have no idea."

"What's happening there? Any chance of a resolution?"

"Hopefully. If not, the council's red tape will make me an old man before my time."

"Why don't you give her a call?"

"Who?" AJ looked at Nate and laughed.

MUNDANE RESPONSIBILITIES

Liz Dobson's Putney High Street office sat above two food businesses. The first, a patisserie selling the best custard tarts Liz had ever tasted, and an upmarket Chinese restaurant where immaculately dressed male waiters plied you with hot towels and kind words between courses. The smells wafting in through the office door floated between the heavenly and the divine.

Liz glanced at the job description in front of her as she tried to ignore the sweet aromas from the patisserie. Could AJ be a contender? And if so, how would their professional relationship play out? He certainly had plenty of physical attributes. Those distinctly outlined lips, his strong imaginative hands, and everything else in between. Liz had never been with a man who possessed such a presence. But she knew nothing about him professionally and still couldn't imagine him as an accountant.

Around noon, after a quick dash past the bakery to a salad bar down the street, Liz ran upstairs to find the man himself in reception waiting for her. She stopped in her tracks, momentarily lost for words.

He stood and offered his hand, shaking hers with an intense

grip. "Liz. Can we have a quick word?" His gaze lingered, moving up and down her form.

She pulled her cardigan over her conservative navy dress and secured the middle two buttons. "Come on in." She held the door open. "Sit down, please."

AJ took the chair offered and leaned back slightly. His gaze never left her face.

"How was the trip?" she asked. "Did you find what you were looking for?"

"You mean myself?"

"Or someone else. Your alter ego perhaps. And the pilgrimage?"

"It was life changing."

"A positive outcome then." Liz shifted in her chair but couldn't take her mind off his long, lean thighs and intense stare. "Anyway, what can I do for you?"

"Nate indicated you have a position available."

Liz hesitated. His scrutiny tipped her off balance. She'd expected the charming man she'd been intimate with eighteen months before. But AJ, the budding applicant, gave nothing away. "I've been giving it consideration."

He sat back, still meeting her gaze. "It seems I've jumped the gun. I understood you were taking applications." Businessman AJ just checked into the building. Liz hadn't seen this side of him before, and a prickly discomfort unsettled her. He acted like Liz was the applicant and he the interviewer.

"You may be overqualified for what I have in mind."

"Surely I should be the judge of that."

"Of course." Liz wondered why on earth she'd given the idea of AJ Tanner, as her first and only employee, credence. His friendly tone from a few minutes ago had suddenly changed. "So, you're interested?"

"To a point. It all depends on what's required, the adjustments I'll have to make, and the salary package."

"I'm sorry, but you've caught me unprepared. I need to give it further thought."

His expression didn't shift from serious. "Okay. If you're not ready to interview, I apologize for wasting your time."

Liz took a business card from the holder on her desk and offered it to him. "Maybe you could email me your résumé."

He reached into his leather satchel, pulled out an envelope and pushed it across the desk. "Take a look and get back to me if you reconsider." He went to stand.

"Actually, I have a spare half hour. We could have a brief chat now." As soon as the words left her mouth, Liz regretted allowing herself to be manipulated.

AJ took his time before he replied. "Sounds good."

His résumé comprised of two pages, which seemed insignificant for such a man. They discussed the position in brief. Liz outlined her requirements before asking if he had any questions.

"If I take the job, I expect to know everything about your financial position," AJ replied, his stance controlled and expression stoic.

His abrupt manner unnerved her, but she kept her reaction in check. "I'm not sure that's entirely necessary."

"Look, Liz, let's be honest." He leaned forward in the chair. "I'm not prepared to be treated like the office junior with no autonomy to do what I feel is right for your business."

"Feel is right, or know is right?"

"I work on instinct a lot. It's only failed me once when I didn't pay heed to my gut."

He'd piqued her interest. She wanted to know about the fail.

"And before we go any further," he continued, "I'd like to know the salary package."

His forthright tone kept surprising her. She didn't expect him to be such a tough negotiator. He displayed a smudge of ruthlessness with a tight ticking jaw to match.

"What are your expectations?"

"Fifty pounds an hour with a maximum of twenty hours a week. I've other business interests, so anything over twenty hours could be problematic. I work days to suit my lifestyle, apart from those times you require me to be in attendance. I'll also need my own office. I don't work well in a team environment." He leaned back, waiting for her reply.

Liz was stunned. "Anything else?"

"Apart from a company credit card for the occasional business expense, I think I've covered everything. My needs are few, however, my terms are nonnegotiable."

He reached into his leather messenger bag again and pulled out another white envelope. "I've summarized my requirements." He pushed the envelope across the desk. "I assume you'll need time to ruminate, so if there's nothing else, I have another appointment."

Liz was dismissed. The arrogance of the man. He was giving her time to 'ruminate.' How very helpful. She wanted to ask if he'd trim his beard and maybe get a tidy haircut while he was at it. Still, he'd probably see that as an abuse of his fundamental human rights.

"I'll need a few days to think things through, or 'ruminate' as you so aptly put it. I assume if I'm able to meet your requirements, you're still interested in the position—to a point."

"I may well be." He stood and offered his hand, his grip once again efficiently painful. "I look forward to hearing from you. Oh, and, Liz…" He waited for her full attention. "I'd like to apologize for coming on strong eighteen months back, and for the way I left. I hope you won't hold it against me."

An unanticipated heat crept up her body. She clenched her thighs together under the smooth lining of her dress. "Of course not. It's totally forgotten," she lied. "I acted out of character and have no intention of mixing my business and personal lives in the future."

He stared at her for several seconds. "Well, at least I know where you stand. I usually don't mix business with pleasure either. I wouldn't want an insignificant night to come between us."

He may as well have slapped her across the face with an open palm. "It's just... Well, I don't want to convey the wrong impression now that I'm in a relationship."

"Of course. I assure you, there's no wrong impression taken. I have no problem acting professionally when required."

Condescending, arrogant, moody bastard. The words *hell no* flashed through her mind. She held the door open. "I'll be in touch."

"I look forward to it."

Sophie, the receptionist, watched AJ run down the stairs and smiled. "Who's that hottie?"

"Anthony Tanner, or AJ as he prefers. He may be my new employee if I can scrape up his sizable salary requirements and tell him my deepest, darkest financial secrets."

"How on earth will you get any work done with him sitting across the desk?"

Liz had thought about that a few minutes prior. "He's not my type. Tattoos and chin bush, I don't think so. I like blonds. Surfer types." She'd almost convinced herself it was true. "Anyway, he wants his own office. Is the one next to mine still free?"

"It is. Shall I pencil you in?"

"Can you give me a week? I have to go over his terms and decide if I can work with the arrogant bastard. It seems like I can't decide on anything these days."

"I'll tell the guys it's on hold."

"Thanks. You're a star."

"What is he anyway? A modern-day hippy who moonlights as a lumberjack?"

Liz laughed. Sophie and Peter held the same opinion, but at different ends of the spectrum. "He's setting himself up as a business advisor."

"Come on. Really? Is he single?"

"No idea. Anyway, you're married, so keep your eyes off."

Sophie fanned herself with a sheet of paper and laughed. "If a piece of candy is within sight, you look, even if you're on a diet or quitting sugar. I'd enjoy a bit of his particular brand of taffy around here."

OPEN INVITATION

IT HAD BEEN two years to the day since Liz had arrived in London —a city where she slept, ate, and worked. A city that didn't belong to her. A borrowed home.

Now, AJ Tanner held an invitation into her world, and he expected her to pay handsomely for the privilege. Thoughts of him peppered every daydream and internal conversation. He'd been so dogmatic at the interview, a stark contrast to his reaction at Munro's. Maybe her refusal to share a drink had annoyed him. But what did he expect? She had a boyfriend.

Rationally, Liz understood hiring AJ was risky. Not because she didn't trust him, but because she didn't trust herself.

Fifty pounds an hour. Really?

That Saturday morning, Liz longed to sleep late but woke around six as usual. She glanced at the photo of her family on her bedside table, picked up the frame and smiled at the happy faces smiling back. She'd turned twenty-five last birthday, but some days still wanted her mother's hugs and words of wisdom—telling her everything happened for a reason and how mistakes made us stronger if we chose to learn the lesson. Her father would beg to differ. He preferred practical reasoning. Believed people made their own destiny through choice, dedication, and hard work. Liz favored a mix of both. Six months before, she'd booked flights to New Zealand for her cousin's wedding, and the thought of going home for two weeks filled her with excitement.

She entered the kitchen an hour later, her yoga halo firmly in place. Nate stood at the counter holding a bowl of muesli and blueberries smothered in yogurt.

"Yum. I might have one of those."

"Here, take this one. I'll make another."

"Thanks." She accepted the bowl and sat at the booth. "Have I ever told you what a kind man you are?"

"No, but I'll take the compliment."

As she ate, she sensed Nate studying her.

"I hear you've had a visit from the enigmatic Mr. Tanner," he finally said.

She moved the crunchy combo around in her mouth. "I have. Did you put him up to it?"

"Course not. He's a big boy. Big enough to look after his own career prospects."

Liz shot him a knowing smile. "Liar."

"And did you grant him an audience, oh Queen of Internet Lists?"

"We talked for a bit. He's so bossy."

"Bossy may be too tame a word."

"And you think I should employ him. Thanks a lot."

Nate shrugged. "He's good at what he does."

"He doesn't want much, just my defunct virginity and first-born child," Liz said with a cheeky grin.

"Yeah, he has a habit of going after what he wants with all guns blazing. Still, you need someone with a strong sense of purpose."

"I guess. But my decision-making process is a little rusty at the moment. Also, I bet Peter won't understand my need for a CFO."

A frown tracked across Nate's forehead at the mention of Peter's name. "His problem, not yours."

Liz knew full well Peter would make it her problem.

"That's why you need AJ," Nate continued. "Someone to mediate your business dealings. A neutral party. When are you letting him know?"

"Early next week. I'm not sure he's right for the job. He's scary when he puts his business hat on."

Nate laughed. "He can be. In the meantime, take a step back and honor what you've been through lately. The rapid growth of any company is a major. Don't underestimate its effect."

"I know, but when you're bogged down with necessity, it's hard to look forward. Still, I'm very fortunate. And I've got my trip coming up."

"Speaking of which, I'm going to make things worse, I'm afraid."

"What do you mean?"

"AJ needs a place to live for a while. I said maybe he could stay here."

Nate's words hit Liz in her already tight gut. She shivered at the thought of AJ Tanner in her private space. "So, have my room while I'm away?"

"Not exactly. The Moscow office want me to start ASAP. AJ suggested taking my room while you're away, to keep an eye on the place."

Liz didn't know what to say. AJ and Nate were friends. Objecting wasn't an option. Still, the thought of living with him… She sucked in a lie. "I don't have a problem with it."

"Truly? Are you sure?"

"Of course. If he's still here for a few days when I come back, well, I'm not home much. I guess he won't be either."

"It's just until he can find a place of his own. He's been living with a friend, and it's not working out. Also, he needs to get back on track financially."

"That won't be a problem with his salary demands."

"Why, what's he asking?"

Liz put her index finger to her lips.

"Go on," Nate said. "I won't tell."

"Fifty pounds an hour plus a company credit card."

"To be honest, he could do better. He's one smart guy. His friends call it the AJ paradox. He's business savvy, can fix anything from a flat tire on a mountain bike to doing a grease and oil change, and he's arty as well."

"A real Jack of all trades."

"And in this case, a master of many."

As Liz opened her laptop on Monday morning, AJ Tanner's follow up email caught her eye. She replied with an invitation to join her at the office to discuss it further and appointed a time.

The following day when Liz entered the lobby after lunch, AJ and Sophie were sharing a private joke. He was early, a good sign, so why did she feel intimidated by his efficiency?

"Liz." He offered his hand along with the cool greeting.

"AJ." *Ouch.* Liz massaged her right hand as she recalled how gentle his lovemaking touch had been. The contradictions kept coming. "Please come through."

"Thank you." He spoke before Liz had the chance to sit. "So, I gather this meeting has a letter of offer attached."

She wanted to tell him outright that she'd given his interest serious consideration and had decided against such a letter. But as he sat in the chair opposite her desk—his presence engulfing every square inch of her office—she struggled to find her business voice. "Actually...I need more time."

He rubbed his forefinger and thumb through his thick beard. His gaze didn't falter. "Okay, fine," he said finally and, if she wasn't mistaken, a little coolly. "I've another offer pending, so I'm afraid if you can't decide by the end of the business day, I'll have to withdraw." He stood to leave. "Oh, and thanks for letting me stay in Nate's room while you're in New Zealand."

"It wasn't my decision. It was Nate's."

"Even so, he said he'd ask you first. I assume he did. Otherwise, I wouldn't have a key."

He already had a key. *Great.* "Yes, he mentioned it."

His expression hinted his amusement. "Anyway, I'd better go. Give me your phone." AJ held out his hand. Liz hesitated.

He stepped closer, invading her space. "I have a new number. I'll add it to your contacts so you can text me yes or no. I won't need an explanation if you decide the latter, so don't feel you have to justify your decision."

Liz handed him her phone and watched as he added his details to her contact list with his beautifully nimble fingers.

"Done." He handed it back, those same fingers lightly brushing hers. "I look forward to hearing from you." He walked out the door, a bemused smile firmly in place.

"Does he get the job?" Sophie asked once AJ had left. "The more you see of him, the hotter he gets."

"Stop it." Liz understood what Sophie meant. A sense of foreboding washed over her. How would she keep herself in check with a sexy hunk of male, intent on a 'no mixing business with pleasure' policy, working for her? She'd convinced herself the wall kiss—and the rest—was nothing more than a passionate moment in time. Her last conversation with Peter flashed through her mind, along with a vague trace of guilt. She shouldn't be thinking about AJ that way, and she knew it.

"Anyway, I said I'll let him know by the end of business, or rather, he insisted on it. Told me he'd withdraw if I didn't. Bossy bastard."

"Well, if you don't need the other office, we have an IT guy after it. But his comb-over, acne, and paunch put me off right away, so please, I'm counting on you. A girl can only take so much."

Liz laughed and returned to her desk. Five minutes later, she was back in reception.

"Decision made. He's the perfect fit intellectually, but I just can't go there. He's way too much…of everything." Liz searched Sophie's expression. "What?"

Sophie shrugged. "For what it's worth, I think you're making a mistake. You need help, Liz. The fact that he's smoking hot is a big fat bonus."

"Maybe, but my lawyer suggested they appoint an advisor attached to his firm. It's a good solution. Less hassle."

"I'm blaming you for comb-over guy."

"Sorry, Soph."

At five twenty-five, Liz phoned AJ to tell him the news. The call went straight to answer. She left a message, using way too many adverbs and adjectives before hanging up. Why didn't she just text him a definite 'no' instead?

MANAGED RISKS

"I TAKE it you've made your decision and AJ's out on the streets begging for food and booze money," Nate said as he and Liz ate dinner a few days later.

Liz chuckled. "With his good looks and unbridled charm, he won't be hungry or sober for long. Anyway, how do you know?"

"He called me just before you walked in the door."

She scooped rice onto her fork. "Do you think he understands?"

"It's business. No tears of rejection. He's already taken another position."

"Gosh, that was quick." Liz sipped her wine. "Anyway, I think Ivan's suggestion has merit. An advisor attached to the law firm means I don't have to employ anyone."

Nate raised a brow. "Any idea who it is?"

"Kelly Armstrong. I met him yesterday. He said you guys go biking together."

"We do. But it won't be Kelly. He crashed his bike on the way to work this morning and ended up down an embankment. He's in traction with a broken leg."

"Really? That's terrible. He seems like a nice guy. I hope I get someone I have a rapport with." She studied Nate's smirking face. "What?"

"I really shouldn't say," Nate said with a chuckle. "But I know who Kelly's replacement is."

Liz frowned as her stomach squirmed. "Who?"

"Take one guess and weep."

"What? No." Liz placed her silverware on her plate and pushed it aside. "You can't be serious. AJ is Kelly's replacement?"

"You didn't hear it from me. They may not even assign him to your account."

Ivan Kingston Law had various divisions, financial services being one of them. Thoughts of AJ working for IKL bombarded Liz throughout the evening, sending her to a place called dread and back again. She tried to reconcile his current persona with the man who'd seduced her eighteen months earlier, and failed.

Liz had dated arrogant men before, the difference being—apart from Peter and a couple of guys back home—she'd never slept with those men. It didn't seem to matter. They had still dumped her without a backward glance. On to bigger and better things.

The day of the IKL meeting, Liz dressed in a sedate skirt, blouse, and cardigan combo, tied her unruly curls into a bun, and applied light makeup with barely a touch of lip-gloss, ready to meet her match.

"I'm here to see Kelly Armstrong's replacement," she said to the receptionist. "Liz Dobson."

"Of course, Ms. Dobson. Please take a seat. What a shame about Kelly. He was so looking forward to working on your account. We've put you in the capable hands of Anthony Tanner. He won't be a minute."

"Thank you." Liz sat on a low chair in the reception nook, a small coffee table topped with business magazines and daily newspapers in front of her. She gripped the straps of her bag and breathed deeply. She didn't want to be in Anthony Tanner's capable hands. She'd had that experience. Sure, his hands were extremely skillful, but still.

Seconds later, the man in question strolled down the corridor toward her. Dressed in casual business clothes and with his beard still long and unruly below his chin, he looked out of place.

"Liz. Please come through."

He led her into a light and airy office and offered her a seat. Liz ran a glance over the large desk and the chair neatly pushed into place. A lone pen sat to the right of the scribble free topper pad. Otherwise, apart from a laptop, there was not a file or hole-punch in sight. Liz never imagined AJ to be so fastidious.

He waited several seconds for Liz to get comfortable, then spoke. "Well, this is a rather interesting position we find ourselves in." He swung back in his chair, a look of amusement firmly plastered on his smug face.

"And that amuses you, does it?" she asked.

"I must admit, the situation has a touch of satire attached to it, don't you agree?"

"No, not really." He was definitely enjoying himself at her expense. "I was expecting Kelly Armstrong."

"I'm afraid Kelly's on sick leave. I've taken over the financial side of his client base for the foreseeable future. As your company is one of Kelly's clients, I'm now head of your advisory team."

Call it instinct or dread, Liz had known as soon as Nate mentioned it that AJ Tanner would be Kelly's replacement. "I see. I had no idea," she lied.

"Neither did I until this morning. Still, I'm positive we can make it work."

"I'm not sure if it's a good idea to tell you the truth."

"Really? Why?"

The guy didn't believe in flowery words. "It's just…"

"You didn't have enough confidence in my abilities to hire me, and now I'm head of your team, you feel uncomfortable. Am I correct?"

Any words of comprehension vanished with her pride. "Kind of."

"I understand. However, I see it as a positive step for both of us."

"How so?"

"From what Ivan's told me, your company is extremely successful with a mountain of untapped potential. I'm interested in your future objectives and would like to assist." He paused to take a breath and catch a pompous thought. "But I fully appreciate your hesitation. We didn't get off on the best of footings, so if you want me to step down, we can arrange an alternative account manager when you return from your break.

"Unfortunately," he continued, "Ivan is away for two weeks, we're short staffed, and I don't want to spoil his vacation. He doesn't know about our initial association, so explaining the situation could be tricky, not to mention embarrassing. For both of us."

Liz hesitated as his meaning became clear. "You're not seriously suggesting telling Ivan about—"

"Our past association. Or rather, how did you put it, our totally forgettable night together?"

"I didn't say that."

"Really? I may have misrepresented your statement, but certainly not the intention."

Smug bastard. He just sat there—his expression forthright, his gaze fixed on hers and his superior attitude up on the pedestal where he apparently thought it belonged. And all the time he spoke, the words *'do you want it bad, Lizzy'* flashed through her mind like an annoying pop-up on a computer screen. The continuation of his response broke into her thoughts.

"And to answer your question—no, I don't make a habit of discussing my private life with my employer. Still, Ivan will want answers. I'll leave it up to you to fill in the blanks. However, if you want to reconsider, I'm interested. I hope you'll feel the same way once we get the ball rolling."

I doubt that very much. Those five words sat on the tip of her tongue, but Liz couldn't bring herself to voice them. "We'll see how the initial consultations go."

"Of course. So"—AJ opened the lid of his laptop—"shall we get down to business? We need to tidy up a few things before you leave for New Zealand."

"Fine." Liz rarely cursed—even in her thoughts—but right at this moment, her thoughts screamed, *fuck that.*

"Perfect. Let's get started." AJ leaned forward in his chair and picked up a sheet of paper typed with text. He skimmed over the page, then looked up, his expression rigid. "Tell me everything."

Liz didn't want to 'get started.' She wanted the whole sorry fiasco to be done and dusted. "What do you want to know?"

"What are your main long-term concerns?"

"That I'll fail miserably."

He huffed a smile. "Most of us fail at some point."

"You make it sound like a rite of passage."

"Failure gives us the opportunity to reevaluate and change aspects of our life. It can be a constructive part of the success process, don't you agree?"

"Are you speaking from personal experience?"

He paused. Liz wished he'd stop staring at her.

"Absolutely. I constantly strive to do better, just like most people. But perfection can be the enemy of progress."

Liz nodded in agreement. She understood how her pursuit of perfection sometimes hindered her advancement.

"Anyway," he said, "I have a list of questions. Let's knock them off in order. That way, we should have all bases covered over the next few days."

She frowned.

"Don't look so worried. I don't bite," he said, then murmured, "Not in a business situation, anyway."

There it was, the heat, returning with sexy vengeance. Not for the first time in his presence, Liz clenched her thighs together, contracting every muscle in the vicinity of her sheer black panties. She'd always planned to do more Kegel exercises, but not in front of Mr. Tanner.

He didn't miss a beat. "Is your accounting program in the cloud?"

"Not yet. It's something I've been meaning to do."

"Right, that's the first thing we need to change. I'll allocate one of our tech team to assist you. You'll find it a lot easier once we switch over. Then you can log on from anywhere in the world." He didn't give her a chance to reply. "Can you set up an administrative banking log in and password for me?"

Liz hesitated. "Is that necessary?" If AJ detected her apprehension at the suggestion, he didn't let it show.

"Just until I reconcile your bank feed after the initial setup. Also, I may want to shift funds around in the first few weeks."

Seconds passed while he considered his notes. She glanced at his hands, studied his long fingers and half-moons at the base of his nails. Recalled his touch.

"What's your immigration status? I see you've been here for over two years."

His words washed over her without comprehension as wayward thoughts continued to distract her. She struggled to remember how it felt to be the object of a man's desire and to desire him back. Peter rarely desired her. In fact, when she thought about it, she'd never felt desired by Peter. Not once.

AJ broke her train of thought again. "I assume you're not working under the Highly Skilled Migrant Program?"

Liz sat upright and mentally slapped herself to attention. "No, my father's English. Born and bred in London."

"Good. I don't have to marry you just yet, then?"

"Excuse me?"

He glanced up from his notes and flashed a grin. "So you can stay in the country."

She felt a blush spread up her neck as she fiddled with the collar of her blouse and pulled her fingers over the skin at the base of her throat. "I have dual passports."

"Okay." He studied his notes again, considering several points, then continued. "Tell me about your internet list. I take it you apply honest business practice?"

"What do you mean?"

"Well, do you sell your list to third parties and spam email addresses you've purchased through third parties?"

"Certainly not."

"Fine, but just remember, I know nothing of your business activities. For all I know, you're a pesky spammer. So, talk me through it. Start at the beginning."

Liz shot him a serious look. "But just remember, I am not a naïve damsel-in-distress."

"Really? I rather like you in that role. It suits you." His focus remained on the twenty-question slip of paper, but an amused smile sat on his smug face. "Please, continue."

The air of his office suddenly felt stuffy and dry, and her face and neck prickled with heat. Liz grabbed a water bottle from her bag and excused herself to use the bathroom. How could she work with this guy? She should have gone straight to Ivan and demanded a replacement, just like any other poor little rich girl.

However, Liz had always been a pleaser, and no matter how hard she tried to assert herself when faced with a strong alpha male, she failed miserably. Her particular breed of 'daddy complex' rose to the foreground once again. Liz loved her father dearly, but he was a tough taskmaster and being the eldest daughter, she frequently endured his unyielding parenting style.

AJ was on the phone when she returned. She waited for him to finish the call, pretending not to listen to the one-sided conversation.

"Sorry, where were we?" He referred to his list of questions. "What's the click-through to purchase percentage?"

"Depends on the product. I have an analytics program, the problem is, I'm often too busy to evaluate the data."

He raised his eyebrows at her like she was a naughty school-girl. "Really? Something to look at." He made notes and continued. "There's no point wasting time on products with unhealthy click-through rates. Do you promote affiliate products only, or products of your own?"

"Mainly affiliate. I have an organic skincare range and baby products that are mine. They sell extremely well."

AJ placed the paper on the table and scribbled something in the margin. As Liz spoke, he kept his gaze focused and listened attentively. They discussed her other business activities at length, including her investment portfolio.

AJ continued along the same lines until her head hurt and her butt stuck to the chair. Liz wanted to step back a few days. Life without a business advisor, slash bossy bastard AJ Tanner, was relaxed and informal. She came and went as she pleased, dictated her own terms, and if her investments weren't earning the best interest rate available, that was her business.

Now it seemed her business was also Anthony Tanner's business.

15

CHARMING AND EVASIVE

NATE AND AJ walked from his studio to a pop-up burger joint where smoky bacon and flamed grilled beef tasted like heaven in a bun, and the temperature of the beer was just right.

By now, the studio radiated AJ's concentrated style, the ghost of his lover's past shifting with each brush stroke, each finished piece. He smiled as he thought about Liz and their current situation. Her efforts to portray herself as a serious CEO—in a tight skirt, sexy-as-hell chignon, and bust-hugging top—stirred his interest even more. Shit, she was pretty. And while he wasn't one to gloat at other's misfortune, Kelly's accident had serendipity written all over it. He must remember to buy him a beer sometime.

AJ had never considered himself the jealous type but seeing Liz with her boyfriend at Munro's had pissed him off big time. The guy had *pompous prick* stamped all over him.

They sat at a small table outside. AJ removed the burgers from the brown paper bag and handed one to Nate.

"Thanks. How's it going with Liz?" Nate asked after tucking into his burger. "I gather you're her new advisor."

"Lizzy the List Maker?" AJ said with a grin. "Good, I think.

She's a bit confronting. She asked me not to treat her like a naïve damsel-in-distress."

"And your reply?"

"I told her it suited her."

"You didn't." Nate shook his head. "You, my friend, are treading on thin ice and about to land on your ass. No wonder you find her confronting. I agree, she's naïve about certain things, like where to invest her fortune, but she's a tough little cookie when she needs to be and works damn hard."

AJ swigged his beer. "Maybe that's what I like about her."

"What? Don't tell me you're still interested after all this time? She blew you off after you walked out without saying goodbye, remember."

Nate obviously knew more about AJ's ill-fated liaison with Liz than he first let on. "I remember only too well. But what can I say? We have an orgasmic connection." He caught Nate's concerned look and burst out laughing. "What? Come on. It does happen."

"I thought you didn't believe in mixing business with pleasure."

"There's always a first time for everything and an exception to every rule," AJ said as he dipped a thick fry into aioli.

"She needs business support, not a fuck buddy. So keep your pen on paper and your dick in your pants."

"You're the one who mentioned fuck buddy, not me. But now I come to think of it, the role has merit. Besides, how do you know what happened?"

Nate shrugged.

"Come on, what did she say?"

"That you had dinner together the night before you left for Japan and she woke a few hours later to a cold and lonely bed. Oh, and she might have used the word *asshole* and maybe *bastard*."

AJ recalled the intense intimacy of that night and grinned. The experience stayed with him as a one-night-stand he wanted to replicate, again and again. "Did she now? I bet she never called me an asshole."

"The implication was made. Besides, you're not her type. She likes clean cut guys—blonds usually—with no facial fluff, short hair, and sans ink."

"Is that so? She didn't seem to mind last time." AJ rapidly changed the subject. "They have excellent food here."

"You're a total prick when it comes to women. Hurt her again, and I'll have plenty to say about it."

AJ didn't take offense to Nate's lighthearted banter. "Me? A total prick? Never. Charming and evasive maybe. Anyway, I've found enlightenment, remember. I'm after a long-term committed relationship, and Liz is otherwise occupied. I'm stuck between a rock and an annoyingly hard—"

"Feck off. I don't need to know."

"Anyway, we've discussed it and agreed to keep things on a professional level. She's very specific about it."

"And…are you? Specific about it?"

"Hell no." AJ's cheeky grin lit up his face. "But time's on my side."

A brief rainstorm greeted Liz on Monday morning, so she arrived at work later than usual, only to find Peter spread out on the sofa in reception reading the *Financial Times*.

"Good morning." Peter checked his watch. "What time of day do you call this?"

"I've been working at home." Liz felt the need to explain, then mentally scolded herself. "What are you doing here?"

"Is that any way to greet the man of your dreams?"

She managed a soft smile. "Sorry, I just didn't expect to see you today."

"Obviously." He folded the paper, tossed it back on the table and stood. "I've something I want to discuss. Thought we could do lunch."

"Great. I need to talk to you about something too."

"Marvelous. I'll make a reservation and text you. Now into your office, young lady and get to work," he said playfully. "But first, come here." He pulled her in close and kissed her on the lips. "You look exceptionally beautiful today." He tugged on a curl. "Even with your hair in curls."

Liz stepped back. It was the first compliment Peter had given her in weeks, and she grabbed it with open arms. "Thank you."

They met at twelve-thirty as arranged. As soon as Liz walked into the restaurant, she knew the bill would be a hefty one. Days like today, when Peter piled on the charm and sincerity, she questioned herself for doubting him. All the same, the thought of explaining AJ's role and the anticipation of Peter's response, unsettled her to the extent where her stomach tightened in knots, and the last thing she wanted was rich food.

"Shall I go first?" Peter didn't wait for her to reply as he tucked into a pea and asparagus risotto while Liz moved a salmon and watercress salad around her plate. "I have an investment proposal for you. I'm starting a new company and thought I'd offer you the opportunity to sneak in on the ground floor. The initial capital outlay would be around half a million pounds for a nine percent share."

Nate's warning flashed through her mind as she wondered if the numbers made sense. A straight out 'no' sat on the tip of her tongue, but she held it there for now, just to keep the peace. "What kind of company?"

"Imports mainly. We're still tweaking the details. You'd be a silent partner—sit back and reap the rich dividends."

"Imports are a new area for you. Do you have additional backers?"

Peter kept eating. "I'm putting out feelers. There's plenty of interest. What do you say?"

"I'm not sure. I'll check with Ivan. Do you have a prospectus?"

He looked up, his fork halfway between his plate and mouth. "Not as such. And honestly, Liz, if you have to check with your darn lawyer every time you sneeze, opportunities like this will pass you by."

"Half a million pounds is a lot of money. I'll have to consult my team."

"Your team? What team? Don't tell me you want Nate in on the deal."

"That's what I wanted to discuss." Liz took a sip of her lime and soda. She inhaled a calming breath. "Ivan's set me up with an advisor of sorts."

"What? You've taken on a business advisor without consulting me. When did this happen?"

"Keep your voice down, you're embarrassing me. Yesterday."

Peter gritted his teeth and leaned across the table. "You went behind my back?"

"It wasn't like that. I've been considering it for ages. I haven't employed anyone. It's all done through IKL."

"I don't believe this. How could you make such a decision without my guidance?"

"I discussed it with Nate."

"Your cousin has way too much influence in your life. I don't trust him." He pulled out his phone. "What's the person's name? This so-called advisor."

"Why do you have to be so rude about it?"

"Me, rude? That's rich coming from you. Name?"

"Anthony Tanner. He's a business advisor with a degree in accounting. We met a couple of years ago. He's Ivan's nephew."

He talked as he typed on the tiny keypad. "An office boy in a family firm is an office boy whatever way you want to call it."

"What are you doing?"

Peter slipped his phone back into his pocket. "What you should have done in the first place. Making a few discrete inquiries."

"There's no need. He works for IKL. He must be trustworthy."

"Is he good looking?"

"What's that got to do with anything?"

"I'm just curious." Peter lifted his napkin to his lips and dabbed away imaginary bits of food. He held her gaze. "Well?"

"I guess."

"Older or younger?"

"Early thirties, maybe."

"You say you met him two years ago. Have you ever been intimate with this man?"

"What? Why would you even ask me such a thing?"

Lie number one.

"I'm struggling to get my head around this ridiculous exercise," Peter said. "If we weren't together would he be your type, hypothetically?"

"But we are together, so it's not a consideration."

Lie number two.

"Does he have access to your bank accounts and investments?"

"At least give me some credit."

Lie number three.

"Fine. You can pick up the check. Your news has ruined an otherwise marvelous lunch."

The moment Liz left the restaurant, uncertainty crept into her thoughts and stuck like glue. What if AJ moved funds without consulting her? He said he wouldn't. Even so, he had the means, and now she had no idea how to rectify the situation.

By the end of the next session with Mr. Tanner, Liz wondered if AJ knew more about her business than she did. Apart from the odd pleasantry, he rarely made small talk. However, Nate had left the day before, and AJ seemed to sense a shift in her mood.

"How did it go yesterday? Did Nate get away on time?"

"He did. It will be strange without him around." Liz stood at the window and looked out to the street below. A lone pigeon strutted along, pecking the pavement in a never-ending quest for tiny morsels of food. Liz loved pigeons—with their plump breasts and beautiful tints of color. Mother Nature sure had a handle on it when blending hues. "He's been such a support to me since I arrived in London."

"Let me know if I can help with anything."

AJ hadn't shown his softer side recently. Now, he was an emotion away from being sweet. However, the words 'sweet' and 'crave' danced together on her tongue. Liz knew the moment she lifted the lid off the jar of caramel sauce hiding in her fridge, half the contents would disappear in an instant. Sweet held too much appeal and should be avoided—at all costs. "Thanks."

He quickly switched moods. "Okay, let's go over your finances. I'm eager to see what we're dealing with."

"Actually, I may have jumped the gun initially." Liz paced the floor, twisting her hands together. The air in the office was slightly cool, and a cold draft whistled through a tiny gap in the window frame. "Maybe we should wait until I'm back before you go any further."

His brows knitted together. "Okay."

"It's just, I don't feel comfortable allowing IKL access to my bank accounts at this stage. We can work on it when I get back."

He hesitated. "No problem. So, is there anything I can take care of while you're away?"

She turned to look at him, appreciating his understanding. "No, I don't think so."

"Fine." His tone was curt. "I'll look into investments and have them ready to table on your return."

"Actually, about that, my boyfriend has offered me an investment opportunity in a new importing business. I said I'd discuss it with you and Ivan. I'm not sure if it's right for me, or if the numbers stack up."

"Do you have a prospectus?"

"Not yet."

"How much is he suggesting?"

Liz took a deep breath. "Five hundred thousand pounds."

"Shit. That's… Well, we'll need to see the details. I'm happy for him to contact me."

"Okay, but it might be better if I ask him to email a proposal."

16

CASUAL VISITOR

AFTER PICKING up a Reuben sandwich from a deli across the street, Liz headed along the Embankment to her favorite seat. Packed with sauerkraut and dripping with Swiss cheese, she savored every mouthful as she shifted her focus from work to the afternoon ahead.

Thursdays mentoring gig gave Liz a chance to give back to the community. Those few hours of interaction with the students—fresh ideas and teenage hormones flowing—left her buzzing with inspiration. But this particular Thursday was also an excuse to have a break from AJ and his interrogation tactics.

Lunch over, she hailed a cab; the driver pulling out into the traffic before she'd hardly had time to shut the door.

As she walked across campus toward her class, Liz wondered about AJ's passions. What inspired him? Was he the type that hated their job but did nothing about it? Or did he plan to leave accountancy and change direction entirely?

Making a career switch wasn't easy when there were bills to pay and rent to find. She'd gathered from Nate that AJ wasn't in a healthy financial position. Liz had been in the same boat once, so she understood.

She entered the classroom and put her bag under the desk, then glanced up and smiled. "Hi, everyone. Please take your seats."

On her way home from school, Liz stopped at the supermarket, filling her basket with just enough food to stretch two days. Once home, she followed her familiar routine. Cooked a simple dinner, cranked up the music and, after the meal, flopped in front of the TV. She flicked through the channels in search of rom-com relief before heading off to bed around ten.

Once in bed, Liz told herself that living alone suited her. It was one of many tales attached to her doubting self, along with the 'good enough, worthy enough, smart enough' mantras she repeated in the shower most mornings. Even so, she missed Nate. The way he'd bound up the stairs and knock on her door with a gentle good-night. Nate was a good guy. One of the best.

Liz woke with a start at a noise coming from Nate's room. The dreaming-of-falling-off-a-cliff kind of start she'd experienced as a child. She grabbed her nightshirt off the floor and tugged it on, then reached for the knob on her bedroom door and locked it.

Shaky fingers fiddled over the keypad of her phone, her heart rate rising rapidly as lonely married scared.

Liz: Someone's here. Please tell me it's you???
AJ: It's me.

Liz stormed out of her room and across the landing. Apart from a pair of tighty-whiteys with a pronounced Y-front, AJ stood naked before her. He looked tired and gaunt. His hair, usually tied in that signature man bun, danced around his shoulders in a mass of black waves. Thinner than she remembered, his lithe, muscular body towered over her. She didn't dare to look down. His underwear left little to the imagination and her imagination was running hot.

"What are you doing here?" She glanced around the room. Clothes, guitars, boxes, and shoes were stacked neatly in place.

He pushed soft curls behind his ears. "Um…is this a trick question? And let's set some boundaries, shall we? It's manners to knock before you barge into a person's room." He cocked a mischievous brow. "What if I had someone with me?"

She craned her neck toward the bathroom door and whispered, "Do you?"

"I live in hope."

"You said you wouldn't move in until after I'd left for New Zealand."

He grabbed an undershirt from the bed and tugged it on. It failed to cover the soft bulge in his underwear. "Yeah, sorry. Change of plans. I arrived earlier to drop off my gear. I meant to text you."

"So, you just stroll on in and make yourself at home?"

"I thought you'd still be awake. But you were sleeping like a baby with a belly full of milk. I didn't want to wake you."

An image of her lying naked on top of the covers flashed through her mind. Being a restless sleeper, Liz hated sleeping clothed. "You came into my room? While I slept?"

"It's not as if I haven't seen you in bed before."

His flippant remark did nothing to help his cause. "Hardly the point."

AJ's expression turned serious. "Look, my housemate had a party last night. When I arrived home, a couple were going for it in my bed." He ran his hands through his hair. "I ended up sleeping, if you can call it that, on the freaking sofa. So, can we discuss this another time? I need to get some sleep."

"You scared me out of my wits. Can't you stay somewhere else tonight?"

"Come on! It's after midnight." He sighed. "Look, Lizzy, it's way past my bedtime and I'm exhausted." He glanced down at the hard points peaking through her oversized nightshirt. "And you're obviously feeling the cold, so either snuggle in with me or shut the door on your way out."

Liz followed his line of sight and felt herself blush at the reference. She shot a glance at the intricate pattern of his mandala tattoo. "In future, stay out of my room. And don't call me Lizzy. Goodnight!"

She slammed the door behind her.

When Liz entered the kitchen the next morning, AJ was gone. He'd eaten breakfast and, like a typical male, left his plate and coffee mug soaking in the sink. What was it about men? Why couldn't they take the next step to open and stack the dishwasher?

As she ate breakfast, Liz realized she knew very little about AJ. Sure, he kissed like crazy and was amazing in bed, but he might be a total control freak. An embezzler, even.

Living with him wasn't ideal; but working with him could be worse.

When AJ left the terrace, shallow torrents of rainwater hurried down leaf-clogged gutters to storm water drains at the end of the street. But by the time he'd unlocked the studio door twenty minutes later, the rain clouds had blown through, leaving a dulled off day to match his mood.

The erotic bookstore remained. He sometimes considered buying a book or two, just to help his tenant out, but couldn't stand the musty smell of second-hand books. And lately, erotica was off his reading list in favor of *Men's Fitness*. Although last night when Liz left his room, he could have done with an article titled, *how to calm an erection and keep it down*.

Once inside the studio, AJ changed into a pair of paint-splattered jeans and a seen-better-days T-shirt. He sat for a moment, gathering inspiration. He'd not slept well the night before, images of Liz in that sleep shirt invading his thoughts. At one point, his persistent erection urged him to tiptoe across the landing to renegotiate the terms of their contract. But then he remembered. Liz was in a relationship.

And he was being responsible.

She'd changed over the past eighteen months, emanating a sophisticated, businesslike air. The clipped corners of her Kiwi accent had all but disappeared, leaving an international cadence to her speech. And even though the light and vivacity of her expression had dulled, when he thought of her, one phrase came to mind: Still as beautiful as fuck!

As AJ grabbed a brush and dabbled with colors on a palette board, he wondered, for the hundredth time, why he'd let Nate persuade him to move in as chief Lizzy-sitter in residence. He'd never thought of himself as the knight in shining armor type. However, he often felt a tinge of protectiveness toward her. He didn't know why. Friends had sometimes expressed this sentiment about their wives and girlfriends, but until now, he'd failed to comprehend the condition.

He moved around the studio, tidying up stray brushes as his thoughts got the better of him. There would be no artistic flow that day.

Half an hour later, AJ wandered back to the terrace, picked up his gym gear, and spent the next two hours pumping iron while releasing copious amounts of sweat along with a distinct case of sexual frustration.

As he left the gym, his phone hummed in his pocket. He pulled it out and hit *Accept*. "Paul, how's it going?"

"All set. I can't wait to shift some art on Friday night."

"Need a hand?" AJ asked.

"No, we're sweet. What's your decision on *Un Beso*?"

"As much as it pains me, I have to let it go."

"What? I thought you wanted to keep it as a long-term investment. I hear Jacobs is one to watch."

AJ laughed. "You think? Unfortunately, if I don't flush my

credit card with a substantial injection of cash, we're about to part company. It makes sense financially."

"And emotionally?"

AJ tried not to think about the emotion attached to his painting. "Let's see if we get any nibbles. Otherwise, I'll reconsider."

"Fine, I'll give it pride of place. I hope you don't regret it."

THE JACOBS

Busy streets full of commuters greeted Liz as she made her way to a small suburban gallery through raw hand rubbing air. She sometimes likened London's cold to the briskness of the ski fields at home. Today was such a day.

Hannah, an artist of notoriety and friend of Penny's for many years, invited Liz to all of her exhibitions. Liz loved Hannah's signature style—large contemporary canvases in vibrant colors—and she planned to purchase one as soon as the right piece caught her eye.

Beautiful bodies packed the basement space with standing room only. Liz searched for Penny as she flashed the security guard her invitation. She pushed through the crowd huddled around the bar where they served free alcohol alongside artistic small talk.

"Liz, you made it." Penny called her over. "Love your dress, hon. I need to borrow it."

"Sure. Not tonight, though. I don't have panties on." Liz scanned the jam-packed room. "What a crazy turn out. The owners must be pleased. How many artists are exhibiting?"

"Five or six. And you're a liar. You never leave the house without panties."

Liz winked.

"Have you heard of a guy called Jacobs?" Penny moved Liz through the crowd toward the back wall. "He's exhibiting for the first time."

"Can't say I have." Liz checked out the small plaque below a Jacobs painting and paused. "Look at this one. *Un Beso Imaginado.* Wow. Is it for sale?"

"It's sold. See the red dot? I've never seen his work anywhere. I wonder if he's here. Apparently he keeps a low profile."

"So, he's a bit precious then," Liz said with a smile.

"I guess. Still, he has the talent to pull it off."

Apart from Hannah's four and two from Jacobs, the other artists' works were a mixed bag. Liz let her thoughts wander to *Un Beso Imaginado,* a large canvas depicting—as the name implied in Spanish—an imagined kiss. The color palette frolicked with muted grays and charcoal on white with a touch of jade and violet—the essence of the kiss weighted down in molten lead, full of want and desire as it floated into fluid passion. She imagined the piece gracing the wall of Nate's living room. Or better still, in her dream home.

Liz noticed AJ out of the corner of her eye, unable to miss the guy with his height, topknot, and horrible bushy beard. He glanced up. There was no recognition, not even a slight smile. He'd deliberately snubbed her.

"Liz, why didn't you tell me you were coming?" A familiar voice had her turning in attention. Peter stood in her halo of space, air kissed her on both cheeks and reached for her hand. "I understood this was an invitation-only event."

Liz inhaled sharply but managed a terse smile. "Silly me. I wish someone had told me. I'd better go before security throws me out."

"Don't be like that." He patted her hand, then cupped her

elbow. "Stick with me and no one will be any the wiser. I thought about inviting you but didn't think it would be your thing."

She pulled away. Sometimes Peter's condescending attitude slotted into the asshole category and she didn't have the energy to deal with him right now.

"Come on, Liz," he said, his tone more patronizing than friendly. "Let's enjoy the evening without you getting all moody on me."

A familiar feeling gripped her gut, setting it on fire. "I was just leaving. I'll see you tomorrow."

"Okay, fine. I want to follow up on that office boy fiasco." It was an off-the-cuff remark, made purely to trip Liz up. Make her question and worry.

"There's nothing to follow up. I've already accepted him as my advisor. I'm not going back on my word."

His expression hardened. "I still can't believe you didn't consult me. It has financial disaster written all over it." Peter took a sip of his wine and scanned the room, obviously eager to network. "Actually, my inquiries have raised several concerns."

"Look, Peter, I've had a long day. I don't want to discuss this now."

"That's your problem," he hissed through gritted teeth. "You never want to discuss anything important but you're all over the trivial. We'll talk at the weekend. It seems your advisor has a somewhat checkered past."

Liz felt sick to her stomach as she watched Peter retreat toward his friends. What did he mean, 'a checkered past?'

She turned to leave, bumping straight into a six-foot-two wall of solid yoga-formed muscle all topped off with a scraggly black beard. AJ reached out to steady her. "Hey. Are you okay?" His frown held mock concern. "Was that guy bothering you?"

"He's my boyfriend."

AJ shot a glance in Peter's direction and frowned. "Sorry, I didn't realize."

"Excuse me, but I was just leaving." Liz pushed past AJ and weaved her way through the crowd.

AJ followed her to the door. "Liz, wait. What are you doing here?"

"Not you too." She slapped her invitation into his hand. "I have to go."

"Liz—"

Rushing past the security guards, Liz ran up the steps to the street above. She reached out to steady herself on the side of the building as her boots hit the frost-covered pavement. Tired and moody, she longed to be tucked up at home in bed.

She raised her hand. "Taxi."

———

Once home, Liz unlocked her phone and dialed her parent's number. Andrea answered with her usual formal style. "Andrea Dobson speaking."

"Hi, Mum."

"Liz, is that you? Why didn't you Skype? How are you, darling?"

"A bit homesick, to be honest. I miss you guys."

"We miss you too. What time is it over there?"

"Ten after eleven. I've been to an exhibition. Now I can't sleep."

"Okay darling, tell me in one hundred words or less what's been happening lately?"

It was a family joke. The 'hundred words or less' challenge. Liz burst into tears. "I want to come home."

"Liz? Are you okay?" Her mother waited. "Liz, say something."

"Sorry. I'm a bit emo at the moment." She laughed through her tears. "Must be the time of the month."

"Why don't you have a mug of hot milk and honey and then

get some sleep. It's only a couple of days until you're home. The break will do you good. Have a safe flight and be at the airport in plenty of time…with your passport."

"Tell Ally and Sydney I can't wait to see them."

"What about Mitch?"

Liz laughed. How could she leave her brother out? "Him too. Is he coming home?"

"Of course."

"Cool. I miss him."

"Yes, well, he's still enjoying himself, that's for sure," Andrea said with a humorous tut-tut in her voice. "I wish he'd find a nice girl and settle down."

"I wouldn't think he'd have any trouble in that department."

"He has no trouble finding them. I just wish he'd keep one."

"Good old Mitch. He's got the looks and charm of a movie star with a twinkle in his eye to match. Usually means one thing —trouble."

"Don't I know it. Anyway, sleep tight. See you in a few days."

"Okay. Bye."

As Liz readied for bed, she played the gallery fiasco over in her mind. She'd overreacted and now felt embarrassed by her outburst. Around midnight, AJ sent her a text with *home safe?* She replied a brief *yes,* then turned off her phone.

The next day, Liz braved shoppers lining the High Street and headed back to the gallery. It looked larger and shabbier during the day; the interior taking on an entirely different ambiance. A young woman, with a shock of pink hair and long gloves that reminded Liz of a scene from an old Audrey Hepburn movie, greeted her. "How may I help?"

Liz stepped further into the space, rubbing her hands together against the chill. "I came to the exhibition last night. I'd like to enquire about a Jacobs piece. The Imagined Kiss."

"Ah, *Un Beso Imaginado,*" she replied in perfect Spanish. "I'm afraid it's sold. Caused quite a stir."

"Is there any chance of a backup offer? I'm willing to pay over the asking price."

"I wouldn't think so. But if you leave your details, I'll have the boss contact you next week. And I apologize about the heating. Our boiler's thrown a temper tanty."

"No problem." Liz reached into her bag and pulled out her business card. "Thank you. The new owner may consider selling for a healthy profit."

"He may, but it's highly unlikely."

Liz glanced around the room at the works on display. Nothing caught her eye.

"We have one other Jacobs for sale if you like his work in particular. May I tempt you with a peek?"

"Was it on display last night?"

"No, we didn't have room for everything and what we did, sold in no time."

The woman with the pink hair and perfectly applied makeup guided Liz to a small room adjoining the main gallery. "There," she said with a flamboyant wave of her gloved hand. "The one on the back wall."

The click of Liz's boots echoed on the hardwood floor and her mouth released a silent 'wow' of vapor as she studied the piece. The rich tones of vibrant color, slapped and scraped on the canvas with artistic enthusiasm, overwhelmed her.

"Isn't it special?"

"Extremely." Liz continued to stare at the work. "Is it priced?"

"A bargain at three and a half. We predict Jacobs will be highly sought after in a few years. I'll leave you alone to get acquainted."

"Thank you." Liz stared. Imagined. Coveted.

Entering the main part of the gallery again, she addressed the assistant. "I'm away for two weeks. If I purchase the work today, will you store it for me?"

"Certainly. Call us when you're ready. We'll have it delivered anywhere in the greater London area. I'm Pearl." She opened a drawer and pulled out a business card. "If you need to contact me, here's my card."

Liz took the card offered. "Thank you. One other thing," she said as she handed over her credit card and office address details. "I'd like to contact Mr. Jacobs. I'm interested in a commission."

"Jacobs is not available to members of the public. And as far as I know, he shuns away from commission work."

"I see. Was he here last night?"

"I have no idea. Apart from a select few, no one knows who he is." Pearl stifled a giggle. "I don't make the cut, although I have my suspicions."

18

CHEATERS AND CHARMERS

LIZ MOSEYED INTO THE KITCHEN, grabbed a handful of clothes from the dryer, and folded them neatly, ready to pack into her luggage. All day, the words 'checkered past' had held court in her thoughts. She wished Peter would show his face so she could quiz him about AJ.

Back in the living room, she inched the sheer curtains open and glanced along the neat row of terrace houses, half-expecting to see Peter's Porsche idling at the curb. But the street was unusually quiet.

He finally turned up just after eight.

"I'm about to make scrambled eggs," she said as he followed her into the kitchen. "Would you like some?"

"Do you have anything else? I don't feel like eggs."

"I'm eating out of the cupboard, so I don't have leftovers." Liz didn't wait for him to decide. She carried on regardless. The last thing she wanted tonight was a dose of Peter's condescending attitude.

"Fine," he said with a sigh. "I'll have mine poached."

"Poached it is." She took a deep breath and grabbed a pan from the cabinet. Entering the living room, Peter turned on the TV, saying nothing more until she called him ten minutes later.

"You mentioned something about AJ when we talked at the gallery."

"I did some discrete digging." Peter sat at the booth as Liz placed two plates of eggs and toast on the table. "He has an accounting degree, as you said, but hasn't been a practicing member of the profession for over two years. He ventured into a property deal gone wrong with a school chum…a Christopher Farrell and his kid brother. Doctor Farrell is a do-gooder with a penchant for making a questionable difference in third world countries. His younger brother is a tradesman of sorts. Plumber, builder, whatever. Either way, neither has any business competency."

He reached for the salt, sprinkled his eggs generously, then scraped his knife across the plate as he cut through the toast. It always annoyed Liz, the noise his knife made when he cut his food.

"The Farrell brothers inherited a financially troubled family business after their father died unexpectedly," Peter continued. "They, along with your so-called business advisor, purchased a rundown property with a heritage listing and planned to do all kinds of weird and wonderful things with it. They soon found themselves in hot water with the council and are now fighting it out in the courts. In the meantime, the property is up for sale with a stop work order attached to the door. Word on the street is, the company they formed will fold. Apparently, the men aren't on speaking terms and it's ugly. It seems Tanner skipped the country to avoid the fallout. As you know, he's back to pick up the pieces and is reportedly in debt up to his eyeballs. You definitely shouldn't trust him."

"Are you sure?" Liz didn't mean to question Peter's sources, but his 'inside' information made no sense. She needed to ask Ivan about it at their next meeting.

He shook his head as he ate and mumbled, "You can take the

girl out of the country, but you can't take the country out of the girl."

Liz didn't know what to do about Peter's increasingly smug attitude, other than finishing with him altogether. And right now, that possibility held merit. "Meaning?"

"You didn't do your due diligence on this chap. So let me offer you some advice. Keep an eye open and move him sideways as soon as possible. Until then, don't trust him with any of your funds."

"He seems so on to it."

"Oh, I hear he can charm the panties off a Carmelite nun and have her screaming his name. He's totally believable. Con men usually are. Also, he has a reputation with the ladies, so be careful how you tread."

"But he's Nate's friend."

"That may be so, but how well do we actually know those closest to us? Most people will cheat if they get the opportunity."

Liz didn't believe that for one minute. Not everyone was born a cheater. Still, Peter had planted the seed, and that seed begged for germination. "Anyway, I don't have time to sort it out now." Liz stood and reached for Peter's plate, then moved to the sink to fill the kettle as he made a beeline for the sofa and the TV remote. "I'll talk to Ivan about it when I get back."

"Oh, by the way," he said as she stacked the dishwasher. "I need your sign off on the investment deal we discussed."

"Can it wait until I'm back? I don't know the first thing about it."

"You have to learn to seize the day, Liz. There's someone else interested, so I need an answer ASAP. And there's still the matter of the directorship. You seem to have conveniently forgotten about it."

"I'll give it some thought while I'm home."

"What's there to think about? The investment is a golden

opportunity with massive returns. We're forecasting thirty percent in the first year alone."

"Wow. Sounds too good to be true." She handed him a cup of tea.

"O ye of little faith."

"Even so, I like to know what I'm investing in."

"The prospectus is in the pipeline. Expect to see an email next week."

Liz sat on the sofa next to him. Experience had taught her to pick her time and place and, her battles. Tonight—with Peter in a chatty mood—seemed like the perfect time to bring up Nate's concerns.

She bit the uncomfortable bullet. "One thing Nate suggested, which I agree has merit, is drawing up an agreement between us to protect my assets if I invest in your new company."

Peter took a sip of the tea. He liked to drink tea out of a china cup with a saucer. The pattern on the cup reminded Liz of after-noon teatime at her grandmother's home—full of shadows and musty aromas. "So, you've already discussed this with Nate?"

The chill of a turned mood made Liz immediately regret her suggestion. "Yes, but only briefly."

He set the cup down. "You make it sound like a jolly prenup."

"That's not what I mean. Why would we need a prenup?"

"Why indeed?"

Liz faltered. She'd practiced the conversation earlier, but now didn't want to rock the boat. "It's purely a precaution."

Peter didn't bother hiding his annoyance. "You come up with some jolly silly ideas, but this protection agreement crap takes the cake."

On the way to Heathrow the following day, Liz dragged her mind kicking and screaming away from Peter and his narcissistic tendencies, and instead, steered it toward the Jacobs. *Un Beso Imaginado.* She murmured the words, repeating the Spanish intonation Google translate provided.

While she waited at the gate for the final boarding call, she imagined how it would feel to be the female in the painting. To have a man desire you completely, like Jacobs so eloquently portrayed. She recalled her night with AJ. He'd had that effect—the effect of desire. Knew how to manipulate non-verbal communication, no doubt about it—even if he'd slipped out afterward without saying goodbye.

Peter had never mastered such a skill.

19

SHADY TREES

"NATE. HOW'S MOSCOW?" AJ adjusted his headset and moved his laptop, so Nate had a better view of his face.

"Freezing. Otherwise, it's great."

"I'll get straight to the point while our connection's good. Liz has a situation with the boyfriend. But this is totally off the record, okay?"

"Understood." Nate said. "Go on."

AJ spent the next ten minutes explaining to Nate about Peter's elusive investment opportunity. He didn't have many details, but he told Nate all he knew. "How well do you know Peter Nichols?"

"I don't." Nate frowned. "I've only met him once or twice. But he seems a bit of a jerk."

"I've done some delving. He tends to lean on the shady side of the tree. It seems nothing he touches ever turns to gold. From what I can gather, he's deep in debt."

"Doesn't surprise me. According to Penny, Liz flashes her card everywhere they go. Even when he took her to Paris for her birthday last year, she booked the tickets and to my knowledge, he's never paid her back."

"Right. It might be time for Liz to invest in the property

market, away from his greedy hands. A nice house in an affluent suburb may be the ticket."

"I couldn't agree more."

"I'll ask Ivan to have a word with her when she gets back. It seems I'm not to be trusted. She's pulled back on my input. I'm now playing office junior to some wealthy socialite who's in the middle of a messy divorce."

"What?" Nate chuckled. "Why's that?"

"No idea. Maybe Peter put her up to it."

"What is she doing with him? And more to the point, what's he doing with her?"

AJ had asked himself that same question repeatedly. "I'd say he's slowly taking hold and squeezing the life out of her. She isn't the girl I remember."

"Yeah, she's lost some of that Kiwi spark. I might talk to her. See what's going on. And don't you come on too strong, will you?"

"Me? Wouldn't dream of it. Still, I have to keep up a certain air of professionalism." He laughed. "Wouldn't want her questioning my abilities."

"She's a sweet kid. You behave."

"That won't be so easy when she comes back. It's bloody lonely in the tiny terrace without her, and my half-empty bed is feeling the cold."

"So you don't see Peter Nichols as competition?"

AJ scoffed. "The cracks are starting to show. I feel it."

"Wishful thinking, isn't it?"

"Wishful fantasizing more like it." AJ chuckled. "Okay, mate. I'd better go and twiddle my thumbs. Talk soon."

"Will do."

AJ clicked the *end call* icon and leaned back in his chair, tapping the baseline of a song on the desk with a pen. It was time to give Peter Nichols a chance to pitch his case.

HER WAY BACK

BACK AT HEATHROW two weeks later, Liz juggled coffee and luggage in one hand, bag and phone in the other, and made her way toward the exit. A driver, holding a card with *Lizette Dobson* written in black sharpie, stepped forward. She smiled to herself at Peter's thoughtfulness.

"I'm Lizette Dobson. Did Peter Nichols send you?"

"Mr. Tanner ordered the car, Ms. Dobson. Here, let me take your luggage." Liz followed the driver through the terminal and out the door. Mr. Tanner had a considerate side. How very nice.

Over the past two weeks, Liz had thought about AJ from time to time. Actually, from hour to hour if she was honest. She'd decided to put her feelings—the like slash dislike—aside and treat him the way she wished to be treated, with respect and admiration for his professional abilities. Her thoughts surrounding his non-professional abilities could stay where they belonged. Dead and buried under a headstone labeled, *Missed Opportunities of Sexual Wants and Needs.*

They drove in silence through the surprisingly light early morning traffic. She'd considered staying in New Zealand more than once over the past two weeks. However, the practical side of her personality understood why she had to return to London, even if her emotional side struggled with the decision. Before she could contemplate the possibility of a NZ U-turn, there were things to consider. Like her father's disapproval. He'd had reservations about her working in the UK right from the start, and Liz felt the need to prove a point.

London. Her father's birthplace. Liz couldn't remember a time when he didn't speak of it. He'd weave tall tales into her childhood imagination, and she'd listen with eyes filled with wonderment. Then he'd smile, ruffle her hair and tell her to go to sleep as the strokes of Big Ben floated through her mind.

Dull light enclosed the waking city. Despite inhaling several deep breaths for an injection of calm, the London air didn't have the same effect as that of the orchard at home, where cornflower blue skies offset rustic poplars ready to drop their leaves at the first hint of cold. Thoughts of autumn reminded her of the Jacobs soon to grace her office wall. He'd captured it well; the gentle softness coupled with the dramatic transformation between summer and winter.

"Number thirty-five, you said?" the driver asked as he pulled up outside the terrace.

The question brought her back to the present. "Yes. Thank you."

Out of the cab, Liz tipped the driver, then trundled her case across the pavement and up the path to the tiny terrace. She opened the door, her eyes adjusting to the dim light of the interior.

The living room looked the same—neat and tidy—apart from an empty sleeping bag draped over the sofa, along with a pillow from the linen closet. AJ hadn't mentioned moving out in the few emails she'd received in her absence. She assumed he would wait until she returned.

As she climbed the stairs, a discrete giggle, the kind one makes when sharing a bed with a playful mate, resonated from behind AJ's bedroom door. Each step brought the sound closer until the distinctive commentary of a couple having sex couldn't be ignored.

AJ was in Nate's room with some girl and he didn't care who heard about it. An unexpected disappointment washed over her. The kind that sticks in your chest and is hard to budge.

Liz wished AJ and his talent for all things erotic would shut up. She needed sleep without interruption for at least twelve hours. By then, he'd realize she was home and his date slash girlfriend, slash one-night-stand, slash whatever, would have hopefully packed up and left.

She opened her bedroom door.

"What the…" Liz stared at the gorgeous male specimen tangled around her sheets and duvet. "AJ, what are you doing in my bed?"

"Shit. Sorry," he said, still half asleep and naked from the hips up. "I thought you'd be another hour at least." He propped himself up on his elbows as he squinted against the light. "I started off on the sofa, but I couldn't sleep. Thought I'd sneak in here where I could shut the door. Your bed's so comfortable. I was out to it."

"Who are the *Kama Sutra* couple in your room?"

"My brother and his wife. They don't get away from the kids much, so were making the most of it, and probably another baby to add to their tribe."

"*Are* making the most of it," Liz corrected with a playful grin.

"I'm sorry, this is embarrassing. If you give me a minute, I'll get out of your way."

"Stay there. I need a shower." She knew why he needed a minute, but quickly pushed the thought of AJ's morning glory aside for later. "Oh, and thanks for sending a driver."

"No problem."

He stretched out on her bed with his hands behind his head and watched her move around the room. As usual, his scrutiny tripped her up a little, and she could feel her nipples tighten just a touch.

"How was your trip?"

"Amazing. I had a great time."

She stepped into the bathroom and locked the door.

Liz turned on the faucet to hot, stripped naked, and slipped into the shower, letting the water wash away the tension of the flight. By the time she'd finished, AJ had made the bed, opened the window, and was gone. Cool air mingled with the distinctive scent of complex new age guy with a bushy beard and a man bun. She flopped on the bed, snuggled into the warm space left behind, and sighed.

Welcome home.

Several days later, the installation of the Jacobs was booked to take place around noon. Liz couldn't hide her excitement. The colors reminded her of home at the end of autumn. The azure of the sky, the russet of the leaves, and the aquamarine of the waves rolling into the sandy shore of the East Coast.

AJ arrived just after two, one hand in his pocket as usual, and sat a coffee on her desk along with a letter for her attention. He'd done this twice lately. Popped in without an appointment, when really, an email would suffice. Still, she appreciated the coffee.

She studied him out of her peripheral vision as he turned toward the large canvas on the side wall.

A slight grin graced his lips. His eyes narrowed as he considered the piece. "I see you've dabbled in the world of contemporary art."

"I have," she replied, more than pleased with herself. "It's a Jacobs original. What do you think?"

AJ stepped back. He tilted his head to one side, then the other. "I've seen him do better."

Smug bastard, she thought. As if his dismissive opinion mattered to her. "Well, I love it. Brightens up my day. The girl at the gallery said Jacobs is up and coming."

"Really? Let's hope it's money well spent then. As long as you love it, that's all that matters. What do you think it means, those bold strokes of brash color?"

Liz thought for a moment. "Autumn, strolling into winter on a murmur."

"Hmm." He nodded as if in agreement, then turned to face her, the ghost of a grin on his lips. "You think? Surely murmur is too lenient a word." He glanced at the painting, then back at her. "It's more of a raucous orgasmic awakening, don't you agree?"

She stared at him, struggling to form a reply.

"Anyway," he said, "I'd better go."

He winked and walked away, leaving her caught off guard and struggling for composure. Now, each time she looked at the Jacobs, she'd be reminded of AJ's ostentatious wink and raucous orgasmic awakenings.

Peter didn't make contact for several days. Rather than a dinner or lunch invitation, he arrived at the tiny terrace unannounced, barged in as soon as Liz opened the door, and went straight on the attack. He didn't bother with hugs or kisses or even removing his hands from his pockets. "What the hell's going on?"

"Sorry? And it's good to see you, too. Do I get a kiss?"

He reached down and pecked her on the cheek, leaving a wet smudge, then followed her into the living room. "Your team—your words, not mine—are digging around in my business affairs. They want to know every jolly thing apart from what I ate for breakfast last Wednesday. I suppose you put them up to this, did you?"

Liz watched Peter pace across the floor, his hands still in his pockets and his voice elevating with each word uttered. She'd nearly forgotten how prickly he could be, or rather, had blocked the trait from her mind. "I left it in their hands," she said calmly, more to appease him than anything else. "You know I wanted a stress-free holiday."

"Of course. It doesn't matter what I'm going through, as long as you get your bloody stress-free holiday."

"I didn't mean that. But I have to protect my interests. I'm not one to make snap decisions."

"So, you mean me, do you?" He raised his voice up an annoyed notch. "Protecting your interests from me? Calling *me* a snap decision? What happened in New Zealand? Lost your senses, did you?"

"Look, I'm sorry. But I won't invest in a company unless I have all the facts. I'm sure you wouldn't expect anything less. It's nothing personal."

"Is that right? Well, tell that office boy of yours to back the F off. Otherwise, you'll have to make a choice. Him or me."

Liz knew arguing with Peter was a hiding to nowhere and she'd learned to pick her battles. "Would you like a drink?"

"What? No, I don't want a bloody drink. I'm trying to help you out here. I can't do it with your dream team breathing down my neck. Tanner even invited me to his office to discuss it. I'm not about to discuss my business affairs with anyone, let alone your jolly lackey."

"Okay, I'll talk to them."

"Fine. Now, how about you take me out to make up for it? I'll pour myself a drink while you go and straighten your hair."

THE FAIRY TALE EFFECT

DESPITE EFFORTS TO THE CONTRARY, Liz struggled with the distraction of Peter and his too-good-to-be-true business opportunity. That morning, she'd left her phone in her bag, too weary to deal with his constant text messages as she worked. But, when she checked around noon, and again on the way home, Peter's usual text chats were conspicuous by their absence.

The walk to the tiny terrace that afternoon took longer than usual. Her mother would say she was dragging her feet. That's exactly how Liz felt. By the time she reached the tiny terrace and struggled with the deadbolt of the front door, a realization had clicked firmly into place with a loud snap.

She grabbed her phone out of her bag and called Penny. "Hey. It's me."

"I gathered that by the caller ID," Penny said.

Liz picked up on the happy cadence of Penny's voice and swallowed the lump in her throat. The tears came anyway.

"Are you okay? Liz?"

"Yeah. Um…not really. Can I cook you dinner? I could do with a dose of Penny's wisdom."

"Yum. I'll be there shortly. Half an hour at the most and I'm starving."

"It will have to be pasta. I don't have much else."

"Pasta's good."

Penny, who never minced her words at the best of times, expected answers as soon as she walked through the door.

"What's going on? You look like you've just sat through a rerun of *Titanic*."

"It's Peter."

"Surprise, surprise. Don't tell me he's proposed." Penny shuddered at the thought. "Wait. You didn't say yes?"

"He doesn't know what a jeweler is." She moved to the cooktop, removed the pasta from the heat, and drained it. Tomato, mushroom, and basil sauce sizzled as it hit the pasta in the pan. Liz closed her eyes and inhaled.

Penny sat in the small booth and accepted her meal with both hands. She poured two glasses of Merlot, pushed one across the table, and waited for Liz to join her.

Liz sat and took a sip of her wine.

"Come on, spit it out," Penny said.

"Well, before I went to New Zealand, I decided to go off the pill for a bit—not that I've ever had unprotected sex with Peter, but a break's good sometimes. Now I feel increasingly unsure about him. It's like I've had the proverbial aha moment. It hit me as soon as I walked in the door at Mum and Dad's."

"Finally. You know that's a thing, right?"

"Sorry?"

"The pill thing. Some women on the pill choose a mate who's unsuitable. Apparently, it's all to do with the male aroma, or their sexy stink as I call it, and the gene pool. I read about it online."

Liz looked at Penny in disbelief. "Sounds like nonsense to me."

"Do you and Peter sizzle between the sheets? No. Do you want to grab his T-shirts and sniff? No! I rest my case. Ask Mr. Google if you don't believe me."

"I will. Anyway, I've thought about it a lot lately. When we're together, I'm miserable. When we're apart, I analyze the shit out of my feelings until I'm numb. It's like I'm a watered-down version of myself. My sparkle's gone flat. Even my 'Hell Yeah' list is under attack with a heavy hand and a red pen."

"I'd use a black sharpie. Lasts better."

"He does have a sweet and caring side." Liz twirled her fork around the fettuccine on her spoon as she thought through her argument. "But other times, he criticizes everything about me—from my hair to my clothes, to what I eat, and my choice of friends. I'm on edge all the time when we're together, and now he wants me to invest in one of his companies. I don't think I can do it anymore."

"So don't."

"It's not that simple, is it?"

"It is from where I'm standing. Look, Liz, I've met girls like you before. Beautiful, gentle souls who give themselves to unworthy men who don't deserve them. These guys wrap you in hugs and kisses initially, lay on the charm and weave you into their sticky web. Before you know it, you're singing the praises of a man whose praises aren't worth singing about. And as for your list, that's easily sorted. Listen to your heart for once."

"I know he cares for me. What if I don't find anyone else who does?"

"Spoken like a true victim. It's called the fairy tale effect. You meet a guy, think he's Prince Charming incarnate, then once you've kissed him a few times, he turns out to be a frog dressed in an expensive designer suit. Look, personally, I can't stand the guy. I've made no secret of the fact, and I'm not the only one. None of your friends approve."

"That's not true."

Penny topped up their glasses, then raided the pasta pot for another plateful. "Isn't it? I'm the only one who has the guts to say it."

"Are people talking about us?"

"Occasionally. You must admit, Peter's a bit of a limp dick when he's out in public."

"I don't understand. He has so many friends."

"Only until it rains on his parade, hon. Then they'll all duck for cover and leave him out in the cold to fend for himself."

"You sound like Mum. Fair-weather friends are a pet hate of hers."

"My Mum's as well. The thing is, at some point, you'll cut him adrift because he doesn't deserve you. The Goddess of Epiphanies has already slapped you in the face and the longer you delay the inevitable, the longer it will take to find your one, true love." Penny clutched her hands to her chest and fluttered her eyelashes in true vaudeville style. "It's time you stood up for yourself. You're the champion of the cause. Just not of your own cause. Think about what *you* want for once."

Their meal finished, the friends moved to the living room, wine in hand, and both sat on the sofa with their feet up.

"Let me ask you one thing," Penny continued. "Does he believe in you? Really believe in you?"

Liz swilled the rich red around in her glass while she considered the question. "Not really. In fact, when I think about it rationally, he's dismissive of my success. Happy to enjoy the monetary benefits, though."

"Sometimes it only takes an honest answer to one simple question to expose the truth. My *babushka* always says: 'It's better to be slapped by the truth than kissed with a lie.'"

"Your grandmother's a wise woman. I'm just...scared, I guess."

"Of what?"

Liz huffed out a sigh. "Loneliness. Rejection. Sitting here night after night with only my crazy thoughts for company while I get fat eating chocolate."

"I won't let you be lonely *or* get fat. Plenty more fish in the sea. And while we don't live by the sea, the market is the next best thing. And believe me, London has one of the best fish markets I know."

"Thanks. I appreciate your enthusiasm for my impending single hood. And another thing." Liz was on a roll. "He's slowly isolated me from my friends, and he doesn't have a good word to say about Nate."

"How dare he, the bastard." Penny fluttered her lashes. "Nate is one of the nicest, sexiest, most charming guys I know."

Penny jumped up from the sofa and made a beeline for the freezer singing, "Ice cream, ice cream, who wants ice cream," while Liz chuckled. Nate would be red with embarrassment if he knew Penny had called him sexy.

"Right, we have salted caramel or rich vanilla bean. Let's get brain freeze and watch *Outlander*. I love a guy in a kilt."

"I'll have both. And a sliced banana…and whippy cream," Liz thought for a moment. "Is it true Scottish men are naked under their kilts?"

"Let's just say, if you run your hands under a Scotchman's kilt, they better be warm and ready for action. Oh, and Liz," Penny called from the kitchen. "Now you're off the pill, give that sexy housemate of yours a good sniff the next time he walks past. I bet you and AJ Tanner are the perfect genetically dissimilar match."

Liz's thoughts returned to the morning she'd arrived back from New Zealand when AJ left his particular 'sexy stink' all over her bed. "Is that good?"

"According to those in the know." Penny handed Liz her dessert. "You okay?"

"Yeah. Maybe I'm going through a phase. I'll probably wake up tomorrow and feel like a new woman. Peter will have missed me terribly and decide we should spend more time together."

"We'll see."

"Can I help you with something, Liz?"

She stood at the entry to the kitchen. AJ hadn't spoken to her all morning, and the air held a distinct chilly note of words left unsaid. "I was wondering if you'll be here next weekend?"

"No idea." AJ's clipped reply and tight facial expression meant spoken communication wasn't altogether necessary.

Liz pushed on regardless. "Is there anything wrong?"

"I don't know." He kept his fingers busy on his phone keypad, not even having the manners to look up. "Is there?"

A familiar unpleasant sensation gripped her gut. Maybe AJ and Peter had more in common than she first thought. "It's just...you seem upset about something."

AJ slid out of the booth and grabbed a bottle of milk from the fridge. Liz winced as he took a swig. He turned to look at her, waited a few moments, then spoke.

"Your boyfriend seems to have taken a personal interest in my affairs. For future reference, if you want to know something, just ask. I'm more than happy to answer questions about my professional abilities, but I can't stand it when people gossip about my personal life behind my back."

Liz didn't need him to clarify. She wasn't one to shy away from an apology when warranted. "I'm sorry. It's just, Peter's concerned I accepted you as my advisor without proper due diligence."

"Peter's concerned? What about you? Or don't you have opinions anymore? The girl I met two years ago made her own informed choices. The guy's a dick. It's a pity you're one of the few people who thinks otherwise."

"I can't believe you just said that."

AJ shrugged. "Just so you understand. My personal business affairs have nothing to do with Peter Nichols."

"I'm sorry."

"Not good enough. You could have just asked me. I'm happy to tell you the whole sordid tale."

"I don't need to know."

"I disagree. You asked the questions, the problem is, you ran to Ivan instead of me."

"I didn't mean—"

"Sit."

Liz hesitated, then did as she was told. She didn't understand this side of him. The angry side. *Sit!* Bossy bastard.

"I gather your boyfriend gave you his version of the AJ Tanner anthology. I'm not privy to what he said, but for your information, I invested in a property venture that hasn't worked out. It's no secret. We're still climbing through mountains of red tape, not to mention a bloody archeological dig on our boundary because our neighbor found some minuscule artifact when gardening. According to Ivan, the gossip on the street is I skipped the country after my relationship with the other investors went sour. That's complete and utter bullshit. And another thing, I may be broke, but that's a far cry from being in financial difficulty."

"I'm sorry."

"Stop being so freakin' sorry all the time." AJ certainly knew how to add a dismissive tone into his voice when he felt the need. "You're a successful businesswoman, not a groveling teenager. Healthy business relationships only work if based on trust. As you no longer trust me, maybe we should call it quits."

"That's not what I want."

He threw the empty milk bottle into the recycling bucket under the sink. "Sometimes it's not all about you."

He stormed out, grabbing his coat on the way.

Liz didn't move from the booth. She looked out the kitchen window to the back garden. The morning had started out sunny, but now, gray clouds covered the sky with an overcast hue. AJ was right. Now he and Peter were angry with her for the same reason.

That night, AJ stayed away.

When Liz arrived at the office the next day, a white envelope, sealed along the back flap and addressed in an artistic hand, sat on her desk. Once opened and unfolded, she flicked her sight over the text. AJ Tanner intended to resign from her account. The words *irreconcilable differences* and *difficult* jumped off the page and slapped her hard in the face. He made it sound like they were in the middle of an acrimonious divorce.

RISKY JUDGEMENTS

THAT WEEKEND, Liz and Peter's date night played out in the following fashion. He arrived at the tiny terrace just after seven with the idea of an early dinner for two. Liz suggested MoMo, to a negative facial response.

"MoMo? I don't do dumplings. And besides, it's always teeming with people."

When Liz asked Peter to pick somewhere more suitable, the reluctant sigh said it all. "No, we'll go to MoMo," he said. "Maybe I need to broaden my palate."

True to Peter's prediction, the place was packed. As they waited to be seated, Liz noticed AJ sitting at a snug table for four with two women—a brunette to his right and a blonde opposite. On recognition, he managed a terse frown before turning his attention back to his friends. A familiar-looking guy, whose sandy colored hair and hazel eyes complemented a take-me-to-bed body, joined them. It took Liz a few minutes before she realized it was an older, and altogether more visually sophisticated version of Ryan, AJ's friend who wanted to eat her for breakfast with blueberries and French toast.

"You know what, maybe you're right," she said to Peter,

willing herself not to glance in AJ's direction. "There are no tables. Let's go somewhere else."

"I'll talk to one of the staff. See what I can do."

She dared to look back. Watched like a voyeur as AJ laughed and chatted with his friends. "Can we just leave, please?"

"Fine," Peter said with an annoyed sigh. "Whatever."

They ended up at yet another expensive restaurant. When their meals arrived, tiny cuts of meat rested on a delicious rich jus, flavored with garlic and tarragon. A small serving of dauphinoise potato, barely enough for a picky toddler, and no more than four stalks of asparagus shyly kept the beef company on the plate. It tasted divine, but Liz could have eaten three times as much and still had room for dessert *and* a truffle with her coffee.

Throughout dinner, Peter relentlessly pitched his business opportunity as Liz listened half-heartedly, void of enthusiasm and bored to tears. She couldn't get AJ's letter and the sight of him enjoying himself out of her mind. When a waiter wheeled past the dessert trolley, she refused to even look at the options. Peace-keeping at its worst.

"Liz, did you hear what I said?"

She turned her attention to Peter.

"I asked you what you've decided about my investment offer?"

Here we go. "Ivan thinks it's not the right time to invest at this stage."

"So that's it then, is it? You're passing on the opportunity of a lifetime because some old fart of a lawyer thinks it's an inopportune time? I suppose that blasted office boy put you up to this, did he?"

Liz leaned over the table and whispered, "Can we not discuss this at dinner?"

"Fine." Peter motioned for the check, then excused himself to use the bathroom without a second glance as the waiter inserted

Liz's card into the slot, and over one hundred pounds left her bank account with the tap of her four-digit pin.

They drove home in silence. When they reached the tiny terrace, Peter pulled his Porsche into the curb and cut the engine.

"How about I stay? I haven't seen you in three weeks."

Liz sighed and turned to look at him. "I'm exhausted."

"You won't even know I'm there."

Peter didn't bother opening the passenger door for her, but once inside, pulled her close for a limp hug. "I'm sorry I was short with you before. I was counting on you, Liz."

"I know." She said nothing more. Nate's warning rang alarm bells in her head as they climbed the stairs, but the desperate clutch persisted.

"I missed you when you were away," he said as he unbuttoned his shirt, not even bothering to look at her.

Liz hadn't seen Peter's softer side much lately, and once again, mentally questioned her doubts. "Did you?"

"Of course. Still, it's hard to feel close, you know, with that fucking Tanner all over my private affairs."

"He's just doing his job. And please don't swear like that."

"The guys an idiot. When did you say his contract's up?"

AJ's letter flashed through her mind as she entered the bathroom and started removing her makeup. "Can we talk about this later? I hate bringing work home."

"And the jerk lives here. What's that all about?"

"It's only temporary. Anyway, it's Nate's decision, not mine." Liz walked back into the bedroom. She wanted to add 'a crazy one at that,' but Peter didn't need to know how uncomfortable she felt with AJ sleeping, probably stark naked, across the landing. She climbed into bed.

"It had better be. I don't like him anywhere near you. Move over." Peter, still in his white cotton tank, boxers, and socks, nudged her with his elbow. "You know I sleep better on the left."

Liz moved over to accommodate his left-of-the-bed preference.

She wondered what would happen if she forced him to sleep on the right side. He lay on his back, staring into space, and made no effort to reach out. It was his thing. He didn't have a passion for her, of that she had no doubt. But maybe Peter had a point when he repeatedly called her needy.

"By the way, who was that scruffy guy you spoke to at the supermarket a couple of weeks ago?"

"When?" She thought back. "Oh. A student from school. Smart kid. We're working on a group project together."

"It's bad enough mixing with these louts at school, there's no need to fraternize with them in public. Understand?"

"That was over a month ago. Why bring it up now?"

"Because that school's a waste of your time and energy."

She sighed. "Peter, it's something I enjoy. My way of giving back."

"The sooner you realize life isn't always about giving back, the better."

"I don't agree."

"Yes, well, that's why you need me in your life." He reached for her hand and patted it. "To save you from your sentimental, do-gooding self. Goodnight."

Having dished out his advice, he rolled over and went to sleep. Liz stared at the ceiling, struggling to find an excuse for his behavior. And indeed, hers.

At first light the following morning, Liz woke to Peter holding her close. His erection—already sheathed—pressed into her back as he moved into position behind her. Clumsy fingers fumbled between her legs as he tried to enter her without preparation. She pulled away.

"What's the matter?" He murmured the words into her neck, his breath cold and wet. "Don't you want to?"

Liz reached to kiss him. "I need a little time to prepare." She guided his hand to her breast. He rubbed his fingers over her nipples two or three times before trying again. She tensed at his touch, uncomfortable at the thought of another mechanical session of unfulfilled sex.

Nothing had changed in all the time they'd dated. Peter seldom wanted to make love at night, feigning tiredness or preoccupation. Yet, when he awoke with lead in his pencil in need of release, Liz provided a convenient means to his end.

"I've never met a girl who needs so much foreplay."

Liz sat upright. She swung her feet to the floor. Her jaw clenched. "I should get up. I have an early meeting scheduled."

"I thought you wanted it. You can't decide about anything. Even sex."

"What?" Her fists tightened, and for once, she gave into the feeling of humiliation. She'd never imagined striking another human being, but right at that moment, Peter Nichols was danger-ously close to a fist in the face courtesy of peace-loving Liz Dobson.

"It doesn't matter. Let's take a raincheck."

Peter stayed in bed. Her bed. Liz allocated herself five minutes in the shower. Every sixty seconds brought with it a new emotion. First, she belittled herself for being sexually undesirable. Then, grief for the type of relationship she wanted swamped her. The third minute, she vowed to improve, to please him more. At the fourth minute mark, tears mixed with droplets from the shower head. By the fifth minute, realization slammed into her with an undeniable mental slap. Peter Nichols was an asshole. One who screwed in his socks and white cotton tank.

Back in the bedroom, Liz sat on the bed. She linked her hands together, her fingertips pushing into the knuckles of the opposite hand, first left, then right. Peter had dressed and was about to put on his shoes.

He glanced up, just long enough to throw an insult. "Your eyes are all puffy. Maybe you need to change your cream."

"I've been thinking." Liz kept her gaze fixed to steady her internal balance.

"Really? That's dangerous."

Jaw clenched, she inhaled sharply. "I'm done here. It's over." She had his attention now, albeit a dismissive version of it.

"Here we go again. Are you due for your period? Is that it?"

"This has nothing to do with my period."

"I see what's going on here. You suddenly come into money and your team—a broke conman and an old fart of a lawyer—tell you I'm no longer required. I made you, Liz. I jolly well made everything about you."

"Is that what you really think?" Despite her inner turmoil, Liz held her voice steady. "That I'm incapable of succeeding on my own merits? Because I have succeeded. Not because of you, in spite of you."

"And what merits would they be?" he said with a smirk. "You arrived in London with very little of anything. Very little panache, a basic education, and a few insignificant ideas all wrapped up in your lackluster Kiwi style. If it weren't for me, you'd be back in boring old New Zealand working as a waitress in some dead-end dump that pretended to be a café."

"You need to leave."

Peter sat next to her on the bed and reached for her hand, his particular form of groveling about to show its face. "Don't do this, Liz. We'll talk later in the week when you're feeling better. I care for you. Especially now I've helped you improve the model." He laughed at his attempt at a joke. "You were a tad unsophisticated at the beginning."

"Yes, well, I'm giving you an out. Find a sophisticated girl with a posh accent and a father with a title. Someone who makes you happy. Someone slim and poised and English."

He hesitated. "Look, the company deal's still on the table. Let's do it. It will bring us closer together. I can't believe you accepted Kingston's advice over mine."

"Take the offer off the damn table." Liz's jaw hurt from the clench. "I'm not, and will never be, interested in investing in one of your companies."

Peter stood, hands in his pockets, his stance intimidating. "Big mistake."

"And as far as me making you happy, only *your* version of me makes you happy. You've never got to know me, Peter. You wouldn't even know what music or books I like, or that gerberas are my least favorite flowers. Or that instead of all those pretentious damn dinners, a night at the movies with street food to follow is my idea of a good time." She stood to leave.

"Liz." He tugged her back. "Stop."

She pulled free. "I'm off to work. Lock the door behind you when you leave."

"Liz. Come back here. Liz!"

Rain pelted the London pavements, the gray sky adding a surreal light to the already dim interior of the office stairwell. Liz had stopped at the patisserie on the way in, buying not only one but half a dozen pastries filled with custard—three topped with apricots, three with strawberries—and two coffees.

"Morning, Sophie. Has AJ been yet?" Liz asked as she walked into reception. "We arranged a meeting for ten-thirty. Our last."

"He can't make it until after lunch. He's been texting you, apparently. You okay?"

"Yes, fine. I bought coffee and Danish." Liz checked her phone and glanced over the lengthy text from AJ before unlocking the door to her suite.

Sophie followed her. "Yum. What's the occasion?"

"Autonomy. Independence. Liberation. Take your pick."

They sat on the small sofa, pastries and coffee on the table in front of them.

"What's going on?" Sophie asked.

Liz dropped her gaze, her hands comforting each other in her lap. Next, she shook her head, and within a few seconds, burst into tears. "I did it. I told Peter it's over."

"About time."

When AJ finally made it to Liz's office around five, a small box—the type used for the transportation of delicious treats—sat on Sophie's desk. Stuck on top, a pink Post-it note held his name. He smiled as he opened the lid and reached for the Danish. Glancing out the window as he ate, he expected to see Liz strolling up the street.

"Afternoon, AJ."

He turned. "You're still here, Soph. Is Liz around?"

"Sorry, you've just missed her."

He reached for a tissue and wiped his fingers as he motioned to the box. "What's the occasion?"

Sophie pretended to zip her lips together.

AJ flashed his flirty smile. "Come on. We don't have secrets."

"You're as smooth as a spoonful of caramel and twice as sweet. Let's just say she's gone home to have a soak while listening to breakup music on Spotify."

"What! You're freaking kidding me. She's finally dumped that prick of a boyfriend?"

"It's not for me to say. She did eat three pastries to my one, though."

"Maybe my exit from her account was a tad premature."

"So why did you? Exit, I mean?"

AJ thought for a moment. "Frustration, disappointment. Stuff I shouldn't even be talking about."

"I get the impression you're not only referring to work," Sophie said with a knowing tilt of a brow.

He grinned. "Beauty *and* brains peppered with perception. Love that about you."

Sophie took a small bow. "Thank you, kind sir. And, AJ?"

"Yes, Sophie."

"Try not to sound so happy about the break-up. It's not an easy time for her."

"Of course. Though you must admit, it's good news from where I'm standing."

"I agree. Still, lover's regret hurts like a bitch, especially when the realization you've stuffed up big time slaps you hard in the face."

23

IRRECONCILABLE DIFFERENCES

IRRECONCILABLE DIFFERENCES. What did that even mean? Why didn't he just cut to the chase: *Liz, I'm done. I don't give second chances or a gnat's ass about you.*

Liz didn't want to take AJ's stance as a personal rejection, but she did. Her self-critique wasn't about the actual issue, but rather her state of mind. He'd texted earlier requesting a meeting. She had no idea why.

He arrived early and offered a polite hello, his expression stoic.

Her hands found each other, fingers moving of their own accord in her lap. "What can I do for you? I thought you no longer worked on my account."

AJ's eyes narrowed as he studied her. "We have a situation. Ivan's requested my input."

"What kind of situation?"

"It didn't take long for that boyfriend of yours to do his dirty work."

"What do you mean? And he's no longer my boyfriend."

AJ nodded. "His lawyer phoned earlier this morning. Peter Nichols plans to sue you for half of your company, including access to your email list."

"You can't be serious. Why would he do that?"

"Because he's an asshole with a Napoleonic complex who thinks he has a chance at taking you to the cleaners."

Liz slumped back in her chair. "I don't believe it."

"Believe it." Any compassion AJ showed toward Liz in the past was nowhere in sight. It was business all the way.

"What should I do?"

"Nothing…except stay away from him. IKL will handle the rest."

Liz rubbed the tips of her fingers across her forehead, trying to lessen the discomfort of a sudden headache as AJ summarized points from the email.

"I need to talk to him," she said, her head in her hands. "Ask him what on earth he's playing at."

"Yep, that will help no end, you…" He stopped midway through the sentence, varying his tone. "Let me make this perfectly clear. You will not, under any circumstances, contact Peter. Understand? Not one text, one email, or phone call. That's what he wants, to manipulate you, and I imagine he'll use any means he can."

Neither of them spoke for several seconds. Liz never believed Peter would stoop to this level. Now, AJ was ready for a fight, and if she wasn't mistaken, looking forward to it. "Does he have a chance?" she finally asked.

"Depends on how many nights over the last two years you spent in each other's beds playing doctors and nurses." He glanced up and down at his tablet like he didn't expect a response.

She shot him a serious stare. "That's none of anyone's business."

"It's everyone's business if he claims you had a common-law marriage."

"That's ridiculous. We were only together for ten months, off and on. We hardly ever stayed with each other."

"Why's that?"

"He wasn't interested. Liked sleeping alone."

"The guy's a freaking idiot," AJ murmured, deep in concentration as he flicked his fingers over the tablet keyboard.

"Excuse me?"

"Doesn't matter. Let's hope that's your saving grace."

He leaned forward in his chair, his expression softening. It reminded Liz of the tenderness he'd displayed two years before. She allowed herself a flicker of retrospect.

"Hey, don't look so worried," AJ said. "You never lived with the guy. What's the worst that can happen?"

"You tell me."

"Worst-case scenario, he'll spin some bullshit yarn about how you were business partners and threaten court action. You'll feel crap about yourself for a while. And I'm pretty sure he'll expect a significant payout." His concerned smile took her by surprise. "We won't let that happen."

"But you're no longer on my account."

"I'll make myself available if needed. Do you mind if I finish up here? I'll be ten minutes max."

"No problem."

Liz grabbed a clipboard and pen, entered the stationery cupboard, and shut the door. Reaching for the light switch, she remembered the bulb had blown last week. She managed three deep breaths before the tears began to well. Her head trash screamed at her for being stupid and her heart hurt like a bitch. Not because she loved Peter, but because she never had, and it had taken her all this time to figure it out.

The mental slaps to the face continued for the next few minutes. Peter was so wrong for her. Liz knew that. But she'd ignored the warning signs out of a sense of what—loneliness, longing, lust? The last thought evoked a shudder. Lust. What a joke. Peter didn't do lust. Even his kisses felt like a slap in the face with a dead mullet. The seconds turned into minutes. Liz had no idea how long she'd stayed in the cupboard until a soft knock of two even beats invaded her pity party.

"You okay?"

Liz flinched at AJ's caring tone. Did he even give a damn? He had a job to do, that was all. A ragged breath filled her lungs. "I'm fine."

"Can I get you anything before I leave? Water?"

"No. Thanks anyway."

AJ paused. "Okay. I have an appointment. Flick me a text if you need me. I'll be back at IKL around four thirty."

Right on five, AJ knocked on her open office door. He'd worried about her all afternoon. If they were ever going to reclaim a common ground, he needed to tread carefully. Curb his jealous outbursts and soften his stance. "Do you have a minute?"

She looked up from her screen, her eyes puffy and red. "Sure."

"Want to grab a drink?" AJ asked out of courtesy only. He knew her answer would be no. "You look like you need one."

She shook her head, her face drawn and blotchy. Sharing a quiet drink and casual conversation in a bar was a ridiculous idea.

"Are you okay?"

She nodded. "Fine."

AJ's eyes narrowed as he studied her. He had no sympathy for her breakup with Peter, not because he lacked compassion, but because he wanted the best for her. Peter Nichols didn't even come close. Still, he understood her pain. If things were different, he'd take her home, feed her, bathe her, and hold her as she wept in his arms. *Shit.*

"Okay, well, I'd like to discuss our living situation, but it can wait until we get home."

"I have yoga later."

Liz straightened her spine, looked AJ in the eye and smiled.

For the first time in weeks, he glimpsed the old Liz. The Liz he'd made love to. The Liz he'd dreamed of while he dragged his sorry butt around Asia.

"We can talk now. Are you moving out?"

"Wasn't planning on it." He sat in the chair in front of her desk, legs wide. "But if the prospect excites you so much—"

"That's not what I meant. But it's not up to me. It's Nate's room." She leaned back in her chair and inhaled deeply as if the weight of the world was on her shoulders.

"He said it was your call."

"You've already discussed it with him?"

"Briefly. Look, if you're not happy, I'll leave. But I'm away a lot, so it makes sense. To me anyway."

"I thought you found dealing with me difficult."

She was making him sweat. Extracting her pound of flesh. "Is that a statement or a question?"

Liz answered with a slight smile. AJ admired that about her, how she kept any overreaction on the down low. She wasn't a fighter, that much was clear.

"I need a place, it's convenient. Our working relationship has nothing to do with it."

"Fine."

AJ stood to leave. "Great. And, Liz?"

She glanced up.

He flashed a grin. "Maybe hold the reluctant sighs until I'm out of the room. Even my ego has a sensitive side."

24

COUNTERCLAIMS

LIAM THE BARBER was a stout Irishman who sported an impressive beard that rivaled AJ's in length and thickness. Holding his scissors still, he offered AJ the opportunity to back out. "You sure about this?"

"Yep. It will grow back."

Liam went to work. By the time AJ walked out the door, his beard was no more than designer stubble, and his hair just touched his shoulders. When he hit the street, a brisk wind assaulted his uncovered neck, and he pulled the lapels of his jacket tighter, wondering what Liz's reaction would be.

Entering the terrace, AJ called her name as he dropped the mail on the sideboard. Even though he knew she'd be at work, a tinge of disappointment surfaced. He enjoyed coming home to find her cooking in the kitchen or on the sofa reading. Their light, albeit brief, conversations—evidence of her ever-increasing strength post-Peter—gave him a feeling of belonging.

AJ bounded up the stairs to his room and threw his messenger bag and two suits he'd collected from the cleaners on the unmade bed. He never imagined those expensive suits from his now defunct corporate life would come in handy again. He showered and washed his hair, removing the product so liberally applied by Liam. As he entered the bedroom, he picked up his glasses from the bedside table and looked over the suits, choosing the charcoal, along with a white shirt and mid-gray tie.

An hour later, AJ entered the foyer of Ivan Kingston Law, ready to partake in the first negotiation process between Peter Wallace Nichols and Lizette April Dobson. AJ loved an intellectual fight. Physical altercations were not his style, but anything with words and intellect was a different story.

The boardroom was a typically utilitarian space dominated by a large mahogany table flanked by black leather chairs. AJ placed his satchel on the table and removed a file.

He addressed the two men sitting opposite. "Gentleman. I'm Anthony Tanner. Ms. Dobson and Mr Kingston will be here shortly."

After an initial greeting, Peter's lawyer excused himself to take a phone call while Peter stared at AJ.

"Where have we met?" Peter stood and offered his hand. "Maybe the Young Professionals' Club?"

AJ shook hands with Peter, albeit reluctantly. "I met you at an art exhibition recently."

"I can't say I remember. Still, my hands were full negotiating a purchase. Are you familiar with the work by a fellow named Jacobs?"

"Somewhat."

"According to those in the know, he's one to watch. As far as I'm aware, he's only exhibited once."

"So I've heard. What piece are you interested in?"

"It's already a done deal. The one of the snog."

AJ wanted to deck the guy. He hated the thought of Peter Nichols getting his hands on a Jacobs original, especially *Un Beso*. He didn't even refer to it by name, the prick.

"You mean *Un Beso Imaginado*? It's an interesting piece."

"Are you part of Lizette's legal team?" Peter asked before the penny dropped at his feet with a loud ding. "Hold on, you're the housemate and office boy."

"I'm Ms. Dobson's business advisor." AJ struggled with his annoyance for all things Peter Nichols. He didn't understand how Liz could allow a guy like Peter to manipulate her.

"Business advisor? What kind of business advisor?"

"I wasn't aware of a distinction."

Peter leaned forward. "Don't tell me you're her new fuck buddy."

AJ's jaw clenched. "This is hardly the time or place to discuss my personal life, Mr. Nichols."

"Let's throw the term 'conflict of interest' out there, shall we?"

AJ and James Mann stood as Liz and Ivan entered the room. Peter's butt stayed glued to the chair. It took Liz several seconds to recognize the handsome guy who greeted her with a brief smile. With designer glasses gracing the bridge of his nose, a well-cut suit, and minus the scraggly beard, AJ looked so different. More attractive than she would have ever imagined. Liz let the hand of regret grab her by the throat, giving her a soft squeeze.

"Shall we begin?" Ivan said. "You start first, James."

"Thank you, Ivan. As I said in my email, Peter and Lizette were in a long-term relationship during the time she registered her company. He assisted with this process and indeed, spent many hours advising her. They'd been negotiating a share offer for Peter along with a directorship. His ink on the dotted line was merely a formality. Under those circumstances, we feel Peter is entitled to compensation for the company he helped found. And, there's the matter of their common-law relationship and Ms. Dobson's internet list, which at a conservative estimate is worth a considerable sum."

"I was led to believe your relationship was purely a dating arrangement," AJ said to Peter.

The sternness of AJ's voice comforted Liz and, by the look on his face, took Peter by surprise.

"Excuse me, tell me why you're here again?" Peter said. "You may call yourself her business advisor, but what has our personal life got to do with you? Have a score to settle, do you?"

"Once we ascertain the nature of your relationship with Lizette," AJ said without reaction, "we'll be in a better position to discuss whatever settlement you feel entitled to."

Peter turned to Liz. "I can't believe you'd let this idiot speak for you."

Liz went to defend herself but paused when AJ bumped her leg under the table with an unmistakable motion to remain silent.

"We're not here to trade insults with Ms. Dobson and her team." James said as he frowned at Peter. "Let's stick to the facts, shall we?"

AJ continued. "Under UK law, a common-law relationship is described as a continual living together situation for not less than two years. According to Ms. Dobson, the two of you never shared a living space, and only dated for a nonconsecutive period of ten months. Therefore, I don't see what claim you have to her company or email list. The mention of a share offer and director-ship are ridiculous."

Liz watched as the men traded arguments on her behalf. AJ's articulate deliberation stunned her. It was a side of him she'd noticed more and more. Cool and ruthless with a touch of hostile arrogance.

"I'm sure Liz will agree," Peter said, "that our relationship was more than a 'dating arrangement' as you put it. We talked about marriage on numerous occasions. In fact, I stayed at her place several days a week, and she did the same at mine. We've known each other for two years."

"I see," Ivan said. "And did this talk of marriage result in a formal engagement with a diamond ring and an announcement to friends and family?"

"No, but—"

"Then we shouldn't pay it any heed. Don't you agree, James?" Ivan glanced over his glasses at Peter and James. "What do you think, James?" he repeated.

"Well," James answered. "Until today, I understood Lizette and Peter had a common-law marriage. I now realize this wasn't entirely the case."

"There's no *entirely* about it," AJ said. "They either lived together in the same household for two years, sharing their lives as a married couple, or they didn't. And clearly, they did not. In fact, Lizette has shared a home with her cousin since moving to London, and to his knowledge, Mr. Nichols was conspicuous by his absence."

"I see," James said.

"It's time for you to put a proposal on paper," AJ replied. "It may be your intention to procure a portion of Lizette's assets, however, under the circumstances, we fail to see what, if any, claim you have on her company." AJ's tone conveyed his disdain.

Peter leaned forward and tapped an aggressive finger on the table. "I helped Liz set up that company and her web-based activities."

"Is that so?" AJ held Peter's gaze, his jaw tight and ticking. "Lizette had already established herself in the internet marketing scene months before moving to London."

"That may be so, but her business was in a sorry state and going downhill fast when we met," Peter said. "I spearheaded several of her larger campaigns and introduced Liz to the right people. People she'd never have had the opportunity to meet while working as a waitress in a two-bit tapas bar."

"So to clarify, you were Lizette's chief mentor?" AJ asked.

"The word mentor hardly covers it."

Liz went to speak but couldn't get a word in as Peter and AJ continued their verbal battle.

"Knowing Lizette as I do, I can't imagine she'd have a need for you in that capacity," AJ replied. "I've seen the way she conducts her business. She's more than competent."

"Think what you like. We wouldn't be here today if it weren't for my contacts. Liz and I were partners in every sense of the word. We'd decided that I'd come on board months ago. As James said, we were about to sign off the paperwork when she broke off our arrangement. It seems she's moved on to duller pastures." Peter looked straight at AJ and smirked.

"I doubt that," AJ murmured under his breath.

Liz shook her head. Why would Peter say such things? He excelled in manipulation. She only wished she'd reached that conclusion earlier in their relationship. How could she let a man like him dominate her? Even now, Peter had a way of taking her power, setting it blazing, and harnessing the energy for himself. She shifted in her chair and tapped AJ's foot with hers. He got the point.

"We're getting nowhere," AJ said. "Let's take a short recess." He checked his watch. "Shall we say ten minutes?" AJ rose from the table, followed by Liz and Ivan. They walked through the floor-to-ceiling office doors and stood in the sunlit corridor. Liz couldn't stop staring at AJ and his new look, struggling to connect his controlled, working persona with AJ the lover. If she was honest, she found this side of him arousing to the point of distraction.

"Are you okay, Liz?" AJ asked with a frown.

"I've been better. That guy's unbelievable."

"So, what he said about promising him half of your company?" Ivan asked. "True or false?"

"No truth in it whatsoever. We discussed two campaigns, that's all. He kept making noises about being a director, but I always ignored him."

"And the marriage talk?" AJ questioned.

"Peter made it clear marriage wasn't on his agenda."

"Prize prick." AJ shook his head. "How the hell did you ever get involved with him?"

"AJ." Ivan gave his nephew the 'behave' look, then turned to Liz. "So, what do you think? Are we prepared to take this to court?"

Liz breathed a sigh of defeat. She'd spent ten minutes before the meeting in tears and didn't know how much more she could take. "Court's a big step. I don't want to go there, to be honest."

"I agree. It's the last thing we want. A complete waste of time and money, and it could drag on for months." Ivan glanced back to the boardroom where James and Peter stood, locked in heated debate. "Let's see if he's prepared to settle."

"What a shame," AJ said. "I was looking forward to seeing you in action, Ivan—squashing the bastard into the ground and stomping him into the dirt."

Ivan chuckled. "Enough of that kind of talk."

"Intellectually speaking, of course." AJ winked at Liz and she couldn't help but smile.

"Do you mind if I sit the next part out?" she said.

"Shall I stay with you?" AJ asked, all concerned and too darn sexy for his own good.

"No, I'll be okay. I just need a minute."

The men resumed their place at the table. Ivan spoke first. "Ms. Dobson is sitting out for a moment if that's acceptable, gentlemen?"

"Starting to get to her, am I?" Peter flashed another first-class smirk.

AJ rubbed his chin where yesterday there'd been thick growth. He stared Peter down as he loosened the designer noose around his neck. "Let's cut to the chase. What's your bottom line?"

"Didn't you get the memo, Tanner?" Peter said. "Fifty percent of her company and access to her list."

Ivan gathered the papers before him and stuffed them into his briefcase with a flourish. "I see we've reached a stalemate. Will that be all, gentlemen? Otherwise, we'll see you in court."

"Now, Ivan, let's not get too hasty," James said. "I'm sure we can come to an arrangement. What's your proposal?"

AJ made no attempt to make eye contact with Peter again. "Ten thousand pounds as commission on the projects Mr. Nichols says he consulted on, subject to the following conditions. Once signed, Mr. Nichols will have no further claim to the assets of Lizette Dobson. This includes, but is not limited to, companies she may be involved in, affiliates, investments, and her email list. Additionally, Mr. Nichols must sever all contact with Ms. Dobson, including approaching her in social situations."

"That's ridiculous. She's worth millions of pounds. And, more to the point, I helped her earn those millions."

"Ms. Dobson's portfolio has taken a haircut over the past year as fallout from the GFC continues. Ten thousand pounds is our limit, I'm afraid," AJ replied. "The offer is on the table for five business days. Otherwise, as Ivan said, we'll see you in court."

"I can't believe Liz hired you." Peter's eyes narrowed as he addressed AJ. "You must have something big between your legs because you've nothing else going for you. Rather you than me, mate. She has no class."

AJ fumed and took several steps forward as Peter backed away. He gritted his teeth. "I think we're done here, don't you?"

"Gentlemen, please," James said. "Peter, that kind of talk is uncalled for." He turned to Ivan. "Thanks for your time, Ivan."

"That went well." AJ smiled at Liz as he walked into Ivan's office.

"You think?" Liz sat in the chair opposite Ivan's desk, chewing her bottom lip, her voice soft and fragile.

"James knows there's no case," Ivan said. "They'll settle."

"I agree," AJ replied. "Although I'm not convinced ten grand will hit the spot. Still, we have a little wiggle room. Now, if you'll excuse me, I have an appointment."

AJ left Liz and Ivan at the office, discussing the formal arrangement of the counterclaim. He hailed a cab and rode to the gallery, still fuming at Peter's smug mouth and smarmy smirk. He wanted to screw him over big time.

As AJ walked down the steps of the gallery and pushed through the door, his thoughts centered on *Un Beso Imaginado*. He only hoped he'd made it in time.

"Dude. What's with the groom-over? You look like a model for a suit maker." Paul Young and AJ Tanner had been friends for over fifteen years. Paul, an all-around good guy and father of one, smiled at the new look AJ. "Where's the bushy growth and the man bun gone?"

"Thought it was about time I conformed. That growth, as you call it, itched like mad." He glanced around the space. "What's happening with *Un Beso?* Has the sale gone through?"

"Not yet. The guy hasn't come up with the cash. I said we'd hold it until the end of business today."

"It's not Peter Nichols, is it?"

"Let's see." Paul moved a few papers around his desk before picking up an invoice. "Here it is. Peter Nichols. He's listed in the address details."

"Right, as soon as it's six o'clock the deal's off. And refund the deposit."

"Do you know this guy?"

"I met him for the second time today. He's a prize prick with a sense of entitlement and no backbone."

"Interesting. Anyway, another customer asked Pearl if she could put in a backup offer. And she's not the only one. There's half a dozen on the list now. I have her details if you want me to flick her an email."

"Anyone we know?"

"Not one of my regulars. Hold on." Paul pulled up a file on the computer. "A Lizette Dobson. She's willing to pay over the asking price and has requested a face-to-face with Jacobs with the view of a commission."

"Lizette Dobson?" AJ nodded slowly and smiled. "I'll hang on to it in the meantime. In fact, I have the perfect wall at Nate's to display it."

"Okay, we'll pack it up tomorrow."

"Thanks. If I change my mind about the backup offers, I'll text you. Sometimes, it's not about the money."

"What about the meeting? Do you think you could persuade Jacobs to consider a commission? It could be a good little earner."

"No chance in hell."

25

BUILDING FRUSTRATIONS

AJ OPENED the ironwork gate leading to the front door and strolled down the path. Lights from the living room and entry hall evoked a feeling of welcome. Of home. As he inserted his key in the lock, he glanced at the hydrangeas Liz had planted in black pots on either side of the door, and smiled.

He loved this part of Putney, and when thinking about it from a purely practical viewpoint, AJ enjoyed sharing Nate's house with Liz. He only wished she felt the same. Of course he wanted to live with her for another reason, but now wasn't the right time to pursue it, for either of them.

Liz glanced up when he entered the living room. Her face held a frown as she set down a bowl of soup on the small table in front of her. To the side of the bowl, toasted ciabatta topped with tomato, avocado, and cheese sat on a plate. He nearly reached forward to steal a slice, but since he'd resigned from her account, an uneasy air stirred between them.

"Are you home for dinner?" she asked.

The smell coming from the kitchen reminded AJ of cold winters and warm fires back in Cambridge. "Yeah, I'll just make a sandwich."

"Help yourself to soup. There's plenty there."

In an imagined life, he would sit on the sofa and explain why their relationship had taken this reluctant turn. Then they would kiss and make up, and end up spending hours in bed, skin to skin, his whispered commands leading them both to rapid pulse release.

But it was too soon post Peter to even consider that possibility.

"Thanks," he said. "Sounds good."

AJ flicked on the gas under the soup and cut a thick slice of bread for the toaster. Not wanting to intrude on her TV time, he sat at the booth, sipped the delicious soup, and chewed hot buttered toast topped with thickly sliced cheese. Liz stayed in the living room—already dressed for bed in gray knit pajamas edged in soft pink piping and monogrammed with a distinctive logo on the front pocket.

For AJ, the sight of her laughing softly at something on the TV, her face free of makeup and hair pinned in a messy knot, conjured up evocative thoughts of that pre-Japan night. One touch of her hands on his face and neck, and the sweet sounds of her arousal, cemented a union of unparalleled lust that stood out in a sea of uneventful liaisons.

Her footsteps broke his train of thought. He glanced up and watched her rinse plates and load the dishwasher. This was now their relationship—one of shared domesticity.

"How are you feeling after today?" he asked.

"Good. Thanks to you and Ivan. I appreciate your support."

"No problem. Only doing my job."

"Even so…"

He sensed her hesitation and softened his stance. "If you need me for anything, I'm available, remember."

"About that… Considering what's happened lately, I wondered if you're still interested in working for me directly?"

"I think it's best if we loosen our professional ties, don't you?"

"I'm happy to meet your salary requirements, plus some."

AJ pushed his empty plate aside. His first instinct was to keep his mouth shut. But before he had the chance to consider that option, he released the jealous asshole out of its cage and let his frustration flow. "It's not about the money. In fact, I don't care about money, so let's drop it, shall we?"

"It's just…I don't understand—"

"Maybe that's the problem. You never trusted me to do my job. And why? Because your boyfriend thought he knew better."

It was her turn to sit and his to stand. "I know it looks that way, but I've had a difficult time lately."

AJ's anger shadowed his compassion. "You knew Ivan, Nate, and I had your best interest at heart, but you ignored our advice. The next thing I know, you've asked Peter Nichols to delve into my personal life."

"I didn't ask him. Quite the opposite."

He picked up his plate and sat it in the sink. "That didn't stop you running to Ivan behind my back."

"Well, to be fair, I knew nothing about you initially."

"Yes, but you've had plenty of opportunities to ask me what you wanted to know, but your communication skills are sadly lacking. You gave me the autonomy to make a difference in your business. Then boyfriend cocks his dirty finger and I'm no longer trusted."

"That's not—"

AJ held up his hand, silencing her. "He then presents you with a too-good-to-be-true investment offer telling you not to delay because this opportunity won't last. It reminds me of that *but wait, there's more* bullshit."

Worried eyes held his. "I never committed to investing. I took your advice."

"And lucky you did, because his shifty scheme to import diamonds from an unreliable African source is at best dubious, and at worst, smacks of goods falling off the back of a broken-down truck in the middle of nowhere."

She frowned, her hand fiddling with the chain around her neck. "Diamonds?"

"So what? He held his hand out for half a million pounds without giving you security or information? He's either dumb as shit or smarter than I first thought."

"Anyway," Liz said, "it's no longer relevant."

"And are you pleased about that? Or do you still think he's a good guy?"

"Of course not, but I don't see the need to A, discuss our relationship or B, talk about him behind his back."

AJ leaned his butt on the kitchen counter. "We all come across assholes who aren't worthy of our respect at some stage in our lives. Don't be afraid to take the lesson here, Liz. Cut the freaking tie."

"I don't understand why you're taking this so personally."

"Don't you? I had a job to do. A job I thought I handled well. But obviously not, since you made an ill-informed decision not to trust me. As far as I'm concerned, once we sort this company bullshit out, our business association is over."

"Fine. I've spent months listening to a control freak of a man. I don't need a rinse and repeat and to wear the damn T-shirt."

AJ opened the fridge, put away the butter and cheese, then slammed the door shut. He stayed silent for several seconds as he inhaled a sharp breath, his glare pinning her to the seat.

"Don't you ever, ever, compare me to that bastard again, do you understand? I may be controlling in certain circumstances, the difference being I have your best interests at heart. I'm a professional and take my work seriously. Sure, I've stuffed up in the past. I thought Ryan, Chris, and I were ten-foot-tall and on our way too easy riches. I've learned from that mistake. We all have. My motto, learn the lesson and move on."

She straightened in her seat. "I apologize if I gave you the impression that I didn't trust you. It wasn't my intention."

He held her gaze for a moment, leaving her apology unac-knowledged. "Maybe, but it wasn't me who asked you for half a million pounds for a trumped-up investment scheme."

"I remained cautious. I'm not the sharpest pencil in the box, but I do have a few clues."

AJ frowned and ran his hands through his hair. Another frus-trated sigh left his lungs. "Look, it's late. I'm tired, and more than a little pissed off. We shouldn't be having this conversation at home. I've probably just ruined your evening, and that wasn't *my* intention. But sometimes, it's important to stand up and be heard."

Her chest tight, Liz went to stand then thought better of it. She watched AJ leave the room, surprised at how quickly his mood had turned. He bounded up the stairs and closed his bedroom door.

He returned several minutes later.

Liz expected him to stroll back into the kitchen and resume their conversation. Apologize even. But he didn't. Rather, he grabbed his coat off the rack and shut the front door on his way out.

AJ was right. Her evening was ruined. Liz hated arguments. Especially with AJ. Living with him and his *pissed off* personality had suddenly lost its appeal. There was no reason for them to share a house. AJ could stay in the terrace as long as he liked. It didn't mean Liz had to do the same.

Tired and upset, she didn't have the energy to think about it now. The sad truth was, she longed for a hug, but had no one to ask.

Liz held the banister for support as she climbed the stairs. Step-ping into her bedroom, she looked at the unmade bed, and sighed. With her favorite linen sheets still in the dryer, she grabbed an old set from the closet in the hallway and tossed them on, not even bothering to tuck in the corners. Sleep came long and slow, in and out—every creak, every slam of a car door, every siren that drifted across from the High Street a reminder of her solitude.

MISUNDERSTANDINGS

IN A SMALL BAR opposite the Thames, AJ warmed a beer with his hands. Why hadn't he stayed and made things right between them? Even though hurting Liz wasn't his intention, he'd overreacted like an arrogant prick. The words he spoke were the truth, but his rising frustration had little to do with their argument.

Warm arms encircled his waist. He caught a whiff of overpowering spicy perfume and knew straight away who stood behind him.

"AJ. Baby. I thought it was you." The woman ruffled his hair. "Been to the barber, have we?"

He turned in his chair and grinned at the familiar face. "Lauren. How have you been?" He pulled her into a tight hug.

"Terrible until now. Aren't you a sight for horny eyes."

AJ chuckled. "I see you still haven't been to that Swiss finishing school your parents begged you to attend years back."

"No need. I've done all the finishing I'm ever gonna do. I'm all about starting from where I left off these days."

AJ sipped his beer, his expression full of amusement. "Same. So, what's been happening with you?"

"Nothing much. Just waiting patiently for you to slip into this bar on a cold and dreary night. How about you walk me home? I'll reward you with a hot toddy."

"An offer I wouldn't usually refuse."

"What? Don't tell me you've met someone."

AJ shrugged. He didn't want to discuss Liz with Lauren, or anyone.

"So why are you all alone at one in the morning in this dive of a bar?"

"Disagreements and misunderstandings get me here every time. I said some asshole things to someone I care about. I'm beating the shit out of myself before going home."

"You understand a little immorality can be healthy for a relationship?" Lauren laughed at the expression on AJ's face. "It's true. I watched a talk about it on YouTube."

"Not my scene."

"Is she the blonde from MoMo a few weeks back?"

He stared at her blankly, then expressed a question.

"I saw you and that buff builder guy, Ryan, out slurping dumpling juice with two beauties as I walked past."

The recollection dawned on him. "No, that's Fiona, Ryan's sister from Scotland. The other woman's someone he's been seeing off and on."

"So where was this mystery woman on the night in question?"

"Having a breakup dinner with her ex."

She grinned. "You've been screwing a chick with a boyfriend? I thought you said immorality wasn't your scene."

"We're not in a sexual relationship."

"What? Pull the other one."

AJ and Lauren had been friends for many years. Long enough for him to sense she needed company. "Come on. I'll see you home and fill you in on the way."

They walked down Lower Richmond Road toward the Embankment. He slipped his hand into his pocket as Lauren slid her arm through his.

"Can I tell you a secret?" she said.

Lauren didn't look at him, so he focused straight ahead, modeling her mood. "Sure."

"I was pregnant last year, for a moment in time."

He stopped walking and turned toward her, the sadness in her expression visible from the glow of the streetlamp. "Really?"

"Yeah. To a guy I met at work. I lost it three months on."

They fell into step again. "That's tough. Are you still together?"

"It's complicated."

"Why? Is he married?"

"No. He wants to marry me. You know me, AJ, I'm not exactly the commitment type. He popped the question at the top of the London Eye. Even had the ring. We rode down in awkward silence after I refused."

"Was this before you lost the baby?"

"No, after. I freaked out when I found out I was pregnant. By the time I lost it, I'd come around to the idea. I even felt a little excited. And then one day…gone. Oh, he kept up the pretense. Said he loved me. Sent flowers, chocolates, the whole shebang."

"Do you have feelings for him?"

"Feelings? Who knows? If you let someone in, how do you know they won't crap all over you? Or that you'll end up hating each other over a bleak breakfast every morning? I never thought I'd be a mother but having a life inside you changes your very core. There's no going back."

"That's the whole point, isn't it? Life's a journey of progression, not stagnation. If we're lucky, a family is part of that. Do you want to wake up when you're sixty, still staggering from bar to bar as you pick up men who couldn't care less? Men who call you a cab at three in the morning, so they don't have to face you in the daylight. You deserve better."

Lauren turned and walked backward so she could face him.

"What's happened to you? Would the real AJ Tanner please present himself?"

They fell into step again. "Cathy's death gave me a jolt. I remember one day, lying on a massage table in Thailand after one of the best massages of my life, and the masseuse suggested a happy ending. This woman touching me intimately made no sense, so I declined."

"Most guys would jump at the chance."

"But would they really?"

Lauren hesitated. "So, this girl—what's the deal?"

"Not sure yet. We're housemates. She's newly single and needs space. In the meantime, my frustration is presenting itself in other ways. I overreacted about some trivial bullshit tonight and stormed out."

He watched Lauren's lips pout then creep into a flirty smile. "Let me help. We're friends. I could be your happy ending."

AJ shook his head at Lauren's blatant invitation and chuckled. "Come on." He took her keys, opened the door of her bedsit, and stood back, allowing her to enter first. "Time for your beauty sleep."

"Anthony Tanner?"

"Yes, Lauren Barker."

"Thanks for the ear. You're a special man."

"Anytime, sweetheart."

AJ finally made it back to the tiny terrace around dawn.

Standing outside Liz's room, he listened for any hint of sound from inside. He turned the knob gently and stepped forward. Liz faced away from him, her body curled around a stray pillow, the duvet hugging bare shoulders, and a thin ribbon of light—courtesy of a gap in the curtain—adding a suggestion of illumination across her back. Her bed was an unruly mess.

He knew she wasn't asleep, not properly anyway, but apart from the gentle rise and fall of the bedding with her breath, she stayed still. He reached out his hand and held it above her face—wanting to touch her, but knowing if he did, he'd never stop.

———

Liz rolled onto her back as AJ closed her bedroom door. He reeked of packed bars, damp air, and overpowering perfume. The type that lingers in the nostrils with a sting, and clings to your collar long after a hug from an enthusiastic friend.

She'd sensed him before, standing by her bed at some ungodly hour of the morning, and wondered why he felt the need to check on her when he arrived home after being out on the prowl.

Now wide awake, Liz watched a tiny spider crawl across the ceiling as she held a conversation between her rational and emotional selves—opening her heart to scrub it raw with a stiff brush as the city stirred.

Later that morning, she caught the bus into the inner city to meet Penny for brunch before a planned shopping trip. They sat in a rowdy café on Oxford Street, eating eggs benedict served with strong black coffee.

"I spotted your housemate out last night," Penny said. "Actually, it was this morning if my watch was keeping time."

"Really?"

"Yep, sitting on a bar stool next to a curvy, plus-size-model-type hanging all over him. She had breast that would make any guy weep with joy."

"It's none of my business who hangs all over him. And I hate the word *plus-size*."

"Jeez, Louise, you're all fired up this morning. Jealous, are we?"

"I am not jealous. AJ was merely a glimmer of hope from my past." Liz sipped her coffee. "Anyway, he doesn't fit with my list."

"No? Why so snooty then? You've been sniffing his T-shirts, haven't you?"

Liz couldn't help but smile. "We had an argument. I asked him to consider working for me and he let rip. I'm a tad fragile. Went to bed and turned on the tears for a while." Liz watched as Penny mopped up hollandaise sauce with a tiny piece of English muffin. "I know what you're going to say."

Penny chewed a few times and swallowed. "What?"

"Toughen up."

"That's the spirit."

"It's just, this Peter thing is still hanging over my head."

"The guy hasn't got a case, you know that. And one more piece of Aunty Penny's words of wisdom. If you want to hook yummy-man-bun Tanner, stop feeling so damn sorry for yourself and start laying on the charm."

"I just told you, he doesn't check my boxes. What makes you think I want him?"

"Come on. It's me. Penny. You want him. Trust me, I know these things. And, if I'm not mistaken," she said, brows rising to meet her words, "he wants you, too."

"How do you know? You've hardly seen him lately."

"I've seen enough. He can't stop staring at you."

"Yet he was with someone else last night. I know it's not my business, but he arrived home just before dawn, reeking of opportunities—either lost or found."

"Stop being so dramatic." Penny shrugged. "A guy has needs. And you're in rebound mode, so he's bound to keep his distance for a while before he makes a move. It's purely relationship etiquette."

"I hate this, Pen. Why are guys so complicated? Why do we play games, dance around the people we're attracted to without saying how we really feel?"

Penny pointed her coffee spoon at Liz. "So, you admit it. You've got the hots for him."

"I'm speaking hypothetically. I'm still getting over Peter, remember."

"Bullshit! You're falling and falling hard. And to answer your question. Guys like a little resistance, a bit of 'want what they can't have' kind of thing. They're like dogs. If you want them to come, you have to play chase."

"Stop it." Liz cracked a broad smile. "Drink your coffee and tell me what's on your Kindle. I could do with a good book."

"Change the subject all you want, your transparency remains." Penny picked up her coffee and sipped. "Wait a week or two, then give him a little taste of his own medicine. Flirt with other guys, go on a date. He'll soon get the message you're available."

"And where am I supposed to find these guys?"

"Tinder. You'll have hundreds of the bastards swiping right in no time."

"Your enthusiasm astounds me. Come on, let's go spend some money." Liz reached into her bag for her phone, checked her texts, and smiled.

AJ: Truce?

"What's tickled your fancy?" Penny asked.

Liz showed Penny AJ's text.

"He's not one for chitchat, is he." Penny grinned like a gossipy schoolgirl. "This guy's the one. I feel it. Send him a tit pic."

"What? I've never sent a tit pic in my life."

"What happens when he decides he wants you? Will he send you a picture of his manhood encased in a wet pair of tighty-whiteys with the word 'screw' attached?"

Giggling, Liz pushed Penny out the door. "Would you stop? Now I have that image in my head."

"And how does he look?"

"Hot as hell."

27

A WHISPERED HINT OF JADE

On the day of the Young Enterprise Awards, Liz left work early and caught a cab back to the tiny terrace to shower and change in time for the seven-thirty start. Except for the occasional breakfast where they'd exchanged polite small talk, she'd had little contact with AJ over the past couple of weeks. He hadn't mentioned their argument and not wanting to tempt fate, Liz decided to leave the ball in his court.

AJ spent the weekends away and stayed out until after eleven most nights. Liz told herself it didn't matter, although it had crossed her mind that he stayed away because of her. Maybe he had a girlfriend. Or several girlfriends. Perhaps he shared a bed with the woman Penny saw him with. Whatever the reason, Liz had texted him that morning saying she'd be out, in case he wanted an evening at home.

Her bag in one hand and dry-cleaning in the other, Liz pushed the door open with her butt. As she turned into the living room, she stopped. Three guys were slouched around the room in front of the TV, drinking beer. On closer inspection, she recognized one as Ryan. His new look still surprised her. From a rugged, slightly scruffy type to the urbane guy dressed in well-fitting jeans and a

Henley shirt stretched across his broad chest. If Penny was here, she'd call him a prospect.

"Hi." She lay her keys, bag, and dry-cleaning down on the sideboard as they all stood and stared. Stepping forward, she offered her hand. "Ryan, isn't it?"

"Liz, hi," Ryan replied. "Sorry, AJ's gone to pick up pizza. He thought you'd be out. We came over to watch the rugby."

"No problem. Hi, I'm Liz." Liz offered her hand to the second and third men as they introduced themselves as Paul, and Ryan's brother, Chris. "I need to get changed. Can you ask AJ to save me a slice? I'm starving." She smiled sweetly before running up the stairs to her bedroom. Liz had wondered about Ryan and Chris ever since Peter weaved his tales of AJ's doomed business affairs. AJ had insisted their friendship was solid. Now, here they were, large as life and as happy as three guys in a shed full of power tools with a cooler of beer.

<hr>

AJ entered the room holding four large pizza boxes and a six-pack of lager. "Okay, guys, let's eat. I'm starving." He frowned in reaction to Ryan's cheeky grin. "What?"

"So is Liz, apparently. She wants you to save her a slice."

He noticed her bag on the sideboard. "Liz is here?"

"Upstairs. How do you sleep at night with that little hottie under your roof?"

"I sleep just fine." Knowing the guys would tease him relentlessly if he told them about his feelings for Liz, AJ kept his response noncommittal. "I hope she didn't freak out when she saw you ugly dudes in her living room."

"She was as sweet as pie," Ryan replied. "Wonder if she needs me to wash her back."

"As if. She's way out of your league, mate."

The men shut up when Liz appeared. Dressed in a capped-sleeve shift with a lace bodice gracing the creamy skin above her cleavage, AJ couldn't help but stare.

She looked directly at him with an expression full of opportunity. "Hi."

Little tease. She wouldn't be so bold if they were alone. "Hi, yourself. I hear you need sustenance before you venture out."

"Just a small slice."

Smiling warmly, he served her a large slice and made room on the sofa. They hadn't seen each other much lately. As he'd said to Lauren, she needed time, but the spark was returning, no doubt about it.

She stayed standing. "Thanks."

The three other men gawked as she took a bite, licked melted cheese off her fingers and let out a soft groan. "Yum. This is delicious."

AJ stuffed half a slice of pizza into his mouth to stifle a laugh and shook his head in amusement.

"Where are you off to tonight?" Ryan asked. "Hot date?"

"I wish. The Young Enterprise Awards at the school where I volunteer."

"You're a teacher?" Chris asked.

"No, a mentor. We have a group who've designed an app that's looking promising. I hope they take out the big prize this year."

"Sounds worthwhile," Ryan said.

"Yeah, it is. Anyway, I'd better go. Thanks for the pizza and enjoy the game." She glanced at the TV. "Who's playing?"

"The All Blacks and England at Twickenham. Starts in twenty-five minutes if you want to stay for the *haka*," AJ said. He often wondered where she went on Thursdays. Now he knew.

"No, I'll be late if I don't leave now. The Kiwis should romp home. Although they've had some injury problems."

"So, you're interested in rugby?" Ryan asked.

"Only for the thighs." Liz faked a swoon. "Those guys are perfection. My brother played at a provincial level, and my sister's boyfriend is an up-and-coming rugby player. So I've had plenty of exposure. To the sport I mean, not the thighs."

The men laughed, apart from AJ who looked at her with his mouth half open. He hadn't seen this side of Liz in a long, long time. He stood as she walked to the door. "Have you ordered a cab?"

"I'll just get one on the High Street. See you later." She closed the door behind her.

AJ turned toward the others and flashed a knowing grin. "Don't say a word. There's nothing going on between us," he said firmly. "I don't think my thighs are big enough for Lizzy the List Maker."

"What's wrong with you, mate?" Ryan asked. "She loves pizza, knows rugby, has a social conscience, and is sexy as hell. Can she cook?"

"You're a sexist pig. And yes, she's a great cook."

"What more could you want?" Ryan continued. "And you can't take your fucking eyes off her."

"Really? And don't let her catch you saying the F-word in her home *or* call her sexy."

"Does she have a boyfriend?"

AJ shook his head. "Recently single. I suspect it's more than a little raw. I'm not interested in being her token rebound guy."

"Text me her number." Ryan pulled his phone out of his pocket. "I'm keen, rebound, or no rebound."

AJ laughed. "Piss off. You're not her type. She likes brooding types with long dark hair and tats."

The usual stilted conversation prevailed over breakfast the following day, but there was no doubt that Liz was finding her way out of the mist. Her spark shone a little brighter when she spoke, and her hands once again accompanied her speech with purposeful animation. Even her face seemed more relaxed.

"How did it go last night? For your school, I mean?" AJ knew to keep his interactions with her light.

"Great. We won. I'm so proud of them."

"I had no idea you were involved in something like that."

Liz shrugged. "It's not only me. There's a whole group of us working on different projects."

"Sounds interesting. I'd love to have a look sometime."

She hesitated, as if the thought of him invading this aspect of her life didn't appeal in the slightest. "Sure."

"Oh, and before I forget. I have a painting arriving sometime this week. Is it okay if I hang it in the living room for a few months?"

"It's not skulls and ugly scenes of debauchery and destruction, is it?"

"Not a skull in sight."

"Good. I couldn't stand evil obliteration greeting me when I came home from work. It's all about Feng Shui."

"Right." AJ grinned as he wondered what her reaction to *Un Beso Imaginado* would be. The piece she'd been prepared to pay over and above the asking price for. "Also, I've considered your offer—the CFO position. I think it's best we maintain the status quo. I'm still assigned to your account at IKL. Until we sort out this Nichols debacle, anyway."

"Of course. It was a silly idea."

When Liz arrived home from work three days later, the artwork in question already held pride of place on the once blank living room wall. She didn't notice it at first as she dropped a bag of groceries in the kitchen, but when she turned around, she came face to face with *Un Beso Imaginado*—and AJ.

"Wow." Liz took several steps closer, then two back, her attention lost in admiration. "I love this painting." She dropped her purse on the coffee table. "It's a Jacobs. From the exhibition. Did you buy it?"

He looked up from plucking a baseline on his guitar. "I'm storing it for a friend."

"I wanted to buy this painting the first time I saw it, but it had the dreaded red dot." She glanced his way. "If your friend ever wants to sell it, I'd be interested."

"Tell me what you like about it."

"It's not what I like about it. I love it, but..." She thought for a moment. "It's how it makes me feel, rather than what I like or don't like."

"And that is?"

Liz couldn't look away as she traced the silhouette of the couple in the air with her hand. "We all have a different interpretation of art."

"And what is yours?"

She tilted her head toward him and hesitated. He held her gaze.

"Private."

"Come on," he challenged. "You can't verbalize your thoughts? Or rather, how it makes you feel when you study it."

She stared at him. What made the man tick? Apparently, he considered himself an art aficionado. Was he interested in her opinion, or trying to make her feel like a naïve country girl? She didn't need to prove herself to him, or any man. So why did she feel challenged?

Liz cleared her throat and stood with her back to AJ, her attention still on the Jacobs. "When I look at it, or even recall the essence of how it made me feel the first time I noticed it, I sensed the desire, the chemistry between the male and female."

"You see them as male and female?"

"The one on the right is more masculine. Look at his muscular structure, it's amazing. But they both have long hair."

"What else?"

She shot him a glance over her shoulder. "It fires your imagination."

"And what do you imagine?"

Liz closed her eyes briefly and lost herself in thought. "Desire. What it would be like to have someone desire you so intently, crave you, like the male in the painting desires the female. For him to hold you, touch your face with his hands and kiss you like he means it. And in that instant, their bodies are totally in the moment. Oblivious of time or space to such an extent that they blend into each other and nothing can tear them apart."

She stopped and considered it more carefully. "It's the colors as well. Black and white with fluid gray and a whispered hint of jade and violet in the woman's top. Nothing else. There's no need for any other colors…"

"Because?"

"Because it is what it is. Resolute."

His chuckle brought her out of her thoughts.

She looked at him coolly, embarrassed by her openness. "I'm glad my opinion amuses you."

It was her own fault, but that didn't stop her annoyance. He'd set her up with his probing questions, and she'd walked right into the ambush with her heart teetering precariously on her sleeve.

"Your opinion doesn't amuse me. It's you who amuses me."

"Really?" Liz turned back to the painting. His manipulation had stripped her bare. She felt hurt and exposed.

"I don't mean it in a derogatory way. You've made an interesting observation."

"In your opinion."

"Well, to be fair, I should know," he murmured.

"So you studied art *and* accountancy?"

"I did, actually." He gave her a tight-lipped smile as he stood, his stance softer—almost thoughtful. "Can I make you dinner?"

"No thanks. I'm going out."

Liz ran up the stairs to her room. She shut the door and flung herself front first on the bed. She hadn't planned to go out. It was Tuesday, and she had nowhere to go. Even so, after a quick shower and change of clothes, she left the terrace on her way to a place called solitude.

The cool London air rallied her. Pulling her coat and scarf tight, Liz hurried toward the cinema near St Mary's. Once inside, she struggled to concentrate on the rapid-fire subtitles that flicked across the screen. Awareness of couples surrounding her intensified. Shoulders touched, hands held, and words of affection floated between lovers' lips. Slipping down in her seat, she closed her eyes as one hot tear tracked the progress of her loneliness.

Her popcorn remained untouched.

The house was empty when Liz arrived home. Sitting in the living room, she stared at the painting. There is a point in everyone's lives where external inspiration moves you forward. Be it an unforgettable novel, movie, moody song, or an inspirational piece of art. It takes you by the heart and dances you around. For Liz, the portrayal of the lovers in *The Imagined Kiss* had the opposite effect. It made her want. The kind of want where you long for a soul mate, knowing they represent home, no matter where life may take you.

Liz woke to the everyday sounds of AJ in the kitchen as he emptied the dishwasher and made breakfast. She stayed in bed and mulled over moments of the last week until she heard the front door deadbolt click tight.

Downstairs in the living room, *Un Beso Imaginado's* imposing presence heightened her senses. Liz felt strangely emotional—not in a melancholy way—but more alive than she'd been recently. She struggled to imagine what life could be like if a man made you the object of his desire, was in awe of your radiance, wanted you with all the lust he could muster, and did something about it. For her, those feelings couldn't be shared with just anyone.

Lust.

The hand of lust hadn't touched Liz in a long time. Not since the old AJ barged his way into her fantasies all those months ago. She longed for his touch again—craved it. While she didn't entirely blame Peter for his sexual malaise, Liz now realized how his manipulation had affected her. Her confidence had taken a hit.

Penny was right. The time to strike back had arrived.

PARCHED AND SPENT

THE FIVE-DAY PERIOD didn't seem to matter to Peter and his team. James Mann had already requested two lengthy extensions, so the threat of court still loomed. According to Ivan and AJ, Peter didn't have a case. However, the worry that he might niggled away in the back of Liz's mind. She thought about it constantly, then admonished herself for her stupidity.

She straightened in her chair as AJ entered her office. He'd requested a meeting for just after one and arrived right on time.

"Are you okay?" He sat in the chair in front of her desk. "You look a little tense."

"Do I? So, what's on the agenda?" Liz could tell he wanted to ask more, but he took the hint in her tone.

"Let's go over your forecast. It's been three months. Time to reevaluate, see if I'm anywhere near the mark with my advice."

"Gosh, how time flies when you're having fun. Three months already."

A cheeky grin greeted her sarcasm. "Gosh," he mocked. "Are you happy for me to continue with your account, and if so, do we look at other business ventures?"

AJ leaned back in his chair, absently clicking the top of a pen as he waited for a response. His gaze never left her face, and she faltered a little, biting her lip in the process. He had an edge, and that edge intimidated her. Liz sensed him more at home as well— considered possibilities, imagined scenarios. Was it her sexual frustration or his that instigated this shift? Either way, it unnerved her.

"Are you back on my account?"

"I'm happy to keep the status quo if you are. But to be frank, I sense you find me confronting."

How observant.

"All healthy relationships require feedback," he continued. "You could be more forthcoming in that regard."

Liz thought for a moment. Should she spread her cards on the table and risk being stung by his businesslike arrogance, or simply say nothing? She mentally reached for her cards. "I do feel uncomfortable around you sometimes."

"Why's that?"

"Because I'm out of my depth and you keep rescuing me."

His expression softened. "All businesses require consultants and advisors. Your revenue stream is not small change. I'm full of admiration for what you've accomplished so far. Still, the opportunity for growth is there. I'm happy to assist, but I need more time."

"I value your expertise. I'm sorry if I haven't conveyed my appreciation adequately."

"Thanks, but please don't feel uncomfortable. We both have our strengths—and weaknesses for that matter. I believe we balance each other out. Opposites of equal strength increasing stability."

"But you think I'm incompetent?"

"I can assure you I think no such thing." All smiles disappeared. "We've established a certain trust. The time's right to purchase property," he said in his authoritative accountant's voice, legs wide as he leaned back in the chair. "Any thoughts about buying a home or commercial space?"

"What, in London? Can I afford it?"

"In my opinion, the property market's a good move for you. I like its solidness. I've a friend who's a realtor. He's sent me a few emails lately with good deals. The other option is New Zealand. The Auckland market is scorching hot right now. It all depends on where you see yourself in a few years' time. Commercial in New Zealand may be worth a look if you plan to return sometime. If you're not keen on Auckland, Queenstown's an option. Invest in the right commercial property and you'll make money all day long."

"With what's happened lately, I'm not sure London's the right fit. Going home unsettled me."

AJ cocked a questioning brow. "Really? Personally, I don't think you're done here. Not that it's any of my business," he added.

"When I was with Peter, I assumed I'd make London my home, settle down and eventually start a family. Crazy me."

"I didn't realize your relationship was on that level."

"It wasn't. I considered the possibility, though. It's a girl thing. We think about babies as we get older."

"You're only twenty-five." AJ cleared his throat. "Anyway, shall we take a look?"

Liz noted the change of subject.

"I can tee something up with Callum for next week," he continued. "Have a think about it over the weekend."

"Okay, thanks."

"Also, Ivan just phoned to say Peter has decided to settle."

"Really? That's great news." A lump caught in her throat; the relief welcomed but emotional all the same. "I don't know where I'd be without you and Ivan."

"As much as I love a battle, it's good we don't have to go to court. We had to up the offer by five grand, but it's a satisfactory result." He leaned forward and put his hand on hers, the brief touch over in a flash as he pulled away. "You okay?"

She took a deep breath and smiled. "Yep."

Liz sat at her desk and peered at the screen in front of her—the victory won in a no-win situation. Peter remained a thorn in her side, one she'd left to fester when she had invited him into her home and her bed. Liz had let Peter's opinion on what was right and wrong in her life cloud her judgment. Now her determination to never let it happen again, colored her dealings with AJ. Her guard had to stay up.

Lately, thoughts of dating held mild interest, a way to rid AJ from her system, perhaps. But Tinder? Really? The phone on her desk buzzed and Sophie's voice came over the intercom. "Liz, Peter Nichols is in reception."

"Oh." Liz noted the time: five twenty-five. Nearly time for Sophie to knock off. "Okay, send him in."

She stood and took several short steps forward. "Peter, what can I do for you?"

He looked her up and down in his usual disapproving way. This time, Liz didn't give a shit about her short skirt, sheer blouse, or unruly curls.

"Liz. You're looking gorgeous as usual. You've heard I've decided to settle?"

"I have."

"How about a drink to celebrate? It's not every day you give me fifteen thousand pounds of your money."

Her flesh crawled, not only because he was a slimy bastard, but also because she'd failed to realize it initially. "Sorry, I'm busy tonight."

Peter narrowed his eyes as if he didn't believe her. "Also, I wanted to ask you something."

Typical. He didn't want a drink date. He wanted information.

"That guy you cheated on me with. Tanner. The business

advisor slash boyfriend or whatever he calls himself. Does he know people in the art world?"

"I've never cheated on anyone in my life." Liz mentally questioned why she felt the need to respond. But when confronted with an accusation, it's human nature to offer a defense. "AJ is not my boyfriend. And as to his acquaintances, I'm not privy to his social contacts."

"I purchased a painting recently. A Jacobs. Thought it was a done deal. When I went to claim it, they'd withdrawn it from sale."

Her heartbeat rushed, and a tightness gripped her stomach. She sat at her desk, the solidness of the timber between them calming her a little. "Why do you think AJ had something to do with it?"

"We discussed it the day of the settlement meeting. He said he'd met me at the exhibition." Peter leaned forward, his hands on her desk. He lowered his voice. "If you know anything about this, I'll be jolly well pissed off, make no mistake."

She remained silent.

"Anyway, let's go for a drink. You can thank me for not going to court."

"I told you, I have something on."

He smirked and shook his head. "Pity. I thought I'd give you the chance to make amends. Still, you never delivered in that department, did you?"

"I guess not." Memories of their last morning together flashed into her mind as she struggled to remain calm.

"What the hell are you doing here?" AJ's elevated voice boomed across the room as he stormed into Liz's office and addressed Peter. "By being here, you're breaking the terms of the settlement. I think you've outstayed your welcome, don't you?"

"I'm talking to my girl."

"Liz is not *your* girl. Now, shall I call security, or are you leaving?"

"The Jacobs, *Un Beso Imaginado,*" Peter said in his pompous tone. "Do you have any idea why it was suddenly withdrawn from sale?"

"Why would I?"

"Once I told you about it, it disappeared off the face of the earth."

"Had you paid for it?" AJ asked.

"I'd paid a deposit."

"Maybe they had a better backup offer."

"And how would you know?"

"Purely an assumption. Now, is there anything else?" AJ held the office door open.

Peter held AJ's gaze. "I expect that fifteen K by the end of business."

"It's in your lawyer's trust account. If you took the time to read the fine print, you'd realize it stays there for sixty days until we're satisfied you've kept your end of the bargain." AJ's voice was cold as steel but steady. "I repeat, by coming here, you're in breach of the agreement. Keep your distance or the offer's off the table."

"Up yours. You're welcome to her." Peter pointed his finger at AJ. "And about the painting, you haven't heard the last of this."

Liz didn't speak until Peter left reception. "What did Peter mean—"

"I don't want to discuss it." AJ's expression remained unsympathetic and his tone cold. "Don't you ever let that jerk in here again. Do you hear me?"

"But—"

He held up his hand. "Liz. What did I say? Get your coat. I'll walk you home."

"I'm not going home," she said, more than pissed at AJ's 'what did I say' tone. "I'm still working."

"Too bad." He removed her coat from the rack and held it up for her to slip into. "Come on. It's getting on for six. You've been here long enough."

Liz stared at him for a moment before shutting her laptop with an exaggerated click of the lid. The draft of his breath prickled her neck as she slipped her arms into the cool satin lining of her coat sleeves. She'd rarely seen this side of him. Angry AJ. Sure, he had plenty of facets to his personality, demonstrating serious businessman down pat. And when they were at home, he morphed into his easygoing, laid back persona. But Liz had never thought of him as the angry type until recently.

Words were left unsaid as they walked home, stored away for when clouds of thought could finally break. The further they walked, the more furious Liz became. Once inside the tiny terrace, she turned to face him.

"What's your problem? Is this you in damsel-in-distress protection mode? Because if it is, I don't need it." AJ wasn't the only one who could spit tacks.

"Tough. I don't want Peter Nichols anywhere near you. Understand? He's a creep, and under the terms of the settlement, you can't see each other. It's for your own protection," he shouted. "What were you thinking? Oh, wait—when it comes to Peter Nichols, you don't think, do you? You go in boots and all with your arms wide open."

"So, you feel you have a right to insult me now?" she yelled back. "I told him I didn't want a drink. What more do you want?"

"The guy was after half of your net worth and not once did I hear you say no."

"I did."

"You said you were busy. I heard you. Don't make excuses to the guy. Learn to say no."

"Don't tell me what to do. That's what he did. He told me what to do all day long." Sobs choked her throat as she struggled to speak. "What to wear, what to eat, or rather, what not to eat. And sometimes, what to even think. He tried to control me, under the guise of... I don't even know what to call it. It certainly wasn't love. Do you honestly think I'd let him back into my life?"

"Shit." He reached to comfort her. "I'm sorry."

She recoiled. "Don't. Please don't touch me. I dealt with his visit the best way I knew how." Her voice softened. "I stayed calm. Didn't yell or cry. Do you know how hard it was for me? I had to mentally glue myself together just to be in the same room as that bastard."

"Liz—"

"And you…you treat me like I'm clueless. You have no idea what he did to me. You can't possibly know. This is not about you and your ego. You don't have to mark your territory around me." She looked up and blinked hard. The tears still came.

"I'm sorry. It's just, he makes me so damn angry."

They stood at the bottom of the stairs, both still dressed in their coats. He reached out and slipped hers off her shoulders, his touch offered as an expression of concern. "I don't know why I feel I have to protect you."

"Yeah, well, you don't. And you did have something to do with the sale of the Jacobs. Now, it's hanging on our living room wall. Every time I look at it, I'm reminded how I stuffed up by giving my affections to that horrible man."

"Liz—"

"Don't. Just don't."

She ran up the stairs to her room and locked the door behind her. Thoughts of Peter, his lack of affection and critical manner, crammed her mind. Maybe Penny was right for suggesting Liz talk to a professional. Could she do it? Admit her mistakes to a stranger? Analyze the why? She thought possibly not.

Liz fell asleep fully dressed and woke around midnight, parched and spent. The lyrics of her argument with AJ repeatedly played in her head. The insensitive phrases and the heated retort.

Slipping into her flannel nightshirt, Liz entered the bathroom, cleaned her teeth and used a warm washcloth to wipe away the grime of her day. She sidestepped the mirror. Her image carried too many painful reminders of Peter's never-ending critique.

She tiptoed downstairs to the kitchen, grabbed a bottle of

water from the fridge and stood at the sink, taking small sips. Outside the window, a spindly ornamental cherry, rimmed by a circular seat and lit in an ineffectual glow by a row of solar lights, stood bare. It would soon be Christmas, one of the loneliest times of the year for many. This year, Liz felt lonely, too.

AJ's presence filled the space before he made a sound. Her hands tightened around the bottle as he stepped closer. Naked from the waist up, his warmth overwhelmed her as he leaned his torso into her back.

"I'm so sorry. You're right, I had no idea." His voice danced on a throaty whisper as his musky scent swirled around her, drawing her in. He ran his hands down her arms, the touch lifting her skin in tiny bumps of want and concern.

"Please don't do this."

"I know it's too soon," he said. "I just want to hold you. Keep you safe."

He rested the tip of his chin on her crown and inhaled her hair like they were lovers. She remembered he'd done this before— inhaled her scent—and for a moment, she lost the strength to resist.

They stayed that way for a few seconds before AJ pulled her closer. His lips caressed her crown as his arms tightened and the unmistakable firmness of him pushed along the junction of her butt. His lips touched her neck. It was more of a peck than a kiss, but the scorch mark lingered.

Liz inhaled sharply and closed her eyes. Just one moment more, she told herself.

"You can't make this right for me," she said, finally gaining enough composure to speak. "I need time and space." She pulled away but couldn't look at him. "I haven't felt secure in a long time. It's not going to happen here and now."

She glanced up.

A look of concern shadowed his expression. "What did he do to you?" He brushed a few wayward curls from her face with an unsteady hand, letting a finger remain in the coil of a ringlet for a moment.

"It doesn't matter. I let it happen. It's up to me to deal with it."

"It matters to me. Come to my bed." He offered his hand. "To sleep, nothing more."

She shook her head.

"I'm not suggesting anything sexual. You need someone in your corner."

"I don't need that complication right now," she whispered. "It may mean nothing to you, to hold me and tell me you care before slipping away without a word. I don't function that way. Don't you understand?"

"Of course, I do. You're hurting. I get it, but don't push away the very people who care about you."

"And you're one of those people, are you? One of my care group?" Liz didn't mean to sound confrontational, but even so, her words and tone conveyed an aggressive tenor.

"You think I'm not?"

"We have a business relationship, that's the extent of it."

"Bullshit. It's not that simple, is it?"

Liz struggled to voice a reply, her thoughts muddled between want and defense. "I need to get some sleep."

He sighed. "I might stay up for a while. Listen to some music."

"But it's almost one."

He shrugged. "I'm suddenly wide awake."

"Yeah. Me too."

"I know what happened between us is water under the bridge, but..." He turned away. "Anyway, you better get to bed."

"Goodnight." She went to leave, then hesitated. "I'm sorry if I sound like a bitch. It's just—"

"Liz don't. Just go to bed."

"I'm trying to explain."

AJ frowned and rubbed the back of his neck. "Yeah, and I'm trying to do the right thing. Go to bed."

Back in her room, hot tears dripped onto her pillow as she waited for sleep. Liz had rarely directed anger toward Peter in the past. Rather, she belittled herself for making a wrong judgment call. Blamed only herself. Now, resentment consumed her. She hated Peter with a passion that shook her core beliefs.

The following morning at the office, Liz got straight to work. The distraction failed to have the desired effect. AJ's firm warmth, pressing hot and strong along the ridge of her butt, was all she thought about. Nothing sexual? Bullshit. He'd screw her in a heartbeat. And she'd be a willing participant. The difference being, she wouldn't be able to carry on regardless after the fact.

When they spoke a few days later, AJ acted as if nothing had happened, bringing Liz a suggestion of relief, accompanied by a measure of resentment.

29

INVITATIONS

For the next few days, AJ continued his performance effortlessly. Their interaction at the kitchen sink wasn't mentioned again. He offered Liz a nice enough, but all the same, stilted version of his personality whenever their paths crossed. He stayed away from the terrace mostly. Liz didn't know where he ventured to. When their working life did coincide, she noticed he focused his attention solely on business, nothing more.

Liz dismissed her disappointment. The grass wasn't necessarily greener on AJ's side of the fence. And yet, she longed to relax on that grass. Smell it and touch it.

The following Thursday, when she arrived home from the market, an unexpected visitor sat at the kitchen table.

"Hello. You must be Liz." The tall, elegantly dressed woman stood and extended a graceful hand dripping with diamonds. "I'm Marielena, Anthony's mother."

"So nice to meet you." Liz couldn't contain her surprise as Marielena kissed her on both cheeks. "AJ didn't mention you'd be calling in."

"I'm in London for an appointment. Anthony's in the shower. He's driving back with me. Charlotte will drop him home on

Monday. I hate driving in the dark and Garry couldn't get away. Some excuse about being too busy at work. You know what men are like."

"You don't look old enough to be AJ's mother. Surely you can't be a day over forty."

"Thank you, dear. I've birthed five babies. I'm definitely well over forty."

"Can I get you anything? Tea?"

"Thanks, but we had coffee at a cute little café down the road." She held Liz's gaze. "So, you and AJ… Just friends, are you?"

Wow, straight to the point. "Yes. And housemates."

Marielena gave a disbelieving nod. "I see."

"He consults for my company as well."

"Yes, he mentioned that. In fact, he's mentioned several things about you."

"Mother, I hope you're behaving." AJ entered the room, his weekender in one hand and laptop in the other. Liz stopped herself from inhaling his freshly washed sexy stink, as Penny called it. "Obviously you've met Liz."

"I have. Anyway, Liz, what are you doing the weekend of the sixteenth?"

"I'm not sure." She hesitated, wondering what was coming next. "Nothing special."

"Good. Come to my birthday party. It's only a small family affair. Since Nate can't make it, I'd love you to take his place."

Liz caught the amused grin on AJ's face. "Thank you, but I couldn't possibly intrude."

"Don't be silly. I insist. Any friend of Anthony's is welcome. I'm sure he'd enjoy showing you around Cambridge, wouldn't you, darling?"

AJ looked at Liz and winked. "What a great idea. You must come," he said, an eager exaggeration in his voice. "It will be so much fun."

Prick. "But—"

"I won't hear another word about it," Marielena said. "You can stay in the cottage. Right, I'll go powder my nose."

As his mother left the room to use the downstairs bathroom, AJ burst out laughing. "Can't say no, can you, Dobson?"

"I can so. She caught me off guard, that's all. I'll phone later in the week with an excuse."

"No, you won't. You'll come, and what's more, it will do you good. If you're well-behaved and take the sour plum out of your mouth for a few days, I might even let you be my date and feed you decadent chocolate cake."

"Bossy bastard!"

He laughed again. "Hurt my feelings, why don't you."

The day of the road trip, AJ arrived at the office without invitation, a fresh vegetable juice in each hand. He placed one in front of Liz and perched his butt on the edge of her desk. "I thought you might need a little sustenance. I asked for extra ginger."

Liz reached for the cup. She loved ginger. "Thank you."

"I'll be ready around three. Okay?"

"Where do your parents live again?"

"A few miles out of Cambridge. They have a small hobby farm. It even has a name. Tancroft."

Liz continued the small talk. "I've never been to Cambridge. I hear it's lovely."

"Are you still angry at me?"

"I wasn't angry at you."

"Really?" He smiled, the kind of smile that's shared between intimate couples. "I get the impression you'd rather jump off Putney Bridge than spend the weekend with me."

She held his gaze, feeling the heat between them.

"So we're good?" he asked.

She nodded. "Yes, we're good."

"Okay. Be ready by three."

Liz reached for a file on her desk and opened it, purely as a distraction. The thought of spending time with AJ and his family held more than a mild interest, but as usual, she pulled back. "Look, as much as I appreciate your mother's invitation, I don't want to intrude on your family time."

"You won't be intruding. The fresh air will do you good. You can hang out with my crazy sisters, drink wine, eat cake, and dance the night away."

"Unfortunately, I have a hair appointment later. Also, we work together. No point in spending weekends together as well."

AJ continued with his argument. "Look, unless you're tossing me out, we have to spend time together away from work. We share a home, remember? Obviously you're not interested in us being lovers, and I respect that, but there's no reason we can't be friends." He sipped his juice, not even flinching at the word 'lovers.' It was all a matter of fact to him. Easy come, easy go.

"About that," she said, steering the conversation away from the lovers' comment and the word 'home.' "I've considered your suggestion—"

"About coming to my bed?" he said with a grin.

A brief smile graced her lips. "About buying a place. If your friend has time, I'd like to look in the New Year. Then I'd be out of your hair."

"Is that what you'd prefer?" he asked, an edge of curtness in his reply. "To live on your own?"

"As you said, it's a sound investment." Liz brought the paper cup to her lips and took a much-needed sip. A hit of ginger tingled on her tongue. Maybe AJ was right. A few days away would do her good. "How long does it take to drive to Cambridge?"

She noticed him relax. "About ninety minutes, give or take. All depends on the traffic. You sound keen."

"I often have trouble saying no, as you're aware. I blame it on my father," she said with a smile. "He had, or has, a robust parenting style. Rarely takes no for an answer. Even now."

They both moved toward the door.

"Thanks for the juice. I guess I'll see you around three. Should we take the Evoque? It could do with a run."

He smiled. "Will you let me drive?"

"Only if you stick to the speed limit."

TANCROFT

As THEY LEFT LONDON, traffic on the M11 moved at a steady pace. AJ talked freely, asking questions about her trip to New Zealand and told funny tales about his siblings. A very different AJ sat behind the wheel than the one she'd experienced lately. Relaxed and charming.

"I wondered if you would do me a favor," she said. "I'd like to buy the Jacobs. *The Imagined Kiss*. Since you know the owner, could you approach him with an offer?"

"Do you now? Last time I checked, it wasn't for sale."

"Would you ask anyway? I'm willing to pay up to ten thousand pounds."

He shot her a sideways glance. "You can't be serious. That's nearly three times the original asking price. Jacobs is a virtual unknown."

"You think I'm crazy?"

He laughed. "I would never admit to such a thought."

"Please. Or give me his number."

"Fine. I'll ask, but I know what he'll say."

"Well, at least he'll know that I'm interested. How much longer do you have it for?"

"A couple of months. I'll give him a call."

"Thanks."

The subject quickly changed. "I have music for the occasion." AJ flicked the switch on the steering wheel and Jason Kerrison's voice filled the vehicle.

"Opshop. I'm impressed."

"I like this album. In fact, I like lots of Kiwi things." They shared a casual glance. "We went to New Zealand and Australia about five years ago on a family holiday. I had a ball."

"What kind of Kiwi things do you like?"

"What, besides the music and the girls?"

The flush of her face went unnoticed in the car's dim interior.

"Hokey pokey ice cream, meat pies. The usual stuff," he said.

"You're making me homesick."

He glanced her way and smiled. "Dad walked in on me in bed with a girl in Queenstown one night. He wasn't a happy camper."

Liz rarely engaged in conversation with AJ that didn't involve work. Now here she was, listening to him share a sexual conquest story. He wasn't bragging about it. It was purely a matter-of-fact account that he obviously found amusing.

He kept his focus on the road. "But that was the old me."

"Do you mean as opposed to the new you?"

"I was a bit of a lad back in the day."

"Are you saying you've changed?"

A brief pause followed. "Maybe there's something to be said for a committed relationship."

"I never imagined you as the commitment type," she said.

"I didn't think you imagined me at all."

Her body tensed. She felt exposed, for want of a better word, and discussing the life and loves of AJ Tanner didn't help. She leaned back on the headrest, her thoughts lost in the lyrics of *One Day* as it streamed through the stereo speakers.

"I love this song."

"Me too." AJ slowed and turned left. "This is us."

Liz sat up straight, peered out the window and took in the view. "Wow." Black wrought-iron gates flanked by a large stone wall covered in star jasmine appeared in the distance. AJ pulled over. The crushed white pebbles gave the driveway a movie set look. "I hope your father doesn't mind me tagging along."

"My friends are always welcome, especially cute ones. Anyway, Mum issued the invitation, and she's the boss. The family rumor mill will be abuzz in no time."

"And that amuses you, does it?"

He chuckled. "Totally."

Anna and Charlotte hijacked Liz as soon as she stepped from the car. They chatted non-stop about life at Tancroft and their older brother. Liz had two sisters back in New Zealand, Ally and Sydney, and the Tanner siblings were just like them. Fun girls who loved a bit of gossip.

"So, you and AJ? Are you seeing each other, you know, in the boyfriend-oh-la-la-girlfriend sense?"

"Anna," Charlotte said. "Stop being so nosy."

"It's okay," Liz replied. "And no, we're not involved 'oh-la-la' romantically, if that's what you mean. We're just housemates, and AJ is my business advisor."

"So, how does that work?" Anna asked. "Living and working together with all that sexual tension floating around?"

Liz shook her head and laughed. "Any tension is usually because he leaves dishes in the sink. The word 'sexual' doesn't come into it, believe me."

"Don't mind her," Charlotte said. "All she thinks about are boys, boys, and more boys."

"It's true. I blame it on hormones." A warm laugh rumbled deep in Anna's throat. "We want AJ to find a girlfriend. He told David he'd met someone before he went to Japan. They only knew each other for a short while."

A rush of disappointment gripped Liz as she recalled meeting AJ before he left. Their connection and ease with each other—and the intensity. "It's certainly not me."

"Then why did he bring you home to meet the family?" Anna said with a grin.

"Your mother invited me, and AJ wouldn't take no for an answer. He thought I needed a few days of country air."

"Really?" Anna giggled. "Usually, a guy takes you home when it's serious. Are you coming back for Christmas?"

"Anna," Charlotte scolded. "AJ may already have a girlfriend. Stop making assumptions. Although you'd be perfect for him, Liz."

"You're probably right about the girlfriend. He spends most weekends away."

"Yes here. He never brings anyone with him though. You're the first female friend we've met in a long while," Charlotte said.

"And," Anna said with schoolgirl enthusiasm, "he asked Mum to put you in the cottage together."

Liz widened her eyes. "I'm not sleeping in the cottage with him, am I?"

The sisters looked at each other and burst out laughing. "Don't look so worried," Anna said. "It has two rooms. And you do share a house in London. Come on, we'll show you around."

A small hobby farm, Tancroft housed chickens, two dogs, three horses, a few sheep, and a fat tabby cat called Norman. Liz expected a circa eighteen hundred country farmhouse, so the contemporary home, with high ceilings and muted light flooding throughout the interior, couldn't be further from her imaginings. Constructed of timber, glass, and natural stone, with polished concrete and hardwood floors to complement the off-white walls, the house oozed elegance and flair. Vibrant art added an injection of color, and slouchy sofas, rustic rugs, and piles of books enhanced the homely feel.

AJ left to collect his mother's birthday cake, saying he'd be back in half an hour. As it turned out, the rest of the family arrived before him. Liz suppressed a smile when introduced to David, the vocal love-maker, and his wife, Zoe. They, along with their children, Max and Indie, had driven from Northampton where they ran a small business.

Liz sat at the farmhouse-style table in the kitchen, drinking tea as she enjoyed a fresh scone with butter and cherry jam. Minutes later, AJ's father strolled in and greeted her with an outstretched hand and a warm smile.

"Hi, I'm Garry." Tall and handsome like his son, Garry had a handshake to match. Way too firm.

"Pleased to meet you. I see where AJ gets his good looks from." Liz immediately wondered why those words left her mouth. She cleared her throat as Gary smiled. "You have a beautiful home. Have you always lived in the area?"

"Pretty much. We bunked down in the cottage for the first few years of marriage. Built the main house when David and Anthony were little nippers. It's a great part of the country."

"Is Mrs. Tanner here?"

"No, she's gone out for a drink with some friends." Garry craned his neck and peered out the window onto the driveway. "What's keeping that boyfriend of yours? I thought he said you guys were going out for dinner."

"Oh…I'm not sure. And AJ's not my boyfriend." Liz said. "I think there's been a misunderstanding."

"Misunderstanding about what?" AJ entered the kitchen and placed a large box on the counter. "One birthday cake, safe and sound. Sorry I took so long." He glanced at Liz. "I see you've met Dad. I hope he hasn't been boring you with talk of the share market."

"Liz was just explaining the nature of your relationship," Garry said with a knowing grin. The same type of grin AJ flashed when amused.

"Was she now?" He caught Liz's eye and smiled so sweetly, she wanted to melt all over him. "And how did she describe it?"

Garry laughed as Liz cleared her throat for the second time. "Did AJ tell you he has access to all of my business activities?"

"No way," Gary replied. "You don't trust this guy, do you?"

"I may have to reevaluate that when we return to London." Liz enjoyed Garry's banter and personality. He had a warmness to him that had relaxed her the moment they'd met.

AJ opened the scullery to put the cake away. "I'm having dinner with friends from college. Keen? I don't want to leave you here with my sisters. They're shameless gossips, all three of them."

The invitation was a take-it-or-leave-it kind of remark. Liz didn't know what to say. She wondered if her presence would cramp his style. "Sure. Sounds good."

"It won't be a late night. Come on, I'll show you the cottage."

Tiny goosebumps prickled the back of her neck, and a contradicting warmth flushed her face as they walked across the path. Anna had apparently sensed sexual tension between them, but Liz knew she shouldn't consider the possibility. She repeatedly told herself she had good reasons for this.

First, Peter had done his best to put a significant dent in her self-worth. The list followed on from there. She and AJ were housemates who also worked together. Everyone knew one of life's most practical rules was to never screw the crew.

Then, there was his admission he'd been a bit of a lad in his younger days. Liz wasn't a sexual prude, but she didn't want to be just one of the many on a lengthy list of conquests. She wanted to be one of the few. To meet that special guy who turned her on her toes, rocked her world, and only had eyes for her.

She often wondered if she could do the casual thing. Separate sex from her need for a relationship. Have a *friend with benefits*. Pursue sex purely for enjoyment and release without a care in the world about commitment, Valentine's Day, or why her *friend* didn't call on birthdays.

Liz quickly dismissed her internal monologue and followed him—sexy, handsome, boot man—through the front door. She took two steps forward and stilled. "Wow. Are you sure we should be staying here?"

"I always stay in the cottage. It's my home away from home." He turned to look at her. "Are you okay? You look a little flushed."

She broke eye contact. "It's a warm day."

AJ frowned, then huffed his amusement. "It's officially winter."

Even though the cottage was tiny, the proportion and placement of the furniture exuded a feeling of spaciousness. The functional kitchenette consisted of six cabinets painted in a soft taupe with an undertone of gray, and a small butler's sink. Above the countertop, a framed casement window looked out onto the garden, and three rustic wooden shelves held white plates, mugs, and bowls and baskets in various sizes. On the top shelf sat a collection of antique wire bird cages, just large enough for a small canary. The door to each hung free.

Liz looked up. "I love the cages with all the doors open."

"Yeah. It's Marielena's symbolic nod to freedom."

Liz nodded in agreement. "I like that."

In the living room, a compact wood-burning stove chugged away slowly, bringing a cozy warmth to the air. A rusted tin bucket full of dried pinecones sat on the brick hearth, and white rose petals lay where they had fallen from a jug of blooms on the coffee table.

A color palette of soft cream, with accents of turquoise and duck egg blue, adorned the walls, doors, and window frames. Various chairs, cushions, and an ottoman followed the blue tones—either in stripes or checks—and wooden floors, grayed off with age, complemented the flagstones in the kitchen and bathroom. The cliché 'shabby chic' came to mind, but there were no faded fabrics or threadbare rugs anywhere. Cute and classic, yet homely.

"What's upstairs?" she asked.

"Just a loft space."

Liz glanced around the room, noticing small details like the leaded glass windows that opened to the meadow, and a stack of vintage hat boxes on the bottom of a wooden bookcase. Elsewhere, low side tables overflowed with hard-covered books and magazines.

"You take the bedroom," he said. "The sofa folds down to a bed."

"Don't be silly. It's your bedroom. I'll sleep out here."

He shook his head. "Would you just humor me and do what you're told? Oh, and if you want a shower before we leave, the towels are in the bathroom. I'll be back in ten."

Liz smiled. "Thanks."

Standing in the shower, she let the warm water sooth her. AJ was right. Being in the country lifted her spirits, and his family's warmth comforted her. A pang of homesickness came and went, and Liz realized she hadn't felt quite so lonely lately.

She dressed in a pair of fitted black pants teamed with suede boots, an off-white button-to-the-neck shirt, and a taupe jacket. An animal print scarf completed the look. The memory of all those stuffy dinners with Peter flashed into her mind, before she quickly pushed all thoughts of him aside.

When AJ arrived back at the cottage, Liz was standing in front of an antique mirror fiddling with her hair. His eyes narrowed; not in a negative way—more like he was summing her up.

"Why don't you leave your hair down? You have beautiful hair, don't tie it up."

Liz struggled with a reply. AJ meant it as a compliment, she knew that. Still, Peter's words of critique whispered in her mind, tipped her up, and slammed her back down again. The word 'thanks' stuck in her throat, unheard.

"Would you mind doing up my clasp?" Liz handed him a fine silver chain joined with a delicate jade heart charm. She offered her wrist. "I can't get it."

He moved closer, his breath soft in her ears and his scent floating around her with anticipation. AJ lifted the bracelet and touched the heart with his fingers. "Beautiful. Is it jade?"

"We call it greenstone—*pounamu* in Māori. My grandfather received a piece of *pounamu* as payment once. He had a medical practice. Many of his patients couldn't afford to pay. Each of his grandchildren, and there are over twenty of us, receive a *pounamu* charm or carving on our twenty-first birthday."

"It's a wonder you dare to wear it."

"Granddad would hate the thought of it stuck away in a jewelry box. He always told us to enjoy the beauty of our prized possessions while we could."

"Smart man. Okay, hold still." His fingers fiddled with the clasp. "There." They looked up in unison, and at that moment, she wanted AJ to kiss her like she belonged to him. To plunge his tongue between her lips and hold her face in his hands, no matter how casual it would be to him.

He broke the spell with a nervous cough. "I'll be a few minutes. I need to jump under the water."

Liz was talking to Max and Indie in the driveway when AJ emerged from the cottage. When they noticed their uncle, they burst out laughing. AJ frowned a question. "What's the joke?"

"Nothing." Indie and Max fell into another fit of giggles. "Just stuff."

"Okay." He glanced at Liz. "Time to go."

"Where are you going?" Max asked. "Can we come?"

"No, mate. Not tonight. I'm taking Liz out to dinner."

"Like on a date?" Indie asked.

AJ chuckled. "We'll catch you tomorrow. You better go inside. It must be bath time." He walked around to the passenger door and held it open. Liz relaxed. Her outfit matched his perfectly. Dressed in dark jeans and a leather jacket over a white T-shirt, and yet another pair of designer boots, he looked like her dream hot date.

Her *Hell No* list was becoming more and more redundant by the day.

The winter air was crisp but not unpleasant. Liz sat back and watched AJ's hands slide around the steering wheel as they drove along the highway toward the city. He wore glasses when driving. She thought for the second time how much they suited him. There had been a shift in their affinity with each other, no doubt about it. It wasn't necessarily the way AJ looked at her, more the instinct one feels when another person shows an interest. The confusion persisted.

"What was that all about?" AJ's question broke into her thoughts.

"Indie wants to be my flower girl."

"Who are you marrying?"

Liz relaxed her head on the headrest, glanced out the passenger side window, and grinned. "Guess."

He chuckled. "Smart kids, those two."

AJ had the role of flirty bastard down pat. No wonder she caved the first time around. But she'd seen him in action, flirting with nearly every available woman in Putney, and realized she was one of the many. Nothing special. Still, the relaxed mood between them continued. Different from earlier in the day when Liz didn't want to leave London. Seeing him with his family helped. It seemed his personality was more complex than she'd first thought.

"Where are we going?"

"To my favorite Turkish place. They have great food. You'll love it. It's just us and two other couples. We all went to university together."

AJ parked in a parking building in the center of town. "It's not far from here. Are you warm enough?"

His concern touched the tip of her heart. "I'm fine. Thanks."

They walked a few blocks. Neither of them spoke until they reached their destination.

"This is it." AJ pushed through the door and into a restaurant bustling with activity. The waiter greeted him like a long-lost friend as he ushered them into a booth at the back of the seating area away from the bar.

"Guys, this is Liz. Liz, meet Andy and Anne, and Rick and Shelia. Liz is Nate's cousin."

The men rose as she shook hands around the table. "Pleased to meet you all."

"So, housemate is it?" Rick said with a huge grin as Liz made herself comfortable. "If you say so, mate."

"Don't mind Rick," Sheila said to Liz. "He and AJ go way back and are always stirring each other up."

AJ knew the interrogation would start as soon as Liz, Shelia, and Anne left the table to use the restroom.

"So, who is this girl?" Andy asked. "Just a friend, is she?"

"I told you, she's my housemate. Also, I've been consulting for her business as part of my role at IKL."

"Interesting," Andy said. "So how is the self-imposed sexile going? You can't tell me you've stayed celibate for two years with Liz sleeping under your roof."

"You're telling the story," AJ said with a grin.

"What does she think about it?"

"Nothing, so keep your mouth shut. Shit, you guys never change, do you? Not all my female friends are fair game for your matchmaking. You're like two old women."

"I've never known you to have a purely platonic relationship with a sexy woman before," Andy said. "Why start now?"

"I've changed, mate. I'm finally open to a long-term thing. And anyway, that's not true. I have plenty of female friends."

"Shit, you have changed. So, what are you saying? Making love to the same woman every night of the week sounds okay, does it?" Rick asked.

"Well, if you're making love to Shelia that often after four years of marriage, it must be special." AJ laughed and took another swig of his beer.

Rick looked at him over the rim of his glass and smiled. "It is. I wouldn't go back to being single for anything. She just gets me."

"Thank you. Now you understand. I'm looking for a committed relationship, not casual sex with nameless girls."

"No way." Andy's look conveyed his skepticism. "But you're right. It's about time you parked your car in the same garage every night, just to see how it feels."

"You like her, I can tell." It was Rick's turn to give his opinion.

"Would you guys shut the F up? I told you—"

"Told them what?" Anne asked as the women sat back at the table. "What are you guys talking about?"

"We're teasing him mercilessly." Rick laughed. "It's too easy."

"It's because he's frustrated over certain things," Andy said.

"Oh?" Shelia replied.

"What, still? So how long is it since you left for Asia?" Anne asked with a grin.

"Coming up two years." It didn't surprise AJ that everyone knew about his abstinence secret. He confided his intention to Andy one moody night after Cathy died. Andy told Anne, Anne told Shelia, and so on. By the time he left for Japan, they all knew, and more than likely, had tabled bets. No one believed he possessed the self-discipline to see it through, least of all AJ himself.

AJ glanced at Liz. He loved the way she rocked her style, casually draping her elegance in the perfect outer layer and finishing it with a delicate greenstone heart.

She returned his gaze and smiled, and for a moment, he would have sworn he had butterflies in his stomach.

31

UNCONSCIOUS EASE

THEY LEFT the restaurant around eleven. Liz almost expected AJ to take her hand and link his fingers through hers as they walked. But his hands slid into his jacket pockets instead. She'd eaten too much, and hated being overly full, even if it took the edge off her sexual appetite for which—at the moment anyway—there was no nourishment.

On reaching the car, AJ threw Liz the keys. "You'd better drive. I've had one too many."

Hundreds of stars shone brightly as she traveled along the highway toward Tancroft. Even in the dark, that special hush of winter stilled the air.

"Your friends are nice people. Thanks for the invite. I enjoyed their company."

AJ chuckled to himself, his head leaning back on the headrest. "Really, even when Andy asked you about your real job? He can be a bit of a dick sometimes, but he's a good guy."

"I didn't mind. I'm used to it."

Her interest in AJ shifted up a notch when they were around other people. The way he conducted himself, his unconscious ease when he made conversation, and his genuine interest in the lives of others without it stemming from idle gossip, intrigued her.

Liz pulled the Range Rover into the driveway and parked in the space for visitors' cars. The air had cooled, and as they strolled the pebbled path to the cottage gate, AJ grabbed her gently by the shoulders, pulled her backward and gestured toward the heavens. "Liz. Look at the stars."

She looked up. The sky was as clear as she'd ever seen it since arriving in the UK and she marveled at the unfamiliar sight. "Isn't it amazing?" she said. "We're standing on the same earth as my family back home, yet the northern sky is as unique as the southern."

He indicated with his index finger, his other hand still on her shoulder. "See that one there? That's Andromeda, then Capella." AJ continued to point. "The little house in the middle is Cepheus, and over there, Vega."

She shivered, the warmth of his touch having the opposite effect to his apparent intention. "You never cease to amaze me."

"Funny," he said. "I often think the same about you."

Liz closed her eyes briefly and let his words wash over her. "It's freezing. I'm going inside."

She felt him let go, sensed him following her, and as the door shut behind them, she considered the possibilities.

Inside, the cottage radiated warmth, the slow burning wood fire doing a stellar job. AJ stood behind her and helped her out of her jacket, the closeness of his breath edgy on her skin. She questioned her decision to come for the hundredth time, his presence overwhelming her sensibility as her desire expressed itself in a conflicting physical nuisance.

"Feel free to use the bathroom first. I'm going to listen to music for a while."

There was no reason for her to sit with him. No reason at all. And anyway, he didn't offer the opportunity. The air remained thick with expectancy. "Okay, thanks. I'll see you in the morning. Goodnight."

He smiled softly. She wanted to reach out and tell him everything—and nothing. To snuggle in bed beside him. To be held in his warmth. She didn't want to sleep alone in his home-away-from-home bed while he slept on the sofa in the living room. Every time her sensible inner voice screamed they shouldn't, her reckless voice told her they should.

"Goodnight, Lizzy," he murmured. "Sleep well."

Liz slipped between sheets warmed by an electric blanket. She hated wearing a nightshirt but didn't want to sleep naked while AJ lounged on the sofa with his headphones on. She often slept poorly in strange beds, but as she snuggled down under the covers, an odd contentment relaxed her.

Saturday dawned a glorious day, with a baby-blue sky and a freshness to the air Liz missed when in London. AJ was up making breakfast in the kitchenette when she bounced out of bed, her headspace uncluttered and clear.

He glanced over his shoulder and smiled. "Morning. How did you sleep?"

"Great. You?"

"Not bad." His expression said otherwise. "I thought we could shoot into Cambridge. Have a look around in the daylight."

"I promised Max and Indie I'd take them for a walk later."

"Okay, they can come too. Give Zoe a break. David's a great dad, but she doesn't get much alone time."

"I never imagined you spending time with children."

"Excuse me. I'm the world's number one uncle—according to them, anyway. We hang out all the time when they're here. Go to movies, eat ice cream and popcorn. They love it."

"I bet."

"I think it's safer to have breakfast here. Less chaos." He offered her a bowl. "Muesli?"

"Please."

AJ sat two bowls on the small round table in the living space, along with blueberries and yogurt.

She helped herself and took a mouthful. "Yum, this is just like mine."

"Busted." He smiled. "I always bring some with me. It keeps me going, if you get my drift."

Liz had almost forgotten how charming he could be when he relaxed. "So that's where it disappears to."

Liz watched AJ's interaction with Max and Indie with amusement. He looked like the same man—same clothes, same hair tied back —yet this AJ displayed none of the dogmatic personality of London AJ. This AJ chased, joked, and laughed, displaying qualities required for the position of a perfect father.

AJ stopped and waited for Liz to catch up as the children ran ahead. "What are you thinking about?" he asked.

You! "You don't want to know."

"Dobson, if I didn't know better, I'd say you're checking out those guys over there."

"What guys?"

"The ones working out."

"I am not." Liz craned her neck. "But now you've pointed them out, it's not a bad view."

"Ever think about dating again?"

She struggled to interpret his out-of-the-blue question. "Sometimes, but not so much after what happened with Peter." They walked in silence for a few minutes, Liz feeling a renewed intimacy between them. "What about you? When was the last time you dated?"

"I'm not really the dating type."

"Uncle AJ?" Indie's call broke the mood, but he'd given her the message. Loud and clear. He wasn't the dating type.

"May we have ice cream if we promise to be especially good?"

"Sure." He grabbed Indie's hand. "Come on guys, let's go find an ice cream truck."

By the time they arrived back at Tancroft, the children were asleep, and the day had cooled along with the colors of the sky. AJ opened the car door and carefully lifted Indie out of her car seat. He carried her inside and lowered her onto the sofa before going back for Max.

"What time are we due at the restaurant?" AJ asked Marielena.

"Around six thirty. We don't want to be late with the children coming."

"How many people are you expecting?"

"About ninety."

"What?" AJ laughed. "That's a real baptism by fire for Liz. You told her it was a small family affair."

"She'll cope, won't you, Liz?"

"I'll be fine. I'm used to large family parties."

"Okay," AJ said to his mother. "We'll be back over around six."

As soon as she entered the cottage, Liz flopped down on the sofa, longing to relax for a few minutes, the hustle and bustle of the week suddenly taking its toll. "I might read for a bit."

"Sure, I'll be upstairs."

She slipped into the bedroom, removed her jeans and top for the sake of comfort, and snuggled under a blanket with her e-reader, not even bothering to turn it on.

The loft held a studio of sorts where AJ worked occasionally. He painted differently in the country. The energy surrounding Tancroft guaranteed it. Sitting on a small stool in the middle of the room, he studied the half-finished works. He thought inviting Liz here might have stirred his artistic imagination, but it had had the opposite effect. The only thing stirring was his sexual frustration.

He came downstairs later to find Liz sound asleep on the bed, her face smooth—minus worry and strain. She looked beautiful in slumber. He longed to paint her naked and lately, images of her reclining on the makeshift bed in his studio, the light from the tiny window above casting angular shadows over her skin, flooded his thoughts. Now the perfect opportunity arose. He reached for his camera, stood at the bedroom door, and clicked off a couple of shots, trying to recall—unsuccessfully—what she looked like under the blanket.

"Hey, come on you." He wiggled her toes. "Time to get dressed."

"Sorry, I must have dozed off." Her voice, husky with sleep, reminded him of the first time they kissed. She reached up into a stretch. His breath caught as she exposed her bra before quickly covering herself. "What time is it?"

He checked his watch. "Nearly five thirty. You use the shower first." He smiled. "Or we could share and save on hot water."

"You're hilarious. Who would have guessed?"

AJ grinned as the locks on both bathroom doors clicked. His small attempt to flirt went okay. At least she didn't seem upset by it.

By the time AJ had finished in the bathroom, Liz was dressed and ready, with full makeup and her dark curls cascading below her shoulders. He'd seen her do this at home. Get ready in five minutes flat. And while she always wore makeup when venturing out of the house, it was usually muted, in both tone and application.

Tonight, sultry plum lipstick—matte and begging to be bitten off—coated her plump lips, and her eyes conveyed untold secrets with the aid of winged eyeliner and a smudge of smoky shadow.

She sported a little black dress, a halter-neck number with a tight-fitting bodice and a full skirt that fell above the knee. A stiff bow, just large enough to make a statement, joined the seam between skirt and bodice. Made from silk-like material, it reminded him of movies from the fifties.

Nude-colored heels with thin ankle straps graced her feet, and pearl drop earrings—vintage style once again—hung from soft earlobes. Earlobes he had once kissed before she called his name repeatedly and came apart beneath him.

"Holy shit," he muttered under his breath. He wanted to reach out and touch her—hold her, kiss her. "Look at you." He noticed an uncomfortable shift in her stance and recalled her words about Peter and his never-ending critique.

"Am I overdressed?" Liz looked at him for approval, her worry turning into a concerned frown.

"Hell no." He laughed as he grabbed her coat from the chair, holding it up for her to slip into. "And smile, Lizzy, serious doesn't suit you." He turned her to face him and planted a light kiss on her forehead. Such a simple gesture, and yet intimate. "Come on. We'd better get out the door before I do something I'll never regret. You look like a gorgeous starlet from a nineteen fifties French movie."

She rewarded him with the most amazing smile. He relaxed. *Let the dance begin.*

On the drive to the restaurant, AJ kept stealing sideways glances at the beautiful girl in the black dress. His sight drifted up and down briefly before returning to the road. Anna, Charlotte, and their older sister, Sarah, sat in the back. They chatted and took selfies, oblivious to the tension radiating from the front seat. Liz sat upright, her hands clasped together. Did she want him as much as he wanted her? It would certainly break the tension—and create a lot more.

The restaurant, which was closed for the occasion, reminded Liz of one she'd seen in a recent movie. Outside, at least a dozen tables and chairs sat under a vine-covered pergola, and an enormous outdoor fire crackled in the background. Colorful lanterns swayed in the light breeze, and in one corner, a band played a mix of easy listening classics. Liz imagined how it would look in the summer, with the vine in full bloom.

She instinctively reached for AJ's hand, but quickly let go once she'd realized her mistake. If he noticed, he didn't seem to mind. As they moved through the crowd, he placed his hand on the small of her back as if that's where it belonged.

"Brad, meet my friend Liz," AJ said as they stopped at the bar. "Another London local."

"Liz, it's a pleasure. I'm AJ's cousin." Brad offered his hand, then stood back in admiration. "I like a girl in a little black dress with a firm handshake."

Liz felt the heat of a shy blush lift the color of her cheeks. She didn't notice much about Brad's facial features, concentrating more on his height and immaculate persona. He had large hands and perfectly groomed nails. The only time Liz had groomed nails was when she left the beauticians. The rest of the time, they were broken, picked at, and chewed.

"Watch him. He's on the lookout for a beautiful girl with a bank balance to match his own," AJ whispered into her ear as Brad's attention turned briefly to someone else. "Okay, what's everyone drinking? Liz, white wine?"

"Please."

"Brad?"

"Yeah, I could go another beer, thanks. And I think Gary wants you for something. Don't worry about Liz. I'll take good care of her."

AJ winked at Liz, gave the bartender their order, then left to help his dad.

Without the smoldering appearance of AJ's Spanish heritage,

Brad looked nothing like his cousin. Even so, he conveyed a certain cosmopolitan charm and an accent that reminded her of Ivan's. *Of course.*

"I know your father," Liz said. "He's my lawyer."

"Well, your affairs are in excellent hands. Ivan runs a tight ship." Brad maintained eye contact as if Liz were the most fascinating girl in the room.

"And he's so sweet."

Brad smiled. "I rarely see that side of him."

It turned out Brad worked as a merchant banker. He and AJ were roughly the same age, but that's where the similarities ended. And as AJ moved between his friends and relatives, Liz hid her nails as best she could and Brad the banker didn't leave her side.

"I hope you don't mind me asking, but are you and AJ an item?"

What could she say? Only in her dreams? "No, not at all."

"Sorry, I assumed you were his girlfriend. Although I've never known him to have a long-term relationship. He's more of a love-them-and-leave-them kind of guy. A serial heartbreaker."

Liz wished people would stop telling her AJ was a player who shattered hearts into tiny splinters everywhere he went. She'd read the memo, even did a test drive and crashed badly. Time to repeat the usual mantra. "We're housemates and business associates, nothing more."

"Okay. In that case, would you like to grab a coffee sometime?" He pulled out his phone from his pocket. "What's your number?"

Liz hesitated, then gave Brad her number as AJ approached.

"What's going on here?" AJ slid his arm around her waist as he addressed Brad. "You're not trying to pick up my date, are you?"

"Would I do that? I suggested Liz and I have coffee sometime soon."

"Sounds like a plan."

Brad chuckled. "You don't make the cut."

"What? Piss off."

Still grinning, AJ reached for Liz's hand and pulled her away from his cousin. "Sorry, mate, we have people to meet." He moved Liz into the crowd, but rather than introduce her to anyone else, made a beeline for the dance floor. He laughed at the look on her face.

"Relax, Lizzy. It's a dance, not a seduction." His left hand slid to the small of her back as he held her close. She pulled back slightly, creating a distance she didn't want to create. He glanced down at her. His smile told the tale. She wanted him, and he knew it.

***

Apart from that one dance, AJ spent most of the evening watching Liz out of the corner of his eye as she partied with his sisters. If he didn't know better, he'd think she'd had one too many wines. Self-conscious Lizzy was nowhere in sight. He never imagined this side of her existed, and he found it arousing to the point of distraction.

AJ noticed the direction of Brad's gaze and went to stake his claim.

"What's the story with you and Liz?" Brad asked, not taking his eyes off her.

"No story. A little narrative, maybe. The chapters are still in my head."

"Do you mind if I ask her out?"

AJ kept his focus on Liz as well. "What do you think?"

"I could say all's fair in lust and war."

"But you won't."

"Let me know when she delivers the rejection speech."

AJ laughed. "It's already been delivered. Still, you know me, mate. Always want what I can't have."

"I didn't think you'd be her type."

"I'm her type. She just doesn't know it yet."

After Marielena had cut the cake and made a heartfelt speech leaving everyone with lumps in their throats, AJ guided Liz back to their table.

"So, boring Brad has your number, does he?" he asked as they ate the decadent chocolate cake that he'd promised.

"That's no way to talk about your cousin."

He shrugged. "I can see the appeal. He's not bad looking, wears preppy sweaters draped around his shoulders at the golf club, and is a serial monogamist." He chuckled. "And he's a nice guy. What more could a girl possibly want."

"He sounds perfect." She flashed him a coy smile. "What's the catch?"

AJ leaned closer. "Well, according to one of my friends who dated him when we were younger, his skills as a lover are sadly lacking. That's not what you want."

"Excuse me? And you have an opinion on what I want, do you?"

"I have an opinion on most things." He grabbed her fork and took a bite of her cake. "You gonna eat the rest?"

She playfully yanked the fork out of his hand. "Yes, I am. Get your own."

Plates of cake in hand, Zoe and the children joined Liz and AJ at their table.

"This is very yummy cake. Very, very yummy," Max said in his proper English accent.

"Share it with your favorite uncle?" AJ pleaded dramatically.

"Where's yours?" Max asked.

AJ patted his stomach.

"Mummy says cake is only a sometimes food, don't you, Mummy?"

"I do," Zoe said.

"What?" AJ grinned. "Surely not."

"Right." Zoe pushed her unfinished plate toward AJ. "It's nearly midnight. Let's get you kids home to bed." She turned to

AJ. "I'm having trouble dragging that husband of mine away. I'd better call a cab. I don't think I'm fit to drive."

"I'll drive you," Liz said. "I'm about ready for bed. We can pick up my car tomorrow."

AJ turned to Liz with a smile. "Are you sure? I won't be much longer. I'm feeling pretty hammered."

32

CONVERSATIONS

IT WAS after three a.m. when AJ crashed through the door of the cottage. Turning on every light he could find, he made a beeline for the bedroom and flopped face down on the bed—drunk and ready to chat.

"Sorry, Lizzy, did I wake you? You weren't asleep, were you?"

"I was. Go to bed. You're drunk."

"I'm not. Well, maybe a bit." He rolled onto his back and placed his hands behind his head. "I had the best night. I love my Mum."

"I'm glad. Now get off my bed. I've made up the sofa."

"I hate that sofa. It's so uncomfortable. Hardly slept at all last night. You don't mind, do you—if I share your bed? It's plenty big enough for two. You're so…kind of tiny. Tallish, but tiny."

"I do mind."

"Really? No, you don't." He waited for her response. "Come on, talk to me. I love our conversations, Lizzy."

"AJ, it's three in the morning."

"Is it? *Shit*. We have to get up soon." He took a deep breath. "I've been thinking about what you need in a man."

"Have you now?" She tried to push his dead weight off the bed. "Save it for another day."

"I like it when you get all physical." He giggled, pushing her back playfully. "No, don't. Don't push me. You're making me feel seasick. I have to say it while it's fresh in my mind. Then I'll go to sleep, okay?" He tried to stay serious. "Okay, Lizzy?"

"AJ, go to bloody bed."

He turned onto his side to look at her and giggled again. Vapors of alcohol rushed at her nostrils. "You're swearing at me. It means you have passion. I knew it. You have passion. Anyway"—he took a deep breath—"you need a man who takes your face in his hands and kisses you like he means it. A man who desires you. One who loves you sooooo deeply, when he makes love to you, you're oblivious to time or space."

Out of the mouths of the drunk and giggly. "Really?"

"Yep. Brad's not your guy. You'd be exchanging passion for stability and a school carpool." He reached for her hand and wouldn't let go. "Anyhow, I have the perfect man for you. I want you to meet him one day soon."

"You really do rate yourself, don't you?"

"We're friends. Friends talk to each other, and I'm only reminding you of your critique of the Jacobs. I bet when you were with that fuck-wit Peter Nichols, you were totally aware of time and space, even in the bedroom. Am I right?"

"You're telling the story." Liz pushed herself off the bed and moved to the bedroom door.

"Sleep with me, Lizzy. Just this once. We could play naughty teenagers and—"

"I don't think so."

"Help me get undressed, then. I love being undressed by beautiful women. Especially one in a"—he looked up, squinting to see what she had on—"blue and white striped flannel nightshirt."

She went to walk away.

"Hey, Liz? Liz?"

She turned back.

"If I wasn't hammered, would you kiss me goodnight? Just this…"

Liz stood at the end of the bed and smiled. He was asleep and probably wouldn't remember much of anything in the morning.

"I would," she murmured and closed the door.

AJ was right. The sofa bed was extremely uncomfortable. After what seemed like hours of tossing and turning, Liz eventually fell asleep, although strange dreams came thick and fast.

Sun streaming through the leadlight windows in the entry door woke her gently. She slipped out of bed and stretched upward, smiling at the sight of AJ sprawled on the bed in the adjoining room.

While in the shower, thoughts of AJ's property suggestion gained interest. Besides the practical advantages of separating their professional and private lives, the prospect of owning a London home excited her. She couldn't wait to start looking.

She cut the water and wrapped herself in a towel.

"Lizzy?" AJ called from the bedroom, his voice no more than a croak. "Liz? I need you."

She found him spread-eagled on his front, upside down on the mattress, one arm dangling over the edge of the bed, the other holding his head. "Are you all right?"

"I need water and painkillers. I have the worst headache." He squinted as he looked at her. "Whatever you do, don't open the curtains. And put some clothes on. Shit!"

Liz giggled and reached for her robe.

"It's not funny."

"No, it's hilarious."

She grabbed a bottle of water from the kitchenette, popped two paracetamol from her bag into her palm, then quickly swapped the towel for the robe.

"Here, take these."

His hand shook as he took the bottle. "Thanks." He relaxed back on the bed and covered his eyes with his forearm. "You're a lovely nurse. It's almost worth the hangover."

"The kids want a story. Shall I send them in?"

"Don't be a bitch. It doesn't suit you. What am I doing in your bed? Shit, Liz, you didn't take advantage of me, did you?" He chuckled at his own joke. "How could you? I was hammered."

"I slept on the sofa."

"Why didn't you push me out?"

"You think I didn't try?"

Bright light flooded in through the French doors and across AJ's face. He looked around the room. Liz's greenstone heart bracelet and pearl earrings sat on top of the chest of drawers, and her dress hung from a hanger on a hook behind the bedroom door. But she was gone.

AJ reached for his watch lying on the floor beside the nightstand. Over four hours had passed since Liz had played nurse, and his headache had returned with a vengeance. He sat on the edge of the bed. A frustrating erection stood like a tent pole in his boxers, and his mouth tasted like he'd eaten a vodka-soaked newspaper. The throb in his head reminded him of why he didn't get drunk often. The throb elsewhere made him question why hungover and horny went together—and not nicely. He needed a cold shower.

When AJ walked into the main house half an hour later, apart from his mother, the place was deserted.

"Morning, Mum. Where's Liz?"

Marielena moved around the kitchen, setting out lunch as AJ slumped at the dining table. "Off for a walk with Anna to pick up her car. And it's afternoon. You look terrible. Almost as bad as your brother."

"Feel worse. I'm never drinking shots again."

His mother raised a brow. "Spare me the resolutions. I'm glad Liz didn't see you in that state."

"Oh, she saw me all right. I woke up this morning in her bed." He rested his head on the table, needing a second to recall what happened after three a.m. "Shit, I can't remember what I said. We had a deep and meaningful conversation about something, though."

"Deep and meaningful? If I know you, Anthony Tanner, a load of obnoxious rubbish peppered with how wonderful you are would be more like it."

"Mum!" He feigned mock indignation. "How can you say that about your favorite son? Anyway, I'll remember it later. Shit!"

"Watch the language." Marielena placed a mug of black coffee in front of him. She leaned on the counter, arms crossed. "She's a lovely girl. Are you lovers?"

"What? Give it a rest, Marielena."

"The way you look at each other... Anyway, everybody thinks you're keen on her."

"Is that right?"

"Aren't you? When are you going to settle down and give me another *nieto*?"

"Mum, we don't need to have this conversation. Liz is nursing hurt from a broken relationship. It's not cut and dried."

"Look, if you want her, make a move. She won't stay single for long. All this rebound rubbish. Why wait if you're perfect for each other?"

Garry entered the kitchen carrying a basket of fresh eggs from the henhouse. "Who won't stay single for long?"

"We were discussing Liz. A private conversation between mother and son."

Garry reached around his wife's waist and kissed the back of her neck. "We don't have secrets from each other, do we?"

"Would you two stop. If you want to fondle, do it in private,"

AJ said, still leaning on the table with his head in his hands. "You're ruining my chaste impression of you both."

"You're just jealous." Garry laughed. "It's time you settled down, Anthony Jacob Tanner. Liz is a nice girl, and she's a Kiwi. Kiwi girls are usually good cooks."

"Not you too. I told you, we're not in a relationship and it's complicated."

"Easily changed," Garry said. "But you better get a move on."

"Yeah, well, my net worth is about zero, so I don't have much to offer, do I?"

"Why should that matter? We had a beat-up V-dub and four hundred pounds when we got married, didn't we, darling?" Garry said.

"That's the whole point, Dad. Liz and I are not in the same financial position. In fact, she's seriously wealthy. Very, very seriously wealthy, as Max would say."

"Is it family money?" Marielena asked.

"No. She's built a company from scratch. All I've got going for me is charm, a few worthless canvases, and a stuck-in-red-tape heritage listed building. Not that I'm intimidated by her wealth, but still—"

"Your modesty knows no bounds," his mother said.

"So, she's wealthy, sweet-natured, and beautiful. Sounds perfect to me." Garry continued to grin at his son. "And your brother and sisters approve."

AJ watched his mother set a platter of baked chicken, various salads, and a basket of fresh bread rolls in the middle of the kitchen table, and swallowed hard. He couldn't stomach a salad.

"Afternoon, AJ," Sarah said as she walked into the kitchen still in her pajamas, followed by Anna and Liz. "You look ghastly."

"So people keep saying. I'm feeling a lot better than I was, thanks to Liz." He gave Liz a faint smile. "She condescended to give me water and painkillers at eight o'clock this morning."

"I didn't condescend," Liz said. "I was very supportive."

"Yeah, especially when you were going to let Max and Indie into the cottage to jump on my bed."

"Serves you right," Anna said. "You boys never learn."

"Cook me bacon and eggs, Anna," he pleaded. "I need grease."

"Mum's made a beautiful lunch," Anna replied. "If you want grease, make it yourself."

"I'm not up to cooking."

"I'll do it." Liz smiled at AJ. "If you don't mind me using your kitchen, Marielena?"

"Of course not, dear. You go right ahead."

AJ shook his head as Liz put the plate in front of him ten minutes later. Eggs—sunny side up—bacon, mushrooms, and hash browns, with two rounds of toast on the side.

He glanced up and smiled. "What did I do to deserve you?"

A hush fell over the kitchen as all eyes looked their way.

"So, Liz." Garry cleared his throat. "Are you joining us for Christmas? We'd love to have you."

"Thank you, that's so kind. But I'm spending Christmas with my aunt and uncle, Nate's mum and dad."

"Of course," Gary said. "Right, let's eat. Anna, go tell the others lunch is ready, would you?"

All through lunch, AJ kept glancing at Liz out of the corner of his eye. He knew he'd held an all-important bullshit conversation with her at three in the morning, but he still couldn't remember what he'd said. It can't have been too bad. She was as sweet as pie as she enjoyed the meal and joked with his family. As he ate, small snippets of their chat, or rather, his verbal diarrhea, flicked through his mind. Just as he remembered asking her to sleep with him, kiss him, and undress him, she looked up, flaunting a sweet smile.

The drive back to London dragged with heavy traffic. Persistent drizzle accompanied by the dull light of the afternoon made visibility difficult. AJ slept most of the way while Liz sang along to Opshop and Hozier streaming from his phone. Once they neared Woodford, Liz pulled onto an off ramp. "Are you up to driving? London traffic makes me nervous."

AJ stretched. "Sure. I'm good." He gave her a quick smile as they swapped places and, once back on the road, glanced her way. "You have a beautiful voice."

"I thought you were asleep."

"Nah, just listening to an angel as I drifted in and out of heavenly bliss." He chuckled. "I had to open my eyes to make sure you were real."

Liz loved AJ's laugh. And, as usual, his smile completely changed his expression, from moody to mellow. "Just drive."

"You don't like compliments?"

"My sister, Ally, is the singer in our family. She sang in bands in high school. She's one of those good at everything kind of kids —sporty, smart, and gorgeous."

"I still like your voice better."

"How can you make a comparison? You don't even know her."

He shrugged. "I'm a budding musician. I know what I like."

Liz looked out the window as the traffic increased in density. AJ sang in the shower occasionally, his voice best described as interesting.

"Stop it," he said with a grin. "You're making judgments about my shower singing."

"I am not."

He laughed. "Liar. One of the most prolific songwriters of our time has a unique voice that one would never call beautiful, but it doesn't mean he's not fascinating to listen to."

"Who's that?"

"Burt Bacharach."

"Bit before my time, but I do have a favorite Burt song."

"Let me guess. *I Say a Little Prayer* from that Julia Roberts movie."

"No. *A House is Not a Home*. What's yours?"

He glanced her way. *"The Look of Love."*

That was the moment Liz realized how much she'd enjoyed the weekend and how much she liked AJ the person. Sexual attraction aside, she realized AJ Tanner was a lovely guy—a very, very lovely guy. "Great song. My mother loves Dusty Springfield."

"Sing it for me."

Liz shook her head. She leaned back on the headrest as she recalled the DJ playing *The Look of Love* at her parent's twentieth wedding anniversary party. She'd loved that song ever since.

When they arrived home, AJ took a second shower for the day, trying not to think about his drunken babble and current horny status.

He entered the kitchen and made a beeline for the curry simmering on the cooktop. "I'm starving." He had a taste, then another one. "This is so good. Did you make it from scratch?"

Liz dished rice into a bowl and placed it on the table. "Kiwi girls always cook from scratch."

"That's an urban legend, isn't it?" He sat in the booth, the aroma of the meal reminding him of home and contentment. "Why are you being nice to me after last night?"

"So, you remember your ramblings?"

"Ramblings? Interesting word," he said as he loaded his plate. "Small snippets. I'd call it bullshit, though."

She slipped into the booth opposite. "It's okay. You'd been drinking. Not that I know what it's like to be drunk, but I understand it makes you say and do things out of the norm."

"What, you've never been drunk?"

"Or stoned."

"You've never smoked a naughty cigarette?" AJ shoveled another forkful of curry and rice into his mouth, smiling as if he had a private joke. "This curry's fantastic. So, you've never been drunk or stoned, ever?"

"Maybe Brad and I would make a good match. We could be boring together."

He shook his head. "Nah. He's not your type."

"Really? You have an opinion on everything, don't you?"

"Don't most people?" AJ mopped up the remnants of his curry with naan bread, then pushed his plate aside. "That was amazing. Thank you."

She smiled. "I'm glad you enjoyed it."

"I could help you get drunk one night if you're up for a new experience. Not stoned, though. Smoked a few joints in college, makes me paranoid and overly…"

"What?"

He cocked a brow, his grin full of cheek. "You know—"

"Hungry? I've heard that."

AJ enjoyed it when Liz got a little flirty. "Yes, that's the term. Overly *hungry*." He winked.

"After what you went through today, I think I'll pass on getting drunk." Liz took both plates to the sink and began tidying up. "What does your friend do for a living?"

"Who?"

"My perfect match. The man bursting with desire."

"Oh, him." AJ picked up the last piece of naan bread from the basket and broke it in half. "He's a struggling artist."

"Hmm. I don't do struggling males, unless he knows nothing about me. Guys can get a bit weird with the money thing."

"You don't *do* them?" His smile lit up his whole face.

She felt the heat creep up her neck. The more they talked, the finer his form became. "Stop it. You know what I mean."

"And how do you feel about it? The money thing?"

"Doesn't worry me. My work isn't about money. Having a steady income is important, but I'd survive without it. It's all about cutting your cloth."

He leaned back and held her gaze. "For a girl, you have few material needs."

"You think? I'm about to go shopping for an expensive piece of London real estate, remember."

"That's different from having hundreds of pairs of shoes and lots of bling. Investing in real estate you're passionate about is a wise move, especially in our market."

"I guess." She checked her watch. "Right, I'm off to bed. Thanks so much for the weekend. I enjoyed being part of a family again. Goodnight."

"Sleep well." AJ watched her leave the kitchen and smiled. The weekend had been a success.

The week before Christmas, Liz met Nate, who was in London staying with his parents, at a small café near Oxford Circus. Liz loved the atmosphere of the inner city at Christmas, even when the day turned dull and dreary after a promising start. They exchanged hugs and hellos, then sat at a table by the window overlooking the busy street.

"How's it going here?" Nate asked. "With AJ, I mean? You never mention him in your emails."

Liz suspected Nate had asked AJ to keep an eye on her. "It's good. He doesn't seem to be moving out anytime soon. Not that he's a problem."

"And what about your love life?"

"No love life. I'm on a man diet." She giggled. "The cravings are a bit of a problem, though."

Nate chuckled and looked out onto the street as he sipped his coffee. "You and AJ make a good pair, then. His friends say he's in sexile."

"What? What is sexile?"

"As it sounds. Sexual exile. He decided that when he went to

Asia, he'd be celibate for two years."

"No way!" As much as she tried, Liz couldn't imagine AJ celibate for two days, let alone two years. She pondered the absurdity of it for a moment before her initial assessment stood. AJ Tanner couldn't possibly be celibate. Could he?

"I shouldn't be telling you this," Nate said, "but to be honest, I thought he may have said something. We give him stick about it all the time."

"Why? That's mean."

"Because he's a reformed man-whore. No one thought he'd follow it through. He won't let on either way, the sneaky bastard."

"Well, he never has anyone back to the terrace. I've seen him flirt lots, though—when he's out."

"He probably takes them back to his art studio to show them his oils."

"He has a studio?" Liz questioned. "You never said."

"Didn't I? He studied art when we were younger. Lately, his focus has intensified. Surely you've seen his work."

She frowned. "No. I don't think so."

"Maybe he wants to keep things on the down low until he's famous."

Liz wondered why AJ hadn't mentioned his studio or paintings. "Maybe, but when you know who people are, what they do, it's easier to channel the respect they deserve. It's not about being nosy, it's about understanding the essence of them as a person."

Nate nodded. "Judgments, eh? They get all of us in the shit at times. Apart from the arty farty side of him, there's nothing much to tell. You know the rest."

"Do you think he's seeing anyone?"

"He's certainly got his boxers in a twist over someone, but he's not saying who. I thought it might be you."

"What? It's not me."

"Are you sure?" A soft grin slipped into form. "Your protest seems a little too eager."

"Don't be ridiculous. He's my business advisor." She giggled. "Although…"

"One word," Nate cautioned. "History."

Liz pulled a face. If history was going to repeat itself, she wished it would hurry up and happen.

"All I'm saying is, be careful. AJ has a certain way with the ladies when he puts his mind to it." Nate laughed at her facial response. "If he has you in his sights, you won't stand a chance. And he did take you to Tancroft to meet the family."

"Would you stop?"

"Your relationship hasn't moved up a notch, then?"

"Definitely not." Liz felt the heat of a blush and wondered if Nate had noticed.

"All that aside, it's good to see you've got some spark back."

"Yes, sometimes you never realize it's gone until you look in the mirror one day at the dull expression reflected back."

33

A PICTURE TELLS...

LIZ WALKED into the living room to find AJ slouched on the sofa, his feet jutting out over the arm, and bass guitar in hand. He looked up and smiled.

"Can you send me some of those photos from the weekend?" She asked. "I'd like to email a couple to Mum and Dad."

"Sure." AJ picked up his phone from the coffee table. His index finger hurried across the screen. "Done."

"Cool, thanks." Liz put the kettle on, then opened the email and downloaded the zip file. She scrolled through the photos. When she came to the one of her asleep at the cottage, she took a second look.

Frowning, Liz picked up the laptop and walked into the living room. "Why do you have these photos of me?"

He didn't look up. "I was taking photos all weekend, of everyone."

"AJ, you took two photos of me asleep on the bed. Why?" Liz looked back and forth from the image to AJ. "I want you to delete them right now."

He hesitated. "You looked so peaceful. I didn't mean any harm."

"What were you thinking? This is a total abuse of my trust."

"What? It's a couple of photos. Get a life." AJ stood and moved into the kitchen. He took two mugs from the shelf above the kettle and added a tea bag to each one.

"It's not only the photos."

"Let it go, Liz. It won't happen again."

"All this...this interest in my private life. I can't live or work with you under these circumstances."

He flicked the switch of the kettle to bring the water back to the boil. "Don't start this again. I suppose you're going to run to Ivan and tell him I've been a naughty boy, are you?"

"Of course not. But lately the line between our professional and private lives has blurred."

"And your point?"

"We need to step back."

"Why? We're friends. Friends do things together. Friends take pictures of one another."

"I'm half naked for Pete's sake. And asleep!"

"You're covered with a blanket," he said as he filled the mugs. "And it's not like I haven't seen it all before."

"You prick. Whether you've seen *it* all before isn't the issue and you know it." She wanted to yell—scream—at him for his insensitive comments but stayed calm. "Did it never occur to you I'd be upset about this?" Liz hated how some men defended themselves no matter what, wouldn't admit wrongdoing or back down. "What's your problem?"

"I don't have the problem, you do. You've tied yourself up in knots and hung yourself out to dry, out of reach of people who care about you."

"And it's your job to make judgments about me, is it?" Emotion caught in her throat and her eyes stung with heat. She looked up and blinked several times, embarrassed by her physical reaction.

He stepped forward, his gaze softening into a pleading request. "I don't know. I feel protective of you."

She stepped back. "Well, don't. I don't need you or any man running my life. I've been there, done that with Peter. In the end, I hated myself—"

"See, this is what I mean." AJ raised his voice up a notch. "Why do you say these things? You're better than that."

"Because... I was never enough for him. Wasn't sexy enough, thin enough, perfect enough. I wasn't enough." A sob greeted the words, but Liz swallowed it down. "And he never wanted me. Do you know what it's like to lie next to someone you're in a relation-ship with and not have them touch you? You question who you are, your essence as a woman."

"Liz... I'm so sorry. Please—"

"And you," she interrupted. "You think you can tell me who I should and shouldn't date. I was flattered when Brad paid me attention. But he's not right for me, apparently. So, what do I do now? Log on to Tinder and hope some guy swipes right?"

"You know why I don't want you to date Brad," he yelled. "If you'll give me a chance—"

"I don't want to hear it," she yelled back. "I can't be around you right now. We need to redraw the line and stay the hell put. You on your side, me on mine."

"Fine." AJ leaned closer. "But just remember one thing," he whispered, his breath hot on her neck. "I'd swipe right for you any day of the week. Understand?"

"And then what? We'd have an unforgettable few hours before you walked out the door at four in the morning without even a backward glance."

"So that's it? You can't let it go, can you? Have to live in the past."

"It's not about living in the past. It's about safeguarding my future."

"Really? Well, I glanced back. You dismissed me with one

swift tap of the decline button. So don't blame me for what happened. I seem to recall you were just as happy about fucking me as I was about fucking you. At least you finally admit it was unforgettable."

He reached over, grabbed his jacket from the back of the chair and stormed out of the house, slamming the door behind him, the two mugs of green tea left to go cold on the kitchen counter.

On her way to work the following day, Liz wondered where AJ had slept, then decided it was none of her business. That kind of questioning smacked of needy desperation. She'd never cast herself as a needy girl, and she wasn't about to start.

Liz usually enjoyed her job, but not today. She hated arguments—didn't need a good old verbal tussle to rid herself of frustration. For her, yelling had the opposite effect. It chewed her up inside. And as she climbed the stairs to the office, she couldn't shake the feeling of regret.

Sophie looked up as she entered the foyer. "Morning. You've just missed AJ. He left you this." She handed Liz a folded note.

Liz glanced at the text.

Liz,
I'll be unavailable for the next few days.
Please call Kelly if required.
AJ.

She folded the paper back in half and slipped it into her bag. The guy had a phone, why didn't he just text her.

"Is everything okay?" Sophie asked. "He seemed distracted."

"We had an argument. He left in a huff after I yelled at him. Then I stayed awake half the night worrying—chewing up my words along with my gut."

"He didn't come home at all?"

"Nope. It may sound silly, but it's comforting to know he's asleep across the hall, even if he doesn't get in until well after midnight sometimes."

"I know it's none of my business, but don't you think it's about time you let him in?"

"Not you too. Why do people assume we're destined to be together? Involved?"

"You're already involved. He looks at you like he holds all your secrets. Like he's yours, and you're his. I assumed you were doing the wild thing already."

Liz smiled, seeing the funny side. "I wish."

Sophie burst out laughing. "So, you've never…you know?"

Liz shot Sophie a sideways glance, her lips pressed firmly together.

"O.M.G. You have so," Sophie said. "It's written all over your openly expressive face."

"It is not."

"So? Was it good, bad, or indifferent? Did he rock your world and send you to heaven? Or did you mentally write your grocery list while staring at the plaster molding on the ceiling?"

Liz hesitated. She knew she shouldn't be discussing AJ with Sophie, but their light-hearted conversation had lifted her spirits. "Let's just say I never thought about the supermarket once, *or* the moldings."

Sophie nodded as if she understood just how good AJ was at 'you know.'

"He did the whole wall thing the first time we kissed," Liz said with a thoughtful smile.

Sophie's eyes widened. "What, pushed you up against the wall and kissed you like he meant it?"

"Yep. I've never told anyone before."

"You lucky girl. What's he like as a kisser?"

Liz scraped her teeth over her bottom lip.

"Shit." Sophie sighed. "He's amazing, isn't he?"

"Yes. But I don't do casual well, and AJ's the casual type."

"But you're hot for him, yeah?"

"Oh, he could lure me into sexual temptation any day of the week, but it's a complication I don't need. Especially while we're living and working together."

"You know what I think?" Sophie didn't wait for an answer. "The guy's mad about you."

"He's mad, but not about me. In fact, he's got quite a temper. We're like an old married couple. We live and work together, and fight like crazy. I even ironed some of his shirts the other day. What was I thinking?"

"Well, we all know what breeds anger. Frustration. He needs to get laid."

Liz laughed. "He probably gets laid most nights of the week and twice on Sundays. He often reeks of the scent of women who give their favors for little more than a compliment."

"We really are feeling dramatic today, aren't we? But just remember one thing. Men need encouragement. They don't always respond to the 'treat them mean, keep them keen' cliché."

"Right. Thanks for the advice." Liz buttoned her coat, still smiling. "I might slip down to the patisserie before I start work. Keen for a delicious Christmas treat?"

"Yeah, why not."

34

THE NEW YEAR

THE DAY DAWNED warmish for winter with an overcast sky, but by midday, a light drizzle cloaked the urban landscape. Liz searched through her closet for something quirky to wear to school. Peter had constantly criticized her style when they were together, leaving her increasingly unsure about her wardrobe choices. Now that he was out of the picture, she enjoyed dressing up again.

AJ was a different story. He threw out the odd compliment about her dress sense, and she appreciated his interest. She liked his style too. But now, it didn't seem appropriate to comment.

Liz hadn't seen AJ lately. He'd been home the day before, made his bed and cleaned the bathroom, and when she opened the laundry room, his sheets and towels were still tumbling in the dryer. She must have just missed him.

On arrival at school, Liz was surprised to see AJ talking to one of the female teachers in his default language—AJ Tanner charm —all laid on under a gray and white striped umbrella and a cocky smile. She knew he'd applied for the mentoring program before the Christmas recess but had no idea when he planned to start. He glanced up as she approached and offered a polite greeting but said nothing more as they walked to class.

For the rest of the afternoon, apart from courteous verbal inter-action when required, AJ ignored her. When the school day ended, he wandered out the gate, chatting with two boys, then disap-peared into the sea of parents and students without saying goodbye.

When Liz arrived at the office the following day, AJ sat in reception—legs wide, phone cradled between his ear and shoulder —talking to someone as he ran his fingers over his tablet keyboard.

Who said men couldn't multitask?

He talked for a minute or two, chuckling with whoever was on the other end of his conversation. He glanced up as she hung her coat on the rack and ended the call.

"Liz," he greeted, a frosty note to his voice as he sank into the chair opposite her desk. "Let's discuss investments and share options." His tone was businesslike and clipped. It took her all her strength not to mention the words 'stick' and 'ass' in the same sentence.

"Also," he continued, "Calum called. He's away until next week but will contact you as soon as he's free. I told him you'll work in with his schedule." He settled his gaze on her.

"Do you plan to join us?" she asked.

"I thought you'd prefer to go alone. We can structure the contract subject to due diligence once you find a suitable location."

"Fine."

Seconds stretched into moments before he replied. "Good." He studied his tablet and resumed. They discussed the share market, with AJ suggesting several companies that showed promise, before he called the meeting to a close.

"Oh, one other thing. You transferred a rather large sum of money to a New Zealand bank account last week. I hope you're not planning a term investment in a finance company over there." His mouth held a slight smile.

Smug bastard, she thought. "Why would you think that?"

"Managing your risk is my job, Liz, and while I realize there's strong recovery in the NZ market, I advise caution. Do you have a purpose for that money?"

Liz hesitated, his arrogant tone annoying her more than it should. "I do." She said nothing further.

He leaned forward in his chair, his expression one of irritation. "Well, are you going to share, or are you pulling back on our business relationship as well as our…well, whatever?"

Liz clasped her hands under her chin. She hated dealing with this side of him. This confronting-asshole-in-serious-business-mode side. "I'm investing in a property with my brother. It has nothing to do with my internet business."

"And you didn't think to mention it?"

"Mitch's lawyers are handling it."

"Fine. I'll leave it in their capable hands." He stood and took several steps toward the door.

"AJ." She waited until she had his attention. "I'm not pulling back on our professional relationship. I appreciate your expertise. In fact, I'd like to discuss a compensation bonus."

He stared at her. Liz couldn't decide if he was irritated or interested. "That's very generous, but there's no need. I'm employed by IKL. Further compensation is unnecessary." He paused. "Oh, and by the way, the Jacobs… It's not for sale. At any price."

35

CONSUMMATE PROFESSIONAL

As she left the dentist, Liz weighed up the options between home or work. She'd been away for the best part of the afternoon and couldn't face an empty office. As she turned the corner of her street, she noticed a black Porsche pulling away from the curb by the terrace.

Two doors down, a group of men in hi-vis vests and hard hats ambled around a cherry picker. Pruned off branches lay on the pavement and across the street, an elderly woman, dressed in a floral skirt and lilac cardigan, dragged her wheeled shopping trolley behind her. Pulling her coat around her, Liz slowed her steps, oblivious to the wolf whistles courtesy of the arborists.

Opening the gate, she noticed a black package the size of a shoe box on the doorstep. Liz held a shallow breath and unlocked the door, ignoring the package as she stepped inside and dropped her bag and keys on the hall table. She turned to pick up the box and carried it into the kitchen.

She lifted the lid. Lying on black tissue were six scarlet roses tied with a length of string. Nothing unusual there, except they were all dead, their half-opened buds drooping onto parched leaves the color of washed-out green, the stems dry and brittle. The box contained no card or inscription, nothing to indicate the sender.

It wouldn't, would it?

Liz unlocked the back door and dumped the box and the roses in the trash. She checked all the locks on the windows and doors, then dragged herself up the stairs, snuck into AJ's room and sat on the bed. Guitars, books, and clothes were jam-packed into every nook and cranny. Liz snuggled into the bedding and did what Penny suggested. She inhaled. Like a bolt into her blue day, the recollection of their lovemaking slammed into her thoughts. Because, to her, lovemaking described the encounter perfectly. It wasn't just sex. She'd never forgotten the intensity of that night and wondered if a man with AJ's skills would ever enter her world again.

Back in her own room, Liz sprawled on the bed, listening to a heavy dose of homesickness in the form of Ginny Blackmore on repeat. But no matter how hard she tried, she couldn't get the image of those roses out of her mind.

Her phone alert startled her. She picked it up and hit *accept*.

"Are you okay, hon?" A note of concern overrode Penny's usually frivolous tone.

"It hasn't been the best day of my life. I came home from the dentist to a box of dead roses on my doorstep."

"Seriously? Any idea who they're from?"

"Peter maybe. I wouldn't put it past him. Do you want to come over? I have a nice bottle of Pinot Gris just begging to be opened."

"I never turn down an invitation for a glass of vino. I'll be there in half an hour."

Penny breezed in and made herself at home, making a beeline for the platter on the coffee table. "Okay. What the shimmy-shit is going on with you and Mr. Man Bun? And what's the goss on the roses? I want all the details, not the glossed-over Liz version."

Liz poured two glasses of wine and handed one to Penny. "Nothing's going on. The roses must be from Peter. Who else would pull a stunt like that?"

"You know what they say, wherever there's a rose, there's usually a prick." Penny sipped her wine as Liz laughed at her quip. "So why aren't you and AJ screwing yet? Shit, hon, this foreplay business has been dragging on for weeks. I'm over it, so how do you guys cope?"

"He's being all aloof and mysterious."

"Making you want and wait, is he?"

"I don't know what on earth he's doing." Liz shrugged. "He did say he'd swipe right for me any day, but that was in the middle of a heated argument."

Penny, always ready with interesting advice, had plenty to say about AJ Tanner. "He wants you."

Liz shrugged.

"I've seen the way he looks at you, remember. So what's the problem."

"What, besides the fact that he consults for my firm, we live in the same house, and he's a shameless flirt?"

"I'd call him more of a man-whore, but that's all part of his charm."

Liz didn't agree on that point. She'd never been interested in men who slept around. "Also, AJ and my 'Hell No' list are almost a perfect match. I'm confused."

"Rubbish. You want him, and he wants you. And I'm not talking movies and popcorn or your pointless, soon to be redundant list. You want the sex, he wants the sex. Where's the problem?"

"That's the problem. The sex. I'd love to have sex with him again, but this situation has hurt and heartbreak stamped all over it."

Penny stopped mid-sip and narrowed her eyes. "Again? What do you mean again?"

"Oops." Liz giggled. "It was a long time ago—on a dark and stormy night." She grabbed a cracker and hummus then said as an afterthought, "Anyway, according to Nate, he's celibate."

"Shut the front door! You mean like a monk?"

"Exactly like a monk."

"No way. If AJ Tanner's celibate, I'm a vestal virgin fanning the sacred fire. And we both know that's a big fat fib."

On Friday afternoon, Liz arrived home early to find a bowl covered in scrapings of pasta sauce in the sink. She opened the fridge. AJ had helped himself to a hefty portion of leftovers. It made her smile. He could hardly speak to her but wasn't too annoyed to eat her spaghetti and meatballs. His bedroom door was open when she reached the landing, so she popped her head inside. He glanced up.

"Enjoy the pasta?" Her offered smile wasn't returned.

"Yeah. Thanks."

"Are you back?"

"Not for long." He moved around the room and stuffed clothes into an oversized duffel while munching on an apple. "What can I do for you?"

Liz bit her lip and let the dose of hurt settle as she breathed through it. "Why are you doing this?"

"Doing what?" His curt demeanor pissed her off. He could barely answer a civil question.

"Shutting me out?"

"I'm shutting you out. Unbelievable. You penciled in a new line, or don't you remember? Told me to step back over my side, redefined our relationship. The ball's in your court. In the meantime, I'm staying away."

"Why? You live here?"

AJ rubbed the back of his neck, an overtly male gesture for 'enough.' His workload often took a toll on his back and shoulders, and Liz wanted to reach out and massage away the tension.

"You know exactly why." He sighed. "You and Peter had a shitty relationship. I get it. He tried his best to screw you over. In the end, you believed his bullshit. That doesn't mean all men are assholes."

"I know that."

"Do you? Sometimes I wonder. I don't need this shit in my life right now. If you want me, Lizzy, you have to come and get me."

"I don't understand what you mean."

"Course you do. That's what this is all about, isn't it? This"—he waved his hand between them—"you and me... The desire and passion. The lust."

"What?"

He reached for her and gently pushed her against the wall like two years before, his lips so close Liz could smell the freshness of the apple on his breath. "You understand completely." His hand reached up and brushed a strand of hair off her face. He dipped his head, forcing her to look at him, then moved to take her lips with his.

The kiss was everything she remembered and more. He increased the pressure, his tongue taking her captive, until her breasts tightened against the cotton lace of her bra.

He let go. "That's 'what.' Remember now?"

Rapid breaths escaped her lungs in gulps as every nerve ending in her body stood to frustrated attention.

He stepped back. "I tried staying on my side of your line, to keep things professional, but what does it matter? Plenty of couples work and live together, happily."

"But we're not a couple, are we?" she said quietly. "You're not the dating kind, remember."

"Shit, Liz. Can't a man change his mind? I told you how I felt about you the second day we met. Told you I wanted you."

"That was two years ago. And just sex."

"Was it? Maybe for you. What were your words? Totally forgettable. Not something a guy wants to hear when one is referring to his skills as a lover, believe me."

"I didn't mean it that way. You left. My only choice was to forget."

"Well, I couldn't forget. I wanted you then and I want you now. But I'm not prepared to spend my life chasing after someone who won't give me the time of day because some other asshole screwed her over, and mixing business with pleasure is not on her agenda."

"It's not all my fault," Liz said. "I remember that day as if it was yesterday. The day you called our night together insignificant. You're equally to blame."

"I don't deny it."

"So why say it?"

"The same reason you did. Self-preservation. Fear of rejection. We both lied, and we both know it." He raised his hand as she went to speak. "I'm going to get out of your hair for a while." His voice softened along with his stance. "Then, we seriously need to start over. Each time we reach this point, I get angry. And I'm usually not an angry person. Decide what you want, then we'll talk."

"When will I see you again?"

"Your call." He picked up his bag, bounded down the stairs and was out the door before she could even say, 'AJ, wait.'

Liz was grateful Christmas was over. The New Year always brought with it a measure of renewal and, in this part of the world, the anticipation of spring. She mulled over AJ's last words, the silence a heavy reminder he'd walked out of her life, and she'd let him. AJ was right. What did it matter if they were business associates and lovers? If she'd taken a different fork in the road, they might have been lovers weeks ago.

Recollections of recent conversations, where he'd flirt and make small jokes, drifted in and out of her thoughts. Their last night at Tancroft came to mind. He was drunk, so maybe it didn't count, but that same night he'd told her she looked sensational, and that he had the perfect guy for her in mind.

Un Beso's magic drew her in, daring her to reach out—to touch, to immerse herself in the feeling it evoked. Even with her left-brain personality, Liz understood the concept of artistic inspiration—were writers told tales so inspiring, they changed your life in an arousing moment, and artists painted colors onto your tapestry that you never imagined belonged to your spectrum. She considered the style of the work. Certain details were exceptionally precise. And yet, as the abstract hand of the painter blurred the lines between reality and imagination, it still left you guessing.

Much like life itself.

Liz let three days go by, giving AJ time to 'ruminate.' One persistent thought obscured all others: she desired him more than any other man she'd ever met.

Home alone on the fourth night, Liz watched a sad movie before listening to old Motown music streaming from her iPad.

Your call. She grabbed her phone and drummed her fingers on the back of the case while she considered those words, then hit the keypad.

Liz: Hi. Could you please forward me the number of your friend, the artist?

In under a minute, he'd sent her a business card contact with the name Anthony J and a number.

Liz often wondered why AJ had two phones sitting side-by-side on his desk. Her fingers touched the keypad before she could stop herself.

Liz: Hi. I'm a friend of AJ's. Would you like to catch a movie sometime? Liz.

Anthony J: Sounds good. Is tomorrow too soon? I'll meet you outside Munro's. Text me a time.

Liz: 7:30?

Anthony J: Perfect. I'm looking forward to it.

The whole situation felt weird. Like she was a fresh-faced schoolgirl off to the movies for the first time with a popular guy she'd had a crush on for months.

Liz stayed awake until after one. She shuffled thoughts and let them fall, then mentally acted out imagined scenarios. He'd mentioned the word relationship. Did he want a relationship? With her?

In the morning, Liz arrived at the office later than usual. A new broadcast campaign with an affiliate company excited her, so her mood was upbeat.

AJ strolled into her office just after one. He looked effortlessly handsome in dark jeans, a stylish jacket, and white shirt, and with his hair secured off his neck. "What time are you leaving for school?" he asked. His offhand manner confused her.

"In about ten minutes. Shall we share a cab?"

"Sure. But first, I have a bank feed question."

Liz glanced at him, then at the screen of her laptop. "I'll bring it up."

She caught the sharp inhale of his breath as AJ moved closer, casually entering her space. He'd made no reference to the events of last week, but as he leaned over, his attention on her screen, his heat radiated down her body and she shivered.

"Cold?" he asked, moving his lips closer to the sensitive spot below her ear.

She closed her eyes for a second. "No, not at all."

"Either someone just walked over your grave, or you're nervous about something."

Liz excused herself to use the bathroom. She looked in the mirror, a knowing grin suppressed by the scrape of teeth over sensitive lips. *Game on.*

Fifteen minutes later, they sat in the back of the cab, sharing the same space but poles apart. AJ reached for his phone from his breast pocket. His fingers hurried over the keypad while the urban world raced by in a maze of streets, traffic, and people. Her text alert chimed.

Anthony J: Looking forward to meeting you tonight.
Liz: Me too.
Anthony J: What will you be wearing?
Liz: Jeans, boots, black jacket over a white top.
Anthony J: Anything else?

He stared out the window, smiling to his smug self. Two can play that game.

Liz: Vintage baby-blue lace.

AJ pocketed his phone and chuckled, pretending to share a private joke with someone. The playful filly had finally returned, much to his relief. He found brash, forward girls a turnoff, but Liz exuded elegance and composure. In certain situations, she could be reserved, almost shy, but as evident at his mother's birthday dinner, she knew how to have fun. He recalled the feeling of sexual excitement they'd shared the night before he left for Japan, and smiled.

Round two couldn't come soon enough.

They reached the school at one forty-five. Their flirty text session lightened AJ's mood and the anticipation of being intimate with Liz again intensified, to where he thought of little else. They walked onto campus, hands close enough to touch, scents close enough to mingle, and steps in stride with familiarity.

"Are you enjoying the mentoring program?" Liz asked after class was over.

"Very much. They're great kids."

"You're highly sought after with your accounting and artistic skills."

He glanced her way. "You make me sound accomplished."

"Aren't you?"

"You have no idea," he murmured as he stepped out from the curb to hail a cab.

They rode back to Putney in silence. AJ asked the cabbie to stop several blocks from the office, where he said his goodbyes and left.

As he walked back to the studio, AJ couldn't shake the feeling that he'd blown it. He'd never played hard to get. Woman rarely spurned his advances, so Liz and her hesitancy intrigued him. He understood her attraction for him was real; he sensed it. But this 'let's be strangers' game could go either way.

Striding along the pavement, AJ reached into his jacket pocket for his beanie and tugged it on. What was he thinking? Texting her under the name of his alter ego, looking forward to their date of make believe like she didn't sleep across the landing of the house they shared. Still, he was determined to be a part of her private world. And the private worlds of Anthony Tanner and Lizette Dobson were about to collide head on.

When he climbed the narrow staircase and opened the studio door, Liz was ever present. In his thoughts, his taste, and his touch.

Her colors flooded his sight as the canvas on the wall pulled him closer. Various shades of green dominated an already cluttered palette board. By the time he took a break, it was almost time for their date.

36

THE DATE

WHEN LIZ STEPPED out of the front door later that evening on her way to meet AJ, she froze. On the doorstep sat another package exactly the same as the first.

A quick scan up and down the street showed no sign of Peter's Porsche, so she crouched and carefully lifted the lid. The snow-white roses, all six open to half bud, were again nestled on a bed of black tissue and had been dead for days.

Her mood heavy—and with the pungent odor of the roses stinging her nostrils—Liz picked up the box, carried it to a dumpster in the driveway of a renovation project, and threw it inside.

In an ideal world, Liz would show up to a date with a smile. And even though she didn't feel like smiling, when she reached Munro's and noticed AJ waiting for her outside, that's exactly what she did. She smiled.

"Hi, I'm Lizette Dobson."

AJ turned to face her. He offered his hand followed by a light kiss on both cheeks. "Anthony Tanner."

Her gaze trailed down his body, taking in the stylish jacket, well-fitting jeans, and boots—always the boots. Dream date check number one; impeccably dressed, smelling gorgeous, and all laid on with a smile. "Sorry I'm late," she said. "I had to take care of something."

"No problem. Where are we going? Do we need a cab?"

"That small boutique cinema off the High Street. Let's walk. It's only a few blocks, and the movie doesn't start until eight-fifteen."

"Sounds good. Are you warm enough?"

"I will be once we start walking."

AJ touched her hand, and as they walked several blocks to the theater, he entwined his fingers with hers, the gesture intimate and one used by lovers all around the world.

"What's the movie called?" He kept smiling, his expression full of amusement.

"*The Dark Horse*. It has excellent reviews. I like to support the New Zealand film industry."

"So, it's a Kiwi movie—to match your accent."

"I don't have a Kiwi accent, do I?"

He smiled. "There's still a slight inflection occasionally."

With their hands still entwined, they sat and watched the credits roll until the very end.

AJ spoke first. "What a powerful film. Do you always cry in movies?" he whispered then planted a soft kiss on the top of her head and pulled her in for a one-armed hug.

Liz took a deep breath. She didn't want to talk. She just wanted to release herself into his warmth. "Depends," she answered finally.

She stood and followed him outside.

"Remind me to take you to a comedy next time," he said as they fell into step.

"I'd like that."

They walked for several blocks—hands held and soft words

spoken. When they arrived at the iron gate of the tiny terrace, AJ turned toward her. His hand reached out to cup her face.

"Thanks for the company." The words coasted on a ghost of vapor. "Is it okay if I kiss you?"

She closed her eyes and leaned into him, the response needing no verbal comeback. He brushed a light touch over her mouth with his, then ran his thumb gently over each lip, tracing the outline of her cupid's bow. "You have the most beautiful mouth."

"Thank you. You do too."

As his fingers entwined in her hair, he swept his tongue into her mouth—soft, warm, and fluid. Another incredible kiss at the hands of this stimulating man.

He held her close, holding her gaze under the dim glow of the streetlight, and smiled. "Finally." He repeated the kiss, then pulled back, his arms encircling her waist. "I've waited, with bated breath I might add, for ages to go on a proper date with you."

"I thought you said you don't date."

"When? We've only just met."

Liz momentarily forgot the game. "Of course. And thank you, I had a lovely time."

"I'm glad." AJ inserted the key into the lock and opened the door. He stayed on the doorstep.

"Thanks for seeing me home."

"Does this mean I have to return to the chill of the dark night?" His play upon words didn't go unnoticed, and she laughed.

"I think it's best." Liz wanted to take it slowly. She sensed he did too.

"Pity." He stared down at her and traced his index finger over her lips once more. One simple gesture, so many complex emotions. "Goodnight, Lizzy. Sleep well."

Once inside, Liz closed the door and peered through the peep-hole, watching him walk away. When he reached the gate, he stopped and glanced over his shoulder before striding off down the street.

After a quick shower to warm up, Liz snuggled down in bed, debriefing the night in her mind. She didn't know where he was staying, but for the first time in days, she felt relaxed and okay about it. When her text alert chimed, Liz grabbed her phone off the nightstand.

Anthony J: Lay back, touch yourself and think of me.
Liz: What are you doing???
Anthony J: Want a pic?
Liz: No, I do not. What is this, foreplay?
Anthony J: Sexting. Everyone does it.
Liz: I don't do sex after a first date…text, solo, or tango.
Anthony J: Really? My memory's shocking.
Liz: I have no idea what you mean.
Anthony J: Come on – you're not still pretending to forget.

She waited several minutes before replying.

Liz: I never forgot.
Anthony J: I know you didn't. Sweet dreams, babe.

Liz fluffed up her pillow and smiled. The new year would be a good one. She felt it in her bones.

Before turning in for the night, she reached for the water bottle on the nightstand and bounded down the stairs for a refill.

A few minutes later when she entered the living room from the kitchen, a full bottle of water in hand, *Un Beso* sat crooked on the wall.

37

OBLIGATIONS

Anthony J: MoMo, 1:30, keen?

A SELF-SATISFIED SMILE played on her lips. Liz quickly texted a reply. Earlier, she'd walked to work with a spring in her step, breezed through a mountain of paperwork, and now, a lunch date with Anthony J.

He arrived at her office just as she grabbed her coat off the rack, kissing her on both cheeks, and then briefly on the mouth as Sophie looked on with an inquisitive stare.

"I hope you like dumplings?" he asked as they walked outside and crossed the street.

"Love them. I love food, period."

"I've heard it said," he murmured as he guided her into the busy eatery, "women who are passionate about food are also passionate about certain other things. Do you agree that's fair comment?"

Nate's words came to mind. Charming AJ was the very man he'd warned her about. Yet, being the center of a man's attention, especially a man like AJ, excited her to distraction. A distraction she'd spent weeks denying. She pressed her lips together to suppress a smile. "I wouldn't know about that."

They sat at one of the few spare tables and waited to be served.

"Hi." A warm smile lit up his face as he reached across the table for her hand.

"Hi." Liz smiled back. "This is nice. I love the food here."

"See, I knew we'd have a lot in common."

"What's something else we have in common?"

He held her gaze for a moment, rubbing the fingers of his other hand through the growth on his jawline. "Let's see. Movies, music, art. And there are other things, but it would be inappropriate to mention them in public."

Her mouth twitched. "Memorable things?"

AJ chuckled. "Very, very memorable."

When the server arrived to take their order a few seconds later, Liz watched with interest as AJ interacted with the young man like they were friends. *Oh, so charming.*

Not long after, a selection of dumplings—more than they could eat—and two bowls of hot and sour soup, were placed on the table.

"What's with the paint-splattered hands?" she asked, the steam from the soup wafting a spell between them.

He reached into the middle of the table with his chopsticks and loaded his plate with small parcels. "I have a project on. Well, it's more a canvas that I'm destroying the shit out of."

"Where do you paint?"

AJ paused to chew. Liz loved watching him eat. His enthusiasm for food knew no bounds. "I have a studio, two actually. One in the loft at Tancroft, and one just off the High Street. I'm working there at the moment."

"Do you sleep there, too?"

"No, although I've slept there the odd night or twenty. I'm staying at a friend's bedsit."

Liz dismissed the question of 'which friend' that landed on the tip of her tongue. She was taking a chance, and sometimes when taking a chance, the details weren't always clear, or essential. "I'd love to see your work sometime."

"Nothing much to see yet," he said, casually dismissive. "These are so good. Do you want the last pork?"

"No, you have it."

"Tell me something trivial about yourself that no one else knows." AJ sucked the broth out of the dumpling before popping the rest into his mouth.

Liz thought for a moment. "One of my favorite songs is *Handbags and Glad Rags*. The Stereophonics version. I don't think I've ever told anyone that."

"That's an oldie. Still, it's a great song. Ryan does an impressive rendition."

Liz frowned. "Ryan?"

"Yeah, we get together and jam sometimes, have a band thing going on. He has a music room in his house."

"Ryan owns a house?"

"Don't let looks deceive you. Ryan's a successful guy."

"Interesting. Are you any good?"

He cocked a questioning brow. "I don't know. Am I?"

Liz laughed. "The band, I mean."

"Terrible, but we still enjoy ourselves. That's the main thing."

They had lived together for months, but when Liz thought about it, she knew little of his personal life, and he knew little of hers. As they sipped green tea, they exchanged small anecdotes about family, and discussed music and snowboarding.

He shook his head and laughed. "Snowboarding, you? Where's the proof?"

Liz pulled out her phone and brought up a short video of her carving up the half pipe. He sat with his mouth open. "I'm impressed." He replayed the video. "But how do I know it's you under that helmet?"

"You'll have to take my word for it. Otherwise, I'm going to Andorra next month with friends from home. You should come."

AJ ignored the invitation and Liz wondered why she'd offered it. Maybe he didn't want a relationship after all. Maybe he just wanted an enjoyable 'fucking' session as he called it—to make beautiful sex.

They talked and drank more tea well into the afternoon, neither of them in a hurry to leave. He laughed and smiled freely. Liz did the same.

"Thanks for meeting me," AJ said. "Unfortunately, I have to go."

He stood and pulled out her chair, their date over. On reaching the street, he leaned down and kissed her lightly on the lips, the tiny flick of his hot tongue just enough to keep her on sexual edge.

"Do you have plans for tonight?" she asked. "I could cook dinner."

"As nice as it sounds, I'm kind of committed over the next couple of weeks. Raincheck?"

"Sure. No problem."

Liz had expected AJ to call over the weekend. He never did. It took her a considerable amount of mental strength to dismiss comparisons between AJ and Peter as ill-founded.

Then, at ten p.m. on Sunday, just when doubt was about to take a firm hold, he texted her a gentle goodnight. She lay back on the bed, phone in hand, wanting to smile. But this time, a frown seemed more appropriate.

First thing Monday morning, AJ strolled into her office and positioned his fine-looking, formed-by-yoga butt in the chair opposite her desk. He enjoyed this game of cat and mouse, she just knew it. She made a brief hello and opened her computer, eager to analyze the latest affiliate campaign.

"How's the analytics program looking?" he asked.

"Good. Shall I print it out?"

"Yeah, a hard copy would be good."

Liz pushed print. The printer produced one page before coming to a halt. "It's out of ink. I'll just grab a new cartridge."

"Stay there. I'll get it."

AJ stood in the stationery cupboard, his neck craned upwards. "I can't find it. Come and have a girl's look, would you?" he called.

Liz entered the narrow cupboard. The cartridge sat on the shelf directly in front of him. "It's right in front of your nose." She picked it up. "Men!"

He grabbed her from behind, his hands slipping around her waist as he pulled her closer. "I love it when you rescue me." He kissed her neck, then moved one hand to cup her breast through her blouse.

"What are you doing?" she whispered.

"Just a little foreplay." He turned her to face him, his passion sinking into her mouth before letting go. He then grabbed the cartridge as if nothing had happened and left. Liz stayed in the cupboard, her body clenched in uncertainty like a teenager who'd been kissed behind the bike shed by a secret crush.

Back at her desk, she stared at the computer screen, trying to recall her next task, her last task, or any damn task as her financial manager from IKL replaced the printer cartridge.

AJ read over the report, calm and composed as he gestured to the front of her blouse. "You seem to have popped your buttons, Ms. Dobson." He didn't even crack a smile as he watched her tug the buttons back through their impossibly tight openings. "But don't feel you have to button up on my account."

Still feeling flushed and warm from the cupboard kiss, she shot him a sideways glance. "Sorry, where were we?"

Silent communication followed as he handed her the printouts. "Someplace rather nice, but I think it's time we got back to work, don't you?"

Further displays of affection were conspicuous by their absence for the rest of the week. No visits, no lunch dates, not even a lousy phone call. But every night at ten o'clock on the dot, his goodnight text would arrive—a tiny teaser she would later call it.

At the office, Liz found herself in the stationery cupboard more than once, looking for nothing in particular as she recalled the feeling of his hands around her waist, his breath soft on her neck, and his kiss, tender yet wanting.

And that tongue...

Late Friday morning, her text alert chimed with four words: *Away for the weekend - x.*

He'd sealed her Saturday and Sunday fate with a single *x* on a phone screen.

38

PREPARATION FOR DESIRE

GATHERING papers into a pile on her desk, Liz thought about the text. Their relationship had turned a corner recently. But now, AJ seemed to be moving straight ahead with blinkers firmly in place, leaving her outside of his peripheral vision. Close enough to touch, yet distant all the same.

Liz held those thoughts while she waited for Calum the realtor to collect her from outside the patisserie. They drove east to Clapham and stopped at a tidy-looking semi only a stone's throw with a robust arm from the Common.

"This area's a little pricey, but I think you'll like its solidness." Calum spoke in such a broad Scottish accent, Liz had to listen carefully to understand. "I've other properties, but this one best suits your brief."

He unlocked the front door and ushered her through. "We've got five bedrooms. I know you only said three, but the single's no larger than a well-heeled woman's closet, so would make a great wee office. And the downstairs bedroom is a guest suite with an adjoining bathroom. You can't go wrong there, especially if you get an influx of Kiwi visitors. There's also a rumpus room of sorts in the basement."

Liz strolled through the entry, switching her phone to silent as she did. The asking price was over her budget, and she needed to concentrate. She glanced up the stairwell defined with a curved, high-gloss black banister, her mind full of ideas.

"The garden will excite you," Calum continued. "It's almost a hundred feet long, and as you can see, the interior has been taste-fully refurbished to a very high standard. Throw in the off-street parking for two cars and a price tag a smidgen over three and a half, and we're onto a wee winner."

"May I look upstairs?"

Calum grinned. "It would be rude not to."

Liz expected him to say, *Sassenach*, even though she knew the term didn't apply to her Kiwi heritage. She asked a few more questions just to hear him speak.

The viewing took under an hour. The gaudy tiles in the master bathroom and the overly patterned flocked wallpaper in the bedrooms would have to go. But apart from those minor details and the canary yellow kitchen cabinets, she loved it.

"What do you think, Liz? Shall we table an offer subject to the usual palaver?"

"I'd like Anthony to take a look."

Calum checked his phone. "Good move. I'm free at one-thirty tomorrow if that suits. But we can't muck about. I already have two other interested parties. You can't be too slow in this market."

"I understand."

Once outside, Liz reconnected to the world and checked her messages. Among the half dozen texts, AJ's stood out from the rest.

Anthony J: Sorry I haven't had time for you lately. Keep next weekend free. We can spend it together.
Liz: I've found a house. Are you available @ 1:30 tomor-row? Shouldn't take more than an hour.

He replied with a yes, nothing else.

As Calum and Liz waited for AJ outside a small bookshop the following day, she wondered where his studio might be, and why he never invited her there, or anywhere. He greeted them both as he slid into the back seat. She turned, looked at his paint covered hands and smiled. "Thanks for coming. I know you're busy."

"No problem. It's good to get out for a while. Where are we headed?"

As they drove, the men discussed the London property market, Scottish football, and share options, all in the space of twenty minutes. As soon as they stopped at the gate, her phone chimed with a text. She glanced at the screen.

Anthony J: Cute as a little button just waiting to be undone.

Out of the car, he continued his conversation with Calum as Liz suppressed a smile. A warm Scottish brogue brought her back to the present.

"Why don't you two have a wee look around?" Calum was saying as he unlocked the front door. "Take your time. I'll be in the garden checking emails."

AJ glanced up at the living room ceiling. "This is a great space. Lots of natural light and the hardwood floors are a plus. It's a little out of your price bracket, but maybe you have to suck it up to get what you want in this area."

"It's huge."

They wandered up the stairs. "Not really. You don't need five bedrooms right now, but you might someday."

"You mean when I have a dreamy husband and six kids?"

"Speaking of which." They moved into the master bedroom, his hand in steering position at the small of her back. "The wallpaper's interesting."

"There's a dressing room and ensuite bathroom."

AJ wandered around the space, his hands in his pockets as he took everything in. "Show me." He made it sound like an afterthought.

Liz motioned to a narrow set of double doors. He followed her into the dressing room, his body too close for comfort. Stepping closer, his energy engulfed her.

"You might have to buy a few more pairs of shoes to fill this monster." He smiled, kicking the doors shut behind him.

"What are you doing?"

"Prep." AJ moved forward, his hands searching for her in the darkness, and held her steady, kissing her with urgency. His grip was tight and forceful, and a faint smell of musk heightened her senses as he moved a hand to cup her face.

He pulled back. "I've missed you."

Apart from a soft 'oh,' Liz couldn't speak.

He ran his hand toward the hem of her skirt before inching upwards past the lace of her stay-up stockings, and brushed the top of her thigh with his thumb. "You wore this little skirt just for me, didn't you? Too cute."

"AJ—"

"Shush," he commanded. "Stay still."

Liz was already breathless and wanting. Her breasts tightened at his touch. "We should go back."

"Not yet." AJ increased the pressure of his hold, bending to caress her neck as her head fell back. "You don't want me to stop, do you?" Needy lips found the warmth of her throat. "Liz?" he murmured, before gently sucking her aroused skin into his mouth, his breath loud and fast.

Pushing his knee between her legs, he rained stolen kisses on her lips. Liz relaxed under his tight grip, the blush she felt super-fluous in the dark. He kissed her twice more, deep and passionate, before he opened the closet doors and entered the ensuite to splash his face with water as if nothing had happened.

Liz fought for composure, her thoughts flying all over the place, trying to catch butterflies. She smoothed down her skirt and raked her fingers through her hair. She was about to leave the room when he pulled her back.

"Come here. Your buttons have popped. How does this keep happening?" AJ motioned to the undone buttons of her blouse as his hands moved to secure the teardrop pearls back into place. "There."

She didn't speak, unsure how to respond to what had just happened. Conflicted feelings remained.

Hot, yet cold.

Unsatisfied, yet content.

Desired, yet hesitant.

"Come on, let's tell Calum you're interested." AJ removed his jacket and draped it over his arm to conceal the evidence of his need.

"You shouldn't have done that."

He smiled down at her, then pulled her into an all-engulfing hug. "Really?" Hot lips caressed her earlobe. "Don't pretend, babe. You love being kissed in a closet."

"We could've been caught."

"That makes it even more exciting."

On the drive back to the office, the text messages continued.

Anthony J: I hope you enjoyed our little trip to the closet.
Liz: Oh, I did. But why are you doing this?

Anthony J: For your need of desire.
Liz: Desire?
Anthony J: You asked for it. To feel desired.
Liz: Did I?

When they reached Putney High Street, AJ asked Calum to pull over. The anticipation of a dinner invitation vanished as he said goodbye, opened the door, and walked into the crowd without a backward glance. Liz sank back in the seat, all alone while AJ traveled to the other side of his life. The side she knew nothing about.

Later that evening, as she slipped into her pajamas, her phone glowed on the nightstand. She sat on the bed, picked it up and smiled.

Anthony J: My imagination is running wild.
Liz: Come over. Please?
Anthony J: Can't sorry. Sleep well, babe.

Liz slumped back, dropped her phone on the duvet and sighed. AJ's games stirred up emotions Peter had done his best to destroy. The need of desire, of want. Suddenly the call of fat, sugar, and salt was too much to bear.

Salted caramel ice cream.

Through the half-closed door of her bedroom, the faint ding of the doorbell chimed. Liz hurried down the stairs, excited by the prospect of seeing AJ wearing tight jeans, boots, and a sexy smile. She peeked through the peephole onto the empty street. Leaving the security chain in place, Liz unlocked the deadbolt. There on the doorstep, another identical cardboard box made an intimidating statement. She pulled her robe tightly across her chest, but her skin still bumped from the cold air seeping through the gap in the door.

Apart from three teenage girls on the opposite side of the street, nothing untoward caught her attention. Cautious hands slid the security chain back. She turned the doorknob, then bent down to pick up the box, keeping her focus on the quiet suburban street where the tiny terrace sat.

Today's roses were pastel pink. Still six, still tied with string, still nestled in black tissue, and still dead.

Ice cream suddenly lost its appeal.

39

HEARTFELT INVITATIONS

SITTING at her desk a few days later, a square brown envelope, crafted from thick recycled paper, stood out from the rest of the mail. Vintage style font, reminiscent of an old-school typewriter ribbon, dominated the center of the envelope. Half expecting another example of Peter's handiwork, Liz carefully prized the flap open. She pulled out the square white card and frowned.

On the front, hand painted flower petals in shades of blue and washed wineberry touched with yellow, overflowed in layers to form the shape of a petal heart. Inside, an invitation—typed on the same typewriter—requested the pleasure of her company at an exhibition the following Friday.

Liz held the card to her nose and inhaled deeply. The smell of gardenias basking in warm sunlight piqued her interest. She noted the date in her diary, then slipped the card into her bag, wondering who the invitation was from.

Peter briefly came to mind, but there was no time to dwell on either him or his lifeless calling cards. Liz had spent months trying to please him. She now thought of him as an obnoxious prick rather than a threat and congratulated herself for this positive step forward.

The following day, Liz met Penny for lunch at a new Korean restaurant a few blocks from her office. The place was packed, but having heard how good the food was, they decided to wait for a table.

"Did you receive an invite to the gallery tomorrow night?" Penny asked.

"I did. It came in the post. I have no idea who from."

"Really? Mine came via a text from Hannah."

Liz rummaged through her bag, pulled out the invitation and handed it to Penny.

"Cute." Penny ran a finger over the petal heart. "Maybe someone has their eye on you. Maybe Jacobs himself."

"Don't be ridiculous."

"Well, you have one of his works." She handed the card back. "And how come I didn't get a fancy ass invite?"

"No idea. It is cute though, isn't it? Are you going?"

"I might show my sweet face for a bit. Check out the talent and the art."

A young man around twenty, approached them, offering a cocky smile and the table he and his friend were about to vacate. As he left, he slipped Penny a napkin with a phone number written on the back and a scribbled message:

Foursome = awesome. Call me.

Penny cracked a grin, showing the napkin to Liz as they sat in the warm seats.

"We've still got the goods," Penny said. "Who mentioned crow's feet and saggy boobs? I love younger men." She watched the men leave. "Especially hot ones."

Liz shook her head in amusement, then quickly pushed the image of a foursome out of her mind with a shudder.

"Come on. Give me a little smile. The world's not about to end yet," Penny said. "And if it does, at least we'll have a tummy full of kimchi and an offer of afternoon delight with two hunks to dream about."

"Always important to have a full stomach if the world's about to self-destruct."

"And knowing you have the attention of handsome hotties." Penny looked up for a moment, obviously imagining the scenario. "You look a little down. What's up with you and AJ?"

"It's complicated."

"Tell Aunty Penny all about it."

"He runs hot and cold. I'm confused. I used to be strong, call the shots and know what I wanted in a man. Now I feel like an emotional mess. It's unsettling."

"I hear you loud and clear, sweetness. I blame that jerk Peter."

Liz skipped over the Peter comment. She didn't want to give him any more mind time. "It went well initially, our new dating thing. I took your advice. Flirted a little with his friends. Then we went to Tancroft and had a great weekend. The next thing I know, he took a photo of me asleep at the cottage. I had PMS and went off my nut. Then we had a big fight about it and—"

"Wait, slow down. I'm all giddy. He took a photo of you? What, naked?"

"No, I was covered with a blanket but—"

"It's only a photo. It's not like he's a creep or anything. He may enjoy taking pics of beautiful women in bed. Like *Humans of New York*. His interest might be *Females in Slumber*."

Liz gave a half smile. "Moving right along, I finally calmed down and asked him to the movies. He was pleasant and sweet— threw in a couple of soft kisses at the doorstep. The perfect gentleman."

"Perfect gentleman? Really? That's the last thing you want. Especially after you've known each other a while and live in the same house. Perfect yes, a gentleman, not so much."

"And that's another thing. He hasn't been living at the terrace lately."

"Where's he living?"

"He mentioned a friend's bedsit. And he has a studio. He paints, apparently."

"So that's why he's at the gallery sometimes." Penny looked up as a server arrived to take their order.

"I wonder if he exhibits," Penny asked as the server left their table.

"I have no idea. It's probably just a hobby."

"Interesting. So, you get the impression he's not keen?"

"We haven't seen each other much over the past week, and when we do, he's in total business mode. He did say he'd be busy for a few weeks and I should keep this weekend free."

Penny frowned. "Well, that's good, isn't it?"

"I don't know, Pen." Liz flaunted a naughty smile. "My thoughts are clouded in sexual confusion. To tell you the truth, it's been one big tease."

"Seriously? You don't want another Peter on your hands. Someone who can't screw to save himself. An ABC guy."

"What on earth is an ABC guy?"

"You know, only screws you on anniversaries, birthdays, and Christmas. Hell, I need a Monday-through-Saturday-times-two-on-Sunday type of guy. ABC guys are definitely on my 'Hell No' list."

Liz laughed again. She'd shared Peter's lackluster bedroom performance with Penny over a crisp sauvignon blanc one cold and stormy night, and since then, Penny wouldn't let it drop. "You have a list now?"

"Maybe." Penny pondered for a moment. "Well, there you go. I thought AJ was gonna be the guy. The one who makes your knees weak, your heart race, and walks over hot coals to be with you. He's so freaking sexy to look at, almost brooding, and then he smiles. *Damn!*"

"Yeah, I thought so too. He's sexy and complex, and... Well

let's just say he unfastens my buttons like no one else. And he said he wanted me. I don't get it."

Penny nodded in agreement.

"What if I sleep with him and find he's not interested in a commitment?" Liz's disappointed expression matched her tone. "Or he's monogamy-shy? That would definitely send my self-esteem over the edge without an abseil."

"Have you asked him?"

"I don't want to be all clingy and needy."

"Just ask him. Simple."

4 0

BOHO CHIC

ARRIVING HOME THE FOLLOWING DAY, Liz struggled with the front door, giving it an extra hard push. Penny was right. The next time she saw AJ, she'd ask him where they stood. Convey her interest.

After toeing off her boots, she walked through to the kitchen in search of something to eat, then sat in the living room munching on an apple. She surveyed the room. Nothing had changed since that morning. AJ hadn't been home in days.

Liz dragged herself up the stairs, changed into a pretty dress, and left the terrace five minutes later to meet Penny for a drink. She didn't want to go out again, but it was better than sitting at home waiting for AJ to throw her a text, and her scrambling to pick it up.

Munro's hummed with punters when she walked through the door. After buying a glass of wine from the bar, Liz joined Penny and friends at their table—a haven in a sea of congestion.

With the conversation centered on the usual after work small talk, Liz found her attention waning as thoughts of AJ's absence took up more space in her head than she could spare. Just as she was about to call it a night, she noticed a group weaving through the crowd toward the bar. Hannah, another woman, and three guys. One Hannah's partner, one AJ's friend Paul, and the man himself.

AJ didn't notice Liz as he laughed with the woman, leaning in close to check out her phone screen. Liz had seen private jokes between lovers before—his hand around the small of her back and her fingers raking through straight strands of polished hair. Such displays of intimate body language held secrets and yet, told no lies.

Liz kept salting the wound. She glanced their way repeatedly at the expense of her self-respect. The woman, with her undeniable mix of boho chic and sophistication all wrapped up into one incredible package, laughed freely as AJ held her attention. Their heights almost matched, their beauty most definitely did, and their interaction conveyed the unspoken.

Her gut clenched as the words *perfect sense* screamed at her. She gave Penny a light nudge and tilted her head toward the group. "I'm off. Busy day tomorrow." Liz slid across the seat as Penny stood to let her out.

"Shit," Penny whispered. "Who's the blonde?"

"No idea but I feel a headache coming on."

Liz slipped right past AJ on the way out. So close, she could have touched him. But not tonight. His preoccupation spoke volumes.

Out of the corner of her eye, Liz noticed Peter strolling toward the bar entrance. He took an unsteady step backward. "Liz?"

She lowered her head and walked past him but stopped with a jolt when he grabbed her arm.

"Hey, what's the hurry? How about a drink for old time's sake?"

She glanced at his hand before yanking free. "I'd say by the stench coming from your breath you've had enough. Now, if you'll excuse me."

"Don't be like that. I just want to talk." With a tight grip, Peter guided her away from the entrance of Munro's to the bolted wooden door of the neighboring building. "At least you can be civil."

"I've tried being civil. You never seem to get the message."

He rubbed his hand up and down her arm. "I get the message loud and clear. Your problem is you don't know what's jolly well good for you. You still want me. I know it. And I've always cared about you."

"You can't be serious? You care about me so much, you leave dead flowers on my doorstep."

"I don't know what you're talking about."

"The hell you don't."

"It's nothing to do with me." His denial held a knowing smirk along with a slight hesitation. "Maybe you should ask your office boy, or fuck-chum or whatever you jolly well call Tanner. That's more his style."

Liz tried to push past Peter without causing a scene. It seemed half of Putney were out and about, yet no one noticed her distress. "Let me pass. You're drunk."

"Don't be a bitch." Peter increased the pressure of his hold. "We need to talk. I miss you."

"Let me go. You're hurting me." She pulled herself free.

By now, several people were looking her way, one of them Ryan Farrell. Liz caught Ryan's concerned stare and relaxed as he quickly pushed through the crowd on the street.

"What's going on?" His voice carried a hard edge but an under-lying note of concern. "Liz, are you okay?"

Peter didn't bother turning to look at Ryan. "Butt out. It's none of your business."

Ryan, standing over six feet and built to perfection from many hours sweating it out on construction sites, grabbed Peter by the back of the collar and slammed him against a wall. "Back the hell off. Now!"

"Or what?"

"You don't want to know, asshole."

"Don't threaten me. This has nothing to do with you."

"Is that right?" Ryan moved closer and whispered through gritted teeth. "She's mine, and I don't take kindly to other men talking to my woman. Keep away from her, or I'll feed your balls to the perch in the Thames."

"Fuck you."

With Peter still against the wall, Ryan turned to Liz. "Grab a cab, babe. I'll be there in a sec."

"*Babe*, how original," Peter said. "Slut would be more appropriate."

"Screw you." Liz pushed past him. "And in future, stay away from me."

"One more word, mate," Ryan said, his slight Scottish accent more pronounced when irritated, "and you'll really make my freaking day."

Peter held up both hands in a mark of retreat. Ryan released his grip with a shove.

"Spoken like a true meathead," Peter said before calling after Liz, "You'll soon come running back when you realize you need me for that two-bit cottage industry you call a company."

He walked away, and as he did, much of her energy followed.

Ryan joined Liz at the curb and ushered her into the waiting cab. He slid in beside her, his concern as readable as his annoyance. "What was that all about?"

"My ex. He thinks we have unfinished business." She sucked in a deep breath, determined not to cry as she wrapped her scarf tightly around her neck.

"I don't believe the gall of the guy. Who does he think he is?" Ryan reached for her hand and held it steady before letting go. "Come on, let's get you home." He gave the cabbie the address.

"He just...takes my stomach and ties it in knots. Every, single, time."

"You don't have to put up with guys like him. And for what it's worth, you stood up to him just fine. I'm proud of you."

They rode the rest of the way in silence, Liz clasping her hands together in her lap. When they pulled up outside the terrace, Ryan dropped the driver a twenty before Liz even had the chance to open her wallet. He ushered her out of the cab and up to the front door.

"Thank you." She handed Ryan the key.

He fiddled with the lock and pushed the door open. "No problem. What did you think of my acting skills?"

"Excellent." She stood in the entry hall and turned to face him with a wry smile. "So, you're not really my boyfriend then?"

Ryan studied her for a few seconds, a half smile on his lips. "I wish, but you're in love with someone else."

Embarrassed by Ryan's candid reply, Liz said nothing.

He cleared his throat and peeked into the living room. "Where's your knight in designer boots when you need him?"

"In Munro's."

Ryan cocked a questioned brow.

"It's complicated," Liz said. "But what is it with those boots?"

"His uncle in Spain is an artisan boot maker. AJ's his perfect male foot model and his London agent, so he gets a ton of samples."

"I never knew. But then, I don't know much about him at all."

"Did he realize you were outside?"

"No. Please don't tell him what happened."

"If you were mine, I wouldn't let you out of my sight."

"You're a sweet guy, Ryan. I bet there are plenty of lovely girls vying for your affections."

Ryan raised a brow. "That may be true. But finding one who's prepared to help carry my baggage and responsibilities isn't so easy."

Liz had never seen Ryan's serious side. She didn't know his

story or anything about him. "Let me shout you lunch one day. We'll talk responsibilities. I'll bring my baggage."

"Sounds good." He followed her into the living room. "Let's do a quick sweep, just in case." They walked from room to room, checking the locks on the doors and windows. "Are you gonna be okay until AJ gets home?"

"He hasn't been living here lately. He has a project on, apparently."

Ryan nodded. "Of course."

It seemed everyone knew about AJ's project except her.

"Okay. I'd better go," he said. "I'll see you at the gallery tomorrow night."

"I'm not sure if I can make it."

"Really? I hear it's going to be an entertaining evening. Anyway, goodnight." He turned away from the door and stepped onto the path.

"Ryan?" Liz called him back. "Thank you." Her index fingers smeared along the bottom rim of each eye, wiping away warm tears. "I feel like a crazy fool...you know, for getting involved with a guy like Peter. It seems my choice of men isn't always positive."

He took several steps forward. "We all make those mistakes. I certainly have. May I tell you a little secret?" Ryan had a mischievous smile with dimples to match and they were on full display.

"Go on then."

"I asked AJ for your number, you know, earlier on. He refused point blank. He's had his eye on you for a long time."

"When was this?"

"The night we came over to watch the rugby. You and AJ have something going on, and as much as I'd like things to be different, well..." Ryan flashed another cheeky grin, then reached out and gave her a tight hug. "Give him a chance. He's a solid choice. And in the meantime, that front door deadbolt needs replacing."

"Yes. It's on our list of jobs."

"Let me know if I can help with that."

"Thanks. And thank you once again for tonight."

"No problem."

Back inside, Liz flopped on the sofa, kicked off her boots, and rubbed a chafe mark on her foot. Her thoughts shot to the woman at the bar—her elegant figure fashioned in the mold of an artist's muse, and the way AJ touched and looked at her.

AJ and Liz had never discussed a relationship. She'd made that assumption aided by his subtle hints. Now the time had come to assume otherwise. She expected to feel relieved by her decision to distance herself. And yet, when she looked up at the blank wall in front of her, all resolve vanished, only to be replaced by an overwhelming sense of loneliness.

Un Beso Imaginado was gone.

COMMUNICATION

JUST AS PENNY grabbed her coat to leave the bar, AJ, also on his way out, pushed through the crowd toward her. "Penny, hi." He offered his hand, then kissed her on the cheek. "How are you?"

Penny stared at him blankly, her body language cold enough to freeze the English Channel.

"You don't remember me, do you? AJ, Liz's boyfriend."

"Sorry. I had a mental blank. I didn't realize you and Liz were an item."

Her curtness only added to AJ's concern. "We've been keeping it on the down low. Still, I'm surprised Liz didn't mention it." He scanned the bar. "Did you see her earlier?"

"She was here," Penny said. "She left about an hour ago with a headache."

AJ nodded. "According to Ryan, Liz ran into a drunk Peter Nichols outside. He caused quite a scene."

"Seriously? I can't stand that guy."

"Yeah. Ryan took her home in a cab. I've tried calling her, but she won't pick up."

"I hope she's okay." Penny looked concerned. "I should go over and check."

"I'm heading home now, so no need. I wished I'd known she was here."

"Maybe she noticed you were busy and thought she'd slip out. Anyway, I'm off home. Tell Liz I'll text her tomorrow."

As AJ watched Penny leave the bar, what was already a minor disquiet turned into full-on worry. He hadn't seen Liz in days, and thinking back, apart from his usual goodnight, he'd hardly even texted her over the last week. AJ understood the importance of communication, both physical and verbal, even if he hadn't been in a romantic relationship for several years.

The tiny terrace was snug and warm when he walked inside. When AJ noticed Liz's coat draped over a chair in the living room and her boots where she'd toed them off, he relaxed.

AJ moved through to the kitchen, flicking on lights as he went. Standing at the sink with a glass of water, he looked out the window to the narrow strip of lawn, the ornamental cherry—almost in bud—and the evergreen shrubs lining the perimeter of the yard. His thoughts turned to tomorrow evening. Excited antici-pation mixed with nervousness clench his gut.

Liz woke with a start to footsteps on the stairs. The eighth riser from the bottom always squeaked when stepped on, usually an encouraging sign Nate or AJ were home. She reached over the bed, grabbed her T-shirt from the floor and tugged it on, the memory of the dead roses and Peter's behavior fresh in her fears. When a thin stream of light glowed under her door, she relaxed. *AJ.*

The stairwell light flicked off in exchange for the one in the bathroom. Liz listened as droplets of water scattered against the connecting wall between the bathroom and her room. Why had he chosen tonight to return? Maybe it didn't work out with the blonde. No matter what she witnessed at Munro's, Liz still craved his closeness. A beam of light from the gap in the curtains cast a soft shadow over the room. She tried to sleep, but her mood was fraught with apprehension. When the doorknob twisted, she froze.

AJ stood at the side of her bed, his hand outstretched as if he longed to touch the life back into her face. Lying half on her back, Liz kept the rise and fall of her breath even. He slid in beside her, reached out and snuggled into her, inhaling with a concentrated breath. She tensed beneath his touch. He wasn't completely naked, but she felt everything.

"Hey, you." Gentle kisses feathered along her nape, dispensed with soft lips and a tender trace of his fingers. "I didn't mean to wake you."

"What are you doing here?" Her voice was flat.

"Penny said you weren't feeling well. Are you okay?"

She didn't turn to face him. He seemed happy to hold her like it was the most natural thing in the world—like they were a couple. "Just a headache."

"Do you need anything?"

"No, I'm fine." She didn't want to look at him, see his handsome face and concerned smile. "I need to use the bathroom."

Liz sat on the toilet with hot tears for company. Why would AJ do this to her? Or rather, why would she let him? She reminded herself of one stark fact. Neither of them had mentioned the word 'exclusive' over the last few weeks. Maybe this was his *modus operandi*. She had considered it—his non-committal, elusive personality. Yet, in certain situations lately, he'd displayed genuine interest. Maybe Nate was right. She was floating in and out of his radar, and right now, his attention was on her.

The bedroom had cooled when Liz climbed back into bed. AJ's silhouette under the covers gave her a brief sense of relief, but if Liz had learned anything from her time with Peter, clutching at straws was a habit she had to break. She wasn't prepared to stand back and let AJ hurt her as he enjoyed his other life in a parallel universe full of sexual opportunities.

AJ reached for her and pulled her into his warmth. "Is it okay if

I stay here?" he murmured. "I know I'm a day early for our weekend date, but I couldn't wait to see you."

One night, she thought. One night of his breath on her neck and his fingers firmly splayed out across her tummy like two years before. Close, yet frustratingly out of reach, and that sensual ache, forever unfulfilled.

"I've missed you, babe." He kissed her neck again, moved in closer, and spooned her until his erection pressed fiery hot against the cotton knit of her T-shirt. "Missed you so much."

Liz buried her head in the pillow. Soft feathers molded to the shape of her face and caught her silent tears.

"Do you have something you want to tell me?" His tone conveyed the obvious. He'd been talking to Ryan.

"No. What do you mean?" Liz swallowed hard.

"What happened tonight outside Munro's?" Demanding AJ was back in the house.

"It was nothing."

"Not according to Ryan. Peter had you pinned up against a wall and Ryan had to intervene. Didn't you see me inside?"

"You arrived just as I was leaving. I didn't want to interrupt. You were busy with your friends. I asked Ryan not to tell you."

"Why, babe?"

Liz swallowed the words on the tip of her tongue. "Because I don't have to be with you all the time. You have your own life, your own friends."

He cupped her face. "Hey, never feel that way. It kills me to think that asshole had you in his grip and I was only twenty feet away, unaware. You should have come back inside."

"I'm sorry. It was freezing, Munro's was packed, and I wanted to get home. And let's not talk about this now. I'm exhausted."

"I'm a shitty boyfriend. It's good Ryan came along when he did." AJ pulled her closer with an exaggerated sigh into her hair. "From now on, promise me you won't keep secrets from me. He could have hurt you."

The words 'secrets and lies' played in her mind repeatedly. "The painting," she murmured, changing the subject as she tried to keep her voice calm. "It's gone."

"Yeah, my friend finally picked it up this morning. He's proposing soon. The painting's a gift for his future wife."

She smiled at the thought. "How romantic. I'll miss it."

"Why's that?"

"It's hard to explain. I'd walk in from an ordinary day and as soon as I looked at it, my senses would come alive."

"I know what you mean. Anyway," AJ's hand reached out to brush ruffled curls off her neck, "go back to sleep, babe. You've been working too hard lately."

He didn't make a move to touch her further but stayed close, his arms possessively wrapped around her until dawn.

Liz had always been an early riser. Her dad said getting up early set you up for a better day, and he was right. However, the following morning she struggled to get out of bed, preferring to stay engulfed in AJ's arms until the world morphed into a better place.

But instead, her feet hit the floor.

Hot water hissed over her skin as she leaned on the wall of the shower, reflecting the many whys of the situation. Why had he shown up? Why couldn't he offer fidelity? Why had she let her guard down?

The concept of an open relationship wasn't new to Liz. But while she'd thought about it occasionally, she couldn't imagine being content with a man who shared his passion with other women. She cringed at the thought of AJ saying 'let's make beautiful sex' to someone else. When she cut the water and stepped out onto the cold tiled floor, the intense buff of her towel and a quick pep talk did nothing to improve her mood.

Liz dressed in her workout clothes, tied her hair in a messy knot, and picked up her bag. AJ had slept through her shower but stirred as she tiptoed to the door.

"Good morning, beautiful," he mumbled, his voice thick with sleep and his hair skimming over strong shoulders in bed-tussled waves. "How are you feeling?" He yawned and stretched, linking his hands behind his head for a better view, his naked chest and mandala tattoo on full display.

"Better, thanks."

"Where are you going?" He sat up and reached forward—a lifeline of delicate fingers that had held her so gently. With that touch of Spanish blood, he really was the most handsome man she'd ever been involved with. "Come back to bed."

"I can't. I have a session with my personal trainer at six-thirty."

"Text and cancel. Come here. Please, Lizzy."

She hesitated. "I have to go. He's waiting for me."

"He?" AJ offered her a fake concerned frown. "Should I be worried?"

She couldn't muster a smile. "I made muesli yesterday. Help yourself."

"Aren't you coming back?"

"I have a busy day at work, so possibly not."

"Pity." He snuggled down in the bed. "Okay, babe. I'll see you later. Hey, Liz." He called her back as she stepped away. "I've something on early evening, then we need to talk."

"What about?"

"Doesn't matter now. I'll tell you tonight." He held out his hand. "Can I have a kiss?"

How could she refuse?

Liz ran all the way to the gym, not to impress her trainer, but to clear her head. AJ had 'something on later.' He always had some-thing on. And what did he want to discuss? The blonde from Munro's?

4 2

GREENSTONE HEART

"Penny, great you could make it." AJ smiled warmly as Penny looked him up and down. "I didn't really know who to invite of Lizzy's friends."

"It turns out you have several strings to your bow. Who would have thought," Penny said, still a little coolly.

"Yeah, it's kind of my coming out party tonight." AJ scanned the room, a light crease on his brow. "Have you seen Liz? I thought she'd be here by now."

"She's not coming."

"What? Is she okay?"

"It might have something to do with the mystery blonde you were getting up close and personal with at Munro's last night."

"Who? Katy?" He frowned, searching Penny's expression. "Are you saying Liz thinks Katy and I are together? She and her husband, Paul, own this place. We've been friends for years." He turned away, looking for answers in the sea of faces. "Shit, shit, shit!"

"Look, AJ, Liz is a good friend and I care about her. I'm not privy to what's going on between you, but I gather you haven't been available lately. Now I understand why. The problem is, Liz has no idea, and that confusion is making her reevaluate."

"We stayed together last night." AJ thought for a moment. "Although now that you mention it, she did seem a little off when she left for the gym this morning."

"Liz is not the type to make waves. But between you and me, she thinks you're not into her."

"What? That's bullshit." He guided her toward the door. "You have to find her. I can't leave now, and she won't answer my calls. Please. I need her here tonight."

AJ fished into his pocket for his keys and a fifty-pound note as he filled Penny in on his plan.

Liz was fresh out of the shower when Penny unlocked the front door and stepped inside.

"Penny! Give a girl a fright why don't you. How did you get in?"

"AJ's key. Have you been crying? You look terrible."

"You have AJ's key?"

"Look, there's no time to explain. We have to hurry." Penny pulled Liz up the stairs and dragged her into the bedroom. "That blonde from last night is the gallery owner." Penny explained who Katy and Paul were, and how AJ had helped them set up the exhibition.

"Come on," Penny said. "You want to see him, don't you?"

"I do, but apart from last night, he's hardly contacted me in the past two weeks."

"And when you see how amazing the gallery looks, you'll understand why. For heaven's sake, go put your face on while I choose a dress. I'm not going back there without you. Go!"

Penny opened the closet and flung dress after dress onto the bed while Liz ran to the bathroom to brush her teeth and apply make-up.

"Here, this one." Penny held up a tight-fitting, nude colored dress with a high neck and three-quarter length sleeves.

"I haven't worn that before. It's too tight. Leaves nothing to the imagination and when I'm cold—" Liz pointed to both boobs. "And my hair's a mess."

"It stretches. Put it on and don't worry about your pert titties *or* your hair. I'll fix it in the cab. Quick."

Penny looked Liz up and down as she shimmied into the dress. "Whoa, I see what you mean. Still, it looks fabulous. But you need a big show of something artistic around your neck, to distract the eye from your boobs."

Liz held up a one-off piece crafted in greenstone and onyx she'd found on her trip to New Zealand. "How about this?"

"Perfect."

Standing outside the gallery, Liz handed the security guard her invite.

"Welcome, Ms. Dobson," he said with a smile. "If you need anything, please ask. As the holder of a Jacobs original invitation, you have special privileges."

"There must be some mistake."

"No mistake, miss. The heart of petals was hand painted by Jacobs for his VIP guest. Enjoy your evening."

Liz turned to Penny. "What on earth is going on?"

"You have one of his works. Maybe all his clients receive a special invitation."

Liz dismissed Penny's knowing smile. "Yes. I never thought of that."

She noticed AJ out of the corner of her eye and glanced his way, watching him mix among the in-crowd as he offered handshakes and easy conversation. He'd tied his hair in a topknot, giving her a small thrill. His sexy sportsman look she called it. She didn't know why. AJ didn't even play sport as far as she knew.

He wore black pants and a white dress shirt rolled up at the sleeves. A notch up from his usual style. Gray herringbone braces added a playful touch and tonight, the boots were charcoal suede with a Cuban heel.

Her confusion increased with each passing minute.

AJ looked her way. This time, instead of ignoring her, he stared openly and smiled. It reminded her of the first time they met, his look laced with intent and the promise of so much more than her imagination could comprehend. He didn't make a move toward her, so she strolled the gallery, eager to view new paintings from Jacobs. There were eight works of his on display, each one as amazing as the next.

Occasionally, Liz snuck a peek at AJ, only to find his focus solely on her.

On the back wall, a large piece entitled *Greenstone Heart,* hung on a black background. A lone spotlight skimmed over the delicate right collarbone of a woman reclining in slumber, her left hand draped across a luminous forehead, palm upwards. Liz studied every inch, every stroke until she noticed a delicate silver chain, joined by a greenstone heart, dangling from the wrist of the muse. If one didn't know what to look for, one would barely notice the trinket as it blended into the visual language of the partially abstract piece.

Liz's fingers caressed the bracelet on her wrist, her thumb and forefinger worrying the greenstone of the heart. She frowned. The model in the painting was wearing her charm, or an interpretation of it.

She sensed him behind her, the smell of his cologne the only clue she needed. "Babe," he whispered as he pulled her in close. "What on earth are you wearing?"

She tensed.

"I've never seen you look more beautiful," he continued as he lifted her hands and kissed them. "Except possibly the day I photographed you asleep on the bed at the cottage."

"What?"

"I know you were mad at me, but when I saw you lying there, a soft shadow cast over the creamy skin of your breasts and your angelic face, radiant in the late afternoon light, I had no other choice."

She cupped her hands over her lips, breathed deeply and let a single tear fall, struggling for exchange as she recalled the time he joked about her meeting his friend, the artist.

He pulled her closer. "What do you think?"

"It's stunning. But I don't understand. Is it me?"

"Of course. Beautiful you."

"So, if it's me, then you're…Jacobs?"

"Occasionally."

Marielena and Garry's arrival at AJ's side broke the spell.

"Liz, so nice to see you again," Marielena said, offering one of her enthusiastic hugs. "Are you all right, dear? You look a little pale."

"I'm a bit overwhelmed, to tell you the truth."

"Stay with Mum." He squeezed her hands tightly. "I'll be back soon."

Liz watched him walk away, her awareness clouded in perplexity.

Marielena grabbed Liz's hand and held it firmly. A proud mother of a talented son. "What do you think of his recent works? He's improving each time he exhibits, don't you think?"

Before Liz could respond, AJ, standing on a small platform at the back of the gallery, caught her attention. He thanked everyone for coming, introduced the other artists in the exhibition, and offered his gratitude to Paul and Katy for their ongoing support.

"Lastly, I want to say special thanks to my parents, Marielena and Garry, who encouraged me to leave my 'real' job as an accountant to work on my art." He looked at his mother and smiled. She blew him a little kiss. "And to my beautiful girlfriend, who entered my world like a caress from the sun one cold, dark night, slowly turning impersonal routines into the personal, acquaintance into friendship, friendship into so much more." He looked directly at Liz. "Thanks for being my inspiration, on more than one occasion."

People turned and looked in her direction as AJ moved to her side. "Excuse me." He reached for her hand. "Hi. I'm one of the artists exhibiting here tonight." His soft voice matched his smile. "A friend of yours thought we should meet. I've been anticipating it for months. He said you love my work. I'm flattered."

"I don't understand. How can you be Jacobs?"

He chuckled. "Sometimes I ask myself that same question."

"And your work…it's amazing."

"Thank you. You sound surprised."

"But you're an accountant."

"Only in my nightmares."

"And I have a Jacobs, in my office. You painted the Jacobs in my office?"

"I did." He grinned. "I don't outsource my work. Let me get you a drink."

The next hour flew by in a flash as AJ moved Liz through the crowd, introducing her as his girlfriend. When he reached Paul and Katy, he left her in their capable hands while he interacted with his family and other guests. She recognized Katy as the blonde from the bar.

"So," Paul said. "We finally meet again, Liz. I always wondered about *Un Beso Imaginado*, but now you're standing in front of me, the resemblance is clear."

"Stop teasing," Katy said. "I'm so happy to finally meet you, Liz. AJ and I have had a few deep and meaningful conversations about you. Did he tell you he's our daughter, Eva's, Godfather?"

"No, he didn't. And what do you mean about *Un Beso Imaginado*?"

"You're the muse." Paul said.

"But I didn't even know him then."

"But you'd met, right? Before he went to Japan?"

Her brows drew together. "Yes, but…"

"Don't look so worried," Katy said. "You're not the first woman in history to be painted by an admirer, and you won't be the last. Let's all have dinner soon so you can meet our little girl."

Her thoughts raced. She was the muse? AJ's muse? "I'd love to, thank you," she murmured.

By eight-thirty, the gallery still buzzed with wine drinking hangers-on. Not wanting to impose on his night of triumph, Liz planned to slip away quietly, go home, snuggle up, and consider. It was all well and good him calling her his girlfriend and having this mysterious other life she knew nothing about, but the fact remained. Liz needed more than AJ was prepared to give.

He stood behind her and braced his hands on her shoulders. "Hey, you. Have you had a good night?"

"A great night. I'm sorry you had to send out a search party."

He turned her to face him, his charming side on full display. "No problem. Don't let it happen again."

She forced a smile. "I might grab a cab with Penny."

"Okay, I'll be home in about half an hour. Are you all packed?"

"Packed?"

"Didn't you get my text about this weekend?"

"Yes, but why do I need to pack?"

"We're going to Cambridge," he said firmly, bossy 'office' AJ coming to the fore. "We need to be away by ten."

Penny caught her attention as she gestured to Liz to hurry up. "Okay. I have to go."

He kissed her goodbye. "See you in a bit."

On the ride back to the terrace, Penny and Liz discussed why the AJ slash Jacobs scenario had never occurred to either of them. Surely Nate knew. So why hadn't he mentioned it?

As Liz climbed out of the cab, Penny called her back.

"Give him a chance, eh? He was so upset when he thought you weren't coming, and he couldn't stop staring at you all night."

"Thanks, Pen. I'm struggling to make sense of anything at the moment. I need time alone to think."

"Okay, hon. Text me over the weekend."

43

FAIR AND SQUARE

As SHE UNLOCKED the door with the usual tug, Liz couldn't stop thinking about *Greenstone Heart,* trying to decide if she liked it or *Un Beso* more. She dropped her phone and bag on the hall table and flicked on the light switch just inside the living room door.

Her heartbeat accelerated in her ears as the moisture left her mouth.

She stayed in the doorway. "What are you doing here? How did you get in?"

"You knew I was coming. I've been leaving my calling cards for weeks."

"How did you get inside?" she repeated.

Peter dangled a key from a short length of black leather. "You let me cut this months ago, remember. Wine?"

Liz glanced at the two glasses of wine on the coffee table—one full, the other almost empty. "I never gave you a key. Please leave. AJ will be home in a minute."

"I don't think so. He'll be out all night celebrating with his arty friends. Turns out your scruffy boyfriend is the very man I've been trying to track down. There's no use pretending he lives here because I know otherwise. Hasn't been here for weeks. He's shacking up with some slut in her bedsit, playing you for a fool. Everyone knows it." Peter patted the lid of the box to his left. "Come here. I've brought you flowers."

She looked at the black box, fear rising in her throat. "I don't want your damn flowers."

"No? You said gerberas weren't good enough, so I decided to up my game. You like roses, don't you?"

"What do you want?"

"Not you, anyway, let's make that perfectly clear. I never really wanted you. I just wanted someone to look good on my arm. Someone to flash around in front of my friends."

"You have to leave." Liz glanced at her watch. AJ had said he'd be half an hour. "Give me the key."

He dangled the key in front of her again. "Here."

Liz stepped forward and reached out. Peter yanked it back. "I want something in return. My painting. The one of the snog. Where is it?"

"I have no idea."

"Really? Until two days ago, it graced this very wall in front of us."

"You've been in here before?"

"Tell me where it is, and I'll leave."

Liz felt the clamminess of her hands as she rubbed her finger-tips over her palms. "As far as I know, it's been delivered to the owner."

"Who is?"

"I honestly don't know."

"I don't believe you. I understand Jacobs is causing quite a stir now people know who he is. Who would have thought you'd turn into an artist's muse for that prick."

"Look, I have no idea what you're talking about. Leave now, and I won't say a word to anyone. No one knows about the flow-ers. It can be our secret."

"Why should it be a secret? It's not a crime to send a friend flowers or visit her with the key she gave you." Peter gestured toward a chair. "Sit."

Liz stepped backward into the hallway, grabbed her phone, and bolted for the front door. It jammed and within a few seconds, Peter's hand pushed on it firmly from behind. Liz felt her muscles tense as he pressed into her back and pulled her hair, his breath reeking of alcohol. "It's a pity you didn't turn me on more, but these curls don't do it for me."

"Peter, please." A tight sob caught in her throat. "Don't do this."

"Shut the fuck up. I'm not here to hurt you." He released her. "You think I'm some thug like your friend Farrell?"

He forced her to look at him, then pushed her into the living room and onto the sofa. "Where's the painting?"

"I don't know. I told you."

"But you knew about it when I came to your office after the settlement. You lied then, and you're lying now."

"I've only just found out about AJ and his connection to Jacobs. I swear."

"Bullshit. You've known all along. You're the muse. That's why I want it. He'll hate the thought of it being with me, knowing how much you loved me."

Liz inhaled sharply. Her next words shot out on an exhale. "Okay. I'll ask him. I promise. I don't know who owns it. He won't tell me. I even wanted to buy it myself. He couldn't broker the deal."

"So, he knew you wanted it, but he wouldn't sell it to you. Some boyfriend."

"It's not like that." She struggled to keep her voice steady. "AJ doesn't own it. He sold it months ago."

"Really? Come over here and open your flowers."

Liz looked up as her phone rang.

"Leave it."

"But it's probably AJ. He'll wonder where I am."

"I said, leave the fucking phone."

As AJ pulled into the curb outside the terrace, he noticed a black Porsche parked across the street. He'd called Liz from the gallery to say he'd be another ten minutes. She didn't answer. Staying in his seat, AJ watched for movement through the living room window, then reached for his phone and shot her a text.

AJ: Call me. Urgent.

He knew if she got that text, she'd call him back straight away. He pulled up his contacts and hit the call icon.

"Hey. I'm at the terrace. We may have a situation here. Is Mike still with you?"

"Yeah," Ryan said. "Want us to swing by?"

"It may be nothing, but I don't have a good feeling about it."

"We're on our way."

AJ didn't make a sound as he tiptoed along the path, through the side gate, and snuck into the back garden. He stepped onto the deck, unlocked the sunroom door and inched it open. He'd made several strides forward before Peter even turned around.

"What the hell are you doing here?" AJ's gaze flicked between Liz and Peter, then at the two glasses of wine on the coffee table.

"We're just catching up, aren't we, Liz? She begged me to come over. Didn't expect to see you here, though."

AJ turned to Liz. "You invited him here?"

"Of course not. He has a key. A key I didn't know he had." Liz stood, her face puffy and red and covered in faint streaks of mascara. "He was here when I arrived home."

AJ moved forward, shielding Liz from Peter. "Go and open the front door and don't come back inside until I call you."

"For fuck's sake," Peter said. "You think it's her I want? Why

307

would I after you've had your dirty paws all over her? And she's just one of the many."

"Charming. No wonder Liz dumped your sorry ass. Liz," AJ said, his gaze still fixed on Peter. "Do as I say."

Liz glanced at AJ and hesitated, then left the room. AJ heard the deadbolt give way with a click just as the headlights of a car flashed across the living room window. He relaxed.

"Oh, very nice. So that's the attraction, is it? You speak, she jumps."

"I'll see you out."

"I'm not going anywhere until you tell me about *Un Beso*. I bought that painting fair and square. You stole it from me. And make no mistake, I'll be taking legal action." Peter stepped forward. He wasn't as tall as AJ, but physically strong.

"Really? What did you buy it with? Monopoly money?"

"I'd paid the deposit. It's mine."

"That painting is not yours. Never was and never will be." AJ pushed Peter with both hands. "Now get out."

"What's going on?" Ryan's voice boomed as he stood in the doorway.

"Mr. Nichols was just leaving," AJ said, his fists tight at his side. "And leave the key."

"You haven't heard the last of this." Peter slammed the key down on the hall table and turned to Ryan's friend standing at the front door. "And who the hell are you? Another thug?"

"Detective Inspector Mike Sweeney. I think it's time you left, don't you?"

"I'm going." Peter addressed AJ. "You'll be hearing from my lawyers." As he pushed past Liz, he grabbed her chin, holding it in a tight grip. "Thanks for the—"

Peter didn't have time to finish before AJ had him pinned up against the wall of the hallway. "Take your hands off her. Don't you ever touch her again, understand?"

"She's all yours, mate. I don't know what she sees in you, but there you go. There's no accounting for taste."

AJ pulled his grip tighter around Peter's collar before Mike intervened. "Okay, break it up."

Mike escorted Peter out onto the street as Ryan and AJ followed. "Keep away from Liz. Otherwise, we'll slap you with a restraining order."

"Fuck you."

"Hey." Strong arms encircled her, pulling her close.

Strangled sobs rose from deep within her belly. She started to shake. "I've never been so scared in my whole life. He…he said he never wanted me. He just wanted someone to…flash around his friends. That's what he said. Flash around his friends."

"Don't cry. It's okay." Lips caressed and hands soothed as she snuggled into him. "He won't bother you again. Not with Mike on his heels."

Ryan and Mike entered the room. "I don't think he'll be back," Mike said. He glanced at Liz. "The jerk's got a nerve using a key to gain entry."

"You okay, Liz?" Ryan asked.

"I'll be fine. Thanks. I really appreciate your help."

"No problem, babe."

"Um, Ryan, less of the babe," AJ smiled down at Liz still wrapped in his arms. "She's my girlfriend, not yours."

"Yeah. Sorry about that," Ryan said with a grin. "Anyway, we better go. Enjoy your weekend and forget about Peter Nichols for a few days. I'll get one of my guys to swing by in the morning and change the lock."

"Yeah, good idea," AJ said. "Send the bill to Nichols."

As Mike and Ryan drove away, AJ sat on the sofa next to her

and reached for her hand. "I'm so sorry. I should've come home with you."

"It's not your fault."

"I felt like punching the shit out of him. Just as well Ryan and Mike turned up when they did."

"I felt like punching him myself." Liz picked up the box and handed it to AJ. "He brought me these."

AJ frowned as he lifted the lid.

"It's box number four," Liz said. "Each one contains six dead roses. The first one arrived a few weeks ago."

He looked up. "And you didn't think to mention it?"

"I figured it was someone playing a joke."

"It's got Peter's dirty signature written all over it. You must have known they were from him. Why didn't you say something?"

"Because I didn't want to worry you."

"Right. Let me make one thing clear." AJ reached for her hands. "We're a couple. If you're worried, I'm worried. And if someone threatens you, I'll do everything in my power to remove that threat. What kind of man would I be if I didn't want to protect you from Peter Nichols and his bullshit?"

"I'm sorry I didn't tell you."

"Don't worry about it now." He softened. "But he won't get away with the stunt he pulled tonight."

"What are you going to do?"

"Get your fifteen thousand pounds back for a start and hopefully, a slap on the wrist for the bastard."

"I don't want the money back. I want nothing more to do with him."

"Anyway, we'll sort it out next week. Right. Are you all set?" He frowned as he posed the question.

"I might stay here." She looked at him with sad eyes. "I need time to think."

"I'm not leaving you alone, not now." He moved closer, tilted her chin and kissed her softly. "You've had a nasty shock. A few days away will do you good."

"Why didn't you tell me about Jacobs?"

"I don't want to discuss this now. You've just been through a terrible ordeal, and I'm exhausted. I just want to go away for the weekend with my girlfriend. So, get your stuff. Otherwise, it will be well after midnight before we get there."

"Why are you always so bossy and officious?"

He grinned, cocking his head to meet her gaze. "Bossy and officious mean the same thing."

"It's not funny." She hesitated for a moment. "And another thing," she continued, "you stood in my office and let me go on about my Jacobs. You even criticized your own work. Said you'd seen him do better. But the joke was on me. And don't even get me started on *Un Beso Imaginado,* or however you pronounce it."

"I'm an artist. We're all tarred with the brush of self-doubt."

She pulled a tissue from the box in front of her. Tears spilled over the rims of her eyes and tracked down her cheeks.

"Come on. Don't cry, babe. I'm sorry. Maybe I handled it all wrong. I can't change that now." He moved forward, sat back on his haunches in front of her and reached for her hands. "It doesn't mean I didn't want to tell you. I wanted to surprise you."

"You certainly did that. And I don't even know where you've been living lately."

"I've been at Lauren's."

"Lauren? The girl at the gallery tonight? The same girl you spent the night with after our argument?"

"How do you know about that?"

"Penny saw you together. So, Peter was right. While you've been pretending to be my boyfriend, you've been going home to Lauren. Saying 'let's make beautiful sex' to Lauren."

"Lauren is away, or was until today. I've been pet sitting her crazy ass dog. We've been friends for years, but I've never slept with her. Shit, she'd chew me up in an instant and wouldn't even bother spitting out the bones. And let's get one thing clear. I love you, Liz. You. You're the only woman I've wanted since leaving for Japan. I haven't had sex since then, and believe me, making love to you is all I've been thinking about lately.

"Do you know how difficult it was to lie next to you last night and not touch you?" he continued. "If you hadn't had a headache, we wouldn't even be having this conversation. I've never wanted another woman like I want you. The more time we spend together, the more I feel that way. I've watched you over the last few months deal with all the shit going on in your life, and you've handled it with dignity."

He reached for her, his lips caressing the skin of her neck and throat. "I've never said 'let's make beautiful sex' to anyone else. Beautiful sex is more than lust, so much more. Beautiful sex is a tender trace up and down the spine, a flutter of your heartbeat, and a sense that you belong to someone who touches your soul," he whispered.

"You love me?"

He leaned back, held her face in his hands, then gently kissed her mouth. "I do. So much. And what's more, you love me back."

"How do you know?" she whispered.

His hands reached for hers—lips barely touching lips—as the soft rhythm of his breath accompanied his words. "I sense what you sense. Every step, every stolen glance, every touch."

"I feel that too."

"Good, because I want to live with you, and not only in a physical sense. Sure, I want us to shower together, sleep together, make love, but also go to movies and concerts and eat beautiful food. And when we're in the car, I want to sing Dusty to you and not feel embarrassed about it, and for you to do the same."

"But you're celibate." The three words fell from her mouth, her last defense to his seduction.

He tried to suppress a grin and failed. "Nate O'Loughlin! I knew he couldn't keep his big mouth shut."

"And your friends. That night in Cambridge, they all joked about it."

"Yeah, well…before I went away, I made a two-year vow of celibacy and was determined to follow it through. It finished weeks ago. I wanted us to be friends. I didn't want it to be just sexual. And you were all mixed up over Peter, so I held back. I don't want to be your rebound romance. I want to be your long-term partner." He reached for her hands. "Believe me, there's nothing more I would rather do right now than to make beautiful sex with you. So, we better get out of here before our first time, second time around, isn't as romantic as you deserve. If you won't come with me, then we'll stay here, but I'm not letting you out of my sight all week-end, understand?"

She nodded. "I'm sorry, it's just—"

"You want me, and you think I'm not interested. I get it, believe me."

"So why all the teasing?"

"I wanted to make you feel desired, to woo you until you lost all conscious thought. Right, are we staying or going? Your choice."

Liz looked down as if trying to decide, then glanced up through her lashes. Their eyes locked. She bit her bottom lip, flirting a smile. "Going."

"Liz, don't."

"Don't what?"

"Look at me like that. I can't wait another ninety minutes. Maybe we should go in the morning."

"No, we'll go now."

He sighed. "Right. Get your stuff."

"You're such a bossy bastard."

"And you're such a damsel in distress."

She chuckled. "I am not."

"Come on. Let me have this fantasy. That's what bossy bastards do. They save damsels in distress." He lifted her chin and kissed her again, then pulled her into his arms and held her for a moment. "Did I mention the family is staying in London for the weekend? We have to feed the animals. It's just you, me, and the menagerie."

"How romantic." She reached up and kissed him. "Thank you for being in my corner."

"I'll always be in your corner." He handed her the keys. "You'd better drive. I've never been so tired in my entire life."

"Okay. Shall we take my car? It has a better sound system."

"Yeah, okay." He looked at her and smiled. "I've missed you. Are we good?"

She nodded. "We're good."

"Right, we'd better get on the road. Otherwise, I will have my wicked way with you over the hood of the Range Rover right here on the street."

44

QUICKSILVER DESIRE

AJ RECLINED his seat and closed his eyes. "Take the next on ramp."

Liz pulled onto the M11 and started laughing.

He shot her a sideways glance. "What's so funny?"

"You. Taking me to Cambridge for the weekend to feed the animals."

"I'm glad my excuse amuses you." He grabbed her hand. "I might doze off. I'll need my strength later."

"Doze away."

Excitement accompanied Liz on the drive north. AJ had said that he loved her, wanted them to be together, and hadn't had sex for two years. She decided to put all negative thoughts and feelings behind her. To make whatever they had work, for however long it lasted.

"AJ?"

He stirred. "Yeah, babe."

"Are you seriously saying I'm the last person you slept with?"

He chuckled. "Yep. Both real and imaginary."

"But didn't you get…"

"Horny. Frustrated. Blue balls?" He chuckled. "So much. It's not something I could ever get used to."

"And did it do you any good?"

"In what way?"

"Are you more spiritually in control of your urges?"

He glanced her way, his hand moving to her thigh. He gave her leg a tight squeeze. "Not one bit."

When they reached the cottage, AJ picked her up and carried her across the path, their luggage forgotten in the back of her SUV. As soon as they moved inside, he pulled off her jacket and threw it on the chair by the bed.

They stood under the low light of the room as AJ tugged free the zipper at the back of her dress. "This dress." He slipped his hands downward and smoothed them over her bottom. "This dress had every guy in the room turning heads."

"Don't be silly."

"It's true. I know I should be jealous, but I'm not. You're mine, and I don't give a shit who knows it."

She cocked a brow. "I'm yours?"

"Yep. Mr. Bossy Bastard, remember." He moved deliberately, his lips soft on the porcelain skin of her neck, then stopped for a moment to look at her. "I'm a lucky man. Let's get this dress on the floor."

The room was warm—too warm. Even so, goose bumps covered her skin and much to his amusement, Liz shivered a little. She stood before him in a short nude colored slip and a silky pair of stay-ups, the scent of her arousal wafting around him. Pulling at the strap of her slip, he whispered, "Take this off. Leave the rest on. Then I'm going to kiss you like I really mean it."

AJ unbuttoned his shirt and tugged it free, his erection bold and ready. Strong arms encircled her waist as he explored her mouth with his tongue. It was the kiss of *Un Beso Imaginado,* and at that moment, he was the *artista* and she the *musa.*

They stepped into the bathroom. His shirt, braces, and pants fell to the floor in a heap as shadows from the lamp in the living room illuminated the mirror with a soft glow. He turned to face her, holding her hands. "By taking this next step, you agree to us having an ongoing relationship, both sexual and otherwise."

She looked at him without a single blink, her lips full of want. "Not casual?"

The fire in his eyes danced with a slight smile. "I want us to be a couple, just you and me. Agree?"

"Just you and me." She reached for the clasp at the back of her bra. It fell to the floor.

Her breasts were more beautiful than he'd remembered. Perfect parcels of authentic desire. AJ held her gaze. "Panties."

As Liz removed her panties, she motioned for him to do the same. "Boxers."

"I knew you'd be feisty." He stood back to look at her, then turned on the shower. "You are one beautiful woman, Lizzy Dobson, but are you sure you're up for it? It could be a little intense."

Her breath caught as he removed his boxers and he laughed at her reaction.

She scraped her teeth across her bottom lip. "I've never been so sure in my life."

"Beautiful *and* brave."

AJ stepped into the shower and pulled her under the water. His hands moved to her breasts. A determined forefinger slowly traced inward, like a spiral pattern of a seashell. He stopped, then gently flicked his tongue over the peak of one nipple as he cupped the fullness of her other breast.

Droplets of steam clung to the windowpane, cocooning the moment as he inhaled the scent of water, body wash, and rain-soaked country air.

He watched her wash him, sucking in a breath as she ran the

soapy cloth between his legs. She was strong, both physically and mentally, and he loved that about her.

"Never let anyone tell you you're not sexy. You are the epitome of sensuality. No question. No doubt."

She reached up to kiss him. "You're such a caring man. I never got that vibe when we first met."

"Yeah, I did come on a bit strong."

"But that's nice too. You know, having someone really interested."

"I thought about you all the time when I was away. Wondered what you were doing and who you were with."

"I thought about you too—not all of it complementary."

He laughed and cut the water. They dried each other slowly, the white cotton caressing ready skin as his intensity hovered like a moody rain cloud about to burst.

Wrapped in a fresh towel, AJ swept Liz into his arms and carried her to the bed. The towel sprawled underneath her as he grabbed her hands and placed them above her head. "Keep your hands here until I tell you." He laughed at the look on her face. "Are you okay?"

"I feel drunk. Sexy drunk."

They kissed slowly—deeply—before he pulled back and considered her. Eager hands cupped her breasts as determined thumbs stroked back and forth over her nipples. "Let's make beautiful sex."

At first, he glided his hands and lips gently across her skin like the brush of a feather. But the more she arched and squirmed, the firmer he touched, pinching tightened nipples as he sucked the base of her neck into his hot mouth to taste the briny essence of her.

"I'm falling," she murmured. "Catch me."

"What?" He chuckled. "We haven't even started yet." His hands stilled. Sitting back on his haunches between her legs, he gently urged her knees apart. He bent down, kissed the soft skin above her belly button and inhaled, then repeated the motion, his lips soft but needy against her core. He wanted to control her—until she lost all coherent thought and the regular rhythm of her breath. Until she couldn't string two words together. He continued to coax, pushing her to the brink and back repeatedly before shifting their position with skillful touch and whispered commands.

"Hands down," he murmured. "Don't touch me below the waist."

Her voice sang on a husky whisper. "But I want to."

"If you touch me, babe, I'll explode. I want to be inside you for that." He reached over and grabbed a condom off the nightstand, tore open the packet, and rolled it on as she watched, eyes wide with fascination.

AJ nestled beside her, his breath cool against her skin, his teeth gently nipping her earlobe. Her tension tightened under his touch as he sucked her fingers into his mouth. "Tell me if it's too much." He shifted his weight, his arms holding him steady. "Okay?"

"Never."

"You really are brave."

They stayed tangled together, lost in each other's form—oblivious of time and space or the soft hum of the rain—as months of frustration hijacked his resolve to take his time. Her climax matched his in strength and speed. Desire and emotion overflowed until he stilled, collapsing on top of her.

After several moments, he rolled them side on and stroked the curls from her face. "I'm sorry I got carried away. I couldn't help myself. I'll last longer next time, I promise." He lay back and laughed. "Holy shit. Two years is a bloody long time to go without sex."

"You don't have to last longer. That was perfect."

AJ swallowed back a sudden rush of emotion. "I've waited

ages to have loving sex with you. And wow. It was mind-blowing."
He kissed her again. "Amazing for only our second time together."

She snuggled under the covers. "It was. You are quite
the lover."

"Yeah?"

"Yeah."

AJ jumped off the bed and entered the bathroom, a contented
smile on his lips. He called back. "Hey, beautiful? Are you
hungry? I do room service." He was acting like a little kid with a
new toy, and while he usually kept this side of himself private,
with Liz, he felt relaxed and in safe hands.

"Room service? From where?"

"I asked Mum to grab us some food. We even have dessert."

"Really?" She perched up on her elbows, sounding as excited
as he was. "What kind of dessert?"

"Layered Chocolate Mousse. Want some?"

"You're teasing."

"I'm not. Will you feed me?"

They sat on the bed, her in a cami and panties, him in a well-fitting
pair of black boxers, feeding each other morsels of delicious food
as they chatted away like the familiar friends they were.

"This famous studio," Liz asked. "Do you lease it?"

"No, I own it. A friend left it to me. Well over two years
ago now."

"You mean in his will?"

He smiled softly. "Yes. *She* died of cancer at the tender age of
forty-six."

"That's so sad. What was her name?"

"Cathy." He gathered his thoughts. Apart from his parents and
Chris, he rarely talked about her to anyone. "We met at an art class
she ran. She'd been married twice, widowed once, divorced once,

and couldn't have kids. Her face fascinated me. The way she wore her sadness for the entire world to see and made no bones about it. Many of us hide our sorrow. Cathy embraced hers."

"Were you lovers?"

"Yes, but not in the 'in love' sense—at least not for me. We were friends with rather a lot of benefits. Being much older, she had an entirely different view of the world than most of the women I'd been with. Her serenity grounded me when my ego spiraled out of control. She taught me a lot about life."

He smiled at the thought. "I never realized how much she loved me until a few days before she died. She had cancer when we first met, but apart from her family, no one knew. We slowly lost touch. I moved on to younger and brighter girls, and Cathy faded away without a word. Then one day, her brother phoned me out of the blue asking if I would be a pallbearer. He thought I knew.

"Everything I stood for crumpled that day. For Cathy to be so humble and unselfish in death because she didn't want me to witness her pain… Well, I felt like someone had shot me through the heart. I spent the next eight days at her bedside. By this time, her once finely crafted body—she was an avid yoga enthusiast and dancer—had been ravaged by the illness. She was so thin, she could hardly stand."

"I can't imagine how anyone could cope with that. She sounds incredible."

"Yeah, she was. When her lawyer contacted me, I thought she may have left me a painting. Instead, she'd left me the studio. Her family insisted I keep it. They spent days clearing out her works, apart from a nude I'd posed for. Afterward, I went to the studio I'd visited so many times before and cried. It's the only time in my adult life I can remember crying. Then, apart from one night when I painted for six hours straight, the night we met at the bar, I locked the studio and left for my trip soon after. I started *Un Beso* that night. It sat unfinished for eighteen months."

He stopped for a moment and pulled Liz closer, kissing her

softly. "Cathy always talked of Shikoku, wanted us to go together. After she died, my life seemed so pointless. I needed a purpose. I was a bit of a player in those days."

"Didn't you ever fall in love?"

"Not really. But I fell in lust, a lot."

"How come you didn't tell me you were Jacobs?"

"I tried that first night at the gallery, but you jumped to the wrong conclusion and stormed off. Then you left for New Zealand, and I didn't have the chance. I wanted to keep the identity of the couple in *Un Beso* private, at least until I knew how you felt about me."

"So, I'm the muse, for *Un Beso*?"

"Of course. And the muse for *Greenstone Heart*. The first time you condescended to talk to me at the bar, I felt an undeniable need to paint you. I didn't even know you were Nate's cousin then."

She smiled.

"As time passed, I wanted to sell my work, so I had something to offer you." He kissed her neck with a playful peck. "It was fun, having a part of me you knew nothing about. I thought my nosy sisters would spill. When I realized they hadn't, I asked everyone to keep schtum. I assumed you'd figure it out."

"I feel stupid that I didn't, and so does Penny."

"Don't say that. I like to keep AJ the accountant and Jacobs the painter separate. It's easier that way. The other issue was my celibacy. I set myself two years. Shit, I nearly stuffed up so many times in those first few weeks at the terrace." He chuckled at the recollection. "I wanted to storm into your room, jump on your bed, and make beautiful sex all night long and again for breakfast. But it was important for us to be friends first. That night when we were in the kitchen, I wanted you so badly. And you left me alone at one in the morning, listening to music with a freaking boner for company."

Liz laughed. "I'm sorry."

He snuggled into her. "I love you, Lizzy. So much."

"I love you too, Mr. Jacobs." She ran her fingers through his light smattering of chest hair. "I've missed you these past two weeks, been a bit lost to tell you the truth. It's the closeness we had…have. I tried hard to keep my distance at first. My self-esteem had hit an all-time low after I broke up with Peter. I didn't feel sexy or desirable or worthy of a man like you."

"Just because he wasn't horny doesn't mean you aren't sexy. That's his problem, not a reflection on you. When I saw you in that dress tonight, I wanted to peel it off and suck you dry."

"Stop it, you're embarrassing me."

"Oh really, because you're so coy and innocent. What is it you Kiwis say? Yeah, right," he teased. "Tell me what happened between you and Peter?" His tone turned serious.

"What didn't happen is more to the point. We only had sex, if you can call it that, a dozen times at the most. He wasn't interested, and I thought it was my fault."

"I've imagined making love to you every day for the past two years, and he had you in his reach and didn't desire you. Stupid prick."

"Still, it doesn't matter now. It's over and I don't want to give it charge anymore." Liz ran her hand up his arm and traced the pattern of his tattoo with her fingers. "I love your tattoo."

"Really? I thought you hated tats."

"Not yours. It suits you."

"Thanks. They hurt like mad, so it's my one and only." He kissed her on the cheek, then returned his attention to the food. "Shit, we have enough food here to last all weekend. Just as well."

"Why? What will we be doing besides feeding the animals?"

He laughed. "Exploring. Movies. Exploring some more."

"Sounds perfect." She picked up a piece of cheese and popped it into her mouth. "How long do you plan on keeping me here?"

"Keeping you here? Aren't you staying of your own accord?"

He reached over and kissed her on her forehead. "Only until Sunday afternoon, or maybe Monday morning. Then, next week, we'll start negotiations."

"What do you mean?"

"You'll see."

45

MOODY AND MOLTEN

"WHAT ARE YOU BURNING?"

Liz closed the door of the wood-burner and offered AJ a flirty smile. "Nothing. Just a silly list."

"Come upstairs. I have something to show you."

"So, I finally get to see the studio where you sketch nude damsels in distress."

"I've never painted a nude. Will you pose for me one day?"

"What, nude?" She frowned. "Um...no."

"Come on, I love your naked body. There's something about a woman with real...attributes." He laughed at her reaction.

Upstairs, filtered light flooded the room through small dormer windows in the roofline, giving the space a sacred feel. Liz glanced at the floor—stained to a rich dark charcoal and splashed with shades from many stories told on canvas. Around the room, two easels sat with partially finished works, sad and empty as if cast aside for labors of more prominence.

The room had a presence—artistic echoes of painted conversations. Crystals hung in random length and order from small hooks on the window frames, dancing their prisms of color across the walls like in the story of *Pollyanna* Liz remembered from her childhood.

"I draw up here a lot. And this is where I painted the work in your office. The room has a unique feel about it, don't you think?"

"It does. I love the crystals." She moved around in awe, daring to touch when she wanted a more tactile experience than her sight conveyed.

"I do too. Seven colors streaming into one rainbow of light."

"These paintings are so vibrant compared to *Un Beso*. More like my Jacobs. Amazing."

"When I painted *Un Beso*, I tried to remember my feelings from the first night we talked and the day we kissed. Then, two years later when I asked you what you thought about it, your assessment was spot on. You got it, probably because I got you, right from the start. Your passion, your desire. You were there in front of me, moody and molten and melting from my grasp, yet I couldn't touch you."

"Who are you? Where has the old AJ gone? The bossy businessman and the casual housemate?"

"There's a time and place for all things. Don't you agree?"

"I do. But you're making me nervous."

He laughed. "Come here to the window. I want to show you something." She stepped forward. "Close your eyes and run your hand over the crystals. Tell me what you feel."

She moved her hand carefully along the line, feeling each crystal with her thumb and forefinger until she reached an entirely different shape.

"This one, it's different." She paused, feeling the circle with her fingers. "A ring."

"Okay. Keep your eyes closed." He removed the ring from the hook and handed it to her. "Describe it for me."

"It has a round center stone, and on either side, two rows of... tiny leaves? The band is fragile. Worn."

"Can you imagine the metal and the stones?"

"Rose gold and diamonds?"

"That's exactly what I do when I paint. I close my eyes and touch, let the subject talk to me. With you, I couldn't touch, so the process was different."

She opened her eyes and studied the ring. "It's beautiful. I love vintage jewelry."

"Me too. I want to paint it. It belonged to my Spanish grand-mother, then Mum and now the oldest son."

"It's a wonder David would let it out of his sight."

"He knows it's safe with me."

They made love three times during Saturday and the early hours of Sunday morning, Liz amazed at his stamina and recovery time. She fell asleep for the last time around five. When she awoke, AJ was gone.

An antique carriage clock on the mantle to the side of the fire-place read ten thirty-five as it marked off the day with an insignifi-cant tick. Liz assumed it was incorrect. She never slept late, but when she checked her phone, the glow of numbers on the screen matched the clock, give or take a few seconds.

Outside, light drizzle peppered the glass, and as she looked out across the meadow, Liz wondered where he could be.

She showered, dressed, and sat on the sofa with a magazine. She was just about to call him when he strolled in with the Sunday paper and a loaf of fresh bread.

He bent down and kissed her. "Good morning, beautiful. How was your sleep in?"

"Great. I'm only just up."

"Feeling okay?"

Liz had asked herself the same question only a few moments ago. She pulled her bottom lip under her top teeth and smiled. "A little edgy."

AJ nodded slowly. "The honeymoon phase only lasts eighteen months. Are you up for it?" He laughed at her shocked expression. "I'm joking. Once I'm back at work, I'll slow down a bit."

She recalled their night together. Each touch and kiss reminded her of the last time, but the improvement he'd showed as the night progressed was worthy of a mental mention. "What have you been doing this morning?"

"Showered, ate breakfast alone." He sat at the table and opened the paper. "Took the dogs for a walk, fed the animals. Now I'm home with my beautiful girlfriend."

"It's a pity it's raining. I wanted a walk before lunch."

"We could have an oral recital if you're keen."

He didn't look up from the paper, the remark so casual, she almost missed his intention. "Excuse me?"

"If you'd rather not, don't worry," he said matter-of-factly as he turned the page and skimmed over the headlines.

She paused. "It's not that, it's... I'm, um... I've never, you know," she whispered, hiding her face behind the cover of *Vogue* so he wouldn't notice her embarrassment.

He looked up now. "What? Either way?"

"You sound surprised."

AJ sat next to her on the sofa, reached for the magazine, and placed it on the coffee table. "I am a bit. What do you think?" Hot kisses rained over her neck and earlobes. "How about a little intro? Oral one *oh* one."

She craned her neck, offering it up to his touch. "I guess it's important in life to be open to new experiences, don't you agree?" she whispered, then started to laugh. "You'll have to talk me through it, and..."

"And?"

"I want to go first."

"Okay."

"Where do we start?" Liz tried not to look at him, but AJ was having none of that. He reached for her and held her face in his hands, kissing her softly. "We start right here." He moved her into a kneeling position in front of him. "Now you take off my jeans and boxers." He gently lifted his butt in assistance. "And then you move to here." He guided her onto the floor and pulled her between his legs as he watched her expression with amusement.

"And then?" Her voice, husky with desire, puffed over his skin.

"And then..." He kissed her, gently plunging his tongue into her eager mouth. "We kiss a little."

"And then...?"

AJ gathered her hair in his hands, leaned back, and closed his eyes as he tried to keep his butt on the sofa. "Shit, Liz. No further instructions necessary. *Fuck*."

It was mid-afternoon. Liz strolled in from the bathroom, towel drying her hair. AJ sat on the rug in front of the coffee table, head-phones on, his back against the sofa. He looked up and smiled. She sat next to him, massaging his shoulders, a white robe loosely covering her body. Leaning his head back, he closed his eyes, enjoying her touch and the flow of the music.

"Do you want to try now?" he asked.

The massage stopped. "Maybe later. When it's dark."

He shook his head as a wry smile slipped into place, then stood and opened the drawer of the dresser, pulling out a black satin sleep mask. He reached forward, held her face and positioned the mask into place.

"Dark enough?"

"I—"

"Lie back." He undid her robe and let it fall, exposing her half-naked body to the intensity of his sight. Hands and lips touched and kissed—her forehead, each eyelid, cheeks, the tip of the nose, her chin. He sucked on her pouty lips, then moved downward to her breasts, belly, and the soft skin on the inside of her thighs.

She tensed.

"Relax, babe." Roaming hands traced over her skin as his breath quicken. "If you're uncomfortable, just say so." He bent her left leg to rest along the back of the sofa.

"Okay," she whispered. "Do I need a safe word?"

"What?" He chuckled at her innocence. "I'll be gentle, I promise. Why are you shaking? I haven't even started yet."

"I don't know. Why do you always find everything so funny?"

"It's a nervous reaction."

"As if."

"We're making beautiful sex. You're safe with me, but you have to shush now because I'm busy."

AJ reached for the stereo remote and pushed play. A chant in Latin flowed softly around the room, the beat resonating with his touch. His rhythm.

Seconds turned to minutes as he explored her in ways he'd often imagined. He looked up, kissed her soft tummy, and darted his tongue into her belly button. "You have a beautiful little butterfly."

She squirmed under his touch. "Don't look."

"You're wearing the mask, not me." He laughed as she tried to close her legs. "I can see everything."

"AJ?"

"Yes, Lizzy?" He moved forward, hot kisses caressing upwards, finding her breasts, hard and wanting.

"Let's make beautiful sex again," she whispered. "Only if you're ready."

He pulled off her mask and grinned up at her. "You're going to ruin me."

"Is that a problem?"

"Hell no!"

HEART AND SOUL

"CAN WE HAVE A QUICK MEETING?" AJ wandered into her office, tablet in hand. "We have a few things to discuss."

Liz looked up from her screen. "Sure. What's up?"

"First, I had a word with Ivan this morning. Peter Nichols has reluctantly agreed to donate fifteen thousand pounds to the school's mentoring program in your name. Also, the police have cautioned him about appropriate break-up behavior. If he puts a foot out of line, he knows you'll take out a non-molestation order."

Liz exhaled. It seemed she'd been waiting for weeks for a resolution to her run in with Peter. "No more roses."

"Let's hope. Also, it's time to talk about an asset protection agreement for you and that Jacobs guy. I'll ask Ivan to arrange something."

"Is that necessary?"

"Absolutely. As your business advisor, it's my job to safeguard your assets. Your net worth is considerable. I'm positive your boyfriend wouldn't want to enter into a serious relationship without adequate safeguards in place. Even if he's a struggling artist, his works may be valuable in the future, so a prenup is a necessity for both parties."

Liz tried to keep a straight face. "Okay."

"This is not something to take lightly, so it's important we get the ball rolling. Don't you agree?"

"Not really, but I appreciate your wise council." Liz grinned up at him through her lashes and casually opened the top two buttons of her shirt. "I'm open to all of your suggestions."

He shot her a cheeky grin back, then cleared his throat. "Okay, what else." He skimmed over his tablet. "Your boyfriend and his associates have received an unconditional offer on the infamous heritage listed property. He's keen to invest in the family home."

"Great news. But we don't have a family."

"Keep flirting like that, and you'll have a family sooner than you think."

She glanced at the fly of his jeans, then flicked her gaze back to his, her finger lightly tracing the outline of her top lip. "I have no idea what you mean."

"Really? The stationery cupboard is looking very inviting at the moment. Want to take a look?"

"I don't need any stationery."

"Is that right, Ms. Dobson?" He adjusted his jeans. "Oh, by the way, a package arrived for you this morning. It's in my office."

Liz frowned her concern. "Do you know what it is? You don't think it's from Peter, do you?"

He took her by the hand. "No, babe," he murmured. "It's not from Peter."

In the corner of his office, a large painting covered with a drop cloth leaned against the wall. AJ carefully removed the cloth and stepped back.

Liz stepped forward. "What? No! How on earth?"

His arms snaked around her waist as he snuggled into her neck. "A gift from my heart and soul to yours."

"You kept it for me? I thought someone already owned it. The guy who bought it for his wife to be."

"That's right."

"What? No!"

"You've said that already." AJ pulled her in closer. *"Un Beso Imaginado.* Where it all began. The imagination of our first kiss."

Her hand reached out and she traced the couple in the air. "I don't understand. Thank you so much."

"You, my beautiful, are welcome." AJ stood back, allowing Liz time to process his gift.

"I love this painting. Have done since the first time I saw it."

"I know. Come over here and sit down."

He guided her to the sofa. She sat. He knelt—on one knee—and pulled a small black velvet pouch out of his back pocket. "Lizette April Dobson. I never imagined I'd find someone who'd want to wear my grandmother's engagement ring." He tugged the cord open and held the ring before her. "After all, my grandfather neither had the desire nor the resources to indulge his future wife in ostentatious displays of affection. And yet, this ring is so you— delicate and beautiful."

Liz cupped her hands over her face as her heartbeat raced.

"I spent many long nights in Asia reflecting on us, our special night, and this moment. I love you and want us to join as we were in my imagination, all those months ago when I painted us in our first kiss." AJ held out the ring and offered it to her. "Will you marry me?"

"I would love to."

He slipped the ring on her finger and kissed her. "I desperately want to make love to you right now," he whispered.

"And here's me thinking you'd turned into a hopeless romantic."

He strode across the office and locked the main door leading into the foyer. "Hey, Liz," he called. "I can't find the new printer cartridge. I need your help."

She stepped forward and smiled. "We can't."

AJ reached out and grabbed her by the hand. "Yes, we can. We can do whatever we want."

"But what if someone comes?"

He grinned. "We won't hear a thing. I promise."

Back at the terrace, AJ slouched on the sofa, guitar in hand as usual. "We'd better Skype your folks."

Liz looked up from painting her nails. "True. Dad's an old-fashioned guy. He'll make you beg for my hand and offer cows as compensation."

"Already taken care of."

"What? You've already asked my dad?"

"Yep. It's been hard keeping the secret."

"How many cows did you have to pay?"

AJ laughed as he recalled the conversation he'd had with his conservative future father-in-law. "A whole herd. He's a tough negotiator, your dad."

She puffed across her hand to dry the polish. "Does anyone else know?"

"Just my parents...and Nate. I didn't want him finding out through the grape vine. He's very protective of you."

"And was he cool with it?"

"Not exactly. I talked him round, though." AJ stood and straightened *Un Beso Imaginado* a fraction. "My sisters will be hysterical when they find out."

"So will mine." Liz held out her hand, admiring the vintage ring. "I still can't believe I have this beautiful ring. I'm so glad Zoe wanted something brand spanking new and showy."

"Yeah. And next weekend we're flying to Spain to visit Mum's family and have you measured up for a pair of my uncle's world-famous boots."

"Really? I've never been to Spain. Do you want me to make the booking?"

"No. All booked and paid for." He moved to her side and kissed her on the top of the head. "Are those nails dry yet?"

She chuckled. "Not quite."

EPILOGUE

TWELVE MONTHS LATER

SINCE ARRIVING in New Zealand ten days earlier, AJ had been dropped in the deep end of the Dobson family experience, and the close-knit clan welcomed him warmly. When he thought about it, they were comparable to his own family, with similar dynamics and values. And just like at Tancroft, privacy was a nonexistent commodity in the Dobson household.

He stretched back on the bed and watched Liz remove her watch and earrings. "Izzy got her flower girl wish."

"You should see her in her dress." Liz glance at him over her shoulder. "She looks adorable."

"I can't wait to see you in yours."

"Not long now."

"Lizette?"

She turned. "Yes, *Anthony*?"

He offered his hand. "If you come over here right now and are nice to me, we could make a baby."

"What? The night before our wedding? You're not even supposed to be here. You need to be back in the guest room by midnight."

He reached out and pulled her onto the bed. "Babe, I'm thirty-three. I don't want to wait." He planted soft kisses along her neck and throat. "After all, baby Tanner will have a dual passport. May as well get the ball rolling while we're on Kiwi soil."

"Sometimes I have trouble following your train of thought."

"That's because I'm artistic, and your brain is full of business."

"Is that right?"

AJ jumped out of bed, switched off the center light, and opened the curtains, flooding the room with the soft glow of a waxing moon. He flicked the lock on the bedroom door, then sat on the bed, staring down at her. "Yep. I know these things," he whispered as he leaned in to kiss the skin at the top of her breasts.

"We shouldn't."

"Why not?" His lips moved to her throat. "You want me. I can almost taste it."

"You always think I want you."

"True." He pulled her closer. "And I have to say, Ms. Dobson, soon to be Mrs. Tanner, the feeling is mutual."

Liz slipped down in the bed, walking her fingers up and down his spine. "I don't want Mum and Dad to hear us."

He nuzzled into her, pecked and sucked her skin, his hands cupping her breasts as he settled between her legs. "Hmm. Can't promise they won't."

"AJ?"

"Babe, you feel so good."

"AJ. Stop," she whispered. "There's someone at the door."

He looked up. "Shit!"

"Who is it?" Liz called as she reached for AJ's T-shirt from the bedroom floor and tugged it over her head.

"It's me, can I come in?"

"Um…hold on."

The door handle rattled. "Liz? Do you have AJ in there?"

AJ shook his head in disbelief, fumbling with his boxers. "Doesn't your sister understand male anatomy?"

Liz giggled. "Behave."

"Come in, Ally," he called, stuffing a pillow over his erection as Liz jumped up to unlock the door.

"AJ. What are you doing here?" Ally whispered. "Can't you keep your hands off her for one night?" She laughed and jumped on the bed. "It's my job as chief bridesmaid to keep my sister in line."

He grinned. "Don't worry, I'm keeping her in line for you."

"So it seems. Anyway, I'm glad you're both here. I want to ask you guys something."

"Are you all right?" Liz asked.

"Not bad." Ally released a sigh and managed a tight smile. "I was wondering if I could come back to London with you."

"Sure," AJ said. "Our guest suite is yours for as long as you want it."

"Hold on a minute," Liz said with a grin. "She's a handful, this one."

"I'll keep an eye on her," AJ said.

"Do you feel secure enough to leave home at the moment?" Liz asked, a note of concern in her voice. "You know, after what happened with Angus?"

"Yes. I don't want to wait. But the thought of taking the flight on my own kind of scares me."

AJ reached for his phone on the nightstand. "I'll email you our flight details."

"Thanks."

"Now, as much as we love your company," AJ said as he smiled at Ally, "I only have a pass out until midnight. So, I'll see you tomorrow at the wedding, and you and Liz can talk over breakfast. Now go to bed."

"Okay, okay, I'm going. You guys behave. Promise?"

AJ and Liz both grinned, shared a glance and said in unison, "We promise."

As Ally closed the bedroom door, AJ grabbed Liz around the waist.

"I love your family, babe, but shit, they can be full on. And Mitch is a little intimidating. I feel like a midget beside him."

"I'm a lucky girl. I have a supportive family, wonderful friends—"

"A sexy fiancée."

"That too."

"Turn around," AJ said.

"It's twenty minutes to midnight. You need to leave. Now."

"Plenty of time to make beautiful sex."

THE END

Not ready to leave London? Next in the series, Ryan Farrell, the buff builder who was crushing on Liz, offers Ally Dobson an invitation:

How About Thursday

"What makes you think I'd be interested?"
"What makes you pretend you're not?"

This contemporary stand-alone romance will have you staying up late just to read one more chapter. So download *How About Thursday* today!

A CEO - A TEMP - AN IMAGINED KISS

"Perfect, my kind of read. 5 stars."

Please read on for the first chapter of
How About Thursday.

HOW ABOUT THURSDAY

SPECIAL DELIVERY

Thursday. A nondescript, 'take it or leave it' kind of day. Thursday couldn't hold a candle to the emotion of Monday, the excitement of Friday, or even begin to touch that day of all days, Saturday.

And yet, Ally Dobson had arrived in London on a Thursday, found a place to live the following Thursday, and secured a temp job two weeks later on yet another Thursday. Maybe her animosity toward the day was misplaced.

But that Thursday, as she alighted from a cab and stepped into a muddy puddle, splashing her skirt and stockings with drips of dirty rainwater, Ally wondered again why Thursday disliked her so much.

She glanced up at the detached Victorian house in front of her. High fencing, hung with the obligatory *Keep Out* signs and warnings about unauthorized entry, surrounded the street frontage of the renovation. She entered through a side gate, ducked under the scaffolding, and knocked on the open door. Receiving no reply, she stepped inside. The large home looked like it had been savagely attacked by an overzealous developer, and the high-pitched whine of a Skilsaw sent a shiver through her veins. In the distance, a nail gun fired, and a radio pumped out 'You Don't Own Me'—the Grace version.

"Yo! What's up?" A young man sauntered toward her, a nasty hickey at the base of his neck and his dreads covered by a hard hat.

"Hi, I'm Ally. Is Jono here? I have a package for him."

His gaze drifted downward, then slowly back up again. "Ally. Pretty name." It'd been ages since a guy had looked at her like a piece of meat, and she struggled to keep her amused mouth shut. "You know he's married, right?"

"No, I didn't know that. What a shame."

"Anyway, he's not here. But I'm the apprentice." He flashed a cocky grin. "So it's me, or me. If you play your cards right, maybe we could meet for a drink later, and I just might have a package for you. I like a bit of cougar, me."

Cougar? At twenty-three? "Really?"

"Yeah. Really."

"Jack, what are you doing? I'm waiting for a lift." The owner of the booming voice—all black tank, muscles, and tight jeans— grabbed a hard hat from the peg on the wall and plonked it on Ally's head without saying another word. Her hair flattened down around her face, and she could hardly see out from under the rim.

"Sorry, mate. Got talking to Ally here."

Black Tank still didn't look Ally's way. "Okay, well finish up and get back to work." He went to walk away but turned back. "And, miss." He looked at her now with the most beautiful hazel eyes that had ever refused to smile. "Next time you come onto one of our construction sites, grab a hat and wear it."

She tipped the hat slightly to get a better view. And what a view it was! Chiseled planes of hard muscle everywhere she looked, and shoulders that could carry a girl through an entire rock concert. On his left wrist sat a large hammer-proof watch and, just to prove he didn't take himself too seriously, a couple of multicol- ored woven friendship bracelets.

"So, where's yours?"

He paused, his expression one of wry amusement. "My what?"

"Hard hat."

Staring at her with narrowed eyes, he rubbed his fingertips over his lips in a gesture of contemplation, any hint of amusement gone in an instant. "You're wearing it," he said finally.

"Very gallant of you."

Shaking his head, he turned to walk away.

"Excuse me," Ally called after him. "Are you the foreman?"

He didn't turn around. "No."

She pulled the package from her bag. "I'm supposed to give this to Jono."

Looking at the apprentice, Black Tank cocked his head in the direction he'd come from. The young man winked at Ally as he ambled past, pulling up his jeans in the process. "Might see you later, sugar."

Black Tank huffed out a heavy sigh and turned to look at her, his expression softening. "That boy has a Casanova complex."

"So I see."

"Jono had to leave early." He looked her in the eye as he reached for the courier bag. "I'll see he gets it."

"Thank you."

The guy went to walk away once more, still all businesslike and looking like someone had just murdered his grandmother. Ally called after him again. "Excuse me, may I have your name?"

He turned and frowned. "For what?"

"Gina, my boss at Farra."

The frown froze on his face, but oh, what a face. He was what her housemate, Jia, would call a 'bells and whistles' kind of guy. Chiseled jawline, light stubble, and full lips that could kiss away a boring Sunday. And those bells and whistles went very nicely with the rest of the package. This guy was built—and not only built—but also tall, with arms that could easily hold a girl the way she ached to be held. Still, he could stand to lose the arrogance.

"Why didn't she just use a courier?"

His question drew her attention to his voice instead of his body. "She tried. They never turned up, so she asked me to drop it off."

He paused for a moment. "Ryan."

Ally pulled out her phone and opened her contacts. "Sorry, did you say Ryan?"

As if he knew she'd heard him correctly, he didn't bother repeating himself.

"And your number?" she asked.

"You're asking me for my number?"

She glanced up. Although his lips had moved a fraction, it wasn't so much a smile; it was more of a 'cat toying with a mouse' kind of expression. "In case we have to get in touch. The last package went missing. Gina asked me to give this one to Jono and no one else."

"Yes. So you said." He grabbed his phone out of his jeans pocket and unlocked it. "How about you give me your number, and I'll forward my details. Name?"

"Ally." She rattled off her number and a few seconds later, her text alert sounded. Ryan went to walk away, but turned back, grabbed the hard hat off her head and put it on his own. He held up the package. "I'll make sure Jono gets this."

"Great. Thanks."

With a satisfied smile, Ally made her way toward the gate, only to find it locked with a padlock and chain. After plonking on another hard hat from the peg, she wandered back through the building looking for Jack—who seemed a safer bet than the stoic Ryan. But as she walked down the hallway, Ryan stepped out of a room, a question on his brow and his mouth pressed firmly shut.

"Excuse me," she said. Ryan stared at her—no smile, no warmth. Ally reminded herself that maybe his granny had just fallen off her perch and he had to attend her wake later. "Someone's locked the gate."

His yellow tape measure flicked back into its case as he

dropped his pencil into the leather tool belt slung low on his hips. "Looks like you'll be staying the night then."

Maybe he was expecting some witty response, but Ally was all out of those right now. "Would you mind asking someone to let me out?"

Ryan walked toward the entry as if expecting her to follow. When he reached the gate, he grabbed a set of keys from his tool belt and unlocked the padlock. He stepped back, leaving barely enough room for her to slip past.

"Thanks."

He reached over and removed her hard hat. "No problem, Ally." The words were softly spoken, as if he'd decided to play nice. He smiled, just a touch. "Watch your step."

"I will. Thank you."

As she relaxed in the back of the cab, Ally felt her face flush. She'd never experienced lust at first sight before, but the feeling was unmistakable—and unexpected.

"Putney High Street now?" the driver asked.

"Yes. Thanks for waiting." Opening Ryan's text, she expected to see a business card contact with his name and number, but when she glanced at the screen, there was only one word.

Click.

Thanks for reading the first chapter of *How About Thursday*. Continue reading Ryan and Ally's story by downloading *How About Thursday* to your Kindle App now! Also available in paperback from Amazon.com.

MANY THANKS

Thanks for taking the time to read *The List Maker*. If you enjoyed the book, please consider leaving a short review/star rating on Amazon and/or Goodreads.

Readers choose books based on recommendations. Leaving a review on Amazon will increase the visibility of *The List Maker* and help other readers find my books.

Good or bad, your reviews matter.

Many thanks,

Frances.

ALSO BY FRANCES COWIE

An Imagined Kiss - The London Series

The List Maker

How About Thursday

Clifton Falls Companion Novels

The Watershed

Field of the White Snow

A Reluctant Kiss - The South Pacific Series

Lime Tree Hill

Available at Amazon.com stores worldwide

in paperback and ebook.

ABOUT THE AUTHOR

Frances Cowie's journey to writing romantic fiction began after waking one morning with the story of an old pump house, and three characters, Rose, William, and Jessa, floating around in her head. That story, *The Watershed,* was her first novel.

Frances resides with her husband in one of the most beautiful areas in New Zealand and has two adult children. For more information, including sneak peeks of upcoming projects, visit Frances online:

www.francescowie.com

ACKNOWLEDGMENTS

One day, while shopping in the village where I live, I came across a large painting in a local gallery of a couple in profile locked in a passionate kiss. I stood in awe, studying how the artist used the colors and the textures to portray their desire.

I hurried back to the gallery a few days later, planning to show my daughter the work. It had been sold. My imagination started running wild—as it does—and *The List Maker* is the result.

I wish to thank the following people. Firstly Laura. I know my manuscripts are in safe hands as you slash your pencil through my overly flowery words. If it weren't for you, AJ would have been a totally over-the-top, new age guy in a pair of tight yoga pants and a tie-dyed kaftan. To Jenny for the initial edit. I appreciate your time. As always, I take full responsibility for any mistakes.

Jane, thank you for giving me many hours of your time as we sit in my office discussing if a sentence works or not. Louise, Abby-Lee, Hilly, Rachel, and Gemma—my beta readers. Kate and Marjorie for keeping me focused and giving me encouragement. To Carole B and Samantha for support and technical information. Thanks also to Nathan for the information on the Shikoku pilgrimage, and to Kyran and Grant for assisting me with my mock-up covers.

Many thanks to Steven Novak, from **www.novakillustration.com**, who completed the final cover.

Lastly, to my readers. Heartfelt thanks for taking several hours out of your busy lives to read my books. If you enjoyed *The List Maker,* please consider leaving a review on your book retailer's site and share my details with your romance-reading friends. Also, if you *Like* my Facebook page, you will have a chance to win a copy of my next effort.

Frances
2017